From the author of
CRIMSON FIRE and NIGHT BIRDS REIGN

BOOK THREE OF

D1647754

HOLLY TAYLOR

Cry of Sorrow

Medallion Press, Inc.
Printed in the USA

DEDICATION:

To my sisters Julie, Kerry and Christine, my companions in joy, in grief and in life. I love you all more than I can say.

Published 2008 by Medallion Press, Inc.

The MEDALLION PRESS LOGO
is a registered tradmark of Medallion Press, Inc.

Names, characters, places, and incidents are the products of the author's imagination or are used fictionally. Any resemblance to actual events, locales, or persons, living or dead, is entirely coincidental.

Typeset in Adobe Garamond Pro
Printed in the United States of America

ISBN#9781933836263

10 9 8 7 6 5 4 3 2 1
First Edition

They sing after thy song,
The Kymri in their grief,
On account of their loss
Long is the cry of sorrow.
There is blood upon the spears.
The waves are bearing
Ships upon the sea.

Taliesin
Fifth Master Bard of Kymru
Circa 275

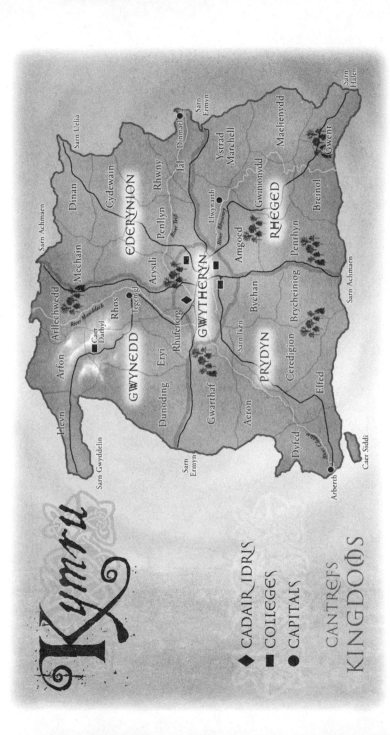

Part 1
The Hunted

Dismal is this life, to be without a soft bed;
A cold frosty dwelling, harshness of snowy wind.
Cold icy wind, faint shadow of a feeble sun,
The shelter of a single tree on the top of the level moor.
Enduring the shower, stepping along deer-paths,
Traversing greenswards on a morning of raw frost.

High King Idris
Circa 129

Prologue

Coed Aderyn
Kingdom of Prydyn, Kymru
Bedwen Mis, 499

Suldydd, Disglair Wythnos--night

Gwydion ap Awst, Dreamer of Kymru, twisted and turned on his narrow, sweat-soaked pallet. His face, illuminated by the shining moon that slipped through the shimmering waterfall and into the cave, was rigid with loss, with grief, with unyielding pain. And the dream unfolded.

He stood in a dark forest, lit fitfully by the pale light of the waning moon riding high overhead. The dark trees surrounded him, hemming him in tightly. The night was cold, and he was alone in a strange place he did not know. The silence hummed loudly in his ears, drumming like thunder with every beat of his heart. Inky black shadows stretched around him, growing and wavering in the uncertain light.

Suddenly the trees shivered as a chill wind blew through the forest, moaning and wailing of loss and despair. Leaves fallen from nearly bare branches rustled around him like the rattling bones of a restless corpse.

Faintly, so faintly he could not be sure at first that he really heard it, a horn began to blow, the note drifting through the forest on the wings of the sobbing wind. Again, he heard the call, coming closer now. And though he thought he knew who sounded that call, it

1

was not the cool, clear note he had heard in times past. It was soft, mournful, as though sent vainly into the air with a dying breath.

The sound of horses' hooves on the ground was muffled, and came slowly. He turned toward the sound, and the aching slowness of it frightened him, until he was terrified of what he would see.

Perhaps they had come to him too late. Perhaps they were dying even now, this moment. Perhaps there would be nothing left of them for him to save.

A faint glimmer of topaz through the dark trees caught Gwydion's terrified gaze. The horse was pale and skeletal. The rider was slumped over the horse's neck, the horn dangling in his hand, forgotten. With an effort, he raised his head, staring at Gwydion with the eyes of an owl. The antlers that grew from his once-proud forehead gleamed faintly in the moonlight. His once-muscular, bare chest was hollow and frail.

"Cerrunnos," Gwydion whispered past the ache in his throat. "Leader of the Hunt. Protector of Kymru."

A rustling of leaves, stirred by the hooves of a black horse, a glimmer of amethyst, and she was there. As her dark horse staggered into the tiny clearing, she slowly straightened and lifted her head. Her once-white tunic was tattered and stained with dirt and blood. Her shadowy hair was tangled and dusty. But her amethyst eyes still had the power to awe him with their pitiless gaze.

"Cerridwen," Gwydion whispered. "Lady of the Wood. Protectress of Kymru."

The two figures stared down at Gwydion but did not speak. Their harsh, labored breathing frightened Gwydion. "What have they done to you? What have they done to you both?" he cried.

"You know what they have done, Dreamer," Cerrunnos replied, his voice hollow. "They came and took Kymru for their own."

"Two years ago they came," Cerridwen whispered. Once, her voice had been like the silvery chime of bells. But no more.

"You . . . you are dying. I did not know that the Shining Ones could die."

"Didn't you?" Cerridwen asked slowly. "For we can. But not

yet. Not just yet. Still do I ride with the Horned God, the Master of the Hunt." She reached out with her pale, wasted hand to the god by her side. Cerrunnos, with a mighty effort, took her hand in his own. The god's topaz eyes fixed on Gwydion, and the Dreamer was startled to see the life that still blazed there. No, the gods were not dead. Not yet.

"Now is the time, Dreamer," Cerrunnos said. "Kymru is crushed beneath the heel of the enemy. The Druids have turned from Modron, and so our Great Mother will not allow the land to be fruitful. The King of the Winds moans of death and sorrow. The Lord of the Sun turns his face from the land. The Lady of the Waters looks upon rivers of blood. The Lord of Chaos is glutted with the souls of the dead. The Weaver cuts thread after thread. And now, the Wheel prepares to turn again."

"And so we have come," Cerridwen said, her voice merely a whisper. "Now is the time, Dreamer. And this is the dream we have promised. The Hunt for the Four Treasures begins. Your task, to make a High King for Kymru, one who will drive the enemy from this land, continues. Look, now, for these are the ones who hold the key." She pointed to the ground at Gwydion's feet. Moonbeams began to gather on the dead ground, forming a silvery pool of light.

Trembling, Gwydion gazed into the pool.

"Complete is the prison of the Queen in Caer Dwyr," Cerridwen chanted. Within the pool Gwydion saw the face of a young woman. Her auburn hair was scattered with pearls, her deep blue eyes filled with anger and pain. Manacles shackled her wrists, and though she twisted and turned, she could not break free. The pool shimmered again, and the face was gone.

"Sorrowful was the exile of the King from Caer Tir," Cerrunnos intoned, and the pool began to cast an emerald glow. Gwydion saw a man with golden hair, lines of pain and sorrow chiseled into his handsome, pale features. His blue eyes were dark with loss and despair as he strained his arms toward something he could not reach.

"Fast was the trap of the woman in Caer Erias," Cerridwen sang, as the pool shimmered again, glimmering like the fire in the heart of

3

an opal. A young girl, with hair of reddish gold, struggled against unseen bonds. A wedding veil spilled from a gold circlet across her brow, and silent screams of horror poured from her blue eyes.

"Many were the girl's tears for the dead of Caer Gwynt," Cerrunnos chanted, as the pool shimmered sapphire blue. The face of a young woman swam to the surface. Her auburn hair was dusty and tangled, and tears streamed from her dark eyes, spilling down her cold, set face.

Then the pool shimmered again, casting a rainbow of light through the trees—silver and green, yellow and blue—sending a glimmer of hope spinning up into the sky. A huge eagle sprang from the pool with a cry of defiance, and followed the light up through the trees, soaring free, unfettered through the dark night.

"Look now, Dreamer, and see what you must see," Cerridwen said softly. Gwydion wrenched his eyes from the eagle's flight, returning his gaze to the pool.

A large, square-cut stone swam to the surface. It was shot through with streaks of silver, which crosscrossed the stone like a net. At each silvery junction a white pearl gleamed.

Cerrunnos said, "Look now at Gwyr Yr Brenin, the Seeker of the King. The Stone you seek."

And though Gwydion did not know it, at that moment Rhiannon ur Hefeydd called out in her sleep. "The water. Please, please, no." Her words echoed hollowly in the cave in which she slept.

In the dream, another object swam to the surface of the pool. It was a cauldron of gold, interlaced with a dizzying array of spirals, the lip of the bowl covered with emeralds.

Cerridwen said, "Buarth Y Greu, Circle of Blood. The Cauldron you seek."

While far away, in Ogaf Greu on the shores of Prydyn, Gwenhwyfar ur Rhoram moaned in her sleep, her blond hair drenched with sweat. "No. The earth. No," she pleaded softly.

Another shimmer and Gwydion saw a spear, the shaft twined with silver and gold. Fiery opals gleamed around its shaft.

"Erias Yr Gwydd, Blaze of Knowledge," Cerridwen said. "The

Spear you seek."

At that moment Gwydion's sleeping body, which lay dreaming on his pallet, twisted in fear. "The fire. Oh, the fire," he moaned.

Another object hurtled to the surface of the pool. It was a sword. The hilt was silver mesh, chased with gold, formed in the shape of a hawk, and studded with sapphires.

"Meirig Yr Llech," Cerrunnos intoned. "The Guardian of the Stone. The Sword you seek."

While far off, in the tiny village of Dinas Emrys, in the mountains of Eryi, Arthur ap Uthyr called out, "The air. No. No. I can't."

And then, to Gwydion's horror, a man he knew appeared on the opposite edge of the pool. He was dressed in shining gold, and his amber eyes gleamed with a terrible need. On his head he wore a helmet fashioned like the head of a boar, with ivory tusks and baleful, ruby eyes. He held a huge sword, the blade carved with boar's heads. The Golden Man raised his head, his amber eyes boring into Gwydion's gray ones. "I will find the Treasures, Dreamer. Find them—and you. I will take them, and enter Cadair Idris. I will kill you all," Havgan rasped, then vanished.

The pool, still glowing at Gwydion's feet, abruptly winked out.

"Now is the time we have spoken of, Gwydion ap Awst," Cerridwen said. "The Hunt for the Treasures begins. We give you these two clues. Remember the Song of the Caers. Use the rings as your guide."

As Cerridwen and Cerrunnos turned their horses to go, Gwydion cried out. "Wait! I have never heard of the Song of the Caers. And I don't know which rings you speak of! Please, you must tell me! Help me!"

"This is a mystery for you to unravel, Dreamer," Cerrunnos said coldly.

"And yours to unravel soon. The Treasures must be found, and brought to Cadair Idris before the year is out," Cerridwen said. "Or Kymru will die beneath your feet, never to return to life again."

"But Cadair Idris is surrounded by the enemy! How can we get through?"

Cerridwen went on as though Gwydion had not spoken. "There

the High King must go with the Treasures in his hands. And there he will undergo the Tynged Mawr, the Great Fate, and, if found worthy, he will have the power to free our land. And so your task begins again, Dreamer. It is time."

As GWYDION WOKE, shivering in the cave, the faces of those seen in the pool burned in his mind. Queen Elen of Ederynion, held captive in Dinmael by the Coranians. King Rhoram of Prydyn, hiding out in the caves of Ogaf Greu, his country ruled by his traitorous brother-in-law. Princess Enid of Rheged, hiding from the enemy with her brother, King Owein. Queen Morrigan, Uthyr's daughter, hiding in the mountains of Gwynedd while her uncle ruled in her stead. These four held the key, somehow, in some way, to finding what he must now seek.

The last words of Cerridwen rang in his mind, fresh and vibrant, as he rose from his pallet and knelt by the sleeping Rhiannon. The moonlight turned the waterfall that stretched across the cave mouth into a curtain of shimmering silver. The silvery light outlined her sleeping face, a face that had become dear to him, though he would not speak this truth aloud. Her shadowy hair was tangled, as though her sleep was restless, too. Gently he reached out and touched her rich hair. He closed his eyes for a moment, then took a deep breath and shook her awake.

And as her green eyes opened and fastened on him, it was Cerridwen's words that rang throughout the cave.

"It is time," he said.

Chapter 1

Eiodel
Gwytheryn, Kymru
Bedwen Mis, 499

Gwaithdydd, Disglair Wythnos—morning

Havgan, Warleader of the Coranian Empire and the self-styled master of Kymru, gazed upon Cadair Idris, passionate hatred on his handsome face.

The deserted mountain hall of the High King remained closed to him. After two years of trying, the Doors would not open. Not yet.

Not ever, a voice inside whispered, a voice that sounded suspiciously like Gwydion the Dreamer, Havgan's most hated enemy. *You are not the High King,* the voice went on. *And you never will be.*

But he would be. When he found the Four Treasures, then the doors of Cadair Idris would open to him, and he would walk into the mountain that defied him. He would walk through in triumph, and the place would be his. All of Kymru would be his.

When he found the Treasures. And he would. He must.

For crushing Kymru beneath his heel had not been enough. Driving the Bards and the Dewin from their halls had not been enough. Killing Kymru's Kings and Queens had not been enough. For even now he could feel Kymru slipping through his fingers, as it had from the very beginning.

His gaze played over the plain from which the defiant mountain sprang. It was early spring, and the day was crisp and cool. The grasses of the plain were brown, yet here and there patches of pale green could be seen. The trees of Coed Llachar, the forest to the west of the mountain stood tall and proud, guarding their green silences closely. The standing stones of Galar Carreg, the burial place of the High Kings of Kymru, loomed coldly, keeping their secrets to themselves.

Far off at the edge of the western horizon, he caught a glimpse of the silvery waters of Llyn Mwyngil, shining clear and cold. A cool breeze blew over the meadow, creating swirling patterns in the grass. But, once again, the message in those patterns eluded him. The wildflowers that dotted the plain were just beginning to raise their heads. Yet even the once-vibrant colors of the wildflowers looked pale, washed out, lifeless. Almost as though Kymru was dying beneath his feet even as he tried to take it for his own.

The harvests for the past two years had been poor, and some of the Kymri had starved. The earth gave food grudgingly, if at all. Oh, he knew what the people were saying. They said that Modron, the Great Mother, was angry that her children, the Druids, had turned from her. In retaliation, she withheld her blessing from the earth.

Not true, Havgan knew. For his God was stronger than the gods of the Kymri. It was obvious that Lytir, the One God, was displeased, and he showed it by the poor harvests. And he must be displeased because the witches—the Dewin, the Bards, and that hateful Dreamer—were still alive, still free, still defying Havgan and his God.

But not for much longer. Today he would meet with his inner circle, to bring to fruition plans that would make his dream a reality, plans that had been in the making for the past two years. Today, the battle for Kymru would begin again. And this time, when the battle was over, his victory would be complete.

It had been the strange dream two nights ago that made him understand victory was in his grasp. For the search for the Treasures was beginning. When Gwydion ap Awst found them, he would turn to find Havgan right behind him.

Havgan's fists clenched in rage as he gazed with hungry eyes at the still-closed Doors to the mountain.

The jewels of the Doors winked slyly at him in the morning sun. The fiery opals of Mabon of the Sun, the cool sapphires of Taran of the Winds, the gleaming emeralds of Modron the Mother, the luminous pearls of Nantsovelta of the Waters all mocked him in their splendor, in his inability to destroy them.

The onyx of Annwyn, Lord of Chaos, the bloodstone of Aertan, the Weaver of Fate, seemed to laugh at him. The diamonds for Sirona of the Stars, the garnets for Grannos the Healer, the bloodred rubies for the Warrior Twins shimmered and danced before his predatory gaze.

And it was then that the topaz of the Master of the Hunt and the amethyst of the Lady of the Wood blazed up fiercely, blinding him with their light. It was then that the many-colored hues of Arderydd, the High Eagle, seemed to shriek at him in defiance.

Havgan did not step back as the light bored into his eyes. He stood his ground before the Doors and vowed that the Shining Ones of Kymru would not mock him much longer.

What was left of them, that is. For they were dying. The god and goddess in his dream of a few nights ago, the two that led the Wild Hunt, glimpsed for one brief moment, had been bereft of power. Wan and pale and—almost—lifeless. He would defeat them.

With a mocking bow to show he was unafraid, he turned from the Doors to gaze upon Eiodel, the black fortress he had built less than a league away. Eiodel, built in defiance of Cadair Idris, in pride, in mockery, gleamed darkly, its shadowy stones rearing proudly to the sky.

One day he would bring Gwydion to Eiodel. He would cast the Dreamer into its deep dungeons. And he would smile at the sound of Gwydion's screams.

But there was much to be done, he thought, as he walked down the broken steps of Cadair Idris. The steps were twined with the brown stems of dead rockrose and alyssum. The low moan of the wind whistled past him, ruffling the golden cloak he wore. The sunlight blazed on his golden helmet. His amber eyes, keen and fierce, flashed with contempt at the sight of the man who was waiting at the bottom of the steps.

"Lord Havgan." The black-robed figure bowed. "I have been looking for you."

"How difficult that must be with only one eye," Havgan replied pleasantly.

Sledda, the Arch-wyrce-jaga of Kymru, supreme witch hunter, flushed an ugly red. The empty socket where his right eye had once rested was stiff and seamed with scars. His remaining eye, pale and colorless, shined with malevolence as Sledda bowed his head in what Havgan knew to be mock humility.

"One day, Lord Havgan, I will find that eagle. And I will kill it."

"You would do better, Sledda, to find and kill the witches who have escaped you. Two years I have been waiting for you to do so."

"The witches are clever," Sledda hissed.

"And you are not. The Master Bard and the Ardewin still elude you. And, worse, yet, you have not brought me the Dreamer or his whore, Rhiannon."

Sledda's one eye gleamed at the mention of Rhiannon's name. "One day I will, Lord. And you will give the whore to me."

"Most probably. After I am finished. Just what is it you want, Sledda? Assuming you have come for some other purpose than to tell me all the things you will do—but have not yet done."

"I come to tell you that they are all here and waiting. It is time."

Sledda's words echoed within him, as he remembered the words of the dying goddess from his dream.

"Yes, Sledda," he said. "It is time."

THE CHAMBER IN the castle of Eiodel was stark. The stone floor was polished to a deadly sheen, its smooth darkness unrelieved by rugs. The walls, pierced here and there with narrow windows, were bare. Torches flickered in their wall sockets, but they could not fully illuminate the shadows that clung to this room.

A fire roared in the huge fireplace set into the south wall. Six high-backed chairs were arrayed in a semicircle before the fire. All but two of the chairs were occupied when Havgan walked into the room, Sledda behind him like a malevolent shadow.

The first man Havgan greeted was Sigerric, now the Over-general of Kymru. The face of Havgan's oldest friend had changed steadily over the years. The joy of life, which had once danced in Sigerric's dark eyes, was gone. His too-thin face was stern, and lines of despair bracketed his once-laughing mouth.

The blue robes of Eadwig, the Archbyshop of Kymru, shimmered in the firelight, straining against his broad, muscular shoulders. His large hands were scarred from the thousands of battles he had fought to claim the life and blood of the bulls in the weekly sacrifices to Lytir. The Archbyshop's blue eyes were peaceful, despite the fact that the Kymri eluded the grasp of the One God. Havgan envied the inner peace in the man's eyes, the peace of a man who knew himself and his place in the world.

Far to the right of the circle sat two of the Kymri, both dressed in brown robes trimmed in green. The hair of the Archdruid had turned even whiter in the past few years, but Cathbad's dark eyes still gleamed with cunning and—on occasion—madness. At his feet was a leather bag, which he touched occasionally as though it held something very precious.

The saturnine features of Aergol, the Archdruid's heir, were unreadable as always. Even his eyes were opaque, giving no hint of his thoughts. If he disapproved of Cathbad's support of the enemy, he did not show it. If he approved, he did not show it. He rarely showed anything, including concern for his family. For Aergol's mother, Dinaswyn, the former Dreamer, was still alive, hiding somewhere. His daughter, Sinend, had run away from Caer Duir two years ago and had not been heard from since. Havgan rarely saw Aergol's son, Menw, whose mother was one of the teachers at Caer Duir. The boy never seemed to be around when the Coranians were there. Aergol never spoke of him. In fact, Aergol rarely spoke at all.

Havgan took his place. The firelight flickered off his golden helmet. His amber eyes shimmered with an inner fire, as he began.

"A few years ago I won the position of Warleader of the Empire, killing my rival, claiming the hand of Princess Aelfwyn. I claimed the power to direct the might of the empire for one reason—to complete the task that God had set for me many years before, the task to conquer the Kymri, to retake this land and cleanse it of the unholy taint of the witches who ruled it. I came to Kymru to bring the might of my God before the people, to reclaim them from their evil ways. To that end I brought with me the preosts of Lytir, as represented by the good Archbyshop." Havgan paused to nod at Eadwig.

"And to that end I brought the wyrce-jaga, our witch-hunters," Havgan continued, nodding at Sledda, who bowed in return. "And to that end I brought with me the finest warrior I have ever known." The bitter lines around Sigerric's mouth deepened as he acknowledged Havgan's praise.

"And when my armies came to Kymru, we were aided in our battles by the Druids, whose support has been invaluable. Of the loyalty of the Archdruid and his heir I have no doubts," Havgan lied. Cathbad, his mad eyes sparkling, inclined his proud head, while Aergol remained impassive, as though Havgan had not spoken at all.

"At first, for all intents and purposes, we had Kymru by the throat. In Ederynion, our forces, led by General Talorcan defeated and killed Queen Olwen. We captured her daughter and made her Queen, to do our bidding. In Rheged, King Urien, Queen Ellirri, and their son, Prince Elphin, all died at our hands. Morcant Whledig, one of Rheged's lords, now sits on the throne, advised by General Baldred. In Prydyn, King Rhoram's brother-in-law rules in the King's stead, guided by General Penda. And in Gwynedd, King Uthyr was killed and his half brother, Madoc, now rules for us with the help of General Catha."

Havgan stood, walking over to stand before the fire. The flames at his back outlined his golden figure. "In Gwytheryn, the Dewin and Bards fled their fortresses. The preosts of Lytir now inhabit Y Ty Dewin, the wyrce-jaga now live at Neuadd Gorsedd."

The room was silent; the only sound was the crackling fire. Havgan walked to the narrow north window, the one that faced Cadair Idris. His back to the room, he said softly, "But Cadair Idris remains closed to me. The Guardian of the Doors denies me entry, because I have not the Treasures."

He turned from the window, his face expressionless, his voice cold. "The Archdruid has explained to me what these Treasures are. They are the Stone of Water, the Spear of Fire, the Cauldron of Earth, and the Sword of Air. By these Treasures a man undergoes what the Kymri call the Tynged Mawr, which means Great Fate. If he survives this test, he becomes High King with command of powers beyond our comprehension. With these powers, the High King may command even wild beasts to do his bidding. He can spy upon the enemy from many leagues away. He can raise fog, call fire to burn an enemy camp, direct a battle by speaking to the minds of his warriors. Such powers would be invaluable."

Havgan circled the chairs, coming to a stop behind Cathbad's. He rested his hand on the Archdruid's shoulder. Cathbad's face spasmed in pain at Havgan's grip.

"And the Archdruid also explained to me," Havgan continued softly, "that somewhere in Kymru there is one who can claim to be High King. Who he is, where he is, the Archdruid cannot say. In fact, this is such a closely guarded secret that none can be found who can— or will—say." Havgan at last released the Archdruid and stood in front of the fire once more. Cathbad closed his eyes briefly at his release.

"In the last two years we have consolidated our hold on Kymru," Havgan continued. "The Druids have journeyed throughout this land with the preosts of Lytir, proclaiming the triumph of our God. And yet, it is not enough. Our work remains incomplete. For though we have Queen Elen, her brother, Prince Lludd, eludes us. Though we have killed King Urien and Queen Ellirri and their oldest son, their second son, Owein, still lives. Though we have taken Prydyn, the former King, Rhoram, is alive somewhere. Though King Uthyr is dead, his daughter, Queen Morrigan, continues to escape our grasp. Cadair Idris remains closed. The Treasures are hidden. I am not High King. But I will be. For I have seen in a dream that the time has come to change this unhappy state of affairs."

Havgan, who had been watching Aergol closely without seeming to, saw the first expression he had ever seen on the man's face— surprise. But why? What did Aergol think it meant that Havgan had dreamed?

He returned to his chair, his words cool and clipped. "Each of you has been given a task. To you, Eadwig, the task of bringing the Kymri to the worship of Lytir. To you, Sledda, the task of finding the Y Dawnus, the witches, who have escaped us. To you, Sigerric, the task of wiping out the warrior bands that continue to defy us. To you, Cathbad and Aergol, the task of finding a way to control the witches. You will tell me now, each of you, the progress you have made. Archbyshop, you may begin."

"As you know," Eadwig said quietly, "one of the first things we did was to burn their sacred groves and build temples to Lytir in their place. Every Soldaeg—or, as the Kymri say, every Suldydd—we call the people to worship."

"And they come," Cathbad said smugly.

"Yes," Eadwig replied hesitantly. "They come."

"You think this strange?" Sledda asked.

"Oh, yes."

"They go to the services because they must," Sigerric shrugged. "This is not so hard to understand."

"I do not think that is why they go," Eadwig said.

"No?" Havgan asked sharply, for he did not think so, either.

"No. I think they go because it amuses them. I think they are laughing at us."

"Laughing!" Sledda exclaimed, shocked.

"Laughing," Eadwig said firmly.

"They are not," Cathbad snapped. "They know it is hopeless to resist. They go because they must, because their Druids tell them to."

At the Archdruid's words, Aergol stirred slightly. As subdued as the movement was, Havgan caught it. "You know better, don't you, Archdruid's heir? Even if Cathbad does not. Tell us, Aergol, what do you think they are doing?"

For a moment Aergol did not answer. Then he said quietly, "They are waiting."

"Waiting for what?" Sigerric asked.

"For the High King to return to Cadair Idris. Then they will drive you from this land into the sea."

"You dare to say such things?" Sledda began, rising from his chair.

"Be quiet, wyrce-jaga," Havgan hissed. Sledda shrank back into his chair. "Go on, Eadwig."

"There is little more to say, my Lord. As you also know, the temples that we build are often burned. These fires are, no doubt, set by the Cerddorian."

"Which brings us to Sigerric," Havgan said.

Sigerric, not meeting Havgan's eyes, began. "The Cerddorian, which, I am given to understand by Aergol, means 'The Sons of Cerridwen,' seem to be everywhere. They are said to be blessed in their efforts to drive us from the land by the goddess Cerridwen herself, the Queen of the Wood, she who leads the Wild Hunt. Bands of Cerddorian burn the temples of Lytir. They attack tribute caravans and small groups of Coranian warriors. Their efforts are not confined to any one area—but we have managed to confirm that their orders are given through the network of witches set up by the Master Bard and his daughter, the Ardewin. Orders are filtered through this network of Bards and Dewin to the chief band in each kingdom. Their headquarters are unknown, yet we have managed to pinpoint their general areas. For example, the band led by Prince Lludd, in Ederynion, is somewhere in the cantref of Arystli—probably in the great forest of Coed Ddu."

"If you know where they are, why can't you find them?" Sledda sneered.

"Have you ever, wyrce-jaga, attempted to find people in a forest that stretches for over ten leagues in each direction? Ever hunted for Bards who could call a warning from mind to mind without a sound? Ever hunted for people who had Dewin who could 'see' you coming from leagues away? But, of course, I am forgetting. You have hunted for such. For two years. And managed to find nothing."

Sledda shot Sigerric a venomous look with his one eye, but said nothing.

"The chief band in Rheged," Sigerric continued, "led by Owein PenMarch, appears to be centered quite close to the capital of Llwynarth, probably somewhere in Coed Addien. The band led by King Rhoram in Prydyn seems to be somewhere off the coast of cantref Aeron. The last band in Gwynedd, led by Queen Morrigan, is probably deep in the mountains of Eyri."

"But," Eadwig asked, puzzled, "surely at one time or another you have caught members of these bands and questioned them. Someone must have told you something."

"We have caught some Cerddorian, Archbyshop. But it has yielded us nothing. Not one man or woman we have captured has spoken one word—not even their names. And not even under the kind of tortures the wyrce-jaga can devise."

"And yet, General, the attacks of these bands are mere pinpricks. The villages, the towns, the cities—all are in our hands," Cathbad pointed out. "These attacks will die down, surely, as my people become reconciled to their lot."

Havgan noticed that something like a bitter smile was tugging at the corners of Aergol's mouth in response to the Archdruid's confident words.

"You know these people, Archdruid," Havgan said. "You know Prince Lludd and his Captain, Angharad. You know Owein and his Captain, Trystan. You know King Rhoram and his Captain, Achren. You know Queen Morrigan and her Captain, Cai. Through you, I know them also. And yet you say they will give up? They will not. Sigerric has done well to—as you say—hold the villages, the towns, and the cities. Done well to even be able to guess where the chiefs of these bands are hiding. Yet they cannot be found and killed. Not as long as the network set by the Master Bard and the Ardewin still functions."

"And that," Sledda interrupted eagerly, "will not be for much longer."

"Which, Sledda, brings us to you. For two years I have heard you say this. And talk is all I have gotten from you."

"My Lord, the time we have been waiting for has come. I have captured a Bard. A Bard who is willing to tell all he knows!"

"Why?" Aergol cut in curiously.

"Because," Sledda replied, his one eye gleaming with cruel satisfaction, "I hold his wife and baby daughter. And he will do anything to have them freed."

"Ah," said Sigerric, the bitter lines around his mouth deepening. "And will you have them freed?"

"Most unfortunately, General, I cannot. For his wife died of injuries sustained when she fought too strongly for her virtue."

"Against you."

Sledda smiled. "Against me."

"What woman wouldn't?"

Sledda's smile faded. "Simply because you have failed in your task to locate the Cerddorian, Sigerric, there is no need to insult me."

"Oh, Sledda, there is always need—and so much cause—to insult you. And the baby girl? What did you do to her?"

Sledda shrugged. "I did not have the means to care for the child after her mother died. I ordered her killed."

"The supreme cruelty. To make a man betray his people to save the lives of those already dead."

"A piece of information that, I trust, you will not share with the Bard? I fear Lord Havgan would be highly displeased."

"Havgan," Sigerric began in a pleading tone.

"Be quiet, Sigerric," Havgan said coolly. "I will use who and what I must to get what I need. Don't be a fool." Havgan gestured to Sledda. "You have the Bard here?"

"I do, Lord Havgan."

"Then bring him in."

Sledda left the room. Havgan said, "Sigerric, I wish that you would leave me be to do the things I must do."

Sigerric smiled bitterly. "And that is something I will never do. As long as you demean yourself with unworthy deeds, so I will speak against it."

"So you will," Havgan agreed equably. "And so I will continue."

"Never have any poor words of mine changed your course. Why should now be any different?

"Why, indeed?"

Sledda returned, followed by a small, lithe man, dressed in a worn tunic and trousers of nondescript brown. The man had sandy hair, pale green eyes, and small, sharp features. His face was tight, his hands clasped into fists, his shoulders tense.

"You will bow to Lord Havgan, Bard," Sledda commanded.

The man hesitated, then bowed slightly.

"What is your name?" Havgan asked.

"I am called Jonas, Warleader," he said softly. "Jonas ap Morgan."

"And you are a Bard."

"I am. Before the war I was the Bard to Diadwa ur Tryffin, Gwarda of Creuddyn, in Gwynedd. Lady Diadwa was killed in the Third Battle of Tegeingl."

"You were in the battles of Tegeingl? Surely, then, you know where Queen Morrigan and her mother, Ygraine, and the rest of her people fled."

"Most unfortunately, Lord, I do not. Before the battles began, the Master Bard called me back to meet with him at Neuadd Gorsedd."

"And then, I suppose, he took you to their hiding place?"

"No, my Lord. He sent me to Rheged, to act as another link in the great chain he and the Ardewin were creating throughout Kymru."

"Then you know where the Master Bard and the Ardewin have gone. You know the final destination of your messages."

"Again, I must say no."

"You are lying."

"Lying," the man said flatly. His fists clenched tighter, his knuckles white. "Lying. Don't you think I would tell you all I knew to free my wife, my baby? I will do anything to have them freed! Anything. If I knew, I would tell you!"

"Then I fail to see, Sledda, what use this man is to us, if he knows nothing," Sigerric taunted.

"Few of the Bards or Dewin know the location of the headquarters of the Master Bard and the Ardewin," Sledda explained smoothly. "The Bards relay spoken messages, mind to mind. The Dewin relay the 'pictures' of what they have seen one to another. Each person knows only one link in that chain."

"Then the chain must be pursued! Capture the next Bard that Jonas knows of, and follow!" Cathbad said, his mad eyes gleaming.

"And that is what we must not do, Archdruid," Sledda said shortly. "The next Bard may not be so—ah, amenable —to sharing information with us. The Kymri might be alerted. I have a better plan. Explain, Jonas."

Jonas took a deep breath, his face pale and set. "No one but me knows that my wife and daughter are prisoners. I will send a message up the chain to Anieron that they were killed, and beg him to reassign me to another post where their memory will not haunt me. He will call me to him, and then I will know where he hides."

"Why should he call you to him?" Eadwig asked. "He could very well simply tell you where you must go next, without seeing you."

Suddenly, Aergol spoke. "Anieron will call Jonas to him because he will be concerned for the Bard's state of mind. He will wish to see for himself that Jonas will recover from the supposed death of his family. And so Anieron's compassion will be his undoing. Isn't that so, Jonas?"

Jonas, unable to meet Aergol's dark eyes, stared at the floor, nodding slowly. "Yes," he whispered.

"Very well," Havgan said crisply. "Anieron calls Jonas to him. What then?"

"Then," Sledda went on, "he will receive his assignment. He will beg to be sent back to Gwynedd, to Rhos, which borders on Eyri, to a place where, for a time, he was happy. We believe that Anieron will send him to the place where Queen Morrigan and her people hide, which we know to be in Eyri. After he leaves Anieron, Jonas will contact us, leaving a message at a prearranged place, which will tell us where the Master Bard is hiding."

"A shade risky, don't you think?" Sigerric pointed out. "Jonas may very well not contact you at all. Wouldn't it be better to follow him to the hidden headquarters?"

"Better, but inadvisable, as you yourself pointed out not long ago," Sledda replied. "We must not give ourselves away too soon. We want Jonas to be well on his way to Morrigan's camp before we move in on the Master Bard and the Ardewin. And you seem to forget that

Jonas has a powerful reason to tell us what we want to know. His wife and daughter, remember."

Sigerric stirred uneasily in his chair, but said nothing. At this Jonas raised his head. "I need your promise, General Sigerric, that when this is done, my wife and daughter will be restored to me."

"My promise?" Sigerric asked in surprise. "Why mine?"

"It is known throughout Kymru that you are a warrior of honor. So I must have your word."

"Lord Havgan's word would, I think, be—"

"No," Jonas said firmly. "Your word."

Havgan waited calmly. The rest might be—and were—tense and uncertain, but Havgan knew what Sigerric would do.

Slowly, Sigerric said, "I promise that, when your task is done, you will be with your wife and daughter."

Jonas bowed his head, and Sledda led him from the room, handing the Bard over to the guards at the door. Sledda returned to his seat, saying, "Well, Sigerric, I suppose I must thank you for that."

"I didn't do it for you," Sigerric said harshly.

"Sigerric," Havgan began, "my friend—"

Suddenly, shockingly, Sigerric laughed. It was a bitter, dark sound.

"Sigerric!" Havgan cried, gripping his friend's arm, capturing Sigerric's dark eyes with his own hawklike gaze. Slowly, Sigerric's laughter tapered off.

"Perhaps," Eadwig said hesitantly, "it would be best if the General got some rest."

"Rest?" Sigerric asked softly. "Rest? Oh, no, I wouldn't miss a moment of this. I must see every step my Lord takes into the arms of Sceadu, the Great Shadow. I've been watching since the beginning. Longer than any of you. Why stop now?"

Havgan's face darkened alarmingly, and his eyes flashed fire. But before he could speak, Eadwig said passionately, "Lord Sigerric, we do what we must do for the glory of the One God! Better for some to die than for all the Kymri to lose their souls. Lytir commands the death of the witches. Did he not speak so to Lord Havgan long ago?"

"Something did," Sigerric muttered. He laughed again, weaker this time. "Never mind about me. Let's hear the end of our plots to bring the Y Dawnus down."

"Lord Havgan," Sledda broke in. "I respectfully request that General Sigerric retire. Or do you think such a man—a man who laughs at you, who seeks to thwart Holy Lytir's will—can be trusted?"

Without even bothering to look at Sledda, without even taking his eyes from Sigerric's tormented face, Havgan replied softly, "You will never again, wyrce-jaga, suggest to me that Sigerric cannot be trusted. Unless, of course, you wish to lose your other eye. General Sigerric stays."

Once again, the men were silent, waiting for Havgan's commands. At last, Havgan turned to Cathbad. "Archdruid, it is time to hear from you. The bag at your feet means, I trust, that you have been successful in your task?"

"It does, Lord Havgan," Cathbad replied proudly, a smile in his mad eyes. "I have, at last, rediscovered the ancient way used to control Y Dawnus. It is a way found long ago, in Lyonesse, the land that sank beneath the sea."

Aergol raised one brow—a look that, for him, spoke volumes.

"You are surprised, Aergol?" Havgan asked.

"I have not confided my experiments to my heir before this moment. What I have to show you will, indeed, be a surprise to all," Cathbad said.

With that, he opened the leather bag. Reaching in, he carefully pulled out a collar of dull gray hue, holding it with the very tips of his fingers. "This," he said proudly, "is what I have made. And with this, you shall have ultimate power."

Slowly he turned the collar over. Tiny spikes protruded from the inside. Delicately, he held it for all to see.

"What's it made of? How does it work?" Sledda asked eagerly.

"It's made of lead. White lead, and quite common. Easily mined. You see these tiny spikes? When a Dewin or Bard is collared, these needles plunge into his or her neck. The victim begins to suffer the effects of lead poisoning. Headaches, nausea, the inability to focus attention. And, eventually, an unpleasant lingering death."

"Yes, yes, but how does that affect their magic?"

"It's a bit difficult to explain," Cathbad said, arrogance in every word. "Druids are scientists, you know, and a layman may find it hard to understand—"

"Try," Havgan said between gritted teeth.

"Well, you see, the brain must maintain a proper balance of fluids of a sort in order to work properly. The brain of a Dewin, or a Bard—"

"Or a Druid," Havgan said smoothly.

"Oh, yes. Or of a Druid, must maintain the proper balance of a particular type of fluid, or the ability is lost. These spikes gouge heavily into a portion of the brain, centered here at the back of the neck, which controls that balance. And, instantly, the talent is lost. A Bard can no longer speak mind to mind. His 'voice' goes no farther than his own head. A Dewin can no longer Wind-Ride or Life-Read. Indeed, they cannot see anything outside the normal range of human vision."

"And a Druid cannot Shape-Move or Fire-Weave," Havgan finished. "And all these abilities will cease the moment the collar is clasped on?"

"They will," Cathbad said in a lofty tone.

"And how many of these collars have you made?"

"Oh, no more than this one, so far. It has taken some time to re-discover how to make them, for their secret was lost a few hundred years ago. There are, indeed, only a very few of these collars in existence."

"Then this is what we will do. We will gather all the Master Smiths—and their families, too, just to keep them working hard. We will convey them to a place easily guarded. And they will turn out these collars by the cartload. Where, Sledda, would you suggest these Smiths do their work?"

"Caer Siddi," Sledda said promptly. "The little island off the coast of Prydyn. No one lives there, and it is easily defensible. Is such a place likely to have the lead you need, Archdruid?"

"Oh, yes. Yes, indeed. Caer Siddi would be the perfect place," Cathbad said, anxious to please.

"Now," Havgan continued, "that we have—at last—found a way to

22

control the witches, we must have a foolproof way to identify them. And for that, we must get our hands on one of their testing devices—those things that the Kymri use to discover magical abilities in their children."

Both Sledda and Sigerric opened their mouths to speak, but Havgan cut them off with an imperious gesture. "No, do not bother to tell me that you have tried. This time there will be no failure. The four Bards who served the former rulers of Kymru must and will be found, for they alone have these devices in their possession. Cathbad, you will call on your Druids to help in this search. Many of these surely know these four Bards by sight. And, as you have explained to me, this is the month when the Bards traditionally begin their travels around each kingdom for what the Kymri call the Plentyn Prawf, the Child Test, where they use these devices to identify young Y Dawnus. The Bards will be on the roads soon."

"But might they not discontinue this practice at such a time?" Eadwig asked. "It is far too dangerous for them to travel. Suppose they do not go on the road? What then?"

"Aergol?" Havgan asked coolly, already sure of the answer to that question.

"They will not put away a tradition that is so important to them. For hundreds of years the children of Kymru have undergone the Plentyn Prawf. The Bards will go." .

"As I thought. And these are whom we seek." One by one, Havgan ticked the names off on his fingers. "Talhearn, who was Bard to Queen Olwen in Ederynion; Esyllt, who was Bard to King Urien in Rheged; Cian, Bard to King Rhoram in Prydyn; Susanna, who was the Bard to King Uthyr in Gwynedd. These four will be found, make no mistake. And, Sledda, I want that Dreamer. Gwydion and Rhiannon also take to the road now. They, too, must and will be found."

"But how do you know this, Lord? The Dreamer has been hiding for two years. How do you know he will come out now?"

"Because," Havgan said, "it is time."

CATHBAD HURRIED DOWN the steps of Eiodel to the horses. As he and Aergol mounted their horses, the Archdruid gazed north to

Cadair Idris. His gaze was no less predatory than Havgan's as he, too, studied the closed doors to the mountain.

"The hunt for the Treasures begins, Aergol," Cathbad said. "Is that not what Havgan has dreamed? Gwydion ap Awst will find them, you can be sure of that. And, when he does, Lord Havgan will take them. Soon Havgan will return to the mountain with the Treasures in his hands. And Drwys Idris will open to him. And you and I will be beside him when he enters Cadair Idris and walks the halls as no one has done for hundreds of years."

Aergol did not answer.

"And the collars! Oh, these collars will give us the power that I have dreamed of. With these collars around their necks, the Dewin and the Bards—and the Dreamer—will be nothing! The Druids will be supreme, as we once were."

Again, Aergol did not answer.

"You are, my heir, angry that I did not confide the nature of my experiments to you? Is that why you are silent?"

The cold wind whipped the grasses of the plain, nipping at the Druids' robes, moaning in their ears, making Cathbad shiver involuntarily as they rode by the mountain.

At last Aergol spoke. "Archdruid, you are a fool."

"A fool! How dare you speak to me that way! A fool because I have found the way to make the Druids masters once again, as we were long ago in Lyonesse? For this you call me a fool?"

"No, not for that."

"For what, then?"

Aergol reached out and grasped the reins of Cathbad's horse, forcing the animal to a stop. He turned in his saddle, facing Cathbad, his dark eyes filled with contempt. "How long do you think it will be, Archdruid, before they clasp a collar around your own neck?"

"They wouldn't—"

"They would."

"I am the Archdruid of Kymru!"

"No. You are a fool. And so am I."

Coed Addien and Llwynarth

Chapter 2

Kingdom of Rheged, Kymru
Bedwen Mis, 499

Llundydd, Lleihau Wythnos—afternoon

Owein ap Urien, eldest living son of the murdered King and Queen of Rheged, gazed upon the dead Coranian warriors lying in the tall grasses by the side of the road. Plumes of smoke rose from the burning wagons to stain the clean, blue sky. The heat of the fire shimmered before his sunken, shadowed eyes, and sweat bathed his lean, tanned face. Still, he did not move. He wanted to savor the sight of the dead.

They must leave soon. The smoke could be seen from many leagues away. Already that false king, Morcant Whledig, and his Coranian watchdog, General Baldred, would know that Owein and his people had struck again.

Owein nodded at Trystan, and his Captain whistled piercingly, like the cry of a hawk in flight. The men and women of Owein's teulu melted back into the forest, moving silently for all that they were heavily laden with the spoils they had won. Foodstuffs, cloth, wine and ale, rich jewelry, and golden vessels—tributes that had been bound for Llwynarth and Morcant Whledig's greedy hands.

But Owein still stood, savoring the burning, savoring the knowledge that he had taken back some of what Morcant had stolen. One day he would take back far more than this. He would wrench it all from Morcant. He would gut the man like a pig and bathe in the blood.

He would do this. He had sworn it to himself when he had learned of the death of his brother. He had sworn it when he had listened to the death song for his parents, a song that had emptied his soul, leaving him to fill it with lust for the blood of his enemies. With each Coranian who died from his arrows, or with his dagger in their guts, his heaviness, his sorrow, his grief lessened.

While his hate grew.

Yet, no matter how much killing he did, no matter how much blood flowed from the enemy to soak the ground of Rheged, it was not enough to blot out the picture he carried in his mind's eye. Not enough to blot out his mother's face as General Baldred's ax had crashed down upon her. Not enough to blot out his father's cry as he had leapt to deflect the killing blade, and died with Morcant's dagger through his heart. Not enough to blot out the way his father's hand had reached out and clasped the hand of his dying Queen in their last moments of life.

He had not seen these things himself, for he had not been in Llwynarth during that last, terrible battle. He had not been there because his mother had tricked him, sending him away in the company of Trystan. But Teleri, his Lieutenant, had been there and seen it all, and she repeated the story to him as often as he asked her to. And he asked often. For it was his hate that kept him strong.

As often as he commanded that story, he commanded to hear another—the story of the night his older brother, Elphin, had died in a midnight raid on Morcant's camp. It was a story he forced himself to hear, for he had both loved and envied his brother, the one passion just as strong as the other. Owein had loved Elphin for his strength, his kindness, his generous heart, and his laughter. And he had envied his brother for Elphin's birthright. For Elphin would have been, should have been, King of Rheged. He would have, should have, married Princess Sanon of Prydyn, and begotten fine children with the woman whom Owein himself had loved from the first moment he had seen her.

Not that such a thing would ever matter to her. For Sanon's heart had been given to Elphin forever. A truth Owein had learned, to his grief, not so long ago.

Only three months ago he and his sister, Enid, had journeyed secretly to Prydyn, to the caves of Ogaf Greu, and met with the fugitive King Rhoram and his band of Cerddorian. There, Owein had offered for the hand of Sanon, Rhoram's daughter, and had been refused publicly by the woman herself. She had declared, in front of everyone, that her heart was dead with her betrothed, and she would never love another.

Even now, as he looked upon the dead, the memory of that moment still filled him with shame. Sanon's burning dark eyes and her golden hair flamed in his heart. For he saw then, or thought he saw, that Sanon knew of the envy he had felt for his brother. Knew it, and despised him for it.

The pure lines of her pale face as she repudiated him still filled him with dread and doubt. For, in one moment, he could be sure that Sanon was wrong. He would know that his love for her was true, and had nothing to do with the brother he had both loved and hated. And yet, in the next moment, he would think he wanted her only because she had belonged to Elphin. And he would know that his soul was a dark and twisted thing that he would reach over his dead brother's body to the woman Elphin had loved.

It was better he should be alone. He understood that now. Better to hate in the silence of his misshapen heart, and never marry, never beget children. Better that he should not pass on such twisted seed. Better that he should keep his hatred, his contempt for himself, hidden far away. For what did he have, really, to offer to any woman? Nothing.

No, he would leave the marrying, the begetting, to his younger brother, Rhiwallon, and to his sister, Enid. Though Rhiwallon was not yet promised, Enid had been betrothed to Geriant, Sanon's brother. Of late, though, Owein wondered if Enid was as happy in that bond as he had hoped. Something he saw in her eyes, a longing that he had thought stilled long ago, still stirred there when she thought no one was looking.

But Owein saw. Why should he not see the darkness, the unbearable longing in the eyes of another? He who was so filled with it himself? Nonetheless, she would marry Geriant, who was a good, kind man, a courageous Prince, and who loved Enid with his entire bright, golden, pure soul. She would marry him, and forget the other one who lurked in the shadows of her heart still.

Owein stepped forward, and turned over the body of the nearest warrior with his foot. The Coranian's sightless blue eyes stared up at him. The blood running from his mouth was fresh and ruby red. So must his brother have looked, the night he died.

"My Lord," Trystan said quietly. "We must go."

Owein nodded. He turned to leave the burning wagons and silently melted back into the forest. And as the shadowy green silence reached out to him, shielding him from the harsh sun, he remembered again something Cerrunnos, Master of the Wild Hunt, had said to him. For the god had clearly read Owein's heart that night long ago, when Owein had stood with Gwydion and Rhiannon in the fields of Rheged, the Hunt spilling around them.

"Be careful what you wish for, boy," Cerrunnos had said. "For you shall surely get it."

IT WAS LATE afternoon by the time they returned to camp and distributed the spoils into the care of Isgowen Whledig, the false King's sister, for she had been steward to the true rulers of Rheged for many years, and was loyal to them still. It was she who parceled out the food, the cloth, and the wine to the members of Owein's band—a harder and harder task as time went on. Two years ago, there had been only a handful to feed and clothe and arm. Now, as time went on, more and more men and women came to him, determined to join him in the fight to take back their land.

The main camp, hidden deep in Coed Addien, was crowded, as always, with the sad remnants of what had once been happy families. Children, some motherless, some fatherless, many both—ran back and forth throughout the trees. In this camp there were few warriors, for Owein set his bands to patrolling the forest itself. At regular intervals, a band would return to the main camp for a time, then set out again.

Though he knew that they were well guarded, Owein still winced at the sound of so many people. Yet he knew that, at his signal, they would fall silent, melting into the forest itself until one would have thought the camp had been a dream. He reminded himself over and over that such a large settlement was in no danger of being surprised. For, at the fringes of this great forest, he had set the Dewin and Bards who had been sent to him by Anieron and Elstar. At the first sign of the enemy approaching their domain, the warning would be sounded, and sounded silently—from mind to mind in both words and pictures. Sounded long, long before the enemy could find them.

It was the same with the other two bands where the Cerddorian of Rheged lived and waged their battles against the enemy. Hetwin Silver-Brow, the Lord of Gwinionydd, and his son, Cynedyr the Wild, led the band in Coed Coch, the forest to the southwest. And far to the southeast, in Coed Sarrug, lived the band led by Tyrnon Twrf Liant, Lord of Gwent, and Trystan's sister, Atlantas, the Lady of Malienydd.

Owein did not smile when he saw Isgowen Whledig, for that was not his way. But the stern lines around his mouth lightened somewhat when he showed her the treasures they had brought back. He held back only one thing from her —a golden bracelet, for he meant to give it to his sister. When Enid finally reached him through the press of people crowding around him, he clasped the treasure around her slender wrist.

"Owein," she exclaimed, delighted. "It's lovely."

"Not enough for a Princess of Rheged, but better than nothing." As always, he spoke with underlying bitterness. And, as always, he did not, could not, say what he really meant. But Enid understood.

"A token, surely, of better things to come." She smiled, but her smile had the tinge of sadness he had seen more and more often in the last few months.

She was small and slight for her eighteen years. Her red-gold hair—so like their mother's—was braided tightly to her scalp. She wore a plain tunic of dark green, and brown trousers tucked into brown leather boots. A quiver of arrows was still slung about her shoulders for, though she had not come on the raid today, she had been scouting the forest to the east in Teleri's company, keeping an eye out for possible Coranian reinforcements coming from Llwynarth.

But her smile faded, and the faint line between her brows deepened. Her blue eyes flickered as she took a deep breath, ready to plead again the cause she held most dear to her heart. "Owein," she began.

But Owein, knowing full well what was coming, did not choose to acknowledge it. "Call the others, will you?" he asked, as he walked past her toward the heart of the camp. "I must know what orders the Master Bard has for us next."

"Owein!" she cried, halting him with an urgent hand on his arm.

He stopped. "Yes?" he asked, feigning puzzlement.

Her eyes searched his face for some sign that he was ready to listen. But she did not find it. "Nothing," she said quietly. "I'll call the others."

OWEIN'S BLUE EYES traveled the circle of people gathered in the clearing. To his right, Trystan, his Captain, stood stolidly, stern and silent, as was his fashion these days. Once, years ago, Trystan's green eyes had danced with laughter. Once, where his eyes would have sought out Esyllt, the Bard of Rheged, now they fastened on Owein with grim intent, to the exclusion of all else.

Esyllt herself sat at one end of a log, on Trystan's right. Her light brown hair was loose, flowing down to her slender waist. She wore a plain gown of blue over a shift of white. Around her neck she wore the Bard's torque of a single sapphire set within a silver triangle. Her beautiful blue eyes were bright with the knowledge of her beauty. Her clear skin, fair and white even after two years of living in the forest, shone translucent, like mother of pearl.

Across from Owein stood his Lieutenant, Teleri ur Brysethach. Her brown hair was cut short, and her gray-green eyes were intent. She was a tiny woman, barely reaching Owein's shoulder. Though petite, she was one of the finest warriors in all of Rheged, and her archery was almost legendary. It had been Teleri who had survived that last battle at Llwynarth, and had brought him King Urien's helm and torque, naming him true King of Rheged, heir to his murdered father.

Next to Teleri stood Gwarae Golden-Hair, the Gwarda of Ystlwyf. A year ago Gwarae had escaped his captors and come to the forest to join Owein's band. Gwarae's green eyes blazed with eagerness, though with the thirst for action or the nearness of Teleri, Owein could not tell. Probably both.

Enid sat quietly on another log, her quiver of arrows discarded, the golden bracelet flashing in the sun that dappled the clearing. Her eyes were shuttered and silent now, but something flickered there that made Owein quake inwardly half in exasperation, half in pity.

Rhiwallon, Owein's younger brother, stood between Owein and Enid. His young, twenty-year-old face was fresh and eager. His red-gold hair was tied back in a leather thong at the nape of his strong neck. His blue eyes were clouded, as always, with dreams of glory— glory for Owein's sake, not his own. How Owein wished that his own heart was so clean and pure.

But it was time to begin. They were waiting for his orders. As he often did, he twisted the opal ring of Rheged on his finger, the ring that Esyllt had brought him, given to her by King Urien himself before that last battle.

"Esyllt," Owein said at last. "What news?"

Gracefully Esyllt rose. "Today I have received a long message from the Master Bard. First, Anieron gives news that Hetwin Silver-Brow, from his base in Coed Coch, has won a great victory over a force of over one hundred Coranian warriors. These warriors had been sent, it seems, to flush out his band from the forest. Every last one of these Coranians is dead. Their commander is still in Clwyd, awaiting some word from his men. He will wait a long time, of that you may be sure."

Owein did smile then, pleasure at the enemy's defeat lighting up his stern face.

"There is word, too," Esyllt continued, "that the band in Gwent, led by Lord Tyrnon and Lady Atlantas, has razed the temple of Lytir in Margam to the ground."

"Good," Owein said shortly. "I hope there were some preosts in it at the time."

"There were, my Lord," Esyllt said, smiling. "And one of the wyrce-jaga was there, also."

"Now that is even better news. One less Coranian witch-hunter in Kymru is Kymru's gain."

"Would that we could come across more ourselves," Teleri said darkly. "That is a gain I would love to help Kymru make."

"You shall get your wish, Lieutenant," Esyllt said. "The Master Bard says there is a band of wyrce-jaga coming up the River Rhymney, passing very close to the forest tomorrow."

"If it will please you, Teleri," Gwarae said grandly, "I shall take their heads and lay them at your delicate, perfect feet."

"That will not be necessary," Teleri said coolly. "Do you think I could let them pass and not be there to greet them myself?"

"Well, then, what if I shoot one straight through the heart, with an arrow to which I have first whispered your name? Then shall you pierce their hearts as you have pierced mine." Gwarae grinned, placing his hand over his heart, his eyes mocking.

Teleri rolled her eyes in exasperation. Gwarae often teased her because, he said, her seriousness amused him. For her part, Teleri declared Gwarae a pest, and ignored him whenever he would let her, which was not often.

"We will all be there," Owein said. "That is great news and an assignment I am happy to fulfill. Is that all, Esyllt?"

"No," she said hesitantly. "There is more."

"Bad news?" Owein asked quietly.

"Anieron warns us that one week ago Havgan called a meeting of his inner circle at Eiodel. It was impossible to hear what went on there, but just after that meeting, urgent messages were sent out to each of his Generals. But what the messages were, we do not know. Anieron fears the worst, for it was reported by a Dewin who was Wind-Riding near Caer Duir that the Archdruid's face, as he rode home from that meeting, was triumphant."

"Nothing much new to that," Rhiwallon said cheerfully. "He's been full of himself for years."

"But Aergol's face was clouded. Now what, Anieron wonders, would be so terrible that Cathbad would be delighted and Aergol would be displeased? Anieron warns us all to be very cautious in the days to come, for surely something of the utmost importance has been discussed, and plans for our further downfall have been laid."

"Does Anieron warn against doing anything?" Owein asked.

"He does not. He suggests only additional caution."

"What about the Plentyn Prawf, then? It is almost time for you to begin your journey to test the children. Perhaps it would be best if you remained here this year."

"I cannot do that," Esyllt said quietly. "The Master Bard would not permit it."

"You asked, of course," Teleri said. "And were grateful he did not refuse you permission." Teleri's words were correct, but her tone was something else again.

Esyllt flushed. "I did ask. And was relieved when he said I must go."

"Yes, that must have pleased you."

"Very well," Owein said hastily. Teleri and Esyllt had never liked one another. "Esyllt, you will leave here to begin the testing next week. I will send Trystan with you as guard."

A sharp gesture from Trystan, abruptly stilled, caught Owein's eye. "Is this acceptable to you, Captain?" he asked, surprised.

"It is," Trystan said steadily, "if that is your wish. And the wish of the lady."

"It is, indeed, my wish," Esyllt said warmly. "To whom else could I trust my life but you?"

Contempt flickered in Teleri's eyes as she looked at the Bard. Well, after all, though Esyllt had a husband, he had been held captive now for two years. What matter if she should continue to take her pleasure in Trystan, as she had done for years?

"Well, tomorrow we go to meet the wyrce-jaga who come up-river, and give them a proper Rheged greeting," Owein said. "An early night, then. If there is no more business—"

"There is," Enid said. Her face was pale, but her voice was firm as she rose to speak. "It has long been on my mind that there is another way to strike at Morcant Whledig. A way to deprive him of someone on whom he depends."

Oh, gods, Owein thought. *Not again.* "Enid—"

"No. Hear me out. Bledri, our own father's Dewin, sits at Morcant's feet in Llwynarth, in his own way a captive, too."

"He is hardly a captive, Enid," Teleri said in exasperation. "He is an advisor to Morcant, protected from the wyrce-jaga by the fact that he, too, is a traitor. Or have you forgotten that he was in on the plot with Morcant from the beginning? Have you forgotten that it was his work that delayed the warriors of Amgoed from reaching your parents until it was almost too late? It was he who prevented Hetwin Silver-Brow from coming to their aid. If Hetwin had come to the final battle, perhaps your mother and father would still be alive."

Enid flushed, but held her ground. "How can we know what pressure Morcant had brought to bear on Bledri? How can we know that Bledri does not now repent of his betrayal? All I ask is that you send someone to Llwynarth to talk to him, to determine if he is happy with the path he has chosen."

"And if he is? Just who do you think should put themselves in that kind of danger?" Teleri snapped.

"I myself will go. I am sure that he would give anything to turn back to us."

"To you, you mean," Owein said harshly. "And just what is it that makes you think he wishes to repent of his traitorous acts?"

"I—I just feel it in my heart to be true."

"No," Owein went on relentlessly, "you just wish it to be true. Because he is handsome and charming and he was always kind to you. But then you were a child. Now you are a woman. Set your heart on the Prince of Prydyn. Leave Bledri to the past. And don't forget his hand had a part in mam and da's death. Don't forget they are dead, in part due to him. Don't forget that Elphin, too, lost his life due to Bledri's treachery."

"I don't forget!" Enid cried, stung. "Who could forget that you wanted all Elphin had, even offering for his betrothed! And she refused you. Rightly, she flung your greed and jealousy back to your face!"

"Enid!" Rhiwallon gasped as Owein turned pale. "You forget yourself!"

"I forget nothing! I am like Owein in that!" Enid spat out, as she ran from the clearing.

THE FOREST CLOSED in around her like a prison. She darted in and out between the trees, but she knew that, no matter how far she might run, she was trapped here, as she had been for the past few years. Trapped, and kept away from Bledri who had won her heart when she was just a girl.

And now, as Owein had said, she was a woman. And a woman with her mind made up. No longer would she try to convince the others of what she knew in her heart to be true. She would show them, instead.

Out of breath, she stopped running. Panting, she clutched at the bark of a sturdy oak to steady herself. She rested her cheek against the rough trunk and dashed the tears from her face. She would cry for Bledri no more. Now she would act.

She knew – oh, she knew—that Bledri loved her. She herself would go to Llwynarth. She would tell him that Owein had forgiven him. And he would return to the forest with her. With Bledri by her side, the wood would no longer be a prison, but a haven instead, a place in which she and Bledri would be together. A place from which they would emerge triumphant and set Owein back on his throne.

But she knew Bledri would not believe that Owein would take him back. Without that assurance, he would not come. She must show Bledri a token, something that would make him believe.

And she knew what that would be. She knew she could take this token from her brother. For didn't the ring of Rheged, the ring her own father had worn, belong to all those of the House of PenMarch? The ring was as much hers as it was Owein's.

She had heard the story from Esyllt. She knew the words that had been passed down from ruler to ruler for hundreds of years. The ring was to be surrendered only to the Dreamer who asked for it using these words: "The High King commands you to surrender Bran's gift." Well, she was not a Dreamer. But she would murmur those words when she took the ring. Just to be safe.

She would take the ring tonight, and be on her way. In three days she could reach Llwynarth. She would find Bledri and hand him Owein's ring as a sign of forgiveness. Why, by this time next week, she might even be returning to these woods with Bledri by her side.

Prince Geriant of Prydyn, her betrothed, was far from her thoughts then. She had only agreed to the marriage to please her brother. And though Geriant was golden and handsome and had looked at her with love, he had not touched her heart. For her heart had been given to Bledri long ago.

And so she turned to go back to camp, her mind made up. And there, as she turned, her eye lighted on a small, fernlike plant, nestled at the base of the oak. And as she saw it, she understood that her decision had been right. For why else would she see valerian, the herb that, when mixed with wine or ale, would bring deep, deep sleep?

Truly the gods were with her. She would not fail.

Meirigdydd, Lleihau Wythnos—midmorning

THREE DAYS LATER, when Enid crested the last rise of Sarn Halen, the main road to Llwynarth, and saw the city in which she had been born, her heart nearly failed her. Almost she turned back, and, oh, what a difference that would have made to so many, she would think later. But she went on.

The walls that circled the city were still broken and torn in some places, even after two years. So hard had her father and mother fought to hold Llwynarth, so hard had Morcant Whledig fought to take it, that the destruction had been even more extensive than she had dreamed.

The last time she had seen the city, when she and her brother Rhiwallon had been sent away before the battles, it had been white and shining, like purest flame in the midst of the golden wheat fields. But the fields had been burned, and scarred, and soaked in blood.

And now they yielded little, if at all. They were nothing compared to what they had once been. Neither was the city. A heaviness, a gloom hung over it. Never, she knew, would the city shine again until her brother came back in triumph to claim his own.

Nervously, she touched the leather strip around her neck from which her brother's ring hung, hidden beneath her plain, linen smock. She had taken the ring (she would not say *stolen*) from her brother's hand as he had slept a deep, unnatural sleep—the result of the valerian-laced wine she had given him.

She was dressed plainly, like a servant girl, for that was the part she needed to play. Her kirtle was of dull brown, and she had wrapped her telltale red-gold hair with a plain linen band. She felt awkward in these clothes and hoped that the woman back at the camp from whom she had taken them (she would not say *stolen*) had not been too attached to them.

They would not follow her, she knew, for she had chosen her time wisely. With the prospect of a band of wyrce-jaga to kill, Owein would not have split his warriors to send some after her. And she had been careful, as she had moved through the forest, knowing the places where the Dewin and Bards were set.

It was so strange to be here on the road in the full light of day. The faces of the people around her were pinched with hunger. Even those who looked better-fed showed another kind of want, as though remembering the days when King Urien and Queen Ellirri held the city and the land was fair.

What she saw as she continued through the gate and up the road toward the marketplace nearly made her weep with rage. In that moment, if she had seen Morcant, she would certainly have killed him and never mind what would have happened to her after. For Nemed Draenenwen, the grove of hawthorn trees, the sacred grove where she and her family and the people of Rheged had celebrated the festivals, the grove where the white petals had shone in spring and the red berries had dripped like fire in autumn, was no more.

Every last tree had been cut down. And in its place a temple now stood, consecrated to Lytir, the god of the Coranians. They had built it on this sacred ground, and it was a wonder to her that the Great Mother had not vomited up the temple, spewing it into the air, to be laced with fire, and blown away as ashes in the wind.

One day, she told herself fiercely, her blue eyes sharp and cold, one day the temple would be destroyed. And the grove replanted, and hawthorn would again flower in the city of Llwynarth.

But today was not the day. So she blinked back her tears of helpless fury and continued on to the marketplace. Compared to days gone by, the market was quiet. Of food there was little, for it was early spring and the harvest last autumn—and the autumn before that—had been poor and meager. But there were other wares there, and she made her way straight to the nearest weaver's booth.

"Fine cloth, my girl, for your mistress?" the proprietor said in a tone that was meant to be cheerful but was forced and tight. "I have cloth made in Tegeingl itself, from Gwynedd. The finest cloth in all of Kymru."

"They still weave in Tegeingl, do they?" she asked absently, her mind still on the destruction of the grove. "I suppose they must keep themselves busy while they wait."

The proprietor paled a little at her words. Then he spoke so softly that only she could hear. "Be careful, girl. We all wait, but we none of us speak of it."

"I'm sorry," she said quickly. What a fool she had been already, and she had just arrived. How little skill she had for intrigue. Too much time in the forest, she thought wildly, among those where she did not have to watch her words.

"Don't be sorry lass. Be careful." He then raised his voice in a normal tone. "You seek fine cloth for your mistress, do you?"

"For my master," she said. "He wants something in silver, perhaps. Or sea green." These were the colors of the Dewin, and she needed a reason to see Bledri.

"Something for your mistress would be better," the man replied swiftly. "Something in green or brown."

Her mistress? Green or brown? Those were the colors of the Druids. Oh, surely not, for the Druids had fought for the enemy.

What was the man trying to tell her?

"Yes. Green or brown," he continued in a firm tone. "Your mistress will surely like that best of all. And will reward you for a job well done."

And then she had it, and wondered what it truly meant. For surely the man was trying to tell her something about Sabrina ur Dadweir, who had been the Druid to her mother and father. Sabrina had fought with them in the last battles, but had in the end bowed to the Archdruid and joined with the enemy after she was captured when the city was lost. Or so they had been told in Coed Addien. Maybe green or brown would be best after all. To start.

So she said she would take something in green. And the proprietor cut and measured and handed her a length of cloth, folded into a square. Another sign, she knew.

"Tell your mistress that Menestyr ap Naw wishes her well."

"I will," she said, smiling for the first time in many days.

"And, lass," he said, very low, "pull your linen cap down a bit. The color of your hair is showing."

"Thank you," she said, as she adjusted the band. "And wish me luck."

"If you're going where I think you are going, you will need more than luck." And with that he turned away, his eyes sad.

ON HER WAY through the city to Caer Erias, she detoured slightly. She had to see Crug Mawr, the burial place of the rulers of Rheged. Her mother and father had been laid here with honor, at the insistence of General Baldred. Morcant had wanted them to be left on the field to be picked over by the wolves and the ravens. But Baldred had overruled him, and the bodies had been interred within the stones.

A company of Coranian warriors ringed around the standing stones. So, it was true. She had heard that Morcant and Baldred had set a guard here. Did they fear the dead? She remembered asking Owein when she had first heard of it. And Owein had said, no, they feared the living. For the people of Llwynarth had begun leaving gifts at the stones. They had often gathered here to mourn—or to call on—the spirits of their dead King and Queen. So Morcant had set his guard, and she could not linger at the stones, for they might have asked her what she wanted there.

So she walked by, with her head bowed, and did not let the tears fall. And silently, in her heart, she said good-bye again—oh, once again—to the mother who had borne her, to the father who had nurtured her, to the brother who had loved her. In this world she would never behold their bright faces again.

She came at last to Caer Erias, which had once been her father's fortress. The gate to her home was swung back wide, and as she walked through, she gazed on the sight of the horse of Rheged, white on a field of red-gold, its mane outlined in opals. Its fiery opal eyes gleamed at her, knowing her, she felt, as one of the House of PenMarch.

And then she was through the gate and into the fortress. It was all the same, yet so different. The servants in the courtyard scurried about their tasks, their heads down, moving as quietly and as unobtrusively as possible.

Warriors drilled outside their quarters, but instead of the red and white tunics of Rheged, they wore the metal, sleeved byrnies of the Coranians. Instead of helmets fashioned like the head of a horse, they wore helmets with the figure of a boar on top. Instead of short spears, they drilled with double-bladed axes.

There were no cheerful greetings being bandied back and forth, no joking, or laughing. Her home had turned into a grim, dark place, and she could barely stand to return here.

A flash of bright color seen out of the corner of her eye caused her to turn, and what she saw made her dart behind the stables. Her heart beating wildly, she peered around the corner.

The flash of color had come from the bright red cloak Morcant Whledig wore as he came out of the King's ystafell, a host of people behind him. Morcant's black, shoulder-length hair shone like a raven's wing. Around his head he wore a golden circlet. Of course, Enid thought. The torque was not here. Owein had it. So they had given Morcant something to show he was a King, like the master throwing a bone to a dog. His tunic and trousers were of red and white, worked with gold thread and opals. She gritted her teeth to see that the traitor of Rheged wore her father's colors.

Beside Morcant stood a stocky, powerful-looking man. His light brown hair was uncovered. In one hand he held a helmet of silver, fashioned like the head of a boar. He wore a byrnie of silver that flashed in the sun. She knew of him, General Baldred, the Coranian watchdog, who let Morcant think he was King.

She recognized the woman standing a little to the side and behind Baldred. Sabrina's beautiful face seemed carved from stone. Her long black hair was worn loosely, spilling over her Druid's robe of brown and green. Her Druid's torque of gold and emerald sparkled at her slender throat.

And then Enid's heart beat even faster as she saw the man she had come so far to find. The muscles of Bledri's broad shoulders strained against the fabric of his sea-green and silver robe. Around his neck the Dewin's torque of silver and pearl was clasped. His sandy brown hair was tied back at the nape of his neck with a fine silver chain. His gray eyes, oh, so charming, so perfect, so arresting, exuded power and intelligence. His almost impossibly handsome face was smiling sardonically as he eyed the General and the King—and the man who was being dragged out of the ystafell.

Enid knew that man, Llyenog ap Glwys, the Master Smith of Rheged. The Master Smith was loaded down with chains. Gray-haired but strong, he straightened up under the load and dug in his heels as two warriors tried to drag him past the King.

"I ask you again, Morcant Whledig, so-called King of Rheged, what is my crime?"

Morcant, his face flushed, began to say something, but General Baldred forestalled him. "You are being taken at my command."

"So, Morcant," said Llyenog, the contempt in his tone clear and biting, "you do not know. You are King of nothing." Llyenog spat on the ground at Morcant's feet.

Morcant stepped forward and would have landed a blow on Llyenog's face if Bledri had not caught his arm. "Leave him be,

Morcant," Bledri said in an amused tone. "He is not worth your notice."

"And besides," Sabrina said, her voice like velvet, "he could probably break you in two, even now."

Morcant shot Sabrina a venomous look, but General Baldred only laughed. "Take him away," Baldred said, gesturing to the two warriors on either side of the Master Smith. "Oh, and Llyenog, your family will be joining you so you won't be lonely."

"And to be sure you do as you are told," Bledri interjected. "Should you give Baldred's men trouble on your journey, or once you reach the place, your family will be killed. One by one, you will watch them die. And be sure that they will suffer exquisite tortures before they do." Bledri smiled a smile that Enid had never seen on his face before, one she hadn't even known he was capable of. "Take him."

Sabrina, her face cold, pushed past the men and began to walk away. As she passed Llyenog, she whispered something to him. At her message Llyenog straightened his shoulders, and marched out of the fortress proudly, escorted by ten warriors.

Morcant and Baldred turned and went back into the ystafell, but Bledri stood where he was, watching Sabrina cross the courtyard. Almost Enid tried to catch Bledri's eye, but she remembered the cloth she still clutched in her cold hands, and what the merchant had said. So, instead, she stepped from behind the stable and faced Sabrina.

"My Lady," Enid said. "I have come with the cloth you wanted."

Sabrina stared at Enid in shock, her face suddenly white. A frantic warning deep within Sabrina's blue eyes leapt out, catching at Enid's heart. Quickly Sabrina spoke, and her voice was querulous. "At last! Come to my rooms and let me see it. What took you so long, girl? I have been waiting half the morning!" She took Enid's arm in a firm grip, rushing her across the yard and into the guesthouse. Swiftly, she led Enid to her room and closed and barred the door.

For a moment, Sabrina stood with her face to the door, then took a deep breath and turned to look at Enid.

"What in the name of all the gods of Kymru are you doing here?"

"I—I have come for Bledri."

"Come for Bledri," Sabrina repeated slowly. "Did I hear you right?"

Enid held her head high. "Yes. You heard me right."

"Oh, child, child, you cannot be thinking this. You cannot do this."

"I am not a child! And I know that Bledri sickens of what he has done."

"What," Sabrina asked incredulously, "makes you think that?"

"I just know it. And Owein knows it, too. See," she said, taking the ring from her bodice, "Owein sends me here with his forgiveness. To bring Bledri back."

"You lie," Sabrina said, her voice flat. "That is Urien's ring. Owein would never, never give that up. Oh, Enid, you must go from here. Now!"

And then she understood. "You're jealous! You're jealous of me. You don't want Bledri to go away!"

"Oh, Enid," Sabrina said, her voice despairing. "What have you done?"

Before Enid could answer, a pounding on the barred door make them jump.

"Sabrina?" Bledri called. "Open up. I want to talk to you."

"Go away!" Sabrina called.

"Open it, Sabrina. Don't make me have the door torn down. You know I will—I have before!"

"Don't make me burn you," Sabrina shouted back, as she frantically looked around the room. "You know I will—I have before!" She clutched Enid's arm, murmuring, "Oh, gods, no place to hide you. And the window is guarded. Here, under the bed."

"No!" Enid cried, tearing her arm away. "I must see him."

"You must not! I swear to you, Enid, you are wrong. Wrong about everything. Please, hide. Then we can talk. I'll think of a way to get you out of here. Please."

"No!"

"Sabrina," Bledri called. "Who is with you?"

"Open the door, Druid," Enid said quietly. "If you don't, he'll bring others to do it for him."

Sabrina looked from the door to Enid, despair written on her beautiful face. Without another word, she went to the door and unbarred it, opening it wide.

"You've been avoiding me again," Bledri said smoothly. "And you know what can happen when you do that." Then his gray eyes lit on Enid, standing in the middle of the room, and he fell silent.

Enid removed the linen band from her head, and her hair came down, falling around her shoulders in a shower of red-gold. She removed the ring from the string around her neck, holding it out to Bledri, who still stood, frozen, by the door.

"This is from Owein, *cariad*," Enid said quietly. "You are forgiven for all. Come with me, and let us go to him. Help us in our fight to take back what was once ours."

Sabrina gave a low moan of despair and sank to the edge of the bed, her head in her hands. Bledri, his face still, held out his hand, and Enid laid the ring in his palm.

"Urien's ring. You have brought it to me," he said, his tone wondering.

"I have. Now come with me. Let us go from this prison. Be free."

Bledri looked down at the ring, turning it this way and that, enthralled with the fiery opal. Almost absently, he said, "It will make a fine bridal piece, Enid. Very fine."

Enid shot a glance of triumph at Sabrina, but the Druid was staring at the floor. And then her heart skipped a beat. She felt cold, colder than she had ever been in her life. Her head swam. Shock, she thought incoherently. This is shock.

For Bledri had continued. "A fine bridal piece, indeed. And a bride from the House of PenMarch will be just what he needs."

"He?" Enid whispered.

"Morcant Whledig," Bledri said. And smiled.

THAT NIGHT THE message sent by the Shining Ones reached into

44

Gwydion's sleep.

At last he had found Y Honneit, the Spear, one of the lost Treasures of Kymru. He had found Erias Yr Gwydd, Blaze of Knowledge. He could see it as it floated within a mighty ring of fire.

The long shaft made of twining silver and gold flashed brightly in the light of the fire. Gleaming opals covered the base and the top of the shaft. The spear point itself was studded with onyx in a figure eight, the sign of Annwyn, Lord of Chaos.

He tried to reach out for it then, but the fire blazed even brighter. The heat made the Spear shimmer before his eyes.

And he cried out in frustration and anger, for he was so close but could not obtain what he so desperately sought.

Then, suddenly, a black raven shot down from the sky. A collar of opals encircled his neck, and his black feathers glowed red in the light of the flames.

In his talons he held a branch of oak leaves. The raven tossed the branch into the fire, where it settled gently on the shaft of the glowing spear.

Ask. The raven's thought echoed through the deepest chambers of his mind. *You must ask.*

At first his pride forbade him to speak, but his need was too great. "I beg you, then. I beg you to help me," he rasped.

Reach, the raven answered.

"I can't," Gwydion cried. "I'm afraid."

Reach, the raven repeated sternly.

And so he stretched out his arms to the fire as the Spear floated serenely through the flames to his waiting hands. And his hands turned to a raven's claws, then back into his own hands, flickering unsteadily from one to the other.

And the Spear came to him as the man/raven reached out and took it, plucking it from the fire. The raven screamed in triumph. The oak branch glowed with the fiery light of the opals around the hilt of the Spear that shone bright and deadly, as he held the Spear aloft in the light of the blazing fire.

Chapter 3

Ogaf Greu and Arberth
Kingdom of Prydyn, Kymru
Bedwen Mis, 499

Llundydd, Lleihau Wythnos—late afternoon

Gwenhwyfar ur Rhoram var Rhiannon, Princess of Prydyn, daughter of the House of Llyr, winced in pain as she scrambled to her feet. Rolling up her woolen skirt, she gravely examined her wound.

Another skinned knee. Queen Efa would kill her.

Even in her thoughts Gwen styled her stepmother as Queen. Efa had always insisted on being addressed by that title. Even though Efa no longer ruled over a kingdom, her insistence had not changed. Actually, she was worse than ever.

Once—and only once—Gwen had made the mistake of asking Efa just what she thought she was Queen of now—the seagulls? Her stepmother's reaction hadn't bothered her in the least, but Gwen had repented of her thoughtless words instantly, for the look on her father's face had almost broken her heart. Once again she had not thought before she spoke, and so had hurt someone she loved. It seemed to happen to her a lot.

But, she excused herself, as she always did, what can anyone expect of a person who had spent the first eleven years of her life in hiding? What could you expect of someone who had grown up in a cave?

She sighed. Not many years after she had left the cave in the forest of Coed Aderyn, she had returned to another cave. This one was on the shores of Prydyn. But a cave was a cave. Full circle her life had come, it seemed.

The cry of a seagull made her look up to track the bird's lazy flight. The waves washed up to shore with a regularity she found monotonous. The sun had begun its flight to the sea, and the shadows cast by the rocks began to lengthen.

Sixteen years old, she thought, as she moved through the sandy rocks, stepping delicately with her bare feet. Sixteen years old, and still hiding. She wondered if the time would ever come when they could go home. Wondered when—and if—she would ever see the fair, white walls of Arberth, the city from which her father had once ruled the Kingdom of Prydyn. She wondered if, in the next raid on the enemy, or the next, or the one after that, someone she loved would die. Maybe her father, whom she loved so. Maybe her half brother, Geriant, who was so kind to her. Maybe Achren, her father's Captain, dark and fierce in battle. Maybe Gwen herself would die.

She would not think of her death now. And she would not think of the dream that had come to her over a week ago. Even now the remembrance of it still frightened her. She would not think of anything except for the fact that she was out of the caves. For she hating living here, hated being inside the earth itself, hated the feeling it gave her. Once, she had loved the caves. Almost her entire childhood had been spent exploring the caverns that laced the earth beneath the forest of Coed Aderyn. But since that day years ago when she had fallen into a pit from which she could not escape, and the dark had seemed to swallow her, caves had frightened her almost unbearably.

But she had not died that day, for her mother had come and saved her.

No. She would not think of her mother. Gwenhwyfar hated Rhiannon ur Hefeydd with all her heart. Her mother had deserted her and gone to the Dreamer. Rhiannon didn't matter anymore. Gwen had her father now, and her brother and sister. That was all she needed.

And they needed her. Her father, who had once been bright, glowing with joy and laughter, had changed. Rhoram was a driven man now. He rarely laughed, rarely smiled. All his will was bent now to loosening Prydyn from the grip of the enemy.

And Gwen's half sister, Sanon, was only a pale shadow of the girl she had once been, ever since her betrothed, Prince Elphin of Rheged, had died in battle two years ago. So changed was Sanon that sometimes Gwen was frightened, thinking that her sister would just waste away. But Sanon had endured. There was still strength in her, enough strength to refuse the hand of Prince Owein, Elphin's brother. Gwen was sorry about that, for she had liked Owein, in spite of the fierce sorrow in his eyes.

And Geriant, though now betrothed to Owein's sister, and head over heels in love with the Princess Enid, still needed his little sister. If Gwen had read Enid correctly, Geriant might very well need a shoulder to lean on. There had been something in Enid's eyes at the betrothal ceremony that had Gwen wondering if she truly loved Geriant. Some hint of reservation, though she had said all the correct things.

"You've gone too far again."

The voice startled her, and she whipped around, her dagger in her hand.

"Good," Achren approved. "Quick, and the stance was right, but you should have heard me coming."

Gwen straightened, returning her dagger to its sheath. "Sorry, Achren."

"Don't be sorry; be careful. Understand this—I will not watch your father's face when they tell him you died because you were careless."

Gwen opened her mouth to retort, but thought better of it. Few people argued with Achren. And Gwen had been wrong. She had walked too far from the caves, and she should have heard someone coming, even someone who moved as quietly as Achren. So she bit back what she was going to say.

"Wise," Achren said. "Very wise."

Achren ur Canhustyr, King Rhoram's Captain, was dressed in a tight-fitting leather tunic and trousers of black. Her long, dark hair was loose and flowing around her shoulders. Her dark eyes flashed, and her wide mouth was set in a firm line. "Come," Achren continued, "it's past time to return."

"I hate the caves!" Gwen blurted.

"I know," Achren replied shortly. "And you know that it is unimportant, compared to the safety of our people. Come."

"Achren . . ." Gwen began, then trailed off uncertainly.

"At last we come to it. You've been holding something back for over a week now. Let's hear it." And though her tone was not particularly sympathetic, Gwen knew Achren very well.

"I had a dream," Gwen whispered, her mouth dry.

"So, you have become a Dreamer now? What will Gwydion ap Awst say to that, I wonder?" Achren's wide mouth quirked.

"The Dreamer was there. I remember that."

"Was your mother?"

"No," Gwen spat, diverted from her terror. "Since when has she ever been there for me?"

"Since the day you were born," Achren said firmly. "But we won't ever agree on that subject, so let's not start again. Go on."

"There was a wood and a pool of water. And Cerrunnos and Cerridwen were there. And, oh, Achren, the Protectors were dying!"

Achren gripped Gwen's arm fiercely. "They were dying?" Achren asked, her voice thin and taut.

"Yes," Gwen whispered. "Oh, yes."

Achren released her grip, but her face was tight. "What else?"

"There was a golden bowl, a bowl with emeralds on the rim. And then I felt as though the earth was covering me. It was dark, and dirt was smothering me. I couldn't breathe."

"And then what?"

"And then I woke up. That was all." It lost something in the telling, of course. How could she ever convey in mere words the fear that she had endured in those moments? Who would ever understand her terror that there would be no one to rescue her this time, if the earth tried to claim her again? Her mother was no longer here.

"Achren," she went on. "Do you think it was a true dream? And if it was, how could I have done that? I am not the Dreamer."

"No, but you have perhaps been caught in his dreams. It happens, sometimes."

"I'm afraid. I'm afraid of what I might have to do."

"Yes, you should be. But when the task comes to you, you must do the best you can. It will be enough, I think. Now come."

Illogically reassured by Achren's cool compliment, Gwen fell in step beside her as they began to walk back to the caves.

"The Protectors were not dead yet, in your dream," Achren said thoughtfully, after a moment. "Then it is not too late."

"No, not too late," Gwen replied softly. Not yet.

As ALWAYS, WHEN she entered the caves, Gwen's fear fell heavily upon her. But, as always, she concealed it as best she could. Bending slightly, she followed Achren through the narrow fissure in the rock face. Momentarily blinded by the shadows, she blinked and went on, knowing that her eyes would soon adjust. She nodded to Aidan, her father's Lieutenant, who was stationed just inside this entrance. There were many entrances and exits in Ogaf Greu, and they were guarded at all times by Rhoram's warriors. Rhoram, though he always had Dewin and Bards watching and listening, had learned to be very cautious in these troubled times.

"You are late for the council," Aidan said gleefully, a grin on his handsome face. "Which means I win the bet."

"And who," Achren replied, "was foolish enough to bet that Gwenhwyfar would not have gone too far?"

"The King."

Gwen winced inwardly. Achren glanced back at her, then said, "So he believed your promise, I see. He thought you would keep your word. He thought you had grown up, all evidence to the contrary. That was foolish of him, now, wasn't it?"

"I said I was sorry," Gwen snapped, knowing she was in the wrong. But she hated being told what to do and how to do it.

"And I told you, sorry wasn't good enough." Without another

word, Achren turned away, striding through another narrow fissure in the cave wall. Aidan gestured grandly for Gwen to go next, then followed.

Torches lit the narrow passage, casting flickering shadows. They passed another guard, who was coming up to take Aidan's place. They walked through cavern after cavern, each one filled with people. Some were warriors of Rhoram's who had survived that last, terrible battle. Others were warriors who had come after, led to this place by Rhoram's people. Gwen saw the men and women of Hywel's band, from Penfro, and from Lluched's teulu of Creuddyn. The warriors from the bands of Anhuniog and Pennardd were absent, sent to the east and south on raiding parties.

The band of Cerddorian here in Ogaf Greu, commanded by her father, was the largest but not the only band in Prydyn. Far to the southwest in the forest of Coed Gwyn lurked another group of fighters, led by Achren's sister, Marared, the Lady of Brycheniog, and Dadweir Heavy-Hand, Lord of Bychan. Dadweir, the father of Sabrina, the former Druid to King Urien, was very difficult to get along with. But Achren said that Marared had her ways, and Dadweir did what King Rhoram wished him to do.

They reached a small cave branching off from the main cavern. Achren lifted the curtain that served as a door and strode in, with Gwen following and Aidan behind. People sat in a ring on the floor of the cave, but Gwen had eyes only for her father.

Torchlight illuminated Rhoram's golden hair and blue eyes, playing off the emerald ring he wore and the hard angles of his taut face. It had taken him many months to recover from the physical wound the traitor, Erfin, had given him during that final battle. Even now, two years later, those lines of pain were still chiseled into his once-smooth face. The other wounds—the wounds he had suffered because Erfin was his brother-in-law, because he thought he had failed his people, because he had survived that last battle—were still raw. Perhaps, Gwen thought, they always would be.

Gwen took her place in the heavy silence, sitting on the rock floor to the left of her father. As she crossed the circle, her half-brother, Geriant, sitting at Rhoram's right, gave her a smile. Geriant was always kind to her, even when she didn't deserve it.

Dafydd Penfro, Rhoram's chief counselor, sat on Gwen's left. His dark eyes, taking in Gwen's torn skirt and slight limp, were quietly amused and not surprised. Next to Dafydd, his brother, Hywel, Gwarda of Penfro, sat stolidly, waiting for his orders. Cian, Rhoram's Bard, sat on Hywel's left. His green eyes were distracted, and he seemed restless. Clearly he had news from the Master Bard he was eager to share.

Aidan had taken his place on Cian's left, with Achren next to him. On Achren's other side sat Cadell, Rhoram's Dewin. Cadell's face showed his habitual worried frown as he nervously plucked at the ragged sleeves of his undertunic. Next to Cadell, his sister, Lluched, Gwarda of Creuddyn, sat, quietly fingering her dagger. Her dark hair was woven into a cluster of tiny braids, secured with small bands of brass, and her almond-shaped dark eyes flickered to Aidan, who returned her glance with a smile.

There was a heavy silence, until Rhoram took something from his tunic, and flipped it across the circle to Aidan. The torchlight flickered off the gold bracelet as it arced through the air. Aidan caught it, one-handed. "It seems, Aidan, that you have won," Rhoram said coolly.

The bracelet soared across the circle again, this time thrown by Aidan into the hands of Lluched. She, too, caught it one-handed, not even dropping her dagger. "It seems, my King, that is it Lluched who has won," Aidan said smoothly.

"You two had a bet? What was it?" Geriant asked curiously.

"A private matter, Prince Geriant," Lluched said gravely, sliding the bracelet up her slender arm. "And bracelets, Aidan, won't buy as much as you think."

Aidan grinned. "A man can dream, can't he?"

At the mention of dreams, Gwen's own smile faded, and Achren cast her a quick glance. Rhoram, so very quick, caught the brief look and turned to Gwen, his blue eyes grave, waiting.

But before Gwen could speak, Achren said quickly, "Well, Rhoram, let's begin."

Rhoram looked over at his Captain, and what he saw in her dark eyes forestalled the comment he had been about to make. Smoothly, Rhoram began. "Within a few weeks, it will be time to start this year's Plentyn Prawf and test the children. Cian, what says the Master Bard about that?"

"He does not warn against it," Cian replied. "But he reminds us that he still does not know what happened last week in the meeting at Eiodel. He urges caution."

"And what do you say to that?"

Cian grinned. "I say, I love to travel."

"Very well. Achren, when he leaves, go with him. I want the best to guard him."

Achren nodded. She had expected this assignment, Gwen knew.

"Anything else, Cian?" Rhoram asked.

"I have received word from the Master Bard there is a tribute caravan coming our way," the Bard said gleefully. "Goods from Gwarthaf bound for Erfin's use in Arberth."

"I have sighted the caravan, my King," Cadell said. "It will be within our provenance by tomorrow."

"How many warriors guarding it?" Rhoram asked.

"Forty."

"Forty?" Rhoram raised his eyebrows. "How insulting. Only forty."

"Erfin always did underestimate you, Rhoram," Achren replied. "It amazes me how slow he is to learn."

"Oh, come. Do you think Erfin is giving orders to the Coranians? It is the other way around," Dafydd Penfro remarked.

"A trap, then," Achren offered, her black eyes gleaming. "For General Penda surely does know better."

"And just as surely he knows how dangerous this area is," Hywel of Penfro put in.

"And hopes to pinpoint our location," Dafydd said smoothly.

"So, what do we do?" Cadell asked. "Do we let it go by?"

"We do," Rhoram said firmly.

"What? How can you—" Lluched began, always loathe to miss a fight.

"And attack it three days after it has gone by," Rhoram continued.

Gwen caught Rhoram's glance at Aidan. Aidan gave a brief nod. *Now what,* Gwen wondered, *was that all about?*

"I will be happy to follow them," Achren said, smiling. "Who goes with me?"

"You do not go, Achren," Rhoram said. Achren opened her mouth to argue, but Rhoram held up his hand and she subsided.

"The band will be led by Geriant," Rhoram continued.

"Thank you, da," Geriant replied, grinning. "Anything special?"

"No, just the usual. Kill them all and bring back what you can comfortably carry."

"Yes, da."

"Hywel, you and Dafydd are to go, also."

Now that was a surprise. Not the choice of Hywel, but to send Dafydd. Dafydd was a counselor, not a warrior. But Dafydd himself seemed to understand and simply nodded.

"That's it?" Achren said in surprise. "What about Aidan?"

"Aidan stays. Oh, and one more thing," Rhoram went on, turning to Gwen. "You may go, also."

"Oh, da, can I really?"

"Why not? Three days' journey from here is about as far as you walk every day anyway."

Gwen flushed. "Da—" she began, then stopped, for she noticed that her father's eyes were kind. "Thank you."

"You're welcome."

"When do we leave?" Geriant asked.

"Now," Rhoram answered crisply. "I want you far ahead of them. Two days from today, stop and wait for them. Once they pass this area unchallenged, they will think themselves safe." Rhoram rose, signaling that the meeting was over. "Oh, and one other thing. I want you to leave without mentioning your destination or purpose. Hywel, just tell your warriors to be ready to leave within the hour. That's all anyone needs to know."

"Why, da?" Gwen asked curiously.

"For reasons of my own," he replied shortly. "Geriant and Gwen,

Dafydd will be happy to help you gather your weapons."

Dafydd nodded, his eyes serene. Gwen opened her mouth, then shut it quickly, seeing the look in her father's eyes. Any questions she asked would not be welcomed. They filed out of the stone chamber in a puzzled silence. Gwen, who trailed last, was the only one who heard the words that passed between Rhoram and Aidan.

"Tonight," Rhoram said quietly. "Be ready."

ACHREN TOSSED RESTLESSLY on her pallet. It was no use. She absolutely could not sleep. Rising, she put on her tunic and trousers by the light of the fire in the brazier, now burned down to glowing embers, for it was very late.

Shaking her long hair out of her face, she lifted the curtain to her sleeping chamber and stepped out into the cavern. It seemed that everyone else was able to sleep. Carefully, she picked her way around the sleeping pallets spread throughout the cave. She needed to walk, to think, so she made her way to the south exit, which led to the beach. Silently, she glided through the tunnels, thinking hard.

Rhoram's behavior this afternoon had been, to put it mildly, peculiar. Such an odd choice, to send Dafydd Penfro on a raiding party. And dinner tonight had been very strange, with so many undercurrents. When Efa had asked where Gwen and Geriant were, Rhoram hadn't even bothered to answer her. He had pretended not to hear, and concentrated on talking with his daughter Sanon. And Sanon had not asked one single question about Geriant's or Gwen's whereabouts. Aidan had flirted with Lluched, as he always did, yet his eyes had flickered constantly to Efa. And Efa, her dark red hair elaborately braided, her slender arms hanging with bracelets, her rich gown of amber shimmering in the torchlight, scrutinized Aidan with her large, beautiful brown eyes as covertly as she could. Rhoram had not seemed to notice. And that was odd, for Rhoram noticed everything.

As she neared the end of the last tunnel, she suddenly realized that something was wrong. The torches nearest the last exit were out, as they should be, for there must be no betraying lights to mark the exit. But just at the very end of the tunnel, she saw the glow of a torch, and heard the murmur of voices. Quietly she crept up to the last fissure. She recognized the voices instantly. Pure rage shot through her as she listened.

"All is ready for me, then?" Efa asked, her rich voice low and seductive.

"Ready, indeed, my Queen," Aidan replied smoothly.

"I do hope you picked good horses. I must be in Arberth within the week. And you have even farther to travel."

"Tegyr's band is only two days away. It won't take me long to persuade them to accompany me to Arberth."

"And then, *cariad*, we can be together. If, of course, you can truly tear yourself away from Lluched," Efa said sharply.

"As I explained to you before, Efa, Lluched is nothing to me. She is only a tool to further our schemes, and throw Rhoram off the scent."

"You play your part a little too well."

"Ah, Efa, there is no woman for me but you. Haven't I told you that often enough?"

"Told me, but never shown me."

"It is too dangerous here. You know that. But when we are together in Arberth, things will be different. You are sure that Rhoram suspects nothing?"

"Nothing at all. He truly thinks I am going to Maen to buy things I can't live without. And that you are going with me, to protect me."

So that was it. Achren had heard enough, and it shocked her to the core. Not that she was surprised Efa was running away to Arberth, deserting her husband and throwing in her lot with her traitorous brother. But that Aidan, her own Lieutenant, would be in league with her!

Slowly she drew her dagger —for even when walking the caves she did not go unarmed. But before she could move, a hand shot out of the darkness, covering her mouth. An arm like a band of steel encircled her waist and pinned her arms to her sides. Before she could even begin to struggle, a voice she knew well whispered into her ear.

"Do not make a sound," Rhoram breathed.

All at once, she relaxed and stopped struggling, as she began to understand.

"What was that?" Efa asked shrilly.

"Ssh," Aidan said. "Keep your voice down. I didn't hear anything."

"I swear, I heard something."

"Then go. Hurry."

As the footsteps receded down the tunnel and out the exit, Rhoram slowly—a little too slowly, Achren thought, even in her distraction—released his grip on her. They stood in silence until they heard Aidan returning.

"She is gone," Aidan called out softly as he came toward them, a torch in his hand.

"Well," Rhoram said cheerfully, "at last! I thought she'd never leave."

"She's going south, to Arberth! Is that why Dafydd Penfro went with them this afternoon? To be sure she isn't stopped by Geriant and the rest?"

"Of course," Rhoram said. "Why else?"

Aidan spotted the dagger she still held in her hand. His brows raised. "You were going to kill me, I take it."

"I still might! What is the matter with you two? How could you let her go?"

"How not, Achren? Did you think I could kill her?" Rhoram asked quietly.

"There are those who can," Achren replied through gritted teeth, "if you are so squeamish. Don't you realize what you've done? She'll call the Coranians down on us."

"My dear Captain, we are moving first thing tomorrow. It will take her seven days to reach Arberth and give our location away. By then we will be long gone."

"Nonsense! She could very well stop on her way to Arberth and tell the next Coranian contingent that she sees."

"Fool," Rhoram said with a smile. "She will not. She will tell only her brother, giving him the credit for capturing us. Of course, as far as she is concerned, I don't have the slightest notion that she plans to betray us, so her absence will not alarm me. I gave my consent to her supposed trip to Maen, indulgent husband that I am. And my consent for Aidan to protect her."

"Then why," Achren said acidly, "hasn't Aidan gone with her?"

"All appearances to the contrary, Aidan is even now traveling east in an attempt to locate Tegyr's band. Aidan is quite sure that he can persuade Tegyr to fall in with his schemes to betray us."

Achren turned to Aidan. "And just where is Tegyr's band?"

"On their way to our new hiding place, of course," Aidan said cheerfully.

"Which is?"

"Haford Bryn," Rhoram replied. "And speaking of the new place, we'd better get moving. Come, Achren, and I will show you the plans for an orderly and secret dispersal."

"Why did you keep this from me?" Achren snarled. "Am I or am I not your Captain?"

"You are the light of my life, dearest Achren," Rhoram said with a grin, "but I did not like to test your ability for intrigue. Your solution to problems is usually to deposit a dagger into them. And," his smile faded, "I could not have Efa killed."

"So instead of that, you make us all disperse? Rhoram, you are a fool!"

"So you keep telling me. You are not the first woman to say so. And you will surely not be the last."

Llundydd, Tywyllu Wythnos—late afternoon
GENERAL PENDA CLIMBED the stairs of the northwest watchtower in the city of Arberth, his brows knitted in thought. He did not return—indeed, he did not even notice—the salutes that his guards gave him. Reaching the top of the tower, he waved the guards down the stairs. He wanted to be alone to think about the messages he had received today.

Instinctively, he gazed north to where the fugitive King Rhoram hid with his warriors—warriors who emerged from their hiding places long enough to ambush, to kill, to steal from the Coranians, then melted back into their holes.

He turned west to see the sea rolling and glittering in the afternoon sun. If only he was taking to the sea himself. If only he was on his way home to Corania at last, on the way home to his father and son, leaving the land of Kymru far behind, then maybe he would be a happy man. If he could forget the things he had done here. But he doubted he ever would.

His face, once so energetic and full of life, was stern and set. His dark blond hair whipped about in the wind off the sea. For a brief moment he closed his brown eyes, pretending he was on the deck of a ship, on his way home.

He knew that it had been a mistake to come up to the tower, that it was always a mistake to stand still long enough to think. When he did that, he always found himself regretting the day he had first seen Havgan. How he regretted—oh, most bitterly of all—that he had ever given his blood oath in the brotherhood ritual. But he had. And his freedom to choose his own way was long gone.

Enough of that, he told himself. He had serious matters to think about—such as the two messages he had received this morning. First came word that the caravan from Gwarthaf had been attacked four days ago. He had expected it. But the attack had come far from the place Penda believed Rhoram was hiding. They had known, somehow, that the caravan was bait. Rhoram's people had waited until the caravan had left the hidden contingents of Coranian warriors far behind. For when the attack had not come, Penda's Captains had called off the plan, thinking they would have to try again. So when the attack did come, the additional warriors were not there. The entire caravan had been stolen, and all his guards had died. Well, he would have to try something else next time, that was all.

It was the second message, the one from Havgan, that had disturbed him even more. Penda had been ordered to arrest the Master Smith of Prydyn, Siwan ur Trephin, along with her family, and send them to the island of Caer Siddi under heavy guard under cover of night. He had not been told exactly why, only that the Archdruid had some kind of plan to neutralize the witches, and that the four Master Smiths of Kymru were to make some type of weapon. If they did not cooperate, their families would be slaughtered.

That was merely puzzling. The second part of the message was the problem. He was to find, somehow, Cian ap Menw, King Rhoram's Bard. The Bard would soon be traveling throughout Prydyn to test the children for witchery. Penda was to apprehend Cian and the testing device the Bard carried, without fail. The Druids would be happy to help in the search. The price for failure would be severe. Havgan, as always, left the details to Penda's imagination.

Footsteps sounded on the stairs. "You sent for me, General?" she asked, her voice cold and clipped, as always.

Ellywen ur Saidi, the former Druid to King Rhoram, returned his gaze, her gray eyes cold as ice. Her brown hair was tightly braided and wrapped around the top of her head like a crown. Her brown Druid's robe was trimmed with green, and her slender hands were hidden inside the sleeves of the robe. She would have been a beautiful woman had there been one iota of warmth in her, one hint of laughter. But there was not. Perhaps there never had been.

"We have been given orders from Eiodel, Druid," he said.

"And they are?"

"We must capture Rhoram's Bard and the testing device he carries. Havgan seems to believe that Cian will be traveling soon to begin the testing, that the Bard will not consider the trip too hazardous and stay hidden."

"Cian will begin the Plentyn Prawf. He was always a fool."

"Where will he go?"

"Everywhere."

Penda sighed. "I mean, where will he go first?"

Ellywen thought for a moment. "Rhoram's Cerddorian are somewhere in Aeron, we know. My guess is, Cian will bypass Maen and travel north."

"Then you must, also."

She nodded. "I will go upriver and be in Cil within the week. I will find him."

"You will take a guard of at least twenty."

"Very well."

"If you find him, take him directly to Eiodel. Havgan will be waiting."

"I shall. I—"

Ellywen broke off, staring to the north. Startled, Penda followed her gaze. He saw a lone rider tearing across the vineyards, making for the north gate. The sun glinted off the diminutive rider's red hair.

"I can't believe it," Ellywen breathed.

"What? Who is that?"

"Queen Efa."

"Rhoram's wife? Erfin's sister?"

"The same. By Modron—I mean, by Lytir—how could Rhoram have possibly let her go? What is he up to?"

Penda shouted for the guards, sending some to alert Erfin of his sister's arrival, sending others to escort Efa through the north gate and into Caer Tir. He had heard much of Queen Efa. He would be very interested to meet her at last, and find out exactly where she had come from.

As PENDA AND Ellywen reached the gate of Caer Tir, Erfin himself came hurrying out of the fortress, followed by Coranian guards. Under Penda's orders, Erfin was not allowed to go anywhere without them.

Erfin's red hair flamed beneath the golden circlet the Coranians had given him to mark his kingship. He was dressed richly but gaudily in a tunic and trousers of dark green trimmed with orange and purple. Penda, though never fashionable himself, thought Erfin's taste was excruciatingly bad. But, he reminded himself, that's what you can expect when you take the dregs of humanity and make Kings out of them.

Erfin's shifty brown eyes were shining as he hurried through the gate. His face, still scarred by his battle with Rhoram two years ago, was gleeful. The Wolf of Prydyn, blazoned on the gate in emeralds, seemed to wink balefully at the upstart King.

"Is it true?" Erfin asked breathlessly. "Is it really her?"

"It is. I saw her myself, Erfin," Ellywen said stiffly.

"How many times," Erfin said crossly, "do I have to tell you not to call me Erfin?"

"It is your name, as I recall," Ellywen replied caustically.

"I am King here. You are to call me—"

"Not now, Erfin," Penda said tiredly. "Here she is."

Efa rode up on a fine, black horse, attended by several guards. She wore brown riding leathers and an undershirt of fine, white linen. The cuffs of her brown leather boots were turned down slightly to show a rich, golden lining. She wore several necklaces of gold and long, golden earrings with amber stones. Her hair was elaborately braided, fastened at the ends with golden clips. She must have stopped a few leagues from the city and freshened up, Penda thought. Nobody travels dressed like that.

As she made to dismount, Erfin hurried to help her. "Sister! I could scarcely believe it when they said it was you!"

"I rid myself of that fool at last!" Efa crowed. "And a long time it took, too." She took Erfin's arm and walked over to stand before Penda. "General Penda, I believe," she said, her large brown eyes suddenly warm and inviting. "I am very pleased to meet you."

Penda bowed briefly. "And I to meet you," he lied. He had expected Efa to be as dishonorable, as calculating, as ridiculous as her brother, and he was right. He had not expected her beauty, or her rampant sexual charm. But he could deal with that easily. He had never been a slave to passion.

"And Ellywen," Efa went on, turning to the Druid. "How delightful to see you again."

"I trust your husband is well," Ellywen said coolly.

"Most unfortunately, Rhoram recovered from the wound that my brother gave him a few years ago," Efa replied, smiling unpleasantly.

"Where is he?" Erfin asked eagerly. "Where have he and those Cerddorian of his been hiding?"

"Ogaf Greu. And if I never see another cave in my life, it will be too soon."

"Then we must ride there! Now!" Erfin turned away to shout for the guards, but Penda forestalled him.

"A moment, Erfin. Before we go wasting time and resources, I need to know how Efa managed to leave."

"You needn't worry, General Penda," Efa said sweetly. "Rhoram has no idea of my purpose here. He thinks I left the caves to go to Maen. He would never imagine that I would betray their hiding place."

"You are a fool," Ellywen said flatly.

"What did you call me?"

Ellywen turned to Penda. "He let her go. They won't be there."

"I tell you," Efa said hotly, "he suspects nothing."

"How were you able to get away?" Penda asked.

"Aidan ap Camber helped me."

"Aidan? Rhoram's Lieutenant?"

"The same," Efa said smugly.

"And why, Efa, would he do that?" Ellywen asked coldly.

"He wants me, that's why. You wouldn't understand."

"I'm afraid it is you who doesn't understand, Efa. Rhoram wanted to get rid of you. No doubt he was tired of having you watched. By the time we get to Ogaf Greu, they will be gone."

"That's not so! Aidan himself left the same night. He went to find Tegyr Talgellawg's band from Pennardd and enlist their help. They should be here very soon."

Well, there was nothing for it. Penda knew as well as he knew his own name that Ogaf Greu would be empty by now. But he had to be sure. "I will send a contingent to the caves as soon as possible, of course. But I must tell you that I also believe Rhoram let you go. But no matter," he went on, overriding Efa's squawk of protest. "We are truly glad you have returned to us. And your brother will no doubt see to it that you will be quite comfortable here. Erfin, I am sure your sister is weary from her journey."

"Oh. Oh, yes. Come, Efa, you can have your old apartments back. I have been saving them just for you." Brother and sister entered the gate of the fortress, leaving Penda and Ellywen alone.

"You will leave tomorrow morning, Ellywen, to seek out Cian. I will be unable to see you off. I must arrest the Master Smith."

"Siwan? What for?"

Penda shrugged. "I don't know. But those are my orders. It has something to do with some scheme the Archdruid cooked up."

"Ah. My master is very clever, indeed."

"You revere him, don't you?"

"Of course. He has restored Druids to our rightful place, preeminent over all of Kymru. Once, hundreds and hundreds of years ago, we were the only Y Dawnus in our old land, Lyonesse, now sunk beneath the sea. Now we are once again supreme."

"As long as you preach the religion of Lytir, abandoning your old gods and goddesses. You should have a care, Ellywen. Your goddess Modron, the Great Mother, must be very displeased with you."

He smiled. But Ellywen did not. Instead, her pale face became even whiter, and she shivered.

"Are you cold?" he asked.

"No," she said shortly. "It is nothing."

"Well, good hunting tomorrow."

"I wish you the same. But there won't be anyone in Ogaf Greu. He let her go."

"Yes," Penda said. "I know."

THAT NIGHT THE message sent by the Shining Ones reached into Gwydion's sleep.

At last he had found Y Pair, the Cauldron, one of the lost Treasures of Kymru. He had found Buarth Y Greu, Circle of Blood. He could see it as it lay at the bottom of a dark pit—a pit that lay in the very center of a maze far beneath the earth.

The cave was hung with torches, and their light glittered off the golden bowl carved with a dizzying array of spirals, like tiny mazes that hurt the eye to follow. The lip of the bowl was studded with emeralds that glowed with an inner light. On one side of the bowl, a figure eight was carved, the sign of Annwyn, Lord of Chaos. The figure was studded with shining black onyx.

He reached down for the bowl, but it was too far below. And he could not climb into the pit, for he had no rope. He would never get back out again.

And he cried out then in frustration and anger, for he was so close but could not obtain what he so desperately sought.

Then, suddenly, a black wolf shot out from the darkness and came to stand by him at the edge of the pit. A collar of emeralds encircled her proud neck.

In her mouth the wolf held tiny white stones, which she dropped down into the pit. The stones clanged musically against the golden bowl.

Ask. The wolf's thought echoed through the deepest chambers of his mind. *You are to ask.*

At first his pride forbade him to speak, but his need was great. "I beg you, then. I beg you to help me," he rasped.

Reach, the wolf answered.

And he stretched down his hands, but they were not his. Instead, he saw the slender hands of a young girl stretched down toward the Cauldron, and the Cauldron floated serenely up from the pit into those outstretched hands. And the hands turned into a wolf's paws, then back into a girl's hands, flickering unsteadily from one to the other.

And the Cauldron came to him as the girl/wolf hands reached out and took it. The wolf howled in triumph and shot back into the maze. The white stones at the bottom of the Cauldron glowed in the golden bowl that shone in his hands, the girl's hands, as they held the Cauldron aloft over the black pit beneath the unquiet earth.

Chapter 4

Coed Ddu and Dinmael
Kingdom of Ederynion, Kymru
Bedwen Mis, 499

Llundydd, Lleihau Wythnos—late afternoon

Talhearn ap Coleas, Bard to the fugitive Prince of Ederynion, listened intently for the Wind-Spoken message he expected any moment now.

Two days ago they had learned that Prince Lludd's mission had been successful, and this morning the Prince's raiding party had been sighted returning to the forest. When they returned to the main camp, Talhearn would have an earful of news to give them. His long life had taught him to be patient, so he continued to strum his harp, absently playing some of the fine airs he had learned in his youth.

Alun Cilcoed, the Lord of Arystli, was less patient. He shifted his weight from foot to foot and toyed with his dagger. His eyes never left the face of the man who stood before him, wearing the tattered robe of silver gray and sea green.

The Dewin who, as Talhearn well recalled, had once been sleek and well fed was now thin and haggard, and just as clearly nervous as Alun—though for different reasons. Talhearn smiled to himself. It was almost worth it to see the man again just to know how hard a life he had been leading these past two years.

The sun filtered fitfully through the dense forest roof of Coed

Ddu, illuminating the clearing here and there with bright patches of sunlight. It was early spring, and the day was mild. The branches shifted in the light breeze, giving Talhearn the feeling that the forest itself was restless. A ridiculous fancy, he knew. But he liked the imagery all the same. Perhaps he might make a tune about it.

The warriors who had been left behind gathered around the clearing, talking quietly among themselves. Eiodar, the Gwarda of Is Coed, sister of Angharad, Lludd's Captain, waited patiently, checking the fletching on her arrows, her red hair dappled by the sun. Llawra, Gwarda of Cynnllaith, whose sister was Susanna, Queen Morrigan's Bard in Gwynedd, sharpened the blade of her dagger by running it over and over her whetstone, eyeing the Dewin all the while.

Talhearn, by virtue of his age was the only one seated. The log was not particularly comfortable, but it was better than standing.

The earlier message he had received today made him grin, for that one had come from Drwys Iron-Fist, Lord of Dinan. Drwys and his Cerddorian were based in northern Ederynion, in Penbeullt. They had recently raided the docks at Ruthin, one of the favored places for Coranian trade ships. Drwys and his warriors had made off with a small fortune in cloth, foodstuffs, and jewels. Talhearn could hardly wait to tell Prince Lludd. First, of course, there would be the matter of the Dewin to discuss.

At last he heard the message he'd been waiting for.

"They're here, Alun," Talhearn said cheerfully. "And you," he went on, speaking to the Dewin, "I hope you're ready."

"Ready to die," Alun growled.

"Now, now, Alun," Talhearn chided. "You can't be sure of that. We have to see what Lludd has to say."

"Lludd was always a fair boy," the Dewin said stiffly. "A good lad. I am confident that—"

"I wouldn't be," Talhearn broke in. "I believe you overestimate the regard he had for you. Besides, the Bard who Wind-Spoke to me says that Angharad is in a very bad temper. And I am certain she will have a thing or two to say about this."

The Dewin paled, and Talhearn grinned, his blue eyes alight in his weathered face.

"What's she so mad about?" Alun asked curiously.

Talhearn shrugged. "The Bard didn't say. But we'll find out soon enough."

A rustling in the undergrowth heralded the group's arrival. One by one they stepped into the clearing.

Prince Lludd, the leader of the Cerddorian of Ederynion, came first. His brown hair was tied at the nape of his neck with a leather thong. He wore a plain tunic and trousers of brown leather. A quiver of arrows was slung across his back. He planted the end of his bow on the ground and leaned nonchalantly on it. His brown eyes seemed amused as he met Talhearn's gaze.

"Everybody duck," Lludd said cheerfully. "Angharad is—" Lludd broke off as he saw the Dewin. "By the gods, I don't believe it."

"Don't believe what?" Angharad, Lludd's Captain, asked in a quarrelsome tone as she stepped into the clearing. Her long red hair was tightly braided to her scalp, and her green eyes snapped with irritation. Behind her, his eyes downcast, came Emrys ap Naw, Lludd's Lieutenant. Emrys's handsome face was flushed. The other men and women in the party stepped into the clearing, most of them grinning.

"The temple is burned, I understand," Talhearn said by way of greeting.

"It is," Angharad snapped. "And we killed three wyrce-jaga besides, in spite of the clumsiness of some people." She shot a venomous look at Emrys. "And if you ever try to 'protect' me again, Lieutenant, I will have you killed. What's the matter with you?"

Talhearn smiled inwardly. He could have told Angharad just what was the matter with Emrys. Anyone could have. But Angharad never saw what she didn't want to see, and always refused to hear what she didn't want to hear.

"I saw a situation I thought you couldn't handle without help," Emrys insisted stubbornly.

"Well, you were wrong," she snapped. "I could have—" Angharad, too, broke off what she had been saying as she spotted the Dewin. "You!" In a flash, Angharad's dagger was in her hands, cocked and ready to throw.

"Wait!" Talhearn cried, then hit on the only argument that would stay her hand. "That judgment is for Lludd to make!"

Slowly Angharad returned her dagger to its sheath. Her green eyes were hard as emeralds as she surveyed the Dewin. "Well, Llwyd Cilcoed, I hardly dared to think we would ever meet again. If my Queen were still alive, she might be glad to see you. Then again, she might not. She felt distinctly uncharitable toward you at the end."

Llwyd Cilcoed, former lover to Queen Olwen, bowed his head. "The news of her death saddened me unbearably."

"Did it?" Lludd's voice cut through the clearing. "Then it is too bad you were not there to comfort her the day she died. She might have liked that."

"I—"

"You what?" Lludd pressed. "You are sorry? Sorry that you ran away?"

"Yes, my Prince. Oh, yes," Llwyd whispered.

"Why have you come here?"

"My brother will tell you," Llwyd said, gesturing to Alun.

Alun Cilcoed said, "I can tell you that he says he has come to join us, that he wishes to help drive the enemy from our land. I cannot tell you if this is true."

"Then guess," Angharad said sharply. "Is he a spy?"

"I think not. Nevertheless, you would be fools to trust him. He should be killed," Alun said quietly, "for deserting Queen Olwen in her last days. He cannot be trusted. He is my brother, to my shame, so I must be the one to kill him."

"No," Talhearn said sharply. "That honor would be Lludd's, should he choose to exercise it."

"Your sister would have him killed," Angharad said to Lludd, when the Prince did not immediately pass judgment.

Yes, Talhearn thought. Queen Elen would, indeed. But Elen was a captive of the Coranians, and it was Lludd who would make the judgment.

"Did you Wind-Speak to the Master Bard about this, Talhearn?"

Lludd asked.

"I did, my Prince. And he relayed the message to the Ardewin."

"What did she say?"

"Elstar said that Llwyd Cilcoed has hidden himself in villages for the last few years, avoiding capture by the enemy, and most likely unaware that the Dewin were watching him. She says he is the kind of man who plays his own game and no one else's. She counsels that, if you let him live, keep a close eye on him."

"And does she say I should let him live?"

"She says she relinquishes that decision to the Prince of Ederynion."

"I see," Lludd said quietly. "Well, then, Llwyd Cilcoed, here is my judgment. In the memory of my mother, who once loved you, you may live."

"Lludd! How could you—" Angharad began hotly, but subsided as Lludd held up his hand for silence.

"You may live until my sister is rescued from her prison. Then she will be the one to pass final judgment on you," Lludd continued. "I believe that you wish the enemy gone, for they have made your life uncomfortable, and comfort was always your aim. I believe that you are not a spy. I believe that you do not have a plan to betray us—yet. But you will be watched very closely, all the same, for I do not believe you to be trustworthy. In time you may earn that trust. And there is always need for another Dewin among the Cerddorian."

"Any oaths you require, Prince Lludd, I will make to you," Llwyd Cilcoed said eagerly.

"I do not take oaths in my name," Lludd said fiercely. "My sister is the true ruler of Ederynion. One day we shall free her, and then you may make an oath to her."

"If she will accept it," Angharad said.

"As I said, Dewin, you will be watched," Lludd went on. "The person I will appoint to guard you will be required to watch you closely. This means that you must accompany them wherever they go. You will be able to test your newfound bravery over and over again, for your guard will go to many dangerous places. And the gods help you should you not pull your weight. You will have to, if you wish to come back alive."

Talhearn began to smile. He knew who the Dewin's guard would be.

"Angharad," Lludd said with a gracious gesture, "I give this task to you."

Slowly, Angharad smiled at Llwyd Cilcoed's horrified dawning expression.

After the evening meal was over, Talhearn withdrew from the celebrating warriors and made his way to a small clearing nearby. A tiny fire burned in the center of the clearing. Talhearn settled himself on a log by the fire, unslung his harp, and waited for the others. Idly, he began to strum an old tune.

> *"They sing after thy song,*
> *The Kymri in their grief,*
> *On account of their loss.*
> *Long is the cry of sorrow.*
> *There is blood upon the spears,*
> *The waves are bearing*
> *Ships upon the sea."*

"That's appropriate," Lludd said heavily as he sat down. "Do you think he knew?"

"Taliesin wrote this two hundred years ago. He was no Dreamer, but he knew Bran the Dreamer well. Yes, I think he knew. I think they all did, the Great Ones of High King Lleu."

"Which was why they hid the Treasures?"

"It is well they are hidden. At least the Coranians do not have them, and so Cadair Idris remains closed to them."

"Tell me, Talhearn. Do you believe what Gwydion ap Awst wrote to us? Do you believe that the High King will come again?"

Talhearn nodded. "Yes, lad, I do."

"Sometimes I am not sure I believe it anymore."

"Believe it," Angharad said as she came into the clearing. "Two years ago I saw Arderydd when I, too, doubted."

"The High Eagle came to you?" Lludd asked in awe.

She sat down on the ground, tucking her long legs beneath her. "It could not have been long after he defied the enemy at Cadair Idris."

"And took Sledda's eye," Talhearn reminded them with a grin. "I wish I had seen that."

"I wish I had done that," Lludd muttered. "I wish—" he shook his head with a rueful smile. "I wish a lot of things."

"Elen is all right, lad," Talhearn said quietly. "You know the Dewin watch over her, and they say this is so."

"She is a prisoner. And I will not rest until she is freed."

"The Coranians don't dare harm her," Angharad reminded him.

"As long as she does what she is told," Lludd retorted.

"Which she will, as long as they have Regan under their control," Talhearn said. "Your sister will not endanger her Dewin's life. Which is the only reason Regan is still alive. They usually kill 'witches.'"

"And yet, I think that Regan would rather be dead."

Talhearn smiled. "Well, Regan was always a brave lass, but I'm not so sure about her wanting to be dead. I understand that General Talorcan takes good care that Regan is as safe and as comfortable as possible. He is an honorable man—for a Coranian."

"General Talorcan is the man who killed my mother," Lludd said harshly. "Just how honorable can he be?"

"I would have thought you would leave the black and white judgments to Elen," Talhearn said mildly. "You know that life is more complicated than that, even though you are only nineteen."

Lludd sighed. "When are you leaving to begin the testing?"

"In just a few days," Talhearn said. "Emrys and I—"

"No," Angharad said sharply. "I will go with you."

"Why not Emrys? He's competent—quite good, really."

"But not as good as I am. Do I need to remind you what Anieron said about last week's meeting at Eiodel? Havgan's planning something, and you can be sure it will be nasty."

"What about Llwyd Cilcoed?" Talhearn asked. "You're supposed to watch him."

"My sister can do it. Eiodar is as fond of Llwyd Cilcoed as I am. Just accept it, old man. I'm sticking to you like bark on a tree."

"If you go to Dinmael, try to get a glimpse of Elen," Lludd urged.

"Lludd," Talhearn said gently, "we can't go near Dinmael. We have to stay out of the settled areas and stick to the forests. The people will bring their children to us."

Lludd was silent for a moment. "I know," he said at last. "It's just that—"

"We will free her one day."

"Yes," Lludd said in a grim tone. "We will."

ELEN UR OLWEN, Queen of Ederynion, sat stiffly in the elaborate, canopied chair, her head held high. The pearls and silver thread that decorated the canopy gleamed faintly in the torchlight. Her auburn hair was held back from her face by a band of silver stitched with pearls. She wore a gown of pure white, and the silver and pearl torque of Ederynion. Her eyes went to the pearl ring on her hand, the ring her mother had given her the day before the final battle, when Olwen had died. The ring was to be guarded at all costs, for one day, in the fullness of time, it would be claimed in the name of the High King. Not that these fools knew anything about that.

Darkness pressed outside the windows, vying with the shadows of Iago's dark brown robe, black hair, and jet-black, tormented eyes. The Druid's forehead was beaded with sweat as he forged the psycho-kinetic bonds that kept Elen in her chair.

Regan, her Dewin, for whose sake she had sacrificed so much, stood across the room, her hands tied behind her, her brown hair loose and tangled. Regan's face was a mask of contempt as the wyrce-jaga held the dagger to her throat. But there was nothing Elen could do. And so, for what seemed to be the hundredth time, she said, disdainfully, without a trace of the soul-chilling fear she kept locked inside, "I don't know."

"You do," Guthlac, the Master-wyrce-jaga of Ederynion insisted coldly. "And you will tell us what we want to know or the witch dies."

Elen did not even bother to look at Regan. She did not need to see in her friend's eyes the longing to die and release Elen from this trap. For two years Elen had followed the dictates of the enemy in order to keep Regan alive. She could not give up now.

"I cannot give you information I do not have," Elen said. She did not add that even if she knew, she would never tell—even if it did cost Regan her life. There were limits to everything. "I do not know where my brother and his Cerddorian are hiding. If you stopped just one moment to think—assuming the feat is not completely beyond you—you would know that I am telling the truth. How could I possibly find out such a thing? I was already captive when they slipped away after the last battle."

"Iago," Guthlac spat, turning to the Druid who had once served Queen Olwen and now served the enemy, "you know about the message we received today. You know how important this is. Make her talk."

Iago, who had been wearily leaning against the wall, straightened up slowly.

"Yes, Iago," Elen sneered. "Make me talk."

"Guthlac," Iago said in a pleading tone. "I—"

"Do it, Druid! Your Archdruid has ordered you to help in this matter any way you can. Do it!"

Iago's tortured dark eyes seemed to plead with Elen to understand, to forgive. But this she would never do, and Iago knew it. She braced herself and waited.

"Iago!" Regan cried, struggling against her bonds. "Don't! Don't hurt her!"

"Do you think I would harm her?" Iago rasped. "Oh, no. Never."

It was then that the hem of Regan's dress began to smolder, then caught fire. Elen screamed, "No!" as she tried to rise from her chair. But Iago's psychokinesis held her fast. Rescue came from another quarter.

The door burst open. General Talorcan did not hesitate. He leapt across the room, tearing off his cloak and wrapping Regan in the heavy wool, beating out the flames. When the fire was out, he helped Regan to a chair. His face tightened when he saw her bonds.

He turned to Guthlac and snatched the man's dagger from his hands. Talorcan then knelt by Regan's chair and cut the rope that bound her, his face dangerous. He paused and briefly touched her face, then rose, turning to Guthlac and Iago.

Very, very quietly, he asked, "What in the name of Holy Lytir is going on here?"

Before the two men could answer, Elen answered for them. "They wished to know the location of the Cerddorian. I could not tell them. And so Iago set Regan's dress on fire, to make me talk."

Talorcan's green eyes glittered as he looked at Iago.

"I did as the Master-wyrce-jaga bade me, General," Iago said stiffly.

Talorcan transferred his stare to the wyrce-jaga. Guthlac licked his thick lips. His black robe with the green tabard was tucked up over his huge belly, and he straightened it with nervous hands. "General, it was necessary."

"After two years, Guthlac, have you still not understood? Queen Elen does not know the answer to your question."

"But, General, you know the messages we received from Lord Havgan today!"

"I repeat to you, she does not know. And you will never again seek to interrogate either one of these ladies. Understand this. I will not tell you again."

"Lord Havgan would surely like to know we are doing all we can to fulfill his orders. He would be most interested in learning that you lack the boldness necessary."

Talorcan laughed, the torchlight flickering off his dark blond hair and the stony lines of his thin, hard face. "Try it, wyrce-jaga," he taunted. "But I think you will not be happy with the results, unless you are truly tired of living. Now get out."

Bowing, Guthlac backed out of the room, hatred in his piglike eyes.

"Your coming was fortuitous, General," Elen said coolly.

"I came to see if Regan would care to take a stroll on the battlements. Another time, perhaps."

"But I would like to," Regan said, as Elen had known she would.

"More than ever, now. I need fresh air."

"But you are burned!"

"I am not. You rescued me too speedily for that."

After a moment's hesitation, Talorcan offered his arm to the Dewin. He glanced at Elen, a rueful smile in his green eyes. As always, Elen got the feeling he knew full well what she and Regan had decided long ago—that they would take full advantage of Talorcan's obvious attraction to the Dewin. Yes, he knew it and let them scheme for his own purpose. Elen often wondered what that was.

It was only now that Elen truly understood.

REGAN UR CORFIL took a deep breath of the night air. It was crisp outside, for it was early spring and the nights were still cold. Overhead the stars glittered. Talorcan gestured at the sky.

"The constellation of Llyr," he said, "the first Dreamer. And Llys Don, the court of the Lady Don, his mother."

"Which in your land would be Fal, the god of light and fire. And Nerthus, the Mother."

"And there is Tarw, the Bull."

"Which in your land would be Bana. Named for the Warleader."

"We have learned each other's stars well, Regan," Talorcan said, his smile sad. "But perhaps I should have named a different constellation."

"That is true enough. I do not like to think of your Bana, your Havgan, the man to whom you sold your soul."

"My soul belongs to me," Talorcan said, his voice suddenly fierce.

"You lie, General. Or you would not be in Kymru."

They stood together on the walls of the once-proud, once-beautiful city of Dinmael. Some portions of the broken walls were repaired, but the work was not yet complete, so great had been the initial destruction.

Regan turned away from Talorcan, her eyes scanning the city, so quiet at this time of night. So quiet, really, all the time now, for the Kymri who still dwelt there were silent and subdued. They fished the waters and sold their wares, as they had always done, but they did it without joy. The glassmakers still spun their fabulous shapes from the white sands, but they no longer sang at their work. Paper was still produced in abundance, for the preosts of Lytir needed the sheets to write the book of their god, but the paper workers moved without life, waiting for the living nightmare to end.

Her gaze moved to the east, to the sea. It glistened darkly as wave after wave washed up to the beach with a hiss, then withdrew.

Talorcan reached out and turned her face to his. His green eyes glittered in the cold light of the stars. "In my land," he said evenly, "the brotherhood ritual is sacred. Once blood has been mingled, there can be no betrayal."

"Have you not already been betrayed? Has Havgan not already betrayed you?"

"His dream is a bright one, Regan. He seeks to claim this land for our God."

"And to kill people like me, to unleash the wyrce-jaga to torture us. To use the Druids to further the schemes of his god."

"The Archdruid threw in his lot with us. He thinks to use us, as we use him."

She said nothing, but turned from him and looked out over the water. Her heart ached at the beauty of the night. She longed to rise up from her body, to float among the stars, to see the beauty of Ederynion from on high. When they had first captured her, she had given her word that she would not Wind-Ride. If she were caught doing so, they said, Elen would die. And she had kept her word, partly for the safety of the Cerddorian who fought on still. For what Elen and she did not know, they could not tell. So she had remained blind, seeing nothing that was beyond her physical sight. And never had she thought to break that word.

Until tonight.

She was so tired of her prison, so tired of being bound to the land, unable to soar. So tired of the fear that any day might be her last. So tired of fighting what she now knew was a wholly divided heart. For she loved Elen and her country and her people and her goddess. And she loved Talorcan, the enemy, with a love just as fierce and true.

She was wounded and without hope, for surely the High King would never come. Surely she and her people would never be free. And if the High King did return, Talorcan would die, and her heart would die with him. And the star-spangled sky was so beautiful. She would fly so swiftly that Talorcan would never even know, until it was too late. She would never return to her body, but would let it die. Their hold over Elen would be broken. And Regan's heart would not be called upon to make that terrible choice she knew was coming to her.

She leaned on the parapet and closed her eyes. She gathered her will, and her spirit began to rise, to float up and leave her body. Tonight she would Ride, and never return. It was time and past time to die.

With a jolt her spirit slammed back into her body. Talorcan loomed over her, his hands gripping her arms.

"None of that, Dewin. You have given your word. What were you intending to do? What word were you going to give to your Ardewin?"

"None!" she spat. "None at all. I was going to . . ." She trailed off, looking up at Talorcan in shock. "How . . ." she gasped. "How did you . . ."

He released her abruptly and turned away.

"How did you know? How did you stop me?" she asked, bewildered. "How could you possibly . . ." And then the answer came to her. After so long, at last she understood. It explained so much. "Oh. Oh, Talorcan, you are Dewin."

"I am not!" he snarled, whipping around to face her.

"But you are," she insisted. "They have such people in Corania. They are called Walkers. And you are one of them."

"Enough!" He grabbed her and shook her, breathing hard, his hands tight on her arms. She struggled to pull free, and he let her go abruptly. She stumbled, fetching up against the wall. With a shaking hand, she smoothed back her tangled hair and faced him. They were silent, looking at each other for a long time.

"I'm sorry," Talorcan at last said, stiffly. "Are you hurt?"

"Not in a place that shows," she said quietly.

He reached out and touched her face. The tenderness of the gesture brought tears to her eyes. She looked up at the face that had become so dear to her over the last two years, looked up into the face of the enemy.

Remember, she told herself fiercely, *remember this is the man who killed Queen Olwen in battle. Remember this is the man who holds Elen captive. Remember, oh, remember, this man is the enemy.* She turned her face away.

Slowly, he lowered his hand, then walked to the parapet, looking out over the water. "Across the sea is my home. There lies Dere, the land where I was born. Would that one day I could show it to you."

"I think not," she said harshly, more harshly than she had intended. But she was frightened of herself now. "I understand from you that the city of Elmete where you lived is not much to look at anymore. Not since the Coranians came and destroyed it. As they wish to do in Kymru."

His voice low and sad, he said, "Ah, but once it was beautiful." Softly, he sang:

"Oh, Elmete!
Here once many a man, mood-glad,
Goldbright, of gleams garnished,
Flushed with wine-pride, flashing war-gear,
Gazed on bright gemstones, on gold, on silver,
On wealth held and hoarded, on light-filled amber,
On the bright city of broad dominion."

"It is," he continued softly, "my mother's favorite song. Once Gwydion and Rhiannon sang it for her. I will be sorry when they are dead."

"You are so sure that Havgan will find them?"

"He does not give up. One day he will find them and kill them."

"And you will watch?"

"It is my earnest prayer that I will not have to."

"Perhaps they won't be captured."

"They will. For now they are on the move again, making the next bid to free Kymru. They seek the Treasures, to make a High King. Havgan seeks the Treasures, too. Their paths will cross. And Gwydion and Rhiannon will die. If they are lucky, they will die quickly. But I do not think Havgan plans a quick death."

"Maybe they will surprise you."

"Maybe they will." He took a deep breath, then turned to her. "Regan, why did you try to Wind-Ride?"

She turned away, shrugging, her back to him. "I just felt like it."

"Did you think I would not guess that you wouldn't return? Why, Regan?"

She did not answer. There was nothing she could bring herself to say. Unbidden, tears began to rain down her face.

"So, you would rather die than be near me?" he rasped. "Do you hate me so much?"

She spun around to face him. "No! Oh, no!" she cried.

He cradled her face in his hands, and she let him. He leaned forward and kissed her cheek, tasting the tears there. With mounting passion he kissed her lips. She moaned softly, and tried to pull away, but his grip was too tight. Just as she was on the verge of surrendering, of forgetting everything except his burning kisses, he stepped back, putting her away from him, his face tormented. "Go now, Regan," he whispered, "for if I escorted you back to your room, I would not leave. Later your heart would break. And then mine would break for you."

For a moment she hesitated. She wanted his arms around her, his lips on her skin, the feel of him down the length of her body. But she knew what would happen to her if she did not stop this thing now. So she gathered her skirts and began to descend the stairs. She did not look back.

AFTER REGAN AND Talorcan had gone, Elen remained in her chair, her knees too weak to allow her to rise. She stared at the wall, her thoughts chaotic. Regan had almost died tonight. And it was

Talorcan who had saved her. Surely now Regan would realize the truth Elen herself had seen. These two loved each other. And they would destroy each other, whether they willed it or no. What would the truth do to her dearest friend, her only ally in this prison that had once been her home? How would Regan choose?

Someone put a wineglass in her hand. "Drink," the voice said.

She blinked and looked up. Of course. Iago. He was still there, still watching her, as he always did.

"What's the matter?" he asked.

She laughed a little wildly. "'What's the matter?' How can you ask such a question?"

Iago flushed and withdrew to the door. "Good night, my Queen."

"I am hardly that, Iago. To say I am your Queen implies you are loyal to me. And we all know to whom you are loyal."

"The Archdruid is my master. He is to be obeyed, no matter the cost."

"As I well know," she said bitterly. "And as Regan knows, too."

Iago said nothing, but neither did he go. He did not look at her with his tormented eyes, but leaned against the door, staring into the fire on the hearth.

"Yes," she mused. "We are lucky you fought with us at all, I suppose. For you did fight with us, before you received the Archdruid's letter. I remember you waiting on the beach with my mother for them to come. I remember you setting fire to their ships at my mother's command. How proud she would be of you if she could see you now! To know that you do not just set fire to ships, but to people, as well."

"It was not my wish, Elen," he said softly.

"What is your wish, then?"

"That you forgive."

"Never."

"Yes, I know that," he said quietly. "I knew that from the beginning. You do not have to be afraid of me. I would never harm you."

"Unless you are ordered to," she retorted.

"No. Not even then."

"I don't believe you."

"No, you wouldn't. But it is true. And you understand nothing about me at all. Years I loved you. And you never even noticed."

"A fine way you have of showing me you love me," she said with bitterness of her own. "Turning from your allegiance to me and working with the enemy."

"You never noticed that I loved you," he went on, as though she had not spoken. "And, gods help me, I love you still."

"You should not say 'gods,' Iago," she jeered. "As a Druid you are now a preost of Lytir. And preosts believe only in the One God. They revile Modron, the Mother. And the land suffers from it! Our harvests are as nothing, now. The Mother turns from us, because of you and your Druids."

"Do not speak of the Mother," he said, looking at her at last. "Never speak of her to me."

The wild agony in his eyes leapt out at her, shaking her to her soul. Without conscious thought, she flinched.

A low moan burst from his throat as he saw her draw back in fear. "You are afraid of me. Oh, my love, you are afraid."

Swiftly he crossed the room and knelt beside her. He took her cool hand and cradled it in his own hot grip. She tried to pull away, but he clutched her fiercely. "Oh, Elen, my true love, don't fear me!"

But she did. She, who had once feared nothing, trembled now before the madness in his dark eyes. His tormented face searched her clear blue eyes, and recoiled in his turn from what he saw there.

He leapt to his feet as if stung. "You hate me," he whispered. "So be it, then."

"What will you do, Iago?" she whispered in her turn. "Will you kill me?"

"No. I will leave you."

"Where are you going?"

"I go to seek Talhearn, the Bard. I know what he looks like, you see."

"I don't see. What does Talhearn have to do with you?"

"We—the Druids in Ederynion—have been ordered to help find him at all costs."

"But why?" she pressed. "Even if you found Talhearn, he would never tell you where my brother and his Cerddorian are. Never."

"What time of year is it, Elen?" he asked gently, as though she were a very dull child.

"Why, it's early spring. Nearly time—" she halted, as understanding came to her. "Nearly time for the Plentyn Prawf. You seek a testing tool. Why?"

"The Archdruid has at last found a way to prevent Bards and Dewin from using their talents. A collar."

"And to identify them, you need a testing tool. Oh, Iago, what if you found Talhearn? Would you really turn him over to the Coranians? He was your friend."

"And you are my love. But that is not enough. It never has been."

"Yes," she said bitterly. "I know."

THAT NIGHT THE message sent by the Shining Ones reached into Gwydion's sleep.

At last, he had found Y Llech, the Stone, one of the lost Treasures of Kymru. He had found Gwyr Yr Brenin, Seeker of the King. He could see it as it floated just beneath the surface of the clear, shining lake.

The large, square stone was shot through with a latticework of silver threads. At each silvery junction, where one thread met another, a single pearl rested, gleaming. On the top of the stone, a figure eight, the sign of Annwyn, Lord of Chaos, was carved and studded with dark onyx.

He reached out for the Stone, but it bobbed away from him in the water, just out of his reach. For some reason he was rooted to the spot on the rocks beside the lake and could not move. He could only watch the Stone floating serenely beyond his grasp.

And he cried out then in frustration, in anger, for he was so close but could not obtain what he so desperately sought.

Then, suddenly, a silver dragon swooped down from the sky to land on the rocks. A collar of pearls encircled her slender neck, and her silver hide glistened like the surface of the water.

In her talons she held a wreath of bright yellow globeflowers. She tossed the wreath into the water, and it settled on the surface, floating just above the Stone.

Ask. Her thought echoed through the deepest chambers of his mind. *You are to ask.*

At first his pride forbade him to speak, to ask for help, but his need was great. "I beg you, then. I beg you to help me," he rasped.

Reach, she answered.

And he stretched out his hands, but they were not his. Instead, he saw the slim, delicate hands of a woman stretched toward the Stone, and the Stone floated gently into the outstretched hands. And the hands turned into silver talons, then back into a woman's hands, flickering unsteadily from one to the other.

And then the Stone came to him as the woman/dragon hands reached out and took it, hauling it up from the water as though it was light as a feather. In triumph, the dragon bellowed and shot up into the sky. And the wreath of flowers, which still floated on the water, blazed like tiny suns in the harsh light. And the water dropped from the Stone like diamonds, as his hands, the woman's hands, held the Stone aloft under the blazing sky.

Chapter 5

Tegeingl, Dinas Emrys and Mynydd Tawel
Kingdom of Gwynedd, Kymru
Bedwen Mis, 499

Suldydd, Lleihau Wythnos—night

Tangwen ur Madoc sat quietly in the great hall. If she shut her eyes tightly, she could almost imagine the hall as it had been a few years ago when her uncle, Uthyr, was King of Gwynedd. Longingly she remembered those days. She remembered Uncle Uthyr's great booming laugh, the camaraderie he had with his warriors, the kindness in his dark eyes. She remembered Aunt Ygraine's beautiful, pale face, her watchfulness, how she rarely took her eyes off her daughter, Morrigan, the only child left to her after her son, Arthur, died.

Tangwen remembered Morrigan most of all. Morrigan, with her mother's eyes and her father's laughing spirit and charm. Morrigan, her dearest friend, was the true Queen of Gwynedd now that Uthyr was dead. But Morrigan was not here in Caer Gwynt, the Fortress of the Winds, her rightful place. Morrigan was hiding with the rest of the Cerddorian, those men and women who fought the enemy still. They raided tribute caravans, burned the hateful temples to the Coranian god, and killed the wyrce-jaga, the most feared and hated of the enemy.

She closed her eyes even tighter, bowed her head even lower, trying to shut out the sight of the Coranian warriors. She tried to make-believe that they were the men and women of King Uthyr's teulu, tried to make-believe that Uthyr himself was sitting next to her, that he was alive again, and still King.

She clenched her fists in the rich, golden material of her gown, then raised her head, shaking back the long hair of reddish-gold that curtained her delicate face. It was no use. Those days were gone, and there was no going back. Instead of the good-natured roistering that her uncle's warriors had always engaged in, the drunken shouting of the Coranian troops pounded at her ears. And the man who sat at the table beside her, though called the King of Gwynedd, was not her uncle. It was Madoc. Madoc, the traitor. Madoc, her father.

Madoc's reddish-gold hair gleamed in the light of the torches that were set around the walls of the hall. As always, he was dressed richly, tonight in a tunic and trousers of dark blue decorated with silver thread and sapphires. On his brow he wore a circlet of silver, for the sapphire torque of Gwynedd had been taken away by Ygraine before that final battle. It was in that battle that King Uthyr had been killed by the man who really ruled Gwynedd—General Catha, whose word was law and whom her father obeyed as a dog obeys its master.

Shame crept on her again, bringing with it misery and hopelessness. What could she hope for? That Morrigan would return and slay Madoc and drive the Coranians from this land? Could she hope for such a thing as that and still love her father? For she did love him, in spite of what he was. Yet, she was ashamed of him. Sometimes she almost despised him. Especially on those days when she went out of the fortress to the city and saw afresh what the enemy had done. Especially on those days when she walked by the Sacred Grove that was gone now, the alder trees destroyed, a temple to Lytir in its place. Especially on those days when she watched the people of Tegeingl go about their business in silence and misery. Especially on those days when the people were kind to her, knowing who she was, forgiving her in her mute anguish.

"Tangwen, Catha is talking to you," her father said sharply, nudging her.

Jolted out of her reverie, she looked up, startled, her blue eyes wide. "I'm sorry, General. What did you say?"

The smile on Catha's handsome face had an edge to it. And there was no smile in his frosty, light blue eyes. "I said, Tangwen, where is the necklace I sent to you?"

"Oh. I, uh, I forgot it." The lie was so obvious that she blushed. In truth, she had left it lying deliberately in her room. The touch of it made her skin crawl. For she knew the reason for the gift. Not content with taking Madoc's mistress whenever the mood struck him, Catha was angling for Madoc's daughter, as well. The fact that she was eighteen and pretty had not escaped him, nor the fact that, as daughter to the King, she was another avenue to power.

"You displease me, Tangwen," Catha said coldly. "You displease me greatly."

"I—"

"General," Arday broke in, "I simply must have a new emerald. I have just received the most heavenly forest-green gown. I ordered it months and months ago, but you know how the people are. They work so slowly these days." Arday, the former steward to King Uthyr, sister of the traitorous Lord of Archellwedd, mistress of Madoc and now Catha—much to Madoc's unvoiced displeasure—smiled as she spoke, laying her slender hand on Catha's arm. Her long black hair flowed down her back, held back from her face by a band of rubies. Her red dress was cut so low that Tangwen wondered why she bothered to wear anything at all. Arday's dark, heavy-lidded eyes glittered hotly at Catha.

Distracted, as Arday had intended (but why, Tangwen wondered), Catha bent toward Arday, lazily tracing her cheekbone with his finger, then lightly running his hand over her breasts. "And what, dear Arday, would you be willing to pay for that emerald?"

"Ah, great Lord, whatever you wish, of course."

"Yet I wish for so many things," he said, taking her hand and slowly kissing her fingers.

"And you shall have them all," she purred. "And more."

Madoc abruptly stood and turned to leave the table. Tangwen

scrambled to her feet to follow.

"Madoc," Catha called. Madoc stopped and turned around, his face flushed. "I have not given you leave to go," Catha said, smiling lazily. "Do you not recall that we have business still to take care of?"

Slowly Madoc again took his seat.

"And your charming daughter," Catha went on, "she, too, must stay. For a little while longer."

"I have told you, Catha," Madoc said sullenly, "that I will do everything I can to assist in finding Susanna."

Tangwen's ears pricked up. Susanna was Morrigan's Bard, now in hiding with the rest of the Cerddorian. The enemy had been hunting them for two years now—all of them, not just Susanna. Why was the Bard so important now?

"You know what she looks like, Madoc. Whereas I do not," Catha went on. "I believe that it would be a good idea for you to think about taking a journey."

"I cannot leave Tegeingl," Madoc protested. "And, besides, how do we know that she will begin the Plentyn Prawf this year? Maybe they will think it far too dangerous."

Oh, Tangwen thought. Surely her father knew better than that. Her people—once his people, too—would never pass by the season for testing the children. To do so would be to give up, to admit defeat. And that was something they would never do.

"You have two weeks to prepare yourself to leave, my King." The contempt that Catha gave the epithet was profound. "In the meantime, there is one more piece of business that you have forgotten. Ah, here it is."

The doors to the hall opened, and four warriors escorted a man through the drunken throng. Though the man was loaded down with chains, he held his grizzled head high. His powerful shoulders strained against his plain brown tunic. As he drew nearer, Tangwen recognized him. With horror she stared at Greid, the Master Smith of Gwynedd. Why, in the name of the gods, had they arrested him?

Madoc, after a glance at Catha, reluctantly stood as the Smith and his Guard came to a halt before the high table. "Greid ap Gorwys," Madoc intoned, "you will leave Tegeingl tonight, in the company of these warriors. Your family awaits you now, to share your journey."

"And to ensure your cooperation," Catha put in.

"Yes," Greid boomed, "I have been able to figure that part out myself. Thanks just the same for pointing that out, boyo."

For the first time, Tangewen saw Catha disconcerted. She almost smiled, but caught herself in time.

"Just a few questions, assuming your wine-soaked wits will enable you to answer," Greid went on. "Where are you sending me? And just what do you think I will do when I get there?"

"You will do as you are told," Catha said sharply. "As for where you are going—that, too, is something you must wait to find out. Know this, old man, you will do your job well, or your family will answer for it. And that would be a pity. For your sons and daughters have such delightful, beautiful children. And the soldiers who guard them are quite inventive. Just imagine how one of those precious grandchildren might call out to you to end their torment, should you refuse to obey."

Tangwen, her face twisted in horror, leapt to her feet. She knew that it was more than foolish, that she might pay for this with her life, but she could not listen to this without doing something. "Da, please. Don't let them do this. Don't."

"Quiet, girl," Madoc hissed.

"General," she began urgently, "I beg you—"

"How delightful," Catha smiled. "Please, do. Offer me what I want, Tangwen, and we shall see."

Tangwen froze where she stood. The hall fell silent as the enemy warriors turned from their drunken games to watch. Tangwen looked to her father, her eyes pleading, but Madoc slowly sat down, his shoulders slumped.

She glanced at Arday, expecting to see hatred or triumph in those dark eyes. But Arday was not looking at her at all. Instead, she was staring at Greid, her lips pressed tightly together. There was a message for the Smith in those eyes, but what the message was, only Greid seemed to know. At Arday's almost imperceptible nod, Greid spoke.

"Never mind, lass," Greid told Tangwen gently. "There is nothing you can do for me and mine. One day the High King will return to us. And then the enemy will be driven out. And, one day, Queen Morrigan herself will come, and kill this upstart General. Leave it be, for now, lass. Leave it be."

Llundydd, Lleihau Wythnos—late afternoon
MYRRDIN WATCHED AS the Coranian warriors led their prisoners through the mountains. The group would reach the tiny village of Dinas Emrys in a matter of moments. He scanned the village one last time to be sure everything was in place. Then he returned his attention to the warrior band, watching their every move.

Not that anyone—unless they were of the Y Dawnus—would know that Myrrdin was watching the warriors. For Myrrdin's body sat by the fire in the tiny hut he and Arthur had shared for so many years. The door of the hut was closed, and he sat calmly in his chair by the hearth. For Myrrdin was Dewin—had once, indeed, been the Ardewin of Kymru—and he was adept at Wind-Riding, at sending his awareness many leagues away from his body. So adept was he that he did not even need to close his eyes, did not need to sit still. Every so often, he would reach over and stir the gently boiling pot hanging on the spit over the fire. Only a stew, and a poor one at that. The harvest had, once again, been meager. But it was better than nothing, and he would at least have something hot to give the two prisoners when they were freed.

He knew them both. The man was Edwy, Bard to the Gwarda of Aberffraw. The Gwarda, Cynwas, had escaped to Mynydd Tawel, as had Edwy, and they were now both members of the Cerddorian, assisting Queen Morrigan in her struggle to regain the rule of Gwynedd. Edwy looked worn, but not too ill-used—not yet, at any rate.

The woman with hair of shining gold who walked with her hands bound behind her and her head held high was Neuad ur Hetwin. Years ago she had followed him around Y Ty Dewin, hoping he would notice her—which he had, of course. Who would't notice a girl as beautiful as Neuad? The others had always teased him about it. But he had not even so much as hinted to her how very aware of her he was. For even then he had been an old man. He had not seen her for thirteen years, since he had left Y Ty Dewin in the dead of the night to come here to this village to raise Arthur in secret.

Once again he scanned the village. Yes, all was as it should be. The men were slowly driving the sheep down from the hills in all different directions. And there, at the village well, the women were gathering to draw water. Already they had several buckets full. Most important of all, a boy with brown hair and a white scar on his face sat casually on the limb of a tall oak tree at the north end of the village. The branches of the huge tree shaded the road. Whistling, the boy was cleaning his nails with a small knife.

The contingent had reached the outskirts of the village now. The late-afternoon sun shone brightly on their iron byrnies and shining helmets. They carried axes and shields depicting boars' heads in the red and gold colors of the Warleader.

Myrrdin continued to content himself with sitting by the fire in his tiny hut. If Neuad or Edwy saw him and recognized him, they might involuntarily betray who he was. And that must be avoided at all costs. He was, after all, supposed to be dead these many years. Still humming under his breath, he waited and watched as the warriors and their prisoners entered the village.

So it began. With impeccable timing, the sheep began to swarm over the road from all directions, breaking into the six warriors and their two prisoners just as they came to a halt beneath the spreading branches of the oak tree. The Coranians began pushing at the sheep with their shields, trying to fend them off. One or two warriors wobbled on their feet, almost thrown off balance by the press. Seeing their moment, Neuad and Edwy began to edge away from their captors.

At that moment, two men of the village began to shout, each accusing the other of trying to hog the road.

"You there. Onnen!" one of the men shouted. "Your sheep are blocking my way! And not for the first time, you weasel!"

"Stow it, Cryn," Onnen bellowed. "I know what you're trying to do—steal my sheep. I'll have you before the law for this!"

A few of the women ran up from where they stood by the well, still carrying buckets of water. One of the women, tall and raw boned, began to shout. "Leave my man be, Onnen, or I'll drench you! That will cool you down somewhat!"

"You wouldn't dare, Marwen!"

"Oh, wouldn't I?" Marwen picked up her bucket and threw. Some of the water did, indeed, splash on Onnen. But most of it inexplicably drenched the Coranian warriors.

Two dogs now entered the fray, snarling and barking. One woman reached Marwen and grabbed her by the hair, flinging her to the ground. "You leave Onnen alone or I'll cut your heart out!" the woman shrieked.

Onnen and Cryn ran to the women and tried to break up the fight. But somehow the two men fell to wrangling instead and, in their struggle, hurled themselves straight at the Captain, bowling him off his feet.

At that moment, with the warriors completely distracted from their prisoners, Arthur dropped from the tree branches and cut Neuad's bonds. Neuad, quick as lightning, grabbed Arthur's knife and plunged it into Edwy's heart. The Bard fell to the ground, his dying moan of agony drowned out by the shouting.

After a moment of shock, Arthur recovered his wits and grabbed Neuad's hand, then the two were off and running, ducking behind the huts, disappearing into the mountains.

MANY HOURS LATER, Myrrdin finally heard footsteps coming up the back path. About time, he grumbled to himself. He had not tracked them with his Wind-Riding for he had been concerned that the fracas in the village not end in bloodshed for the villagers. After Arthur and Neuad had escaped, Myrrdin had gone charging out of the hut, shouting imprecations at the villagers, breaking up the fight, soothing the Coranian Captain, and mourning, with as much sincerity as possible, the death of Edwy. He had no idea why Neuad had killed the Bard, but he was sure Neuad had her reasons.

The Captain had, at last, left the village with his men, taking the body of Edwy with them. At first the Captain had been enraged, calling on his men to take the heads of everyone in the village. But the number of men and women who had stolidly faced the Captain and his five men had dissuaded him. Myrrdin had offered the Captain food in compensation for the trouble they had caused, explaining all the while what a sorry accident it was. And so the Captain had allowed himself to be mollified, and the warriors had left some hours ago. As near as Myrrdin could tell from the Captain's comments, the man had no idea that he had captured a Dewin and a Bard. Just who he thought they were, why he had taken them prisoner, was not clear.

Well, Myrrdin thought with a sigh, he was about to find out. He had told Arthur not to bring Neuad back here. But the boy had quite obviously ignored that request.

The door leading into the hut from the sheep byre opened, and Arthur entered, followed by Neuad. Her tunic and trousers of brown leather were torn and stained, and her golden hair was tangled. There were lines of care on her face now, and her cheekbones stood out starkly. She was thin, far too thin. But her blue eyes lit up with the same glow he remembered from long ago when she saw him.

"Myrrdin," she said, wonder in her soft voice. "You're alive!" She ran to him, and before he could stop her (and he didn't think he even wanted to), she had her arms around his neck, hugging him tightly. Without conscious volition, his arms came up and encircled her slim body. After a moment he realized that though he might be sixty-two years old, his body had forgotten that important fact, and he pulled her arms from his neck and set her away from him.

"Neuad, child," he said, deliberately reminding them both that he was old enough to be her father, "how glad I am to see you."

"And I to see you, Ardewin," she breathed, her heart in her eyes.

"But you have not, Neuad," he said sharply. "I am not the Ardewin, and have not been for many years. Nor have you seen this boy. You saw an old man and his grandnephew. And that is all you saw. Do you understand?"

She shook her head, "I—"

"Do you understand?" he asked, harshly.

She glanced at the boy who stood so quietly by the door, then back at Myrrdin. Her eyes held questions that she would not ask. But then her gaze went to Arthur again. As her eyes widened, Myrrdin saw that she did, indeed, understand. She had, after all, been the Dewin for King Uthyr and Queen Ygraine for many years, and their echoes were clear on their son's face for those who had eyes to see.

At last she turned back to Myrrdin, then nodded. "Yes, I understand. An old man and his grandnephew helped me to get away."

"Good," he smiled.

"This is my story to everyone?" she inquired delicately.

"To everyone," Myrrdin said grimly. "Including my sister."

"Dinaswyn does not—"

"No. Only the Dreamer. And so it must remain for a time yet."

"But Ygraine? Morrigan?" she asked, naming Arthur's mother and sister. At the question, Arthur turned his face away, the scar on his cheek whitening as he set his jaw.

"No one," Myrrdin repeated.

Neuad nodded, then abruptly sat down on the rough bench against the wall.

"You are tired, my dear," Myrrdin said gently. "Hungry and thirsty, no doubt, also. Arthur, will you get our guest something to drink?" There was no use using another name for the boy. It was too late for that.

Arthur, his young face tight and set, nodded, crossing the tiny room to the wooden cupboard next to the hearth. He poured a measure of ale for Neuad into a plain wooden cup, then sat next to her on the bench, holding the drink up to her.

Smiling—oh, gods, she did have such a beautiful smile—she took the cup. Arthur's face relaxed a little as she murmured her thanks. Myrrdin ladled the stew into trenchers of bread and set them on the table, gesturing for Neuad and Arthur to eat.

Neuad ate ravenously, not speaking until Myrrdin had filled up her trencher twice. At last she slowed, then smiled apologetically at them both. "Please excuse my rudeness. I haven't been eating too well lately."

"When did they take you?"

"Three days ago, on the border of Is Gwyrfai and Rosyr. We were coming back from Dolbadarn."

"What were you doing there?"

"Spying out the town. Taking stock. They just finished a temple there a few weeks ago. The Master Bard and the Ardewin sent word that they wanted to know how the defenses stood. So Edwy and I went. We were only a day away from Mynydd Tawel when we were taken."

"Why did they take you? Did they know who you were?"

Neuad shook her head. "No."

"Then why did they take you?"

She shrugged. "We had no excuse to be where we were. They thought we were Cerddorian. They were taking us to Tegeingl, to Madoc."

"To Catha, you mean," Myrrdin corrected. "Madoc has no power there but what Catha gives him. And the General gives him precious little."

"Madoc would have recognized me, though. I was Uthyr's Dewin for thirteen years. If worse had come to worse, I could have committed suicide by Wind-Riding, killed myself simply by not returning to my body."

"Why did you kill him?" Arthur asked suddenly.

"Edwy? I watched him. I knew that when we got to Tegeingl, he would start talking."

"But if you hadn't killed him, we could have rescued you both!" Arthur exclaimed. "And there would have been no danger of him giving anything away."

Neuad shook her head. "But if we had been recaptured—and it was a possibility—he would have broken. There are too many people in Mynydd Tawel, too many Cerddorian in Gwynedd, to take that risk. Edwy was a Bard, and he knew a great deal—enough to be dangerous, since he couldn't be trusted. Trust is too important among the Cerddorian to be taken lightly."

"Why are you one of them?" Arthur asked.

Neuad glanced at Myrrdin in bewilderment, but he kept his face noncommittal. She turned back to Arthur. "Do you mean, why do we fight for our freedom?"

"Yes."

"Because the Dreamer told us to. He promised that, one day, the High King would come back to us."

"Gwydion!" Arthur spat. "You trust him?"

"Why not? He is the Dreamer."

"He plays his own game. He uses people. He throws them away and doesn't care. He lets them die, if it suits him." Arthur's brown eyes held the sheen of tears.

"King Uthyr chose to stay and face the enemy," Neuad said gently. "I have heard tell that, when Gwydion and Rhiannon came to warn him, the Dreamer begged Uthyr to leave Tegeingl, begged him not to fight."

"But did the Dreamer tell King Uthyr that he would die?" Arthur challenged.

"He didn't have to. Uthyr already knew."

Arthur turned his face away, but Neuad gently took him by the chin and made him look at her. "You look so very much like him," she said softly. "And like your mother, too. Those are her eyes. Tell me, where did you get that scar?"

The scar on Arthur's face whitened. He jerked his head away, but answered her question. "A bird attacked me. Two years ago."

"A bird?" Neuad's brow rose. "What kind of bird?"

"Yes, Arthur," Myrrdin said gently. "Tell her what kind of bird."

"An eagle," Arthur said sullenly.

"Not—" Neuad began.

"Yes," Myrrdin said. "Arderydd. He came to the boy on the mountain. And marked him."

"And still," Neuad said softly, "you question why we fight? And still, you don't believe the words of the Dreamer? Oh, Arthur, is it nothing to you that we live in bondage? Nothing to you that we want to be free?"

Myrrdin leaned forward slightly. He knew the boy better than anyone else in the world, but still he did not know how Arthur would respond.

But Arthur did not answer.

CAI AP CYNYR, Captain of the Cerddorian of Gwynedd, scanned the surrounding mountains from his perch on the top of Mynydd Tawel. It was foolish, he knew. There was nothing he could see with his eyes that the Dewin could not see better while Wind-Riding. But still he had come up here to the very top of the highest mountain in Eryri, looking for signs of their return. Neuad and Edwy were long overdue.

Susanna had contacted the other band of Cerddorian, in Coed Arllech, led by Isgowen ur Banon, the Lady of Arfon. But neither Isogwen nor her people had seen or heard from the Dewin or the Bard.

The dying rays of the sinking sun edged the surrounding mountains in bold relief, their purple hues fading to black. Soon he would have to go back down and join the others. The wind ruffled his shoulder-length brown hair and caused his dark cloak to billow around him. It stung his tanned, lined face and he narrowed his brown eyes, as he searched for signs that they were returning. But there was nothing to see.

Perhaps Neuad was dead. If he could still weep, he would have. But he could not. He had wept too many tears at the deaths of his wife and son to have any left now. Two years had passed since the battle when Nest and Garanwyn had lost their lives. Yet still the wound was as raw and fresh as if it had happened yesterday.

Poor Neuad was so young and so beautiful. She had been a good friend to him for many years. She had been the Dewin in Tegeingl while he had been Uthyr's Captain. He had not really known just how lucky he was in the old days. A wife and son whom he loved. A King who had been his friend. Men and women under his command, companions for many years.

And now? His King was dead. His wife and son were dead. Many of his friends had died in the final battle—the battle in which Uthyr had not allowed him to fight. He had done what Uthyr wanted. He had taken Queen Ygraine away. He had served and protected Morrigan, Uthyr's daughter. He had gathered the survivors together to continue their fight from these mountains. But it had gained him nothing. All love and laughter had gone out of the world two years ago, never to return.

Until lately. It had been coming for a long time. It was hard to face the fact that he loved again. But love again, he did. He loved someone with hair of red-gold. He loved someone with beautiful blue eyes. He loved someone with a voice as rich as cream, with a wide smile and ready laughter. Someone—

"Ygraine says it's time to come down. It's too dark to see anything now."

Quickly he turned. He should have heard her coming. It was true that she always moved softly and gracefully. And it was true he had been preoccupied. But there was no excuse. He was silent for a moment, taking her in. Her red-gold hair was loosed from its braid and tossed about by the breeze. Her wide blue eyes smiled at him, and her mouth quirked in amusement. She wore a simple tunic and trousers of brown leather. Her cloak of dark green streamed behind her in the wind.

"Cai?"

"Yes, Susanna?"

"Is something wrong?"

"No," he snapped. "Yes, of course, there's something wrong. Neuad and Edwy."

"Maybe they will send us word tonight," she said, her voice soothing. "I could hear Edwy, if he called. So could Gwrhyr. And Dinaswyn could receive a message from either one of them. You don't know that they are in trouble."

"Of course, they are in trouble, Susanna," he said impatiently. "Let's not pretend about that."

"All right, I won't." Her voice was patient, but her blue eyes were beginning to snap. "But standing up here on the mountain won't help them, will it?"

Cai shook his head, then motioned for her to go ahead of him. On the way back down, he never once took his eyes from her.

THE EVENING MEAL over, Cai waited for the rest of them to settle around the fire. Small fires glowed here and there among the trees that lined the mountain slope. Soon the men, women, and children who sheltered here would retire to the caves that pockmarked the mountain. There was no danger from lighting fires. For one thing, this valley within Mynydd Tawel was thoroughly sheltered by the surrounding mountains. For another, the Bards and Dewin who lived here were on watch. They would be able to spot a potential intruder many leagues away—even at night.

Duach, Uthyr's former doorkeeper, was already here. Duach was now the Lord of Dunoding since his father had been killed in the invasion. Dywel, the Gwarda of Ardudwy, was the next to come to the fire. Dywel's gray eyes were fierce, and the lines that bracketed his mouth were deep, as they had been since word had first come that his brother, Bledri, had betrayed King Urien and Queen Ellirri in Rheged.

"No word from Neuad yet, uncle?"

Cai looked up to see his nephew settling down beside him. Though only twenty-three, Bedwyr had been Uthyr's Lieutenant in Tegeingl. Bedwyr's handsome, strong face always reminded Cai of his own brother, Bedrawd, another loved one who had been lost in the fighting. His nephew's brown eyes were steady as Cai shook his head.

Gwrhyr, Susanna's son, came up then and sat down at Cai's feet. The boy had the red hair and freckled face of his Druid sire, Griffi, who had died in the last Battle of Tegeingl. But Gwrhyr's eyes were blue, like his mother's. He was fourteen, tall and gangly. He had just recently come to Mynydd Tawel from the hidden place where the Bards and the Dewin lived. Susanna had requested the Master Bard to let Gwrhyr come to her, and Anieron had acquiesced, knowing how much Susanna needed to see her son.

Cai smiled at the boy, for Gwrhyr reminded him of his own dead son. He was fond of Gwrhyr, in spite of the fact that the boy clearly thought Cai should be his new father. And Gwrhyr was not subtle about it.

"Did you know that mam was the one who dressed the mutton tonight? I thought it was very good, didn't you?" Gwrhyr asked, his young face eager.

Bedwyr hid a smile, but Cai gravely answered, "I thought it very good, indeed."

"She's really a very good cook. I—"

At that moment Morrigan arrived, followed closely by her mother, Ygraine. Morrigan was fourteen now. Her slender body was beginning to fill out, straining here and there against her tunic of forest green. Her rich, auburn hair was tangled, and as always, there was a smudge of dirt on her face. Her dark eyes held laughter and mischief. They were so like Uthyr's eyes that Cai sometimes had to look away until the tightness in his throat eased. On her hand she wore the sapphire ring of Gwynedd, the ring that Uthyr had given her the day he had sent her away to safety.

"Did you hear how good I was at target practice today?" Morrigan asked as she sat down cross-legged on the ground. It was hard to remember sometimes that this girl was the Queen of Gwynedd.

"I'm afraid I did not," Cai said, trying to keep his face stern. "And it is very bad form to brag."

"She did do quite well," Bedwyr said with a smile.

"See? It's not bragging if it's true," she pointed out. "Is it, mam?" she continued, turning to her mother.

Ygraine sat down on a log, as stiff and straight and formal as if she sat at the high table in Caer Gwynt. The former Queen of Gwynedd's auburn hair was braided and wound around her head. Her gown of dark blue was spotless, and her dark eyes were cool and watchful. As always her smooth face showed nothing of what she was thinking. "Morrigan, I told you to wash your face."

"I will. But—"

"Bedwyr told me you did very well at practice today," Susanna said as she came to the fire and sat down next to Ygraine. "It reminded me of your da."

"Really?" Morrigan asked, delighted. "As good as him?"

"No, Morrigan," Ygraine said coldly. "No one is as good as Uthyr was."

Morrigan's face fell. Almost as if it was against her will, Ygraine relented, and smiled. "But you come close, daughter. Very close, indeed."

"Soon I'll be good enough to go with the rest of you," Morrigan said eagerly, turning to Cai and Bedwyr.

"No!" Ygraine said harshly. "You are not to go with them."

"But, Im —"

Cai took a deep breath. In truth art he, too, did not want Morrigan to be exposed to danger. But he knew it was inevitable. Morrigan was Queen. Ygraine would have to remember that. "You may go with us, Morrigan. On our next raid."

"And I say no!" Ygraine replied swiftly, her dark eyes flashing fire.

"Morrigan is Queen now, Ygraine," Susanna said gently. "She has a duty to her people."

"She has a duty to stay alive!"

The arrival of Dinaswyn and Arianrod stopped the argument. Somehow no one, not even Ygraine, argued in front of Dinaswyn, the former Dreamer of Kymru. Dinaswyn's dark hair, frosted with gray, was twisted into a loose braid, cascading down her stiff back. She wore a tunic and trousers of black leather. Her cool gray eyes surveyed them all.

"I have news," Dinaswyn said crisply.

But before she could speak, Arianrod started in. "I tell you, Cai, I won't stand for one more minute of it!"

"One more minute of what?" Cai asked blankly.

"I told you before! I want to go to Tegeingl. My clothes are in rags."

Come to think of it, Cai realized, she had told him that already. But he rarely paid attention to anything she said. There seemed to be nothing she would not complain about, and nothing she didn't think a man would do to fix it. Her honey-blond hair was loose and flowing down to her slender waist. The bodice of her red gown was tight against her smooth, white skin. Her almond-shaped amber eyes and high cheekbones gave her the look of a hungry cat. Elaborate golden earrings dripped from her ears.

For the hundredth time, Cai wondered how Gwydion had put up with this woman for all those years. Even her magnificent body would not be payment enough for having to listen to her constant complaints. Cai should know—he had sampled that body. Though not for quite some time now.

"Arianrod," Cai began wearily. "I told you—"

"Oh, stop whining, Arianrod," Susanna said sharply, reaching up and yanking on the Dewin's arm, forcing her to sit down abruptly. "Hush," Susanna went on as Arianrod opened her mouth to argue. "Go on, Dinaswyn. What news?"

"Neuad is alive."

Morrigan yelled out in glee. Ygraine actually smiled. Susanna jumped up, threw herself into Cai's arms, and hugged him tightly. Before he could say a word, Susanna let him go. "What happened?" she asked Dinaswyn breathlessly.

"She and Edwy were captured," Dinaswyn answered. "On the way to Tegeingl, they stopped in Dinas Emrys. The people of the village distracted the warriors, and Neuad escaped with the help of one of the village boys."

"And Edwy?" Bedwyr asked.

"She killed him," Dinaswyn said briskly.

"He talked?"

"She thought he was going to. She will return to us in a few days."

"Excellent," Cai said, smiling. "Our next raid will be to Dolbadarn, assuming the news Neuad brings is good."

"And you, Susanna," Ygraine said, "had best make ready to travel. It's time for the Plentyn Prawf."

Susanna nodded. "I thought I should leave in a few days."

Cai's heart began to pound. She would leave. Go out into the world where the Coranians waited. Unless— "What does the

Master Bard say about this?" he demanded. "In light of the meeting at Eiodel, and the fact that we don't know what they are planning, I don't think—"

"The Master Bard says I must use my judgment. And my judgment is, I will go."

"Not alone," Cai said quickly. "I won't allow that."

"Maybe you should go with her," Gwrhyr said, his freckled face innocent.

Yes, Cai thought. He had made up his mind. He must go with her. She must be protected at all costs. Yet, even as he opened his mouth to say so, something else came out—something that showed him quite clearly just how frightened he truly was. "Bedwyr will go with you."

And as Gwrhyr's face fell and Susanna's face tightened, an Arianrod smiled and Bedwyr looked at the fire, Cai silently cursed himself for a fool.

THAT NIGHT THE message sent by the Shining Ones reached into Gwydion's sleep.

At last he had found Y Cleddyf, the Sword, one of the lost Treasures of Kymru. He had found Meirig Yr Llech, Guardian of the Stone. He could see it as it floated majestically in the air at the edge of a cliff, borne up by the cool, clear wind.

The long, shining blade flashed silver in the harsh light of the sun. A twisting serpent was carved into either side of the glowing blade. The handgrip was of silver mesh, chased with gold. The hilt was in the shape of a spread-winged hawk with sapphire eyes. The round pommel at the end of the hilt was carved with a figure eight, the sign of Annwyn, Lord of Chaos, studded with shining, black onyx.

He reached out for it then, but it bobbed away from him, and he almost fell. The sword hung in the air, just out of his reach. He could not reach any farther, for he knew that the air would never bear his weight. He would fall, dash himself on the rocks far below.

And he cried out in frustration and anger, for he was so close but could not obtain what he so desperately sought.

Then, suddenly, a pure, white eagle shot down from the sky to land next to him. A collar of sapphires encircled its fierce, proud neck, and its white feathers glowed.

In its talons it held a blue, woolen scarf. The eagle tossed the scarf into the air, and it settled gently onto the proud hilt of the flaming sword.

Ask. The eagle's thought echoed through the deepest chambers of his mind. *You are to ask.*

For a moment his pride forbade him to speak, but his need was great. "I beg you, then. I beg you to help me," he rasped.

Reach, the eagle answered.

And he stretched out his hands, but they were not his. Instead, he saw the slim, unlined hands of a boy stretched toward the Sword, and the Sword floated serenely into his outstretched hands. And the hands turned into an eagle's claws, then back into a boy's hands, flickering unsteadily from one to the other.

And the Sword came to him as the boy/eagle hands reached out and took it, plucking it from the air. The eagle screamed in triumph and shot up into the sky. And the blue scarf glowed with the light of the sapphires around the hilt of the blade that shone bright and deadly, as his hands, the boys' hands, held the Sword aloft under the blazing sky.

Chapter 6

Allt Llwyd and Peris
Kingdom of Rheged, Kymru
Bedwen Mis, 499

Gwyntdydd, Tywyllu Wythnos—afternoon

Anieron ap Cyvarnion, Master Bard of Kymru, was walking down the rocky beach when the call came. He liked to walk by the sea this time of day, listening to the Wind-Spoken messages that came to him, passed from mind to mind, along the length and breadth of the intricate chain he and his daughter, the Ardewin, had set around Kymru.

He frowned as he listened to the messages that poured in, for once again there was no word on the whereabouts of the Master Smiths. In all four kingdoms, the Smiths and their families had been taken away under heavy guard. More than just taken, they had disappeared. Not one Dewin had seen them, although the Wind-Search for them had been extensive. Not one Bard had heard the slightest rumor of them. Which did not surprise Anieron that much. He simply did not have enough Y Dawnus to cover the entire span of Kymru. The Smiths had obviously been moved by stealth, probably traveling only at night, avoiding towns and cities, taking hidden trails. But trails to where? For what purpose?

Surely this was a vital part of Havgan's plans to defeat the Kymri once and for all. No doubt it was something that had been cooked up at the meeting in Eiodel. But what the plan was, what the purpose was, what other plans had been made, no one knew.

The gray cliffs of Allt Llwyd, which masked the extensive network of caves where those Y Dawnus who had escaped from Y Ty Dewin and Neuadd Gorsedd hid from the enemy, glistened in the afternoon sun. The sea-green water hissed onto the shore, retreated momentarily, then reached out again. The sun was just beginning its descent to meet the water, for it was early spring and the days had just begun to lengthen. The salt air whistled past his ears, ruffling his shoulder-length silvery hair. The lonely cries of the gulls added a sense of pleasant melancholy.

He grimaced slightly. He was truthful to himself—if not always truthful with others. He knew that the work the Bards, the Dewin, and the Cerddorian were doing was almost useless. It was not enough. But there was no need to say it. Certainly not to these two girls who followed him down the shore, their parchments and quills at the ready, taking down the words he dictated.

Cariadas, the daughter of Gwydion the Dreamer, followed him closely, her small face serious and intent on not missing a word. As always, her red-gold hair was tangled, for she often wrapped it around her fingers when deep in thought and went for days on end without brushing it at all. He glanced back at her and her gray eyes—so like her father's, but without Gwydion's coldness—glanced up at him.

"What?" she inquired anxiously. She had begged for the job of assistant, and took her duties very seriously. "I got the last message. 'Owein's band has killed the entire force of wyrce-jaga coming up-river. There were six of them, along with four guards. When Sledda heard about it, he bit his tongue in a rage.'"

"I know you have it perfectly, my dear," Anieron said mildly. "I was only looking at you."

She grinned up at him. "You're not going to say that I need to fix my hair, are you? Elstar says that all the time."

Anieron smiled back at her. His green eyes were sharp and keen. "No, Cariadas, I won't tell you to fix your hair. But, as the heir to the Dreamer, you might consider following the advice of the Ardewin.

Elstar very much dislikes it when you ignore her suggestions."

"They're not suggestions. They're orders. And I don't ignore them," she protested. "I just forget."

"Sinend will have to remind you, then," he said, glancing over at his other assistant, Sinend ur Aergol, the daughter of the Archdruid's heir.

Sinend was thin and pale. The sun coaxed the red highlights from her brown hair as she cast her gray eyes down and smiled shyly. She did not reply, for Sinend rarely spoke. If there was one thing Anieron would like to do, it would be to make Aergol and Cathbad pay for what they had done to this sweet girl. Over two years since the invasion, and still Sinend could barely seem to raise her head for shame that her father and the Archdruid were aiding the enemy.

"She does remind me," Cariadas said, smiling at her friend. "But I still forget."

"Well, now. That seems to me—" Anieron began, then stopped, as the last call of the day came in. He halted so abruptly that the two girls almost ran into him.

"What?" Cariadas began, but Sinend laid a gentle hand on her arm and Cariadas subsided.

Master Bard. We are coming.

It is time, then, at last? It begins again?

It begins again, Anieron. We will be there within three days. Just before Alban Awyr.

You and she will be most welcome.

They were on the way here. The time had come to reclaim Kymru at last. Anieron rejoiced that he was still alive to see it begin again, though he had his doubts that he would live to see the ending.

He turned back to the girls, who were watching him with wide eyes. "I didn't hear a thing," Cariadas said in wonder. "Not even an echo. The person who Wind-Spoke to you was very skilled."

"Very. Child, your father is coming."

The joy on her face made him smile, even as his heart ached for her. For he knew Gwydion ap Awst very well, indeed.

LATER THAT EVENING, Anieron retired early to his quarters deep in the caves of Allt Llwyd. After two years, the caves were still beautiful to him, still fascinating, still more than worthy of songs. The torches set in brackets at intervals along the passages made the walls glisten, picking out the shimmer of crystal, veins of silver and gold, onyx, and other stones.

He walked slowly, deep in thought, nodding absentmindedly at the Y Dawnus he passed. He almost had not needed Gwydion to tell him the time had come. He felt it in his bones. Events were moving again, and the die was being cast. Only the gods knew—if even they did—how the game would come out. Not that Anieron minded that; he was good at games. Now, if he could just figure out the latest one, the one that bothered him more than he was willing to admit, he might be able to sleep through the nights again. What was Havgan up to now? What had happened at the meeting in Eiodel a few weeks ago?

In the four kingdoms, events were moving again, moving far beyond the usual raids and pinpricks the Cerddorian managed to give to the enemy.

In Rheged, Princess Enid had left Coed Addien and gone to Llwynarth in a mad scheme to persuade Bledri, Morcant's traitorous Dewin, to return with her. But the scheme had backfired, as anyone with sense would have guessed, and Enid was now a prisoner of King Morcant.

The question to be answered now was, what were Morcant's plans for Enid? Anieron had sent his brother, Dudod, to Llwynarth to find some answers, and Dudod was due back within a few days. Owein had so far refused to move the Cerddorian from Coed Addien, even though Anieron and others were putting pressure on him to do so. Enid had been a prisoner now for two weeks, and though she had, apparently, not yet betrayed her brother, she couldn't hold out forever.

In Prydyn, Queen Efa had finally made good her desertion of her husband, and King Rhoram's entire band had moved east to Haford Bryn before Efa could betray their location. The new location was secure, and the Cerddorian were now settled there. Prince Geriant and Princess Gwenhwyfar had pulled off a successful raid on the caravan

General Penda had used as bait and had gotten clean away with the loot. Soon after Queen Efa's return to Arberth, the Druid Ellywen had left the city, traveling north. Anieron did not know why, but it surely had something to do with the letter from Havgan that General Penda had received.

In Ederynion, Prince Lludd and Angharad had completed a successful raid on the temple in Ymris, returning to discover that Llwyd Cilcoed, Queen Olwen's cowardly lover, had returned. Lludd had not killed the man, and Anieron's estimation of the Prince of Ederynion had risen even higher with that news.

In Dinmael, Elen and Regan were still captive. General Talorcan was still taking pains to see that they were well treated. Iago had left the city, traveling east. So there was another Druid on the road now. Why?

In Gwynedd, young Tangwen, Madoc's daughter, was clearly on the side of those who despised the enemy, but there was little she could do. And yet, she would be a very good tool for the Cerddorian. His agent in Caer Gwynt was doing well, but another set of ears and eyes never hurt. He would think on the best way to approach her.

But the best news out of Gwynedd was that the people of Dinas Emrys had rescued Neuad from her captivity. The message made mention that the greatest help had come from an old man and his grandnephew. Anieron had a pretty good idea of just whom that really was, but he had declined to speak of it. He would say nothing even to Elstar, his own daughter. He trusted her, but there were some things that must be guarded so closely they remained locked in the heart, in the place where hopes are born.

He reached his quarters, pulling aside the woven curtain of bardic blue trimmed with silver that hung over the cave mouth. There was a fire burning in the brazier—Cariadas's work, no doubt. The girl did her best to take care of him. He smiled to himself, thinking of her impulsive generosity, her bright spirit. One day she would be the Dreamer of Kymru. His smile faded, leaving his face lined and sad. Would her brightness become tarnished by what she saw in her dreams? Would she become as her father—cold and hard? Yet it was not the dreams that had made Gwydion that way. It was something inside of those who refused to face their wounds, and so built walls to stay safe. Dinaswyn, Gwydion's teacher, had done the same.

With a sigh, he sat down on the piled cushions of his pallet. His bones ached, living this close to the sea. But he would not trade it for anything. It was so beautiful. He reached out and picked up his harp, plucking out a new tune, another song of the beauty he found here.

"You should be asleep."

He didn't even look up, but said gently, "Elstar, my dear, so should you."

Elstar, the Ardewin of Kymru, sat down at the edge of the pallet. Her light brown hair was loosened from its customary braid and fell in shimmering waves to her waist. She wore a plain robe of sea green, and her blue eyes were dimmed and tired.

"I was on my way to bed when a message came. Jonas ap Morgan has arrived."

"Ah, poor Jonas. Perhaps I should see him now, if he's not too tired."

"He doesn't look at all well, da."

"I would think not. The deaths of his wife and baby daughter have no doubt torn his heart to shreds. May the wyrce-jaga's black souls live long and long under the hand of the Lord of Chaos," Anieron replied, somewhat more forcefully than he had intended.

"You are tired, too."

"So I am," he agreed, for there was no use arguing the point.

"Perhaps you should see him tomorrow," Elstar began.

"I will see him now."

"What are you going to do with him?"

"I'm not sure. I may keep him here for a while. On the other hand, I need another Bard in Gwynedd since Neuad killed the last one. I'll know better what to do when I see him."

"Very well, I'll bring him to you. Oh, by the way, how are your Bards doing with the Plentyn Prawf? Any news?"

"In Rheged there is none yet—Esyllt just left the camp and isn't even out of Coed Addien. Trystan goes with her."

"Humph. Is that why she is so slow?"

Anieron grinned. "She was never one of my bravest. But she does what I tell her. In Prydyn, Cian is somewhere near the city of Cil. Achren guards him, and there is no one better. So far they have found one candidate for the Bards and two for the Dewin."

"And the others?"

"In Ederynion, Talhearn and Angharad are near Sycharth, having already located one Bard, two Druids, and a Dewin."

"And what in the world are we going to do with these baby Druids?"

"For them, we wait. When the enemy is defeated, when Cathbad is dead, we can build up the Druids again, using Sinend. I believe we can count on her to train a new generation of Druids in the right way."

"And in Gwynedd?"

"Susanna has already identified two Bards and one Druid on her journey. She and Bedwyr are now approaching Tegeingl."

Elstar's brows went up. "Is that wise?"

"They will do some testing in the wool works outside the city. They should be safe enough. Now, let me see Jonas."

"All right. But I warn you, the poor man is stretched tighter than a drum."

"I'm warned. Now bring him in."

Elstar left without further comment, and a few moments later the curtain was again drawn back as Jonas entered the room. The Bard was thin and slight. He had sandy hair and eyes of pale green. His clothes were patched and worn, and his face was tight with misery and sleeplessness. Anieron gestured for him to sit, and Jonas settled gingerly on the pallet, erect and tense, as though ready to spring up if the situation called for it.

Anieron put the harp aside and gently said in his rich voice, "Jonas ap Morgan. You are welcome here. I was so sorry to hear of the deaths of your wife and baby."

Jonas swallowed hard and nodded, but did not speak.

"You are welcome here for as long as you like. Perhaps a rest would do you good."

"What would I do here, Master?" Jonas whispered.

"Well, there are messages to pass on. Records to keep. Children to teach—"

"No!" Jonas said harshly.

"Yes, all right. I understand."

"Master, I . . . I wish to get away from Rheged. A change of scenery might . . ." he trailed off uncertainly, staring at the floor, his thin, pale hands clenched together.

"Before the war, you were the Bard to Diadwa in Creuddyn."

"Yes," Jonas said hesitantly. "I was happy in Gwynedd. We were close to Tegeingl and used to visit King Uthyr's court often. Diadwa was a gracious lady, and she often had guests. So much singing then, and so much laughter."

"You would like to go back there? Yet you know as well as I do that things are different there now."

"I was happy in Gwynedd," Jonas said quietly. "And it is far from Rheged."

"Well, then, to Gwynedd you shall go. But not to Creuddyn."

"I—"

"One of the Bards who served the Cerddorian in Gwynedd has recently met with an accident. He must be replaced. I will send you to Morrigan and Cai."

Jonas glanced up quickly, his pale eyes gleaming, then swiftly looked down.

"They have need of you there," Anieron went on. "Will you go?"

It would be some time before Anieron fully understood why the smile Jonas had given then had been so bitter.

Addiendydd, Tywyllu Wythnos—midmorning

DUDOD AP CYVARNION was only slightly disconcerted. A man less used to getting out of tight spots might well have been horrified. But Dudod was not such a man. He recognized, of course, that this might be the end of a long and satisfying life, for he knew very well that he could not afford to be taken alive.

Up to this moment, his trip had been relatively uneventful. He had spent many days in Llwynarth, trying to discover the Coranians' plan for poor Princess Enid. But he had not been able to find out, and had at last given up. In a lifetime of trusting his feelings, he simply knew that he could not afford to stay in Llwynarth one more day.

The day before he left Llwynarth, he had seen Sabrina, King Morcant's Druid, in the company of Bledri. They had come to the marketplace on an errand that Dudod had not been able to determine, due to the fact that he had melted away as quickly as possible. Yet he was sure that before he could do so, Sabrina had seen and recognized him. The interesting thing was that as soon as his eyes had met hers, she had turned away, gabbling at Bledri to see the jeweled comb she wanted, distracting the Dewin from looking over in Dudod's direction.

He had shadowed the couple for as long as he had dared, hoping for a chance to talk to her. She of all people would surely know what the plans for Enid were. But there had been no opportunity to talk. After the marketplace, they had gone straight to the temple of Lytir, which stood in what was once the sacred grove of Mabon, Lord of the Sun.

He didn't think he would ever forget the expression on her face when she emerged from the temple after having assisted the preosts in the worship services. She had returned to Caer Erias and ridden out of the gates of Llwynarth a few hours later. She was unaccompanied and clearly expected—the Coranian guards at the gate let her pass without comment.

Whatever her errand, Dudod had not liked the look on her face. His attempts to find out where she was going had been useless. So he had left Llwynarth soon after and traveled east, as far as Peris, the last city on the way to Allt Llwyd. Invoking the law of hospitality, he had gone to one of the houses in the city and simply knocked on the door.

They had let him in, fed him, and sheltered him for the night. He had not been asked his name, nor had he given it, but just after dinner the master of the house had silently handed Dudod a harp. And Dudod had taken it and begun to play. He would never forget the bright smile of the little girl who had sat at his feet, listening with all her might to the music he made. Nor would he forget the face of the lady of the house, the mix of joy and fear that passed across her face like sunshine and shadow.

If only he could get word to Anieron! His brother must know what Dudod had just now discovered, here on this road outside of Peris. But Dudod was too far away to Wind-Speak to Allt Llwyd. Only another five leagues or so, and he would be close enough. If he could escape this trap just long enough to send a message, the Coranians could find his corpse for all he cared. For what he had seen here was part of the answer to the questions that had troubled them all since the meeting in Eiodel.

Patiently, as though he had nothing particular on his mind, he waited with the rest of the eastbound travelers for his turn to be questioned. No doubt the pack on his horse would be opened and examined, but that was no problem. He was posing as a peddler, and the pack contained nothing that should not be there. He wore a simple tunic and trousers of brown leather; his green cloak was threadbare and clasped at the neck with a plain bronze brooch. His tanned skin was stretched tightly over his high cheekbones. He did not wear a cap, for he was vain of his sun-streaked brown hair, which was just now beginning to gray (the fact that Anieron's hair was almost completely silver gave him much satisfaction). His green eyes were sharp and clever, but that was in character for a peddler who must make a living. All was as it should be and he could get through this—unless, as he suspected, they knew who they were looking for.

Apparently he had been seen in the marketplace after all.

Well, just in case he got out of this one, he used the time to examine as closely as he dared the collar that the black-robed wyrce-jaga held.

He had recognized its purpose the moment he saw it. It was an enaid-dal, a soul-catcher, and the sight of it made his blood run cold, as nothing else had ever done. As a Bard he knew there had been times in the history of Lyonesse when it had been necessary to subdue a recalcitrant Y Dawnus. But the collars made to do that were few, and very old. But this one was recently made. This was the reason for Cathbad's smile after the meeting in Eiodel. This was the reason for the disappearance of the Master Smiths and their families.

A distraction was all Dudod needed. Carefully, he began a soft call, Far-Sensing to determine what animals might be within reach of his telepathic communication. The forests nearby were sparse and the wolves few there. Not good enough. Horses would do, but Coranians did not ride them often, and he would need quite a few. There was the horse he was riding, of course, but he would need the animal to get away.

Far-Sensing as hard as he could, he did not notice at first that the travelers behind him were moving up quietly ahead of him, crowding him out of his place in line, screening him from the sight of the wyrce-jaga and the guards. A slight jostle on his elbow as one man moved ahead of him dropped him out of his light trance. The man, a farmer by the look of his strong arms and leathery face, said nothing, but looked at him sharply for a brief moment before turning away and planting his body squarely in front of Dudod.

Dudod looked around to see that he was now the last man in the line. A brief respite, but one that might make all the difference. Silently he blessed these travelers in the name of Taran of the Winds. Then he Far-Sensed again.

Ah, at last. A flock of ravens heading this way in response to his call. How very appropriate, he thought, almost grinning. How absolutely perfect.

He moved forward a few steps. There were only three men ahead of him on the road now. The women had been barely questioned and were now standing to one side, waiting for their menfolk, talking quietly among themselves. The man who had jostled Dudod was now being questioned.

"Name?" the wyrce-jaga asked officiously.

"None of your business," the farmer replied in a belligerent tone.

The wyrce-jaga, apparently not used to such answers, gaped at the farmer for a moment. The men and women who had been questioned already but who, for some reason, had not yet departed, moved forward slightly, once again crowding Dudod out of the sight of the warriors.

"You will tell me your name or you will die," the wyrce-jaga threatened, recovering from his surprise. The black-robed man had meant for his voice to sound menacing, but it shook slightly. The three Coranian warriors were standing alert and ready, but the grins on their faces showed what they thought of the wyrce-jaga.

"You tell me why you want to know, and I'll tell you my name," the farmer replied, his bluff, good-natured face now set in a scowl. "Fair is fair."

Once again, the people watching moved in even closer. One woman put her hand inside the covered basket she carried. Dudod thought he saw the gleam of metal there. Time was running out—he didn't want these people to pay for his escape with their lives.

At last they came. To the north the sky darkened just behind the guards. Then the flock of ravens dropped out of the air and began to feed. The screams of the guards and the wyrce-jaga echoed across the plain, the raucous caws of the birds mingling in a strange, horrifying harmony. The other travelers grimly stood their ground, watching the birds as they covered the Coranian bodies, ready and waiting to ensure that the work was done properly.

"Hurry, man," the farmer called. "Who knows how many other Coranians might be in the area! Ride!"

Dudod grasped the reins of his horse. "My thanks to you all," Dudod said. "Oh, wait, I almost forgot." At a silent word from him, the birds parted from the screaming wyrce-jaga just long enough for Dudod to wrench the collar from what was left of the man's hands. Then the birds closed in again, continuing their dreadful feeding.

With distaste, Dudod stowed the object in his pack. "The blessings of Taran of the Winds on you all. And a good Alban Awyr!" Dudod called as he mounted his horse and shot away to the east, riding like the wind.

As ANIERON PASSED the cavern where the daily lessons for the young Dewin and Bards were taking place, he paused a moment to listen, hovering in the shadows. If the children realized he was there, they might be nervous.

One group of hopeful Bards sat nearest the cave mouth in a ring, reciting the Triads at the prompting of their teacher. "What are the three birthrights of every Kymri?" the teacher asked.

Answering in unison, the children replied, "The right to go where he pleases, the right to protection by his ruler, the right of equal privileges and equal restrictions."

Anieron smiled. Some of the younger ones had trouble with the words *privileges* and *restrictions*.

"For three things a Kymri is pronounced a traitor and forfeits his rights. What are these three things?"

"Leaving Kymru, aiding the enemy, surrendering himself and living under the enemy." At this one of the boys raised his hand.

"Yes, Olan?" the teacher prompted.

"How can that be? We are all living under the enemy. Are we all traitors?"

"We do not live under the enemy, Olan. We wait."

"Ah," the boy said, and subsided, satisfied.

Anieron turned his attention to another group nearby who were learning the history of the Kymru. "And these were the Great Ones of the fifth generation," the teacher said. "Bran the Dreamer, Taliesin the Master Bard, Mannawyddan the Ardewin, and Arywen the Archdruid. And these four served High King Lleu Lawrient. When Lleu was killed at the hands of his wife and her lover, these Great Ones hid the Four Treasures at the direction of Dian, saying that, when the need was greatest, they would again be found."

Well, the gods knew that the need was greatest now. He could only hope with all his heart that Gwydion ap Awst knew what he was doing.

Over in the far corner, a group of children were sitting upright in a light trance state, their short legs extended and their tiny hands resting on their thighs, as the teacher recited softly. "And now the crown of your head is filled with light. You are a vessel of light, lifted by the Wind of Taran. You are weightless, floating in the air. Now, Wind-Speak to me. Tell me your names."

With a bell-like rush, Anieron heard their names ringing in his mind. Tears came to his eyes as each child named themselves in wonder and awe, listening to the sound of their name reverberating from mind to mind. Their bright laughter, their joy, sounded in his head. Clearly he remembered the day—oh, so long ago—when he had first Wind-Spoken his own name for the Bards to hear.

He had used that gift in joy, in delight, all his life. These little ones would have the same chance he had, he swore to himself. One day they would not have to hide away in this cave. One day they would emerge into the sunlight and proudly Wind-Speak their names to all of Kymru. He would see to it.

He would have liked to stay, but he had lingered long enough already. Elstar and Elidyr would be waiting for him. He slipped away, making his way to the meeting room. As he lifted the curtain that marked the entrance to the cave, he saw his daughter, Elstar, and his nephew, Elidyr, spring apart.

"You don't have to stop for me," he said genially.

"I didn't see you coming," Elstar said, her eyes bright and her cheeks flushed.

"Some Dewin you are. I grant you, however, that you were distracted."

"I'd certainly like to think so," Elidyr replied with a grin.

"You two are married, you know. No need to be coy."

"Elstar's shy. Even after all these years and two children, she doesn't want anyone to think she likes me."

"Elidyr, *cariad*, that's not true!" Elstar protested. The twinkle in Elidyr's light brown eyes stopped her. She lightly swatted his arm.

"You see?" Elidyr asked. "You see how she treats me?"

"As your own father would say, Elidyr, no doubt you deserved it."

"And speaking of my da," Elidyr began.

Anieron shook his head. "No word from Dudod yet. But I don't think that's cause for alarm. He was given orders to stay in Llwynarth for as long as it took."

"Yes, but you know that sometimes he cuts things a little too close. I'd just feel better if we heard from him, that's all."

"I would, too, lad. But I learned a long time ago that it was futile to worry about Dudod. He's fine, I'm sure. Now, down to business."

For the next few hours, they talked and planned. All the reports from yesterday were sorted and noted. When necessary, they marked the large map that hung on one rough wall with the latest dispositions of the Coranians, their tribute caravans, new temples to Lytir, and the movements of the wyrce-jaga. They planned the raids for the next week and composed messages to be passed from mind to mind to the Dewin and Bards who waited to pass on the orders to the Cerddorian.

"So, still nothing about the Master Smiths," Elstar said, frowning.

"Not a word," Elidyr replied, running a hand through his sandy blond hair.

"Hmm," Elstar said, absently scanning the map. "Well, we'll just have to hope for more information. In the meantime, let's think about how in the world we are going to get Owein to move his people out of Coed Addien. Now that the Coranians have Enid, it won't be long before she talks."

"Owein will come to his senses soon, Elstar," Anieron said. "I am sure of it." He felt oddly distracted. Strangely tense. Something was coming. Something was badly wrong. He rubbed the back of his neck and briefly closed his eyes.

"Da?" he heard Elstar say, as though from a great distance. "What's the matter?"

"Nothing. I don't know. I—"

The frantic message came crashing into his skull. Dudod did not, apparently, have time for subtleties.

Brother! Hear me!

Dudod! What is it? What's happened?

Listen to me. The Coranians have an enaid-dal.

An enaid-dal. A soul-catcher. Oh, gods, no.

Cathbad rediscovered how to make them.

Dudod! That is why they have taken the Master Smiths.

To make more of these things. Yes. But, Anieron, think of this. What good does it do them to have these collars unless they know whom to put them on? They need a way to determine who is of the Y Dawnus.

They would need—

A testing device. As many as they could find.

And that is why Ellywen left Arberth, why Iago left Dinmael.

Yes. And why Sabrina left Llwynarth a few days ago.

They are looking for the Bards. They need the testing devices.

Dudod, come back as quickly as you can. Cut off all communication with me unless you want your head to be blasted apart.

Anieron, don't try it! You—

But it was too late. He cut off his brother, and, turning to Elstar and Elidyr, he ordered them to shield their minds, saying he would answer questions later. At the look in his eyes, they did not question him, but did as they were bid.

Anieron gathered every bit of his considerable mind-strength. The message must go, and go now. With a silent prayer to Taran of the Winds, he crafted the Mind-Shout, the Shout that was used so rarely that few could do it. Books and scrolls had written that it could not be done. But it could. And he would prove it. Now.

The Shout shot away from him clear and clean, riding the winds, making nothing of the hundreds of leagues between the Master Bard and his people. The four Bards, scattered throughout Kymru, heard the call as though Anieron were right beside them.

Esyllt, Talhearn, Susanna, Cian! Turn back now! The enemy comes!

Chapter 7

Kymru
Bedwen Mis, 499
Addiendydd, Tywyllu Wythnos

Coed Addien, Kingdom of Rheged

Tight-lipped and uncommunicative, Trystan trudged through the forest of Coed Addien. He had not wanted to come on the Plentyn Prawf, but Owein had insisted, and Trystan had obeyed.

His eyes were on Esyllt's slim back as she walked ahead of him. Unwillingly, he remembered all those times he had run his hands down that elegant spine, had kissed that lovely, long neck and those delicate white shoulders, had—

He forced his thoughts away from those memories. He almost winced when he thought of how many years he had been Esyllt's dupe. Eight years? Nine? How in the name of all the gods had she been able to fool him for that long? Stupid question, really. He knew the answer to that.

She had been able to fool him because he had wanted her to.

All those years, she had managed to keep him on a string, promising to divorce her husband. But she had never delivered on those promises. March had been captured at the last battle of Llwynarth and had not been seen since. If she was concerned over his fate, she concealed it well. In the past two years, no one had heard her so much as speak her husband's name.

Why only now, after all this time, had he realized the truth about her?

Another question to which he knew the answer. For the last two years had been sheer torment to him, and Esyllt had not been willing, or perhaps had simply not been able, to comfort him. For the first time since he had known her, he had turned to her for help, for guidance out of his anguish. But she had not even tried to understand the nature of the wound that was slowly killing him—the wound he suffered because he had been the Captain of King Urien's teulu, and his King had died. Yet Trystan had not.

Grimly he hung on to the memory that sustained him these last two years—the memory of Arderydd, the eagle, whom he had seen in the forest the day he had determined to take his own life. The contempt in the eagle's eyes—for there was no mistaking that—had stopped his blade that day. And the memory of it had stopped him many days since.

It was midmorning, and overhead the sun was shining through the leaves of the trees, splashing on the cold ground. Three days from now, it would be Alban Awyr, the time when the Kymri honored Taran, the King of the Winds, the time to celebrate the coming of spring. The day was mild, with just a slight breeze playing through the tree branches. Just ahead, the forest ended, and the misty hills beckoned. Over the hills lay Sarn Halen, the great north-south road that extended the entire length of Rheged. Once on the road, they would travel south, away from Llwynarth, which lay a few days north.

Esyllt halted, waiting for him before stepping from the forest. Her gown was plain brown wool, and she wore a rough linen smock beneath it. Her abundant light brown hair was twisted loosely around a white linen cloth, spilling down her back. Her beautiful blue eyes caught and held him.

"You do not look at all like a farmer's wife," he said gruffly. And that was true. Her skin was too white, her hands too smooth—even after living in the forest for two years. Esyllt was always very careful of her fine, white skin. "I told you to dirty your hands and face some."

"I will," she said absently, scanning the hills. "Do you think it's safe?"

"Safe? Of course not. No Y Dawnus is safe these days." Seeing her flinch, he almost regretted his harshness. Almost.

"I—" she began, then stopped abruptly as his hand shot out to cover her mouth. He grabbed her arm and hauled her behind the nearest tree. Speaking so quietly he barely made a sound, he whispered, "Movement in the trees, to the north. Stay here."

He crept to the source of the sound. Someone was moving through the forest. Silently he had made his way, not one twig snapping beneath his feet to betray his presence. There it was again, a slight rustle to his left. Drawing his knife, he put the blade between his teeth, then leapt into the thicket.

His captive's struggles were quickly subdued. But not before she had delivered a kick or two to a very important place. By the time she realized it was useless to fight anymore, he was furious. The pain had not been pleasant.

"What are you doing here?" he growled.

"Looking for Owein," Sabrina gasped. "What do you think? Take me to him."

"You are mad if you think I will take a Druid into his presence. How did you know to come here?"

"Enid, of course."

He gripped her arms even tighter, drawing her face within inches of his own. She was dressed in a leather tunic and trousers of black. Her dark hair was braided tightly to her scalp, and her blue eyes were wide with urgency, but not fear. He said nothing, searching her face. Her wide mouth quirked under his close regard.

"It's nice to see you again, too, Trystan. But perhaps we could continue this some other time," she continued.

A rustle in the bushes heralded Esyllt's arrival. "You!" Esyllt cried. "Kill her, Trystan, and let's get out of here."

Trystan spun around to Esyllt, not certain he had heard her right.

"She must have brought others with her, you fool," Esyllt went on. "She—"

"I did not bring anyone with me," Sabrina snapped.

"Then why did they let you leave the city?"

"They thought I was going to find you, of course. They sent me to find you. They are looking for you everywhere —they want a testing device very badly. Now take me to Owein. I have news of Enid that cannot wait."

"She admits that she is in league with the Coranians, and you just stand there, Trystan! What is the matter with you? I told you to kill her."

Well, there were a couple of things wrong with killing Sabrina. And none of them, surely, had to do with Sabrina's blue eyes and raven hair, or his memories of the way she used to look at him. "That's Owein's decision," he said curtly, releasing his hold on Sabrina's arms.

"I can't believe this," Esyllt cried. "Here stands a Druid, one who would give anything to know where the Cerddorian hide, and you invite her to—"

"They do know where the Cerddorian are," Sabrina cut in. "That's part of what I have to tell Owein. There isn't much time. Two days at the most."

"She talked," Trystan said, his throat tight.

"She couldn't help it," Sabrina replied. "She held out as long as she could."

"And you let them do that to her?"

The blood drained from Sabrina's face, and her blue eyes clouded. "I couldn't stop it. There was nothing I could do."

Gently he reached out and touched her shoulder. "I know. I'm sorry." Before Esyllt could erupt again, he turned to the Bard. "So much for the testing. For today, at least. We must—"

But now it was Esyllt's face that paled, her hands flying to her forehead. She gave a low moan, and dropped to her knees. Shockingly, Trystan heard the echo of a Mind-Shout as it reverberated through the clearing.

Esyllt, Talhearn, Susanna, Cian! Turn back now! The enemy comes!

"You see?" Esyllt whispered. "I told you so. She betrays us."

Sabrina swiftly moved to Esyllt's side. Motioning for Trystan to take the Bard's other arm, she said, "Hurry, I must see Owein. If you believe that I have betrayed you, then kill me now. If not, we must go."

The three of them returned to Owein's camp just before dark. They had been spotted long before they reached the camp, Trystan knew, and he was not surprised when they were met by Owein and his Lieutenant, Teleri, the moment they entered the clearing.

Esyllt, who had not spoken a word since that morning, sank down with a sigh onto the blanket that was spread before the fire.

"Sabrina ur Dadwell," Owein said, taking her hand. "I regret that I cannot fully say you are welcome here." Owein's eyes cut to Trystan. "We heard an echo of the Shout this morning. Why, I don't know."

"Because there were Bards around," Esyllt said wearily. "The Shout was so strong it reached every single Bard in Kymru, no doubt. And spilled over to anyone else in the vicinity. To any other Kymri, I should say. A Coranian would hear nothing."

"I didn't know it could be done," Owein said in awe.

"Neither did I," Esyllt replied. "Neither did most of us. The Master Bard is full of surprises."

"King Owein, this cannot wait," Sabrina said urgently. "I must tell you— —"

"Yes, you certainly must. Sit down by the fire. And tell us what you know."

"All that you know," Esyllt said harshly.

Trystan saw Teleri smother a grin. He remembered that Teleri and Sabrina had been good friends. And that Esyllt and Sabrina had always disliked one another. Just what the cause of the antipathy was, he never had known.

Sabrina sat, gratefully sipping the cup of warm wine Trystan had fetched for her. He had not really meant to do that. It had just happened.

"Owein ap Urien, var Ellirri, true King of Rheged," Sabrina

began formally. "I bring you news of your sister."

"Is she all right?" Owein asked anxiously.

"No. But she is alive. First, you and your Cerddorian must leave Coed Addien. She has told them where you are."

"Don't be a fool, Owein," Esyllt said harshly. "You have no way of knowing this isn't a trick. Maybe they are waiting for you to move. So they can take you."

"I have thought of that, Esyllt, thank you," Owein replied, not taking his eyes from Sabrina's face. "There is more. Tell us."

"She is to wed Morcant in four months' time. With her as his wife, he will have a true claim to the rule of Rheged."

"Four months," Owein said softly. "Why wait four months?"

Sabrina swallowed hard. "He must wait to be sure she is not pregnant with another man's child."

"And whose child might she be carrying?"

"Bledri's."

"I see."

"I'm not sure you do," Sabrina said sharply. "She is a prisoner. She has been forced to name your location, forced to agree to marry Morcant."

"I know my sister. You don't need to tell me that." Owein's jaw clenched, a muscle jumping on his cheek. His blue eyes were bleak, and enraged. "Morcant will pay for what he has done to her. And Bledri, too. Neither of them will escape me."

For a time no one spoke. The Cerddorian who were gathered around the fire began to slip away, one by one. Silently they began to gather their belongings. At first light they would go.

"Tomorrow we begin our move to Coed Coch," Owein continued, turning to Sabrina. "You shall join us. We owe thanks for your warning."

"Fool!" Esyllt spat. "You trust her?"

"Queen Ellirri did," Teleri said coldly.

"The Queen is dead!"

"And I am very much alive," Owein said. "And intend to stay that way."

Sycharth, Kingdom of Ederynion

The rolling hills that surrounded the city of Sycharth were faded and brown. In any other year, Angharad remembered, the hills would be green by now. Tiny tufts of clover, bright primroses, rich blue forget-me-nots would have dotted these hills. But spring was slow to come this year. It had been the same the year before.

The people said it was because Modron, the Great Mother, had turned against the Kymri because the Druids now worshiped the god of the Coranians. And Angharad, for one, did not doubt it.

Her sharp green eyes scanned the hills ceaselessly, looking for signs of movement, for the glint of sun on weapons. But so far it had been quiet. She glanced behind her for a moment, to see Talhearn taking the last child on his lap as he sat on a convenient log.

"You see, little one," Talhearn said soothingly to the tiny girl, "this is called the testing device." He held out a little silver box that had a small opening at one end. The top of the box was covered with jewels. At the center was a group of onyx stones, arranged in a figure-eight pattern around a bloodstone. Grouped around these stones were a pearl, a sapphire, an emerald, and an opal. At the far corners, other jewels nested—amethyst, topaz, ruby, and a diamond next to a garnet.

"Now, this is how we tell if you have a special gift," Talhearn went on. "You put your finger in this opening here, and the jewels will glow. The amethyst and the topaz will light up for you because you are one of the Kymri. Maybe one of the other stones will light, too. If they do, it tells us that you have a special gift. And if they don't, it won't matter, for you are a child of Kymru, and that's the most important thing of all."

The child stared at the box, then looked up at her father, who stood next to Talhearn. The father nodded, and the child put her finger into the opening of the box.

Instantly the amethyst and the topaz began to glow. Then the pearl started to shine with a luminous radiance. A low humming sound began, and Angharad stiffened. Quickly, Talhearn pulled the child's finger out of the box. For a moment they were all still. The child stared at the box, astonished. The father had tears in his eyes. And the other parents and children who had made the secret, dangerous journey smiled, then began to murmur in delight.

Talhearn stood up, and handed the child to her father. "She is Dewin. In two years, when she is old enough, we will return here on Alban Awyr and take her. She will be safe with us. She will be loved and treated well. She will be happy. We will take her to the place where the Ardewin waits to greet her, and teach her how to use her gift for the good of the Kymri."

The father swallowed hard, then hugged his little girl. "Her mother died not long ago. Could you not take her now? I will give anything for her to be safe. Anything."

Talhearn glanced at Angharad, and she shook her head. He knew as well as she that they could not care for the child on their long, dangerous journey throughout Ederynion. And he knew they could not take the time to deliver the girl to the Ardewin.

"I am sorry, boyo," Talhearn said gently. "We cannot take her now. But here now, she will be safe enough. No one else knows her for Dewin but those of us gathered here. Surely you can trust them."

The man nodded thoughtfully. "Yes," he said with no uncertainty in his tone. "It's just that—well—you understand."

"I do," Talhearn replied. "Believe me, I do."

"Talhearn," Angharad said over her shoulder, still scanning the road. "It's time to move on. We must be leagues away from here by nightfall. And these people must return to their homes. Now, listen, all of you. Those who have to return to Sycharth, do so in small groups. Go back into the city by different gates. Those of you whose farms lie elsewhere must also split up. Everyone understand?" She knew her tone was preemptory, but she couldn't help that. Too many years of ordering her warriors about, she supposed, left her unable to modify her tone now.

"You see, good folk, what capable hands I am in? Oh, if only I was!" Talhearn's languishing glance behind her back (she knew perfectly well what he was doing) made the people chuckle. But they were Kymri, and knew the importance of what they did. And so they did not linger, but seemed to melt away in groups of two or three, until even Angharad would have been hard-pressed to show that a group of thirty men, women, and children had recently stood in this spot.

"Come on, old man," Angharad said, making for the road. "As my grandfather and a barely successful peddler, you should at least try to sell some of your wares today."

"My dear," Talhearn said smoothly, "I believe we had agreed you would be my daughter, not my granddaughter. Far be it from me to point out that you are too old—"

"Keep your opinions to yourself."

"But you do look very fetching in a skirt. I don't believe I have ever seen you wear one."

Angharad scowled. The skirt irritated her almost past bearing. "I consider it useful," she said sourly as they stepped onto Sarn Uelia, the north-south road that bisected Ederynion. "If anyone who knew me saw me like this, they would never recognize me."

"Unless, of course, it was your Lieutenant, Emrys. He would recognize you no matter what. For love looks with the heart, not with the—"

"I told you to keep your opinions to yourself," she snarled. "I have no time for them."

"Or for Emrys."

"No. Nor for Emrys, either. He wants too much, and so must have none."

Talhearn stopped and studied Angharad. "You know, my dear, I believe you are right. It's astonishing to find actual wisdom in one of your impetuous nature."

Though the words might have been insulting, the tone was not. And Angharad was not a fool, so she took it for the compliment it was. But before she could reply, her sharp eyes spotted a cloud of dust just rising from the road in the far distance.

"Someone's coming to Sycharth," she said.

"Not unusual. It is a fairly large city."

No, it wasn't unusual. So why did she feel so tense? "I think we had better—"

"Too late," Talhearn said calmly, slinging his peddler's pack onto his back and assuming an old man's stoop. "They've seen us. They're too far away to fully identify us, but if we run off the road, they will think something is wrong."

Angharad hefted the basket onto her left arm, her right hand holding on to the cover. "Don't forget what we agreed on at the beginning of this venture," she said to Talhearn as he began to shuffle forward. "If anything starts to go wrong, you run. As far and as fast as you can. Remember."

"I remember," he said.

Something in his tone left Angharad feeling uncertain that he would obey those orders. Oh, well, maybe they wouldn't have to fight. Their disguise was good and had gotten them through many leagues already. No reason why—

The man who rode toward them sat stiffly in his saddle, his back erect, his head of black hair bared to the midmorning sun. His brown robes with green trim fluttered around him. And when his black eyes saw them, Angharad's heart skipped a beat. Twenty Coranian warriors fanned out behind the man. Their metal byrnies flashed in the sun. Their shields were red and gold, with the boar's head stamped on the center.

And the man who was now bearing down on them was surely the last man she ever wished to see—unless, of course, she had a dagger in her hand. And she did, beneath the lid of the basket. It might be worth it to—

"No, Angharad," Talhearn said quietly, lightly touching her arm. "There are too many of them for that. Best we run, I think."

But before they could so much as turn, Talhearn cried out softly, and Angharad's head almost split with the Shout that sounded in her mind.

Esyllt, Talhearn, Susanna, Cian! Turn back now! The enemy comes!

And then the enemy was upon them. She could have cursed the Master Bard and his timing, but she knew it wouldn't really have mattered. It had already been too late, even before the Shout.

The man who led the group of warriors reined in his horse, looking down at them with mad, gleeful eyes. She returned his gaze squarely, holding a weakened and disoriented Talhearn so he wouldn't fall to the ground.

Then Talhearn raised his head, and his eyes slowly focused on the man who stared down at them.

Angharad would always remember that their fate changed the moment when the man met Talhearn's eyes. Perhaps it was the compassion and the wisdom in the Bard's eyes. Perhaps it was the remembrance of all the years they had known each other. Perhaps it was the shared love for a certain auburn-haired captive Queen. Whatever it was, it changed everything.

"What's the problem, Druid?" one of the warriors asked of the man, gesturing at Angharad and Talhearn. "Thinking of buying something?" The men laughed, but the Druid's gaze did not waver.

"Your father looks ill," the Druid said softly, ignoring the warrior's taunt. "A hard life for you both, on the road."

"Better than no life at all," Angharad said sharply, then silently cursed herself for being so abrupt.

But Iago merely smiled sadly. "Yes, so it is."

And then he rode on, followed by the warriors. He did not look back.

Tegeingl, Kingdom of Gwynedd

BEDWYR STOOD SILENTLY just inside the door of the dye shed, looking out at the compound. The door was open only a crack, but it was enough for him to keep an eye on the wool workers as they went about their tasks.

The large hall where the prized wool of Gwynedd was dyed was warm from the heat of the fires that were laid beneath each huge vat. The dyes boiled and bubbled as the workers thrust at the floating wool with long-handled poles.

Bedwyr glanced back over his shoulder. The room was smoky, and he could barely make out the red-gold of Susanna's hair from where she sat in the far corner, surrounded by children and their anxious parents.

Silently, Bedwyr breathed a prayer to Cerrunnos and Cerridwen, the Protectors. He was a fine warrior, and he knew it. But he had never liked the idea of coming so close to Tegeingl. Both he and Susanna had lived here for many years and had been recognized instantly, in spite of their disguises. They had expected that, of course. And they had taken all proper precautions before coming here, to the wool works outside the city.

The compound was busy—busier than normal, for Bedwyr had asked for a certain amount of distracting movements, just in case any Coranians took it into their heads to come here. Men and women were sorting and washing the raw wool, beating it thoroughly in tubs of water. Wool hung on poles to dry until ready to be combed and oiled. Finished wool was being spun into thread with distaffs.

The door to the spinning shed across the compound was open, and a great many people were assisting the warpers as they arranged the threads into strands and cut them. The spoolers wound the thread into bobbins to use on the huge shuttles. The looms were clacking furiously, each one worked by two men. All eight looms were busy.

Huge water-filled troughs were laid out in the center of the compound. The wool cloth was dumped into the troughs and tread on to thicken it. Then the cloth was hooked onto frames and stretched out to dry.

All of this was being done with a great deal of noise and bustle. Good enough, Bedwyr thought, satisfied. Once again, he scanned the compound. Lots of noise, lots of movement. Perfect. And that was when it all started to go wrong.

A mighty Shout echoed through his head, fit to split it in two.

Esyllt, Talhearn, Susanna, Cian! Turn back now! The enemy comes!

He whirled around, speeding through the stunned wool workers to reach her. Some of the children began to cry. The faces of their parents were white and shocked. Susanna was slumped on the stool, but she had not fainted. Bedwyr knelt down next to her, lifting her up.

"Was that—?"

She nodded weakly. "The Master Bard. There is danger."

"We've got to get out of here. Now."

"I haven't finished," she protested.

"Oh, yes, you have." Without bothering to continue the argument, he wrapped her cloak around her and pulled her behind him out the door. Just then, one of the women ran up, out of breath. "Madoc! He's on his way here, with his daughter. You must go!"

Bedwyr whirled around to head out of the compound, but the glint of sun on steel at the gate stopped him.

"General Catha's warriors," the woman panted. "Catha won't let Madoc go anywhere without them."

"Not much of a warning," Bedwyr said, exasperated.

"It was too fast. No one expected him to come here. He never does."

Swiftly, Bedwyr set Susanna on her feet, whipped off her cloak, and snatched off the cloth tied around his neck, wrapping it over Susanna's bright hair. "Get your shoes off," he hissed, slipping off his boots. "Hurry."

Susanna kicked off her shoes and kilted her skirt, baring her legs. They leapt into one of the troughs and began to tread on the wool cloth.

Slowly kneading the cloth, Bedwyr bent his head, turning his face away from the sight of Madoc and a young girl coming through the gate. But not turning away fast enough to prevent him from getting a good look at Madoc's daughter.

Tangwen was beautiful. Her red-gold hair swung down past her slender hips. She had wide-spaced blue eyes, fringed with dark lashes. Her skin was fair and smooth, but she was too pale. There was a kind of listlessness in her movements that tugged at his heart. Her gown was pale blue, embroidered with silver thread and tiny sapphires.

He caught only a glimpse of Madoc; his face set in a scowl, dressed in his usual elaborate finery—cloth of silver, with a silver circlet on his golden head.

"Tangwen looks very sad, doesn't she?" Susanna murmured.

"Don't look!" he hissed. But he stole another glance and found himself agreeing with her. Tangwen did look sad. Well, who could blame her with a father like that?

Susanna poked him surreptitiously in the ribs. "Don't look," she mocked, using the tone he had used earlier.

Madoc strode arrogantly through the compound as the Master Weaver rushed up to greet him. Personally, Bedwyr thought the man was overdoing the obsequiousness a little bit, stopping just short of parody. But Madoc didn't seem to notice. He cut the man's effusive welcome short.

"I have just come from the marketplace and have failed to find the cloth I want. I need a perfect shade of ivory. It is to set off some new pearls I have bought. You will make the shade I want and have the cloth delivered to me by tonight."

"Tonight!" the Master Weaver repeated, aghast. "But, my King, that is not possible."

"It is possible. And you will do it, or I will see you hanged."

"My Lord, allow me to say that ivory is not your best color—"

"It is not for me, fool!"

"Ah. Well, your daughter will look charming in a pale rose I have just finished—"

"It's not for her, either! It is for Arday."

"But, you see, General Catha has commissioned a cloth from me in just that shade already for her."

From the busy crowd, there was a wave of mocking laughter. Madoc flushed. "Then you will give it to me."

The Master Weaver hesitated just long enough to stop shy of insult. "Certainly."

Bedwyr risked another glance, though he knew he shouldn't—he was far too close to laughter. But what he saw sobered him instantly. The sight of Tangwen and her white face, pinched with misery and shame, was almost too much for him.

And then she turned her head and looked him full in the face. And he did not—he could not—turn away. Her eyes widened as she saw him, and then she looked straight at Susanna. Her jaw dropped open, and Bedwyr got ready to run. But Tangwen shut her mouth with a snap and looked away.

The Master Weaver had gone to find the cloth, and Madoc stood impatiently tapping his foot. His eyes began to wander around the compound, and the men and women there suddenly found themselves very busy.

Bedwyr bent his head again, solemnly treading the wet cloth. Beside him Susanna did the same. Her voice barely audible, she whispered, "She recognized me."

"Yes, but she turned away."

"She was always a good girl. Too good for a da like that."

"Do you think she'll—"

"Not a chance. We're safe from her."

But not from Madoc, for he had begun to pace with impatience. And he was coming far too close to the trough where they stood. Idly, Madoc scanned the crowd. His gaze skipped right over them. But then he stiffened. He looked again. He took one step toward the trough for a closer look.

But one step was all he took.

He fell facedown in the dirt, tripped by his own daughter. She flung herself down next to him, apologizing for her clumsiness. But just as she helped him up, she stumbled again, and they both went down. Bedwyr only saw her next move clearly because he was watching for it. And sure enough, her elbow managed to hit Madoc right on the nose. Very, very hard.

"Oh, Da!" she cried. "You're bleeding. Here, tilt your head back." Ruthlessly, she tilted his head, and he began to choke. "Oh, dear," she said. She grabbed a water bucket and threw the water in his face. "Is that better?"

Madoc sputtered, blowing water from his mouth. He wiped his streaming eyes, and stared at the trough where Bedwyr and Susanna had been.

But they were no longer there. Obedient to the slight motion of Tangwen's hand when she had grabbed the bucket, they had quit the trough, and now mingled in the center of the crowd that had stopped to gape at Madoc as he sat in the dirt, his fine clothes water-soaked, blood streaming down his chin.

"You there," Tangwen said haughtily to one of the grinning Coranian warriors. "Take the King back to Caer Gwynt. I'll stay here, Da, and get the cloth for you. If you touched it now, it would be ruined. Go on."

Disoriented, Madoc rose to his feet, assisted by one of the warriors. He stumbled out of the compound without another word, shocked by the shambles his daughter had made of his dignity.

Half of the warriors remained with her as she waited for the Master Weaver to return with the cloth. And so Bedwyr never had a chance to speak to her that day. But he caught her eye as she turned to go, the cloth clutched tightly in her hands. She did not smile, but the light that sprang into her eyes as she saw him once more was blinding. He hoped she saw the same light in his own eyes. For he knew it was there.

Cil, Kingdom of Prydyn

THE DAY HAD begun badly, Achren mused, and was on its way to worse. Any day that included the sight of Ellywen was sure to be a bad day.

Restlessly she paced the forest floor, continually circling the perimeter of the clearing where Cian was testing. Twenty men, women and children filled the clearing, silently waiting to hear Cian's verdict for each child. They knew the danger—both she and Cian had explained that to continue with the Plentyn Prawf now would be even more perilous than usual. But they had come anyway. Not that Achren was surprised, for she knew her people. Brave, stubborn, they never gave up.

She wished Cian would hurry up. All her senses hummed that disaster was imminent. But she had not been able to persuade Cian to turn back to Haford Bryn.

The sight of Ellywen, Rhoram's one-time Druid, in the village of Cil that morning had shocked her. And had enraged her, too. Just looking at Ellywen—cool and collected, escorted by twenty Coranian warriors armed to the teeth, with her fair hair and her icy gray eyes, her haughty bearing—had made Achren want to put a knife straight through the Druid's black heart. She had not forgotten—and she never would—that the Druid had once done her best to kill Rhoram in the First Battle of Arberth. And though Cian had been sure they had not been seen, Achren was not so positive. But Cian had insisted he be allowed to carry on with the testing, and Achren had acquiesced. How she now wished that she had not.

For something was coming. Something was—

Esyllt, Talhearn, Susanna, Cian! Turn back now! The enemy comes!

The Shout that echoed through her mind made her dizzy, and she clutched at a tree for support. In that moment she heard something else. She froze, trying to identify the source of the sound. And then she knew. She whirled back to the clearing.

"Get out now! They're coming." She spoke in a low tone—no need to give the Coranians exact directions. She grabbed Cian's arm and hauled him to his feet.

But Cian wrenched his arm from her grasp. His eyes were narrowed in pain from the aftermath of the Shout. "Lead them out of here, Achren," he gasped, gesturing to the families. "If the Coranians capture them—"

"It's you they want!" she snarled.

"I can take care of myself. The children can't."

Cian was right, and she knew it. She would have to be sure the people got safely out of here and back to their homes. "What about you?"

"I'll go west and circle back. Meet you on the road, just north of Cil. Achren," he went on as she hesitated, "please. You must get them back."

She nodded. "Go!" Cian left, slipping through the trees. "Everyone carries a child," she said to the men and women. "Follow me. No talking."

The group was silent. Even the children did not make a sound. Already they had learned. They were too young to have learned that. But they had.

Her keen ears tracked the progress of the warriors, leaving them far behind, as she guided her people through the forest without incident. When they reached the outskirts of the village at the edge of the forest, she motioned for them to stay where they were. She scanned the streets carefully, then gave the signal for them to break from the woods. In groups of twos and threes, they walked quickly and quietly back to their homes.

Still there were no threatening movements from the village. The warriors must all be in the forest. And Ellywen must be with them.

A muffled shout from far behind her made her heart sink. No, oh, no. She whirled around, running back into the forest, moving swiftly and silently, tracking the source of that shout. Sounds of struggle, then a cry of triumph reached her ears. They were coming this way, and she melted back into the foliage, eyeing the path, hoping against hope that she would not see what she expected.

Twenty warriors, their shields at the ready, their battle-axes drawn, came down the path. And in the midst of the knot of men, Cian stumbled. His head was bleeding, and his arm was bent at an unnatural angle. His face was ashen, and his eyes were trained on the small silver box that one warrior held in his hands. The testing device. They had captured it.

Just behind them, she saw Ellywen, her face frozen, a peculiar look in her cold, gray eyes. Strange, Achren would have expected signs of triumph. The Druid had certainly caught her quarry.

Achren followed them through the trees. She had to know where they were taking Cian. Maybe, somehow, she could rescue him. Or, if nothing else, she could kill him. He would want that, she knew. More important, maybe she could retrieve the testing device. The thought of it in their hands—

The warriors were leaving the forest, their captive in their midst. But Ellywen halted, motioning for the warriors to go on. "I must have a few moments by myself," she said, her voice cold as always. "Get my horse, and one for the Bard. He cannot walk." One warrior opened his mouth to protest, but shut it when she looked at him. The warriors marched away, dragging Cian with them.

Left alone on the fringes of the forest, Ellywen turned and called softly. "Achren ur Canhustyr, I know you can hear me."

Achren did not answer. Ellywen surely had not expected her to. Slowly, Achren drew her knife, cocked her arm back, and prepared to throw.

"Before you attempt to kill me, let me remind you that as a Druid I am a Shape-Mover. I can prevent the knife I am sure you have in your hand from reaching me. You know I can do this."

Yes, Achren knew. But that was no reason not to try.

"They are taking him to Eiodel," Ellywen continued, her voice unsteady. "To Havgan himself. The Archdruid has found the ancient formula to make the enaid-dals. The soul-catchers."

Oh, gods. This was worse than she had thought.

"And now they have a testing device. And they will know who are the Y Dawnus. And that means that the Master Bard and the Ardewin must be warned. Go to Rhoram and get him to use his Bards to relay the message. And hurry. For the sake of Kymru."

"A little late for you to be worrying about that now, isn't it, Ellywen?" Achren asked, stepping from the shadows of the trees, her knife at the ready. "Repenting of your part in this?"

"Yes," Ellywen whispered.

"Cian was always kind to you," Achren said harshly. "He's a good man."

"I must go. I must return to Arberth."

"Can't stomach watching what they will do to him in Eiodel? Don't you want to receive your reward?"

Ellywen turned away, then stopped with her back to Achren. "I'll have my reward, Achren, when you kill me," she said quietly, not turning around.

"Just for that, I'll let you live."

"Somehow that doesn't surprise me. You always were cruel." Ellywen left the forest, and did not look back.

Eiodel, Gwytheryn
HAVGAN FROZE WITH the wine cup halfway to his lips. He expected the others to stop talking, to make some reference to the cry he had

heard, but they did not. Sigerric and Sledda continued to argue, banging on the table to emphasize their points.

He never really knew what instinct kept him silent. The knowledge, perhaps, that if they had heard nothing, then he should not have heard it, either.

But he had. Clear as day. *Esyllt, Talhearn, Susanna, Cian! Turn back now! The enemy comes!*

No. No, he hadn't heard a thing. He took a sip of wine and carefully laid the gold cup on the table. The rubies that lined the rim glistened like fresh blood.

Nothing. He had heard nothing. And he never would.

Part 2
The Treasures

Death comes unannounced,
Abruptly he may thwart you;
No one knows his features,
Nor the sound of his tread approaching.

From Bran's *Poems of Sorrow*
Circa 275

Chapter 8

Meriwdydd, Tywyllu Wythnos—late afternoon

Gwydion rode down the quiet beach, casting sidelong glances at the woman who rode beside him.

Fool that he was, he was always doing that. He rarely looked directly at her, but he always seemed to keep her in his sight. He knew he did that, but he could not seem to stop. There was something about looking at her that both ruffled and eased him, something that fascinated him, something that fed him even as it frightened him. It had been like that for a long time. The sight of her, he knew, would be the most of her he would ever have. And that was his fault, and his alone.

Rhiannon's long, dark wavy hair lifted in the slight breeze coming off the sea, fanning out behind her. Usually she braided it, but this morning she had unbound it and combed it out in anticipation of reaching their destination. He had watched her then, pretending to see to the horses, wondering how it would feel to run his hands through her silky hair. Her profile was sharp and clear in the afternoon sunlight, from the high forehead, to the stubborn chin and slender neck. As always, her back was straight, and she carried herself well—for all that, they had been traveling steadily for over three weeks.

She turned to him, a question in her emerald green eyes. Yes, there was no doubt about it—he was in love with Rhiannon ur Hefeydd. Much as he had twisted and turned against it, much as he had struggled and run, the truth was there for even him to see.

He had fallen in love, for the first time in his life, and had discovered it too late. Too much had happened between them that she resented. He had pried her from her safe hiding place to search for the sword of the High King. He had forced her to leave King Rhoram just as she had discovered that the King still loved her. He had forced her to leave her daughter, Gwenhwyfar, and the girl now hated her mother for it. He had blamed her for Amatheon's death. He had dragged her to Corania on a dangerous mission. And in the last two years he had avoided her, leaving her on her own as much as he could.

Yes, he loved her. And he could never, ever tell her so. He had been a fool for these past years, treating her coldly, always holding her at arm's length, reserving the right to hide behind his defenses. Well, now he would begin to pay for his foolishness. Now the price of the walls he had built around himself was becoming all too apparent. It hadn't mattered when he had felt safe inside those barriers. It only mattered now, when he wished to reach beyond them and couldn't.

"What?" he asked, having missed her question.

"I said, why in the world did we have to—"

She broke off as what seemed to be a tiny whirlwind burst from the rocks and descended upon Gwydion, pulling him from his horse, almost tumbling him to the sand, and gripping him about the neck in a hold so tight he almost choked. But he didn't mind. He hadn't seen her for so very long.

"Da!" Cariadas cried. "Oh, Da!"

He returned her embrace with fervor, then held her gently for a moment as her shoulders shook and she shed a few hot tears on his shoulder. He gently stroked her hair, murmuring over and over, "Daughter. Cariadas. Oh, child."

At last she pulled away from him and studied his face so intently he laughed at the scrutiny, laughed for the joy of seeing her again, laughed because he loved her so, and now she was here. She had been the only bright joy in his life for so very, very long.

"Da, where have you been? And you're safe—really safe. Oh, Da!" She hugged him again. Finally, remembering her manners, she stepped back and looked over at Rhiannon, who had dismounted and stood to one side, smiling.

"How do you do?" Cariadas said, now all dignity. It wouldn't last long, Gwydion knew. "I am Cariadas ur Gwydion var Isalyn."

"Of course, you are," Rhiannon replied gravely, but with a smile in her eyes. "The Dreamer's heir. I am Rhiannon ur Hefeydd var Indeg. And I'm very pleased to make your acquaintance at last. Your da told me so much of you."

"He did?" Cariadas's face beamed. "What did you say, Da?"

"That you are the most wonderful daughter a man could ever want. That you bring love and joy into a lonely man's life. That you never comb your hair," he teased, ruffling the tangled curls.

Cariadas grinned. "Oh, that. No one's perfect." She turned to Rhiannon. "I hope I didn't startle you." She hugged Gwydion again, then continued. "It's been so long since I've seen him, you know."

"I know," Rhiannon replied. "And I hope that girl who is still behind the rocks is a friend of yours. Otherwise—"

"Oh," Cariadas said. "I forgot. Sinend, come out!"

Shyly, the other girl drifted out from behind the rocks. Gwydion frowned for a moment. He didn't like knowing that the daughter of the Archdruid's heir was hiding out with the Dewin and the Bards. The girl was a Druid, after all. But as he studied the girl's face, clearly marked with lines of grief and shame, he was inclined to forget his reservations—for the moment.

In the time that he had hesitated to greet the girl, Rhiannon had already stepped forward and introduced herself. With a sharp glance at Gwydion, Rhiannon turned to him. "I believe you two know each other."

"We met once, Sinend, at Neuadd Gorsedd, a few years ago, very briefly. I hope that my daughter has not been making your life too miserable—she can be anything but relaxing."

"Da!" Cariadas exclaimed, lightly swatting his arm. "What a thing to say!" Her infectious grin was like a tonic to him. He grinned back. It felt strange to smile again after so long.

"By the gods, Cariadas," Rhiannon said, mock awe in her tone, "Gwydion's actually smiling! How did you do that?"

"My natural charm," she replied flippantly.

"But, of course," Rhiannon replied, her tone solemn.

"Come, all of you," Cariadas said eagerly, linking her arm in Gwydion's. "Anieron is waiting to talk to you both. We got the word this morning that you would be coming, and so I begged him to let me greet you."

"Ah," Gwydion said gravely, "so it's the Master Bard I have to thank for that exuberant greeting. And I thought he wanted to be on my good side."

THE TUNNELS TWISTED this way and that, branching off into a dizzying array of paths beneath the surface of the earth. The walls glistened with crystal and other gems as the light of the torches set at regular intervals along the tunnels shimmered and shifted.

At last Cariadas stopped before a curtain of blue stretched over a cave opening. "They're here," Cariadas announced, flinging back the curtain.

The three people in the small cave rose from their chairs. Anieron was smiling with genuine delight. Elstar looked tense, though she, too, was smiling. Elidyr looked as though he had swallowed a hot coal. Just the kind of welcome Gwydion had expected.

"Thank you, child," Anieron said. "We will call if we need you."

Cariadas grinned at Gwydion. "Sorry I can't stay. I know that, deep in his heart, Anieron wants me to. But I have so much to do—"

"Out!" Anieron said playfully, as Gwydion kissed her forehead and sent her on her way.

The chamber was small, barely large enough for the stone table that was placed in its center. A few tapestries hung over the rough walls, bringing a sense of warmth and cheer to the tiny cave. Across one entire wall hung a map of Kymru, marked here and there with tiny flags of varying colors. There were braziers scattered by the walls, with fires burning in them to take the chill off the stone. Five chairs were placed around the table, cushioned with pillows worked in blue and sea green.

Anieron kissed Rhiannon. "You are well, niece?"

She clung to him for a moment, then said, "As well as any of us can be, these days. And I have missed you sorely."

The Ardewin rose, her smile stiff. No doubt Elstar was thinking the same thing Gwydion was thinking. That, but for the fact that Rhiannon had fallen in love with King Rhoram and had run away and hidden herself for years, Rhiannon would be the Ardewin now. *Does Elstar always remember that she was second choice?* Gwydion wondered. *Worse still, does she know that her husband, Rhiannon's cousin and childhood playmate, was once in love with Rhiannon? And perhaps still is?* Gwydion thought he knew the answer to those questions. Knew them very well, indeed.

While Elstar formally greeted Rhiannon, Gwydion glanced at Elidyr. His face was set in a smile, but there was something in his eyes . . . He came forward and hugged Rhiannon briefly, then let her go, almost abruptly. Elstar's blue eyes gleamed with displeasure, but she retained her smile.

At Anieron's gesture, the five of them sat down around the table. If Rhiannon had noticed anything amiss in her greeting—and Gwydion was sure that she had—she gave no sign.

"But where is Uncle Dudod?" Rhiannon asked anxiously. "I thought he would be here. Is he all right?"

"My da is well," Elidyr answered.

"And on his way back here," Anieron continued. "We expect him in time for the Alban Awyr celebration tomorrow night."

"We heard your Mind-Shout," Gwydion said quietly. "What happened?"

"It was news from Dudod that did it. The enemy has enaid-dals. And so they want a testing device, which had to be prevented from falling into the Coranian hands at all costs."

"And?" This must be the reason for his dream last night, for the Shout heard that morning had echoed in his dreams. In spite of all his training, the dream had faded the moment he had awakened, and he had been left with a feeling of dread, a feeling something very precious had been lost.

"Susanna and Bedwyr escaped Madoc's clutches with the aid of Princess Tangwen."

"Madoc's daughter?" Rhiannon asked. "That's quite a turn of events."

"And a fortunate one, too. I have uses for young Tangwen, now that I know where her heart lies."

"Be careful, Anieron," Gwydion warned.

"I'm always careful, Dreamer. Talhearn and Angharad encountered Iago, but he chose to let them go, another lucky turn of events. Angharad credits it to the fact that Talhearn was always kind to the Druid. I cannot say if there was more to it or not. Esyllt and Trystan had not even left Coed Addien before the Shout, and they encountered the Druid, Sabrina, whom they brought back to Owein."

"Did they really? For what purpose?"

"She brought word that Princess Enid had finally talked. The Coranians were on their way to Owein's camp and would have caught them had it not been for her warning. They have since moved to Coed Coch. And taken her with them."

"Sabrina is with them? Is that wise?"

"There is such a thing as a good and decent Druid, Gwydion," Anieron said sharply.

"But they're few."

"Granted. But look at Sinend."

"Sinend. And do you think her a fit companion for my daughter?" The words were arrogant, harsh, but the tone was not. "It would break her heart to be betrayed."

"Sinend is a loyal friend. Have no fear on that score."

"And Cian?" Rhiannon asked.

Anieron was silent. It was Elstar who answered, her voice sad.

"Cian was taken. As was his testing device."

"Oh, gods. Where have they taken him?"

"To Havgan. In Eiodel."

"And Achren?" Rhiannon asked anxiously.

"She survived. She even had a few words with Ellywen, who led the warriors in Cian's capture."

"Ellywen let Achren go? Why, she's the last person on earth I would have thought would do so." Rhiannon frowned. "Why would she do such a thing?"

"The word is that Ellywen, having been faced with the enormity of what she had done, has repented of it."

"Very nice, but too late to help Cian."

"So it is. Achren is on her way back to Haford Bryn. That's where Rhoram and his folk have gone, since Queen Efa returned to her brother."

"She would," Rhiannon said, contemptuously. "Any fool would have known she would do that."

"I don't believe Rhoram was too surprised," Elidyr said mildly.

"By now even such a fool as Rhoram wouldn't be," she snapped.

If there was anyone Gwydion didn't want to talk about, it was Rhiannon's former lover. Particularly now, when, under Kymric law, Rhoram no longer had a wife. Without a doubt Rhiannon was seeing herself back by Rhoram's side. The thought was bitter—too bitter for him to dwell on it.

"So," Gwydion said, "the collars were part of the plans discussed in the meeting at Eiodel. But it is not enough. There must be more."

"I am sure that there is," Anieron said heavily. "But we do not know what."

"We will. I only hope that when we do, it won't be too late."

"You have dreamed nothing of it?"

"Nothing directly related to it. But my dreams do say it is time to begin the hunt. The reason we have come here—"

"We wish to know that, of course," Anieron broke in smoothly. "But we also wish to know where you have been."

"I," Rhiannon said quietly, "have been in my old cave in Coed Aderyn. Gwydion has been traveling all over Kymru most of the last two years."

"Doing what?" Elidyr asked, turning to Gwydion in surprise.

And how could he possibly answer that question? Because, truthfully, he hadn't been doing anything more than trying to avoid being near Rhiannon. He had known—oh, even as far back as the journey to Corania—how dangerous that was. For sooner or later he would have told her how he felt about her. And only the gods knew what would have happened then. How could he trust her? How could he trust any woman? He had let his mother ruin all. And he knew it. But now he felt powerless to master the damage he had done to himself, so his voice was harsh when he said, "Traveling. Keeping an eye on things. That's all."

He had an uncomfortable feeling by the look in Anieron's wise eyes that the Master Bard knew exactly what he had been doing.

"So, the task begins again," Anieron said. "To make a High King and to drive the enemy from our land. What can we do to help you?"

"We have come in search of a song," Gwydion said.

Anieron's brow rose. "A song? What song?"

"I had a dream. And in the dream the Protectors came to me. They told me to seek the Four Treasures. And they told me to let the rings be my guide. And to seek the Song of the Caers. Do you know the song?"

Anieron thought a minute, then shook his head. "No, I do not."

"Anieron, no games. This is serious." Gwydion couldn't believe there was a song in the known world that the Master Bard did not know.

"I am not lying, Gwydion," Anieron said softly, but his eyes flashed. "I do not know the song. Do you know who wrote it?"

Gwydion shrugged. "I assumed it was Taliesin. He was the Master Bard when High King Lleu was killed and the Treasures were hidden. All I know is that the song holds clues to the whereabouts of the Treasures."

"You are welcome to search our library," Anieron said. "It is extensive. We saved every single book from Neuadd Gorsedd. Search as much as you like. Elstar, Elidyr, and I will be happy to help. And I hope the gods guide us to what we seek."

"So," Gwydion said, "do I."

IN THE DEAD of night, Gwydion flung the book away from him. Rhiannon picked it up, smoothed its pages, and returned it to the shelf. She said nothing, but he sensed her annoyance. And she was right. It was a stupid, childish gesture. But then, he was feeling stupid and childish. Anieron, Elstar, and Elidyr looked up from the books they had been perusing, but they, too, chose to remain silent.

Between the five of them, in the past fifteen hours they had pulled every book from the shelves that had been built around the vast cavern in the heart of Allt Llwyd

There was no Song of the Caers here. He had been so certain they would find it. Without the song, they could not even begin to search for the Treasures. And without the Treasures, there would be no High King. And Havgan would rule a defeated Kymru forever.

No, that was no way to think. There was one more thing to try. He had not done it before. Dinaswyn had taught him how, of course. But Dreamers only did it if there was no other choice. It was dangerous, for there was a chance the Dreamer could be trapped in the past and not be able to return. But there was no choice now. Mundane means had not sufficed. Now he would try something different.

The floor of the cave had been scattered with carpets for the ease of those who came to read the books. But he must not lie on the carpet itself. He must not cut himself off from the earth. He picked up the candle on the table. Fire. He would have that. Earth and fire both—only those two for this dream.

As if already in the dream, he rose from his place before one of the bookshelves, carefully holding the candle, then walked across the cavern until he stood directly in the center. The center of the circle. The best place to begin.

"Gwydion?" Rhiannon called as if from a great distance. Yet she was there, standing just in front of him. But she seemed so far away.

"Gwydion, what are you doing? Answer me!"

But the effort seemed to be too much. Already so much of him had gone on the journey that lay before him. Slowly, he dropped to his knees, then stretched out on the floor of the cave, peeling back the carpet so that his back was against the stone, setting the candle down beside him.

Elstar, Elidyr, and Anieron came and stood over him, as Rhiannon knelt by his side. Gwydion could see by Anieron's eyes that the Master Bard knew what was happening. There was sadness there. And fear. And courage. Courage, yes. Gwydion would need it.

"Gwydion," Anieron said, his voice soft. "Is there no other way?"

"None," he replied, his voice drowsy. The Otherworld pulled at him, pulled him down, down into the center.

"What's he doing?" Elstar whispered.

"Time-Walking," Anieron said. "The Walker-Between-the-Worlds is going back to the past."

"Taliesin himself will sing me that song," Gwydion whispered. "He must."

"Gwydion, don't. It's dangerous. You yourself have said that to me more than once." Rhiannon's emerald eyes held him. Did he really see the sheen of tears there? Surely not. Something to do with the light, perhaps. Yet she reached down her cool hand and put it to his cheek. Without even thinking, he languidly reached up and grasped her hand, turning his face to imprint a kiss on her palm.

And then he began the Dreamer's prayer:

"Annwyn with me lying down, Aertan with me sleeping.
The white flame of Nantsovelta in my soul,
The mantle of Modron about my shoulders,
The protection of Taran over me, taking my hand,
And in my heart, the fire of Mabon.
If malice should threaten my life,
Then the Shining Ones be between me and evil.
From tonight until a year from tonight,
And this very night,

And forever,
And for eternity."

Then the dream took him.

He found himself in a dark wood. The sun, bared by the thick, interlaced branches, barely penetrated the gloom. A shaft of light managed to break through here and there, dappling the forest floor. A light breeze filtered through the trees, making them shiver as the patches of sunlight wavered, then steadied. There was a tiny stream running past his feet, the water shallow and clear. He began to follow its course, knowing that it would lead him to the place he must go.

As he followed, he heard a rustle on the branches overhead, and, knowing it was not the wind, he looked up in time to see a black raven perched in the branches, its eyes red as blood. With a caw, the raven bounded into the air and was lost to sight among the branches. Slowly a dark feather drifted down and floated into his waiting hand.

He followed the stream to the edge of the forest. Stepping out of the wood, he found himself on a plain of long, wavy grass. The grass was green, dotted here and there with white alyssum, with forget-me-nots of rich blue, with yellow globeflowers and fiery red rockrose. The wind blew the grass into whirling, swirling patterns—patterns whose meaning hovered just at the edge of understanding.

The stream flowed through the plain, and, still following, he at last came to a deep pool. The water shimmered in the sun, bright and clean. Gravely he presented the raven's feather, then dropped it on the surface of the pool, where it vanished. A flash of light caught his eyes, and he turned to see a cup made of purest crystal sitting by the side of the pool.

His offer accepted he grasped the cup and drank deeply. Then waited.

HE WAS IN A VAST, shadowy chamber. As his eyes adjusted to the darkness, he knew where he was—the throne room deep inside

Cadair Idris, the mighty fortress of the High Kings of Kymru.

The shadows wavered in the uncertain light of four torches set around the dais where a great throne of gold stood, studded with precious stones. The armrests were shaped like eagles, their upswept wings forming the high back of the chair.

Eight steps led up to the throne, each step covered with gems representing the Shining Ones of Kymru. The first step, that of Annwyn, Lord of Chaos, was covered with black onyx. The second was covered with rubies for Y Rhyfelwr, the Warrior Twins, Camulos and Agrona. The third and fourth were for Cerridwen and Cerrunnos, the Protectors, one step of amethyst, the next of topaz. Then came emeralds for Modron, the Great Mother, and then sapphires for Taran of the Winds. Next were pearls for Nantsovelta of the Waters, and last, opals for Mabon of the Sun.

He was not alone in the throne room. On the dais, four figures stood, unmoving, their backs to him, facing the empty throne. The very lines of their bodies spoke of grief and loss, yet they stood straight and tall and did not bend before their unspeakable sorrow. One of the men, a man with light hair, was singing the Kymric death song in a rich, beautiful voice.

> *"In Gwlad Yr Haf, the Land of Summer,*
> *Still they live, still they live.*
> *They shall not be killed, they shall not be wounded.*
> *No fire, no sun, no moon shall burn them.*
> *No lake, no water, no sea shall drown them.*
> *They live in peace, and laugh and sing.*
> *The dead are gone, yet still they live."*

HE STUDIED THE four figures clustered around the throne, and recognized them. He had seen them before, in the flames the day before Arthur's birth. And one of them he had seen in visions during his quest for Caladfwlch. Though they had died over two hundred years ago, he knew them to be the Great Ones, beloved of Lleu Lawrient, the last High King.

And as he knew them, they turned to him, facing him gravely.

The first man dressed in robes of black and red was Bran the Dreamer. His long, auburn hair was caught at the neck in a clasp of fiery opals. His deep-set gray eyes were filled with grief, and the lines on his face spoke of a burning rage.

The second, the man who had sung, was dressed in robes of blue and white. Taliesin, the Master Bard, had blond hair, so light to be almost white, which hung about his shoulders. His green eyes (oh, so like Anieron's eyes) brimmed with sorrow, and with hard-won wisdom.

The third, dressed in robes of silver and sea green, was the Ardewin, Bran's brother, Mannawyddan. His hair was light brown; his eyes, a mild blue. An air of stillness, of patience, of calm even in his grief radiated from him.

The fourth, dressed in robes of brown and green, was the Archdruid, Arywen. Her black hair hung to her waist, and her cat-like hazel eyes were beautiful and sad.

Each held something in their cupped hands. As Gwydion came closer, he saw that the torque of the High King rested on the empty throne. But the emerald, the opal, the pearl, the sapphire, which should have been part of the necklace, was gone.

"I grieve for your loss," Gwydion said softly. "Lleu Silver-Hand is dead. And you mourn his passing. I, too, honored him. But I knew him only as a memory. Know that we, in the Kymru of the future, do not forget him."

"Gwydion ap Awst," Bran said, his harsh voice ringing through the empty chamber. "You have come."

"I have come. There is need. Great need."

"Yes," Bran nodded. "There is."

Taliesin began to chant, his voice pure and sad.

"They sing after thy song,
The Kymri in their grief,
On account of their loss,
Long is the cry of sorrow.
There is blood upon the spears.
The waves are bearing
Ships upon the sea."

"You knew," Gwydion said.

"Yes," Taliesin replied. "Bran told me. He told us all. And that is why we hid the Treasures."

"Which I have been charged to find."

"Ah, Dreamer," Arywen said, her mouth quirking, "did you think we should have made it easy for you? If easy for you, it would have been easy for others."

"Lady, you mock me."

"No, I only speak the truth."

Gwydion nodded. "That is fair. But now I have come to you, because the clues were not enough. I must know—where are they? Where are the Spear, the Sword, the Cauldron, and the Stone? I must have them, for the High King has come again."

"For these things you must hunt. So I have dreamed," Bran said.

"Even for you, Gwydion ap Awst, the hunt will not be easy," Manawyddan said. "And there are others who must hunt with you."

"I have dreamed of the others," Gwydion replied. "I know who they are—Rhiannon ur Hefeydd, Gwenhwyfar ur Rhoram, and Arthur. Arthur ap Uthyr, our High King."

"If you can make him so," Bran said tightly. "My dreams have never told me this."

"The Protectors came to me in a dream. They said, 'Seek the Song of the Caers.' And they said, 'Let the rings be your guide. But it is not enough. I do not know which rings. I cannot find the song. Will you help me?"

"The rings, Dreamer, are here," Arywen said as she opened her cupped hands and held out to him a ring with a stone of emerald.

"And here," Mannawyddan said, holding up a ring of pearl.

"And here," Taliesin said, holding up a ring of sapphire.

"And here," said Bran, lifting a ring of fiery opal. "These are made from the jewels of the High King's torque. You have come in time to watch us as we now set within them the key."

"The key?"

"Recognition of the one who, in time, will claim them. The opal is for the Spear. When claimed by the right man, the opal will guide him to that Treasure. Watch now, and listen." Cupping the ring in his hands, he closed his eyes. "You have been made to guide the Knowledgable One to Erias Yr Gwydd, the Spear of Kymru. This is his face, and this is his soul. On his hand, you will be his guide." The opal ring flared briefly in Bran's hands, then subsided, leaving a fiery afterimage in the shadows.

Bran nodded to Mannawyddan, who cupped the ring of pearl in his thin hands, then began to recite. "You have been made to guide the Great Queen to Gwyr Yr Brennin, the Stone of Kymru. This is her face, and this is her soul. On her hand, you will be her guide." The pearl glowed, shining through the Ardewin's now translucent hands, then faded.

At Bran's nod, Arywen cupped her ring of emerald, then spoke, "You have been made to guide the White One to Buarth Y Greu, the Cauldron of Kymru. This is her face, and this is her soul. On her hand, you will be her guide." The emerald flared in a verdant burst of light, then dimmed.

Bran gestured to Taliesin, who cupped the ring of sapphire. "You have been made to guide the Great Bear to Meirig Yr Llech, the Sword of Kymru. This is his face and this is his soul. On his hand, you will be his guide." The sapphire shone a glittering blue, then subsided.

"These, then, are the rings that you and the others must gather," Bran commanded.

"From where?" Gwydion asked.

"You do not recognize them?" Bran asked. "These are the rings that will be given to each of the royal houses of Kymru. The pearl will go to the House of PenAlarch in Ederynion. The emerald will be given to the House of PenBlaid in Prydyn. The opal goes to the House of PenMarch in Rheged. The sapphire will be taken to the House of PenHebog in Gwynedd. To each of these rulers in my time, I will give a ring. And I will give them the words that will allow you and the others to claim them."

"And the words are?" Gwydion asked.

"You will know them, when the time comes."

For a moment Gwydion considered losing his temper, for it would not be easy to gather these rings. The pearl was on Queen Elen's hand, and she was a captive of the Coranians. The opal was now in the grasp of Morcant Whledig, thanks to Princess Enid's treachery. The emerald, at least, was in King Rhoram's hands. And the sapphire was in the keeping of Morrigan, Uthyr's daughter. He would have to get these rings—in two cases, snatching them out of the enemy's hands. His silver eyes—eyes so like Bran's—blazed into the face of his ancestor. But what he saw there halted him. Bran knew the difficulties. And he did as he had dreamed. Gwydion could do no less.

"Very well," Gwydion said quietly. "And the Song of the Caers?"

"Ah," Taliesin said with a smile. "My best song."

"Your most obscure song," Gwydion retorted, "since I can find no one who has ever heard of it."

Taliesin whipped around to face Bran with an accusing stare.

Bran shrugged. "It had to be protected."

"My very best song, and it has been forgotten!"

"Not forgotten. Just in hiding. Now, Taliesin, I'm sorry, but—"

Taliesin continued to mutter. "All those hours of work. And no one sings it."

"Artists," Arywen said, her tune musing, "are so unreasonable."

"Come, come, Taliesin," Mannawyddan said quickly, "no doubt, when the Treasures are restored, the song will be sung again. Sung by all the Bards throughout Kymru, as part of the story of triumph over our enemies. And, of course, all your other songs are, no doubt, very, very popular in Gwydion's time. Isn't that so, Gwydion?"

"Um, yes," Gwydion said, anxious to get the conversation back to his need. "That is so. But what is this Song of the Caers? Can you tell me how to find it? And quickly?" He couldn't stay here much longer. Already he felt the pull to return.

"It can't be found, Gwydion," Bran said quietly. "It can't be written down. That's how I protected it. But it is still sung, though the singer may not know it. Taliesin will give you the tune. You must carry it back with you. It will be recognized. Now, give him the tune, Taliesin. Then, Gwydion, you must go. You have tarried here almost too long."

Taliesin, throwing off his sulk, began to hum. A complex tune, it seemed to burn itself into Gwydion's mind, as though pulling at a memory already there, striking chord after responsive chord deep within.

The tune completed, Gwydion turned to Bran. "I must go. Yet, one word more. You have never dreamed of the outcome. I heard you say so. You do not know if we will succeed. Have you—have you no word of hope for me? For us? Have you seen nothing?"

Bran was silent for a moment. The shadows seemed to press down on the four Great Ones as they stood on the dais, looking down at him with pity in their eyes.

"I have seen nothing," Bran said at last. "Hope is all I have. I would give that to you, if I could."

GWYDION OPENED HIS eyes to meet Rhiannon's anxious gaze. Anieron, Elstar and Elidyr still stood, looking down at him. He hadn't been gone long. The candle had barely burned down at all.

Rhiannon put her arm beneath his shoulders and helped him to sit up. Short as the dream had been, he was weak and lightheaded. He felt drained. Empty. But not quite empty. For the tune was still with him.

He hummed the tune, and it echoed against the cavern walls, rising up to the roof. And now it was no longer familiar to him. He did not know the song any longer. But Bran had said there was one who would recognize it. He looked up at Anieron, for, surely, the Master Bard would know it. "Recognize it?" he asked.

Anieron shook his head. "No. It means nothing to me."

Nothing! Even the Master Bard did not know that song. But Bran had said—

"I know that tune," Rhiannon said quietly. She hummed the

melody. "That's it, isn't it?"

"The words!" he cried, grasping her arm. "What are the words?"

She shook her head. "I never heard the words. I didn't know the tune had any."

No words. Oh, gods. Now what?

"But," Rhiannon went on, "the one who used to hum that song to me surely knows them."

"Who?" Gwydion asked. "Who?"

"Uncle Dudod."

"Who is—"

"On his way back here. He will be here tomorrow."

Chapter 9

Allt Llwyd
Kingdom of Rheged, Kymru
Bedwen Mis, 499

Alban Awyr—afternoon

The tangy sea breeze rushed through Rhiannon's hair as she walked the deserted beach. Occasionally she stooped to pick up a shell, delighting in their delicate tints, in their unexpected curves and sharp angles. Delighting, too, in these moments away from Gwydion.

She had not spent much time with him over the years. For most of the two years from the time between the invasion of Kymru and Gwydion's latest dream, she had been waiting in the cave in Coed Aderyn for Gwydion to return from one trip or another. Of course, she knew why he left her on her own so much. It was obvious how much he disliked her.

She knew he despised her—he always had. For the millionth time she told herself that she didn't care about that. She told herself that she hated him just as much as he hated her. And she willed herself to believe it. Again.

She had known him for so long, yet after all this time she still did not really know how she felt about him. He drew her to him, like a moth to a flame. But she was no moth—she was a woman who knew the ruin a man could make of a woman's heart—if she let him.

161

She knew what loving someone as dangerous as Gwydion ap Awst could do. For Gwydion was aloof, cold, separate from the rest of the world. She had decided long ago that tearing down his walls would not be worth her time—deciding that the man who hid behind them would be no prize. And often she wondered, even after all this time, if she had been wrong.

From behind her she thought she heard the faint sound of her name carried on the wind. She turned, and two girls came rushing up.

"Rhiannon," Cariadas panted. "We thought you might like some company." The second girl, Sinend, said nothing, but smiled shyly.

The sight of these two girls tugged at her heart. They were close to the age of her own daughter. And she missed Gwenhwyfar so. "Thank you both. That was thoughtful. I would like your company."

Cariadas grinned. "You're just being polite, aren't you?"

"No, indeed. You remind me of—" she stopped, her throat suddenly tight. Her fingers brushed over the bracelet at her wrist. It was a leather band on which a heart of white, polished ash wood dangled.

"Of whom?" Cariadas asked.

"Of her daughter," Sinend said quietly.

"How did you know?" Rhiannon asked.

Sinend shrugged, looking down at the sand.

"She won't tell you this herself," Cariadas said in a confidential tone, "but Sinend's very smart about people. She always seems to know what they are thinking. Tell Rhiannon what you said about my da, Sinend."

Sinend reddened and looked away. Cariadas turned to Rhiannon. "Sinend says that my da can't take his eyes off you. You do like him, don't you? He sure likes you."

"I'm sorry?" Rhiannon asked blankly. "What did you—"

"He watches you all the time. Didn't you know that?"

"No, I didn't. And I think, Cariadas, that you would do better to keep that observation to yourself." Rhiannon's tone was cold. "As well as your wild guesses, which have no basis in reality."

"Oh, I've made you mad," Cariadas said, her face falling. "I'm sorry."

Rhiannon got a grip on herself. "I'm not mad, Cariadas. Truly.

But I am surprised by what you say, and I don't believe it. And even if I did, I wouldn't know what to make of it."

"Really? It doesn't seem that mysterious to me," Cariadas said, her voice gleeful. "And it would be so nice to see da happy."

"Cariadas," Rhiannon began firmly, but the voice in her head stopped her.

Well, well. Who have we here? And where have you been, my sweet niece?

Uncle Dudod! Where—

Just over the dune, my dear.

With a cry of joy, she ran down the beach toward the man who was dismounting from his horse, ran toward the only real father she had ever known, ran toward Dudod's waiting arms.

WHEN THEY ENTERED the cave, Rhiannon's hand in Dudod's, Sinend and Cariadas trailing behind them, Anieron and Gwydion were already there to greet them.

"So, brother," Anieron said, his light tone fooling no one, "once again you have returned unscathed. It is less than you deserve after cutting it too fine. But, then, you always do."

Dudod grinned. "They almost had me, true. But luck was with me."

"Luck is always with you," Anieron replied, gripping Dudod's shoulders. "But for the sake of the gods, Dudod, don't let your luck run out."

"The Weaver is not so fond of me that she will cut my thread so soon. Hard to believe, isn't it? When everyone else loves me so?"

"Dudod," Gwydion said abruptly, "we must meet with you in private—Anieron, Rhiannon, and I. Now."

Dudod's brows raised at Gwydion's commanding tone. "Now?"

"It is vital."

"Gwydion," Rhiannon said, exasperated, "give him a few moments, will you? He was almost captured only a few days ago. And he has ridden far. He's worn out."

"The day Dudod is worn out is the day they bury him. And not before."

"I'm telling you, Gwydion—" she began, her tone dangerous.

"Thank you, Rhiannon," Dudod said smoothly, "for your concern. It is appreciated, of course. And you are right, I am a little weary. Dreamer, I believe I will have to meet with you later. I need to rest. And tonight is Alban Awyr, and I don't want to miss that. I will meet with you after the festival." Dudod moved off, with Anieron following.

"You have such a way with people, Gwydion," Rhiannon said, turning on him. "He's not as young as he used to be. And you pressured him the moment he got here. He has the song. And he will still have it later tonight."

"Your support, as always, touches my heart," Gwydion said bitterly. "Do you think I am playing a game here? Do you think we have all the time in the world to search? If the Treasures are not found and the boy isn't inside of Cadair Idris before the year is out, our chance is lost forever. Forever. Do you understand?"

"Do you understand that a few hours won't make any difference? You may be perfect, but the rest of us have human needs. Little things like rest, like food, like companionship. Things you wouldn't understand."

His face whitened with anger. "There is much you think I don't understand. And you are wrong. But, then, you are so often wrong about me."

Without another word, he turned and stalked down the tunnel.

LATER THAT EVENING, Rhiannon stood between Dudod and Gwydion, waiting for the Alban Awyr ceremony to begin. She wore the customary Dewin's robe of sea green, and silver ribbons were woven through her long black hair. Around her neck she wore her Dewin's torque of pearl. Her green eyes sparkled with the joy of seeing her uncle again—safe and sound, as always, though she had come close to losing him.

Every few moments she reached out and lightly touched Dudod's arm, to reassure herself that he was really here. And whenever she did that, Dudod would turn to her and smile. He understood her need for reassurance, and did not begrudge it. Dudod had always been kind to her.

Unlike some people she knew. For Gwydion virtually ignored her. After greeting Dudod coldly, he had turned all his attention to his daughter. And what had he meant this afternoon when he said she was wrong about him? If there was one man she understood only too well, it was Gwydion ap Awst.

Gwydion, dressed in a black robe trimmed with red, his Dreamer's torque of opals and gold flashing fire, held his daughter's hand, an abstracted frown on his handsome face. His eyes often cut to Jonas, a Bard who had recently come to Allt Llwyd. There was nothing particularly remarkable about Jonas, as far as Rhiannon could tell, nothing he had done that would bring that frown to the Dreamer's face. Jonas was a slight, tense little man, and his eyes were filled with pain and sorrow.

In the old days, this festival would have been celebrated by the Bards in their college of Neuadd Gorsedd beneath the stars, in the sacred grove of birch trees. In the old days this festival would have been joyfully celebrated throughout Kymru, people openly laughing and singing. But now the Kymri must celebrate in secret.

The round cavern, situated in the center of the extensive caves of Allt Llwyd, was full of men, women, and children. All the Y Dawnus here had gathered to honor Taran, King of the Winds. Each person carried a birch branch—branches that had been scavenged from the countryside by night at the risk of their lives.

At the north end of the cavern, a stone altar rested. A golden bowl full of seeds and a silver goblet of wine were laid on top of the stone. Eight unlit torches had been placed in brackets around the altar. In the very center of the cave burned a huge bonfire made of birch wood.

At last Anieron entered the cave with Elidyr behind him. The Master Bard wore a magnificent mantle fashioned with the feathers of songbirds—thrushes, nightingales, and sparrows. He carried a branch made of gold, hung with dozens of tiny, golden bells. As he stepped up to the altar, he shook the branch. The clear ringing sound echoed throughout the cavern, swirling up to the shadowy roof.

In his deep, powerful voice, Anieron began the festival. He gestured to the eight unlit torches. "This is the Wheel of the year before us. One torch for each of the eight festivals when we honor the Shining Ones." As he gestured and named each one, Elidyr lit the torches. "Calan Llachar, Alban Haf, Calan Olau, Alban Nerth, Calan Gaef, Alban Nos, Calan Morynion, and Alban Awyr, which we celebrate tonight."

Again, Anieron shook the branch, and the bells sang. "We gather here to honor Taran, King of the Winds, who woke the Great Mother from her enchanted sleep that the earth might be fruitful."

"We honor him," the Kymri murmured softly, the sound of their hushed voices like that of a gentle breeze.

Anieron continued, "Let the Shining Ones be honored as they gather to watch the Great Awakening. Mabon, King of Fire. Nantsovelta, Lady of the Waters. Annwyn, Lord of Chaos. Aertan, Weaver of Fate. Cerridwen, Queen of the Wood. Cerrunnos, Master of the Hunt. Y Rhyfelwr, Agrona and Camulos, the Warrior Twins. Sirona, Lady of the Stars. Grannos, Star of the North and Healer."

Again the Y Dawnus responded, "We honor the Shining Ones."

In the silence, young Sinend spoke, her shy voice carrying throughout the cavern. "Why do we mourn? Why are we afraid?"

And Anieron answered, "We mourn because Modron, the Great Mother, cannot be found. We are afraid because spring cannot come."

"How can Modron be found?" the girl continued. "How can spring begin?"

"Behold," Anieron said solemnly. "Taran, King of the Winds, is searching for Modron, his beloved. He sends the winds to search the world over. And, at last, Modron is found. She sleeps in the sacred grove and cannot awake. The winds bring this news to Taran, and he flies to her. See how the winds rustle the trees of the grove, and the leaves speak with the wind." Anieron shook his branch of bells. "See how the sounds of the air have awakened Modron."

It was then that the wind began. A gust of air swooped through the cavern, setting the bonfire to dancing. "See now how Taran is with us," Anieron proclaimed, his voice ringing through the cave. "With us now and forever." The wind whipped around the people, carrying with it the tang of the sea, the smell of hope, the hint of freedom.

Gwydion stepped forward and lifted his hands. The wind whipped his black robe. "Taran has not forgotten us as we do him honor. One day we will reclaim Kymru from the enemy! And Taran's winds will blow them back to the sea!"

At Gwydion's words, the wind blew harder, then softened, streaming over the people like a benediction, then dying down gently.

"Taran is, indeed, with us," Anieron agreed. "And blesses us this night." He reached into the golden bowl on the altar and tossed the seeds onto the floor of the cave, then poured wine over the seeds. "The earth has awakened, and spring has come! Blessed be Taran, King of the Winds. See now how he blesses us. See now how, when we have regained our land, Modron will return!"

"Blessed be Taran!" the crowd shouted.

Anieron began the Alban Awyr song, and the crowd joined in gleefully.

"Spring returns, the air rings with the song of birds.
The blameless nightingale, the pure-toned thrush,
The soaring woodlark, the swift blackbird.
The birds sing a golden course of fame and glory
In the countless woodland halls. Spring returns!"

AFTER THE SONG was over, the Bards began to dance in a ring around the fire. Behind them, the Dewin formed another ring, dancing in the opposite direction.

Some Bards began to tell the first stories in the great storytelling contest that would go on all night. "This story is a true story, and I had it from Dyved who had it from Cenred. Whoever doesn't believe me had better go from this company than hear the story unbelieving. There was once an old man who lived all alone on Mynydd Gwyr, the highest peak in Gwynedd. By night he was a mighty hawk . . ."

Another began to recite one of Taliesin's songs:
"I have been a speckled snake on a hill,
I have been a viper in the Llyn.
I have been a bill-hook crooked that cuts,
I have been a ferocious spear."

Rhiannon noticed that Cariadas was saying something earnestly to Gwydion, but she could not hear what in all the noise.

Rhiannon turned to Dudod, who had started off for the ale barrel, already humming. "Oh, no," she said, playfully grabbing his arm. "Time for our meeting, Uncle."

"Just give me a few minutes," Dudod protested. "I want to have a little fun."

"No time for that. Remember, Gwydion said we must slip away right after the ceremony to meet with Anieron."

"Gwydion never lets anyone have fun," Dudod grumbled. "What would it hurt him to at least dance and sing a little? But, no, it's get right to work."

Rhiannon opened her mouth to reply, but the light pressure of someone's hand on her arm made her turn around. Gwydion bowed. His gray eyes were alight with some emotion she could not identify.

"Dance with me," he said. Without even giving her a chance to reply, he grabbed her hand and led her into the ring.

SOME HOURS LATER, Rhiannon followed Gwydion down the tunnel to Anieron's chambers. Dudod had gone on ahead an hour or so before. But Gwydion had refused to leave the celebration, insisting on dance after dance with her. Rhiannon had noticed that Cariadas had been watching them, a self-satisfied grin on her impish face.

"Did you and Cariadas have some kind of bet?" she asked curiously as they neared Anieron's chambers.

"What do you mean?"

"Since when do you like to dance?"

"How would you know if I like to dance or not? We've never celebrated a festival with a group of other people before."

"Well, I . . ." she floundered.

"We're here. Try to restrain your curiosity for just a little while, will you? We have more important things to discuss," he said coolly.

He lifted the curtain that hung across Anieron's chamber and went in, dropping it behind him. Rhiannon yanked it up again and entered, muttering under her breath.

Anieron and Dudod looked up from the map spread across the rough floor. Both men sat cross-legged on cushions, tankards of ale by their elbows. Dudod cradled a harp in his arms and was idly strumming it.

"What did you say, my dear?" Dudod asked.

"Nothing," Rhiannon answered sourly.

Gwydion shot an amused glance, then turned to Dudod. "Rhiannon says you know the words to an old tune. You must write them down for us. It is the tune that holds the key to the Treasures."

"What tune?" Dudod asked.

"It's called the Song of the Caers."

"Oh, that one." Dudod shrugged. "All right." He reached for the quill and parchment Anieron handed to him. He stared down at the paper, quill in hand, unmoving.

"Dudod?" Anieron asked in concern. "What's wrong? Don't you know it?"

"Yes," Dudod snapped. "I know it. Just give me a minute, will you?"

Rhiannon looked at Dudod in surprise. Anieron's brow raised, but he said nothing. Gwydion tapped his foot impatiently. And Dudod brought the quill to the parchment, but again wrote nothing.

"I can't," Dudod said at last, laying down the quill. There was no anger in his voice, only bewilderment.

"What do you mean, you can't?" Rhiannon asked, puzzled.

"I mean that I can't. It won't let me write it down."

"Well," Gwydion said dryly after a moment of silence, "at least we know we have the right song."

"I don't understand it," Dudod complained.

"I do," Gwydion said quietly. "It was something Bran the

Dreamer said to me when I Time-Walked. He said that he had to protect the song and keep it from being written down. Tell me, where did you learn that song?"

"Why, I got it from my da, Cyvarnion, who got it from his mam, Feldelma, the ninth Master Bard."

"Who got it from . . ?"

"Who got it from Beli, who got it from Selyf, who got it from Merfryn—"

"The son of Mannawyddan, the fifth Ardewin," Gwydion finished. "And one of Taliesin's dearest friends. One of the Great Ones of Lleu Lawrient."

"But why did da teach the song to you and not to me?" Anieron asked.

Dudod grinned. "He always liked me best."

"Ha, ha," Anieron said flatly.

"Sing the song, Dudod," Gwydion said quietly.

Dudod, with a last wicked grin for his brother, began to play and sing. The haunting melody, written in a minor key, twisted and danced around the tiny chamber.

"I will praise the Brenin, the heir of Idris,
Who will extend his dominion over the shores of the world.
"Complete was the prison of the Queen in Caer Dwyr.
Under the gravestone
In the land of glass
The serpent lies coiled.
Beneath the water lies the seeker,
Pearls and silver glimmering, shimmering.
The Great Queen went into it;
Except four, none returned from Caer Dwyr.

"Fast was the trap of the woman in Caer Erias.
Within the dark forest
In the land of honey
The hill of oak stands.
Within the storm lies the blaze

170

Opals and gold gleaming.
The Knowledgable One went into it;
Except four, none returned from Caer Erias.

"Sorrowful was the exile of the King from Caer Tir.
Down the cavern's twilight road
In the land of wine
The maze of blood awaits.
Within the center lies the circle
A ridge about its edge and emeralds.
The White One went into it;
Except four, none returned from Caer Tir.

"Many were the girl's tears for the dead of Caer Gwynt.
Down the dark path
In the land of mountains
The black stone looms.
Beneath the seeker lies the guardian
Sapphire of sky and silver of storm.
The Great Bear went into it;
Except four, none returned from Caer Gwynt.

"I will praise the Brenin, the heir of Idris,
Who will extend his dominion over the shores of the
world.

"The enemy congregules like dogs in a kennel,
From contact with their superiors they acquire
knowledge.
They know not the course of the wind, or the water
of the sea.
They know not the spark of the fire, or the fruitful-
ness of the earth.
I will beg the Brenin, the High One,

*That I be not wretched, a prisoner in my own
land."*

"Well," Gwydion said when Dudod fell silent. "That seems clear
enough."

"Oh, right," Rhiannon said, her voice sharp with sarcasm. "No
problem at all. It's a wonder that the Treasures haven't been found
before this."

"Now, now, don't be impatient," he went on, his tone maddeningly calm. "If we take it bit by bit, I think we will find that it
contains all the clues we need. Now, Dudod, chant the first stanza
again, please."

*"Complete was the prison of the Queen in Caer Dwyr.
Under the gravestone
In the land of glass
The serpent lies coiled.
Beneath the water lies the seeker,
Pearls and silver glimmering, shimmering.
The Great Queen went into it;
Except four, none returned from Caer Dwyr."*

"It's about Ederynion, isn't it?" Anieron asked. "Caer Dwyr
is the Queen's fortress in Dinmael. And Queen Elen is certainly
imprisoned by the enemy."

"Yes," Gwydion said. "And the 'land of glass' clinches it—the
glass blowers of Ederynion are masters of that craft. And Ederynion
belongs to Nantsovelta of the Waters. And she is the goddess of the
Stone. So, it tells us where and how to find the Stone—Gwyr Yr
Brenin—which means 'Seeker of the King.'"

"'Beneath the water lies the seeker,'" Rhiannon said suddenly.
"The Stone is in a lake? But what lake?"

"That will doubtless become clearer to us later. The 'Great
Queen' who must retrieve the Stone is you, Rhiannon," Gwydion
said sketching a bow. "*Rhi*—meaning 'great,' and *Annon*—Queen."

"But how do I find it?" Rhiannon asked. Now was not the time to mention how she felt about water, how much she feared and loathed it.

"One other thing I learned when I Walked-Between-the-Worlds. As the legend says, the Great Ones took the jewels from Lleu's torque and made rings of them. They gave each ring to the ruling houses of Kymru. This is what the Protectors meant when they said to let the rings be our guide. The ring given to the House of PenAlarch was a pearl. We must retrieve that ring. What the legend does not say is that the ring itself will guide you. When you put it on your finger, you will know which direction to go."

"Just one little problem with that, Gwydion. Elen has the ring. And she is a prisoner of the Coranians. Exactly how will I get ahold of it?" she asked tartly.

"We'll think of something. Do you think we have come so far, you and I, to be turned back by a little problem like that? Now, Dudod, the next verse, please."

"Fast was the trap of the woman in Caer Erias.
Within the dark forest
In the land of honey
The hill of oak stands.
Within the storm lies the blaze
Opals and gold gleaming.
The Knowledgable One went into it;
Except four, none returned from Caer Erias."

"Caer Erias—the King's fortress in Rheged," Rhiannon mused. "Rheged, the land of honey—the land that belongs to Mabon of the Sun. So this must be about the Spear—Erias Yr Gwydd—Blaze of Knowledge."

"'Within the dark forest,'" Anieron quoted. "Which one?"

Gwydion shrugged. "No idea—yet."

"And, 'Fast was the trap of the woman in Caer Erias,'" Anieron continued. "Poor Princess Enid is held there now. And doomed to marry Morcant."

"Don't pity her too much," Gwydion said with some asperity. "She has set us a hard task. She had the ring when she so foolishly went to Llwynarth with her pathetic plea to Bledri. And that's the ring we must somehow retrieve, the opal given to the House of PenMarch."

"So, somehow we have to get the ring back from Morcant," Rhiannon said.

"Yes. Won't that be fun?" Gwydion asked sourly.

"Do you think we have come such a long way, you and I, to be turned back by such a little problem?" Rhiannon said flippantly. "I'm sure you'll think of something. It's really your job, isn't it, Gwydion—oh, 'Knowledgable One'?"

"Somehow I knew you would think that was funny."

"Children, children," Anieron said. "No squabbling. Dudod, next verse, please."

"Sorrowful was the exile of the King from Caer Tir.
Down the cavern's twilight road
In the land of wine
The maze of blood awaits.
Within the center lies the circle
A ridge about its edge and emeralds.
The White One went into it;
Except four, none returned from Caer Tir."

"CAER TIR—RHORAM'S fortress in Prydyn. And Prydyn is the land of Modron the Great Mother. So this is about the Cauldron—Buarth Y Greu," Rhiannon said.

"The Circle of Blood," Gwydion said. "And Prydyn is the land of wine. And the ring given to the House of PenBlaid is in Rhoram's hands—'the exile of the King from Caer Tir.'"

"'A 'maze of blood,'—I don't much like the sound of that," Rhiannon said.

"But that won't be your job," Gwydion pointed out.

"Who's the White One?"

"You don't know?"

"I haven't the advantage of your dreams, Gwydion."

"Gwenhwyfar. Your daughter."

"Gwen? But she hates me. She won't go!"

"She will," Gwydion said firmly. "The four of us will go on this quest, and find these Treasures. 'Except for four, none returned.'"

"What four? You and I, and Gwen, and—who?"

"Ah, for that we shall need to learn the next verse. Dudod?"

"Many were the girl's tears for the dead of Caer Gwynt.
Down the dark path
In the land of mountains
The black stone looms.
Beneath the seeker lies the guardian
Sapphire of sky and silver of storm.
The Great Bear went into it;
Except four, none returned from Caer Gwynt."

"CAER GWYNT, THE fortress in Tegeingl in the 'land of mountains;'— Gwynedd," Anieron began.

"Yes, Caer Gwynt, what was once Uthyr's fortress." Gwydion's face was tight with pain, but his voice was controlled. "And he gave the sapphire ring of the House of PenHebog to his daughter, Morrigan, when he sent her away to safety before the invasion."

"'Many were the girl's tears'—poor Morrigan," Rhiannon said softly.

"And Gwynedd is the land of Taran of the Winds. And he is the god of the Sword. Meirig Yr Llech— Guardian of the Stone."

"'Beneath the seeker lies the guardian'— another mystery."

"For the moment," Gwydion said. "And the Great Bear—"

"Is Arthur. Arthur ap Uthyr var Ygraine of Gwynedd," Anieron said.

For a moment everyone was silent. At last, Gwydion spoke. "So you knew. Both you and your brother."

"We knew," Anieron said quietly. "We have known for many years that Arthur did not die as a child, and neither did Myrrdin die. We knew that they both live in Dinas Emrys, waiting in safe obscurity for the day to reclaim Kymru."

"And who else knows this?" Gwydion asked tightly.

"Why, besides us, just those who were at Tegeingl the day you came to take him away—Ygraine, Susanna, Duach, and Cai."

"How did you know?" Gwydion asked.

"We put together the pieces throughout the years. I do not think anyone else could have followed the trail you left."

"And you never said."

"We never said. It was so obvious, Gwydion, that you didn't want us to know. It would have disappointed you so," Anieron said genially, but his eyes gleamed.

Gwydion shocked Rhiannon by actually grinning. "How kind of you."

"Arthur hates you," Rhiannon said to Gwydion after a moment. "Almost as much as Gwen hates me. What fun this will be."

"No one said it would be easy," Dudod quipped.

"And speaking of easy, you must sing that song again and again until Gwydion and I have it by heart."

"And sing it now—all night, if necessary," Gwydion said. "For tomorrow I leave to fetch Arthur from Dinas Emrys. And Rhiannon must get Gwen, in Haford Bryn."

"Gwen won't want to come," Rhiannon warned.

"Neither will Arthur," Gwydion said shortly. "But they will come with us all the same. We will meet in Sycharth five weeks from now. That should put us all there by the beginning of disglair wythnos in Gwernan Mis. Rhiannon, travel very carefully. Havgan and his men have your description."

"And yours, Gwydion. He wants you even more than he wants me."

"You always did have a way with people, Dreamer." Dudod grinned.

"Funny," Gwydion said flatly. "Just sing the song, will you?"

Anieron stood. "I must go and bid Jonas farewell."

"Jonas?" Rhiannon asked. "Oh, the Bard whom you're sending to Morrigan in Gwynedd. The poor man whose wife and baby daughter were killed by the wyrce-jaga."

"Anieron," Gwydion said suddenly. "There's something about Jonas that bothers me."

"Something you dreamed?"

"No. I only wish I had."

"Then what makes you think—"

"Just a feeling. There's something very wrong with him."

"His wife and child are dead. What do you think could be wrong with him?"

"It's more than that. I know it. You must keep a close eye on him. You must keep him here."

"I must? Gwydion, may I remind you that I am the Master Bard—and you are not. Jonas is my concern, not yours."

"I see," Gwydion said stiffly. "Well, then, there's nothing more to be said."

RHIANNON HELD THE bridle of her horse as she waited on the rough sands for Gwydion to finish taking leave of his daughter. Rhiannon had already said her good-byes to Anieron and Dudod. There were tears in Cariadas's eyes, and even Gwydion's cold gray eyes glittered as he gently held his daughter in his strong arms.

At last, the farewells said, Anieron, Dudod and Cariadas waved one last time, then reentered the cave and were swallowed up by the shadows.

"Well," Rhiannon said as she turned to mount her horse. "Have a safe trip, Gwydion. I will see you in Sycharth." The words were cold, but she didn't know what else to say. She did not think he would appreciate any show of emotion.

Gwydion's arms went around her, and he lifted her onto the horse's back, settling her in the saddle. But he did not draw away. He stood beside the horse, not loosening the grip of his hands on her waist.

"Take care, Rhiannon," he said softly. "A safe journey to you."

"And a safe journey to you, Gwydion," she said evenly, though she was startled at his nearness, and her heart seemed to be beating a little too fast.

He seemed about to say something more, but then he released her abruptly and mounted his horse. Without another word, he rode north.

Turning her horse to the west, Rhiannon rode away. She did not look back. And so she did not see that Gwydion halted, looking after her, until the curve of the earth shut her away from his sight.

Chapter 10

Allt Llwyd and Coed Coch
Kingdom of Rheged, Kymru
Eiddew Mis, 499

Llundydd, Disglair Wythnos—early morning

Cariadas followed the Master Bard closely, her quill at the ready, poised over the parchment. She liked to be busy, to be thinking of something other than how much she missed her da, even though he had been gone for only one week.

She sighed to herself. Would there ever come a time when he would not go away? Would there ever be a time again when she did not fear for his life? She remembered the days when she was a child at Caer Dathyl, when her da played with her, helped her to pick flowers, and showed her how to weave them into a necklace. He had laughed with her then, picking her up in his strong arms, holding her close and telling her story after story. But that was long ago, before she was sent to Gwytheryn to learn to use her gifts, before her da went to Corania. If the Warleader ever caught her da . . .

Next to her, Sinend, silent as a ghost, waited for the Master Bard's measured phrases. It was Cariadas's task to note the news spoken on the wind that filtered through the minds of the Bards in the chain stretched across Kymru. But it was Sinend's job to note down the phrases that might come to the Master Bard—snippets of songs, bits of poems, such as they occurred to him.

"Cariadas," Anieron spoke, "the Bard in Margam says that the temple to Lytir has risen again from the ashes of the old. Make a special note—I want Atlantas's folk to burn it down no more than two days from now."

Then the Master Bard continued. "Sinend—pale emeralds flash fire in your eyes." Sinend noted the phrase, another line in a song he was composing about Modron, the Great Mother. Modron, Anieron claimed, had been deserted by her children, the Druids, and needed special attention if Kymru was ever going to be fruitful again.

Anieron paused in his walk down the beach, head tilted, listening. Some of the wind-speech filtered through to Cariadas.

Master Durd, I have still heard nothing from our Bard in Maenor Deilo. The Dewin, too, passes on no information. And today there is no word from Peris.

Cariadas frowned. The message from Cenrith, the Bard of Mabudryd, stationed no more than five leagues to the west, troubled her. This was the third day in a row there had been no word from the northeast cantref in Rheged. And now there was no word from Peris. What could be happening? She knew that Anieron was as troubled as she, but his mind-voice was cool and calm.

Very well, Cenrith. I have noted it. Tell—

Oh, gods! Anieron! They're here! The Coranians slipped by me in the night. Oh, gods, they know where you are!

Cenrith! Where are they?

Run, Anieron. Run—

The message was cut off abruptly, in a way that made Cariadas shiver.

Dudod! Elidyr! Elstar! They are coming! We evacuate the caves, now!

Even as Anieron sent this thought, he was running back to the caves, his silver hair streaming behind him, hurrying to get his people out before their death came for them.

Sinend, not hearing any of what had passed, stared after Anieron, stricken. "Come on!" Cariadas screamed, grabbing Sinend's cold hands, forcing her to run.

As they ran, Sinend panted, "Cariadas, what is it? What's

happening?"

"The Coranians. Less than five leagues away! They got Cenrith."

"But how? How could they sneak up on us like this?"

"Traveling at night, hiding in forests, going in small groups. There aren't enough of us to watch everything. And the Coranians are coming here! They know where we are!"

"How could they know?" Sinend cried, her face blanched and shocked. "Who could have told them?"

"I don't know," Cariadas said. More to herself than to her friend, she continued, "But when I find out, I'll kill him."

THEY BURST INTO the cave, momentarily blinded by the shadows. Scurrying forms, the sound of booted feet slapping the rocks, the smell of fear assaulted their senses. A hand shot out from the darkness, grasping Cariadas's arm in a vise grip.

"Cariadas! Sinend! Come on. You two are in our group."

She turned to face Llywelyn, Elstar and Elidyr's eighteen-year-old son. "Who goes with us?" she asked.

"Anieron, and Dudod. My da and mam. And Cynfar. Come on."

She and Sinend followed Llywelyn down the dark tunnels filled with hurrying people. Many carried armfuls of books and scrolls. Some carried packs of food and water. They burst into Anieron's chambers. Cynfar, Llywelyn's younger brother, was bundling Anieron's cloak of feathers into a woolen sack.

"We can't take that!" Llywelyn cried. "We're taking too much as it is!"

Cynfar, his usually sunny sixteen-year-old face now set in stubborn lines, continued to stuff the cloak into the sack. "We will take it," the boy said fiercely. "It's granda's. One day it will be da's, and one day it will be mine."

Llywelyn opened his mouth to argue, but Cariadas understood. "Here, then, Cynfar, put this in, too." She snatched up the golden branch with its tinkling bells. The bells shifted, ringing with jeweled undertones in the stone chamber.

"You fool!" Llywelyn cried, snatching at the branch but missing it. "The sound will give us away!"

"Not if we wrap it up tightly," Cariadas said grimly, bundling the branch into the sack and tying it shut. "There, Cynfar. Now, hoist it up and try it."

Cynfar lifted the sack, wrapping the ties around his shoulders. He purposely shifted it, and it did not make a noise.

"See?" Cariadas said. Llywelyn was always so bossy, always thought he knew best, always looking at her as though she would never measure up to anyone's expectations.

The Ardewin hurried into the chamber. Her light brown hair was unbraided, cascading down her back. Her face was calm, but her hands were clenched tightly on the scrolls she carried.

"Mam!" Llywelyn exclaimed. "Cynfar here is trying to take the cloak and the branch. It is too much! We'll be caught before we move one step."

"Better they should be destroyed, perhaps, than to fall into the Coranians' hands," Elstar said as she bundled the scrolls into another sack. "Here, Cynfar, give them to me."

"No, mam," Cynfar said stubbornly.

"Cynfar," Elstar began, straightening up, her hands on her hips. "Leave them be."

"Let him try, *cariad*," her husband said as he entered the chamber. Elidyr's voice was mild, as it always was, but his wife and oldest son did not argue. Elstar said nothing, only looked away and continued her work. Llywelyn muttered that it was foolish—but he was not speaking loud enough for any but Cariadas to hear.

Elidyr picked up a sack and motioned for Cariadas to turn around. He tied the sack to her back. The weight was light, easy for her to handle. They would save the books, the scrolls, the poems, and the histories of her people. Save them for a time when Kymru belonged to them again. Then they would sing these songs, chant these poems, tell these stories under the light of the sun, the breeze playing around them as they stood on green earth, with water sparkling and playing at their feet.

"Here, Llywelyn," Elidyr said, "take some of the food." Elidyr tied the sack to his son's back, then briefly ruffled his hair. "Don't worry, boyo. Anieron, your mother and I have planned many, many nights for just such a happening. Already small groups are slipping out of Allt Llwyd, carrying our treasures, guarding our children. We make for Coed Coch, and there we will begin again."

Anieron entered, followed by Dudod. "Is everyone ready?" he asked gravely.

"Anieron," Cariadas said, her voice hushed and small. "Do you think—do you think my da made it out in time? And Rhiannon?"

"They left over a week ago, child. I am sure they are well."

"But Rhiannon went west."

"Rhiannon will be fine," Elstar said sharply, her eyes cutting to her husband, then darting away again. "She is one who can take care of herself."

"Her journey would not take her near Maenor Deilo," Anieron said smoothly, as though Elstar had not spoken, "nor near Gwytheryn—from where these Coranians surely came. And your da has gone through Ederynion, to cut across to Gwynedd. No, they are both far from harm, child."

"Which is more," Elstar said, her blue eyes flashing, "than I can say for us. Are we to go now?"

"Yes, daughter," Anieron said quietly. "Now we go. All the others are already on their way."

"And the enemy is at the cave mouth now," Elstar said, her head cocked to one side. "I see them in my mind's eye."

"Then we go," Dudod said, stuffing his harp into a half-empty sack, then swinging the burden onto his back. "Come."

THEY WALKED THE tunnels silently, their footfalls making no sound. From far off they heard the rumor of death—harsh voices, the faintest wisp of smoke. The warriors had found the library. Some books had been left behind, and now they were burning.

Elstar's mind-voice spoke. *I see them. They have surrounded the caves. They have captured so many of us. They knew the ways out!*

How many have gotten through?

No more than five groups—maybe fifty of us, all told. But there are hundreds already in enemy hands. The Coranians are forcing the captives to drink something—hawthorn, I think—to make them sleepy, useless. They will never be able to rescue themselves! And there are not enough free ones to rescue them.

Look ahead, my girl. What about our exit? Guarded?

I see no one here. But that does not mean—

I know.

Cariadas shivered. They slowed as a dim light winked at the end of the tunnel. Silent as ghosts, they crept nearer and nearer.

Elstar paused for a brief Wind-Ride. *No one I can see. Still, they might be hiding.*

Search, then. Do your best, daughter, Anieron's mind-voice said.

Nothing. But there are trees not far away. They could oh, the sun flashes in the trees! They are there.

This, then, is what we do. I go first and run north, drawing them off. When you see they're after me, run south. As quickly as you can.

Da, no! They want you most of all!

And that is why they shall have me. If I get away, I will circle around to the south and meet up with you all.

Dudod reached out and gripped Anieron's arm. He shook his head. *No, brother. Let me do it.*

No. Your task is to get the others to safety. Do you remember whom we have here? We have the Ardewin, the next Master Bard, and the four Great Ones of the next generation. Sinend, who will be Archdruid, and Cariadas, the Dreamer. Llywelyn, who will be the Ardewin, and Cynfar, the Master Bard. They must be protected at all costs. I am old. I have done much. Their chance has not yet come.

Anieron—

Dudod, I have decided. Let me go.

Slowly, oh, so slowly, Dudod released his grip on his brother's arm. Anieron straightened, shedding his pack. He reached out and cradled Elstar's tear-streaked face in his hand, kissing his daughter one last time. He grasped Elidyr's shoulders, pulling his son-in-law and nephew to him for a last embrace. He fixed his wise, green eyes on Sinend, on Cariadas, on Llywelyn, on Cynfar. "You four," he said quietly, "will be the Great Ones of the High King, one day. I will not say his name, not even to you. But this will be so. Remember that. And be worthy of it."

At last, Anieron turned to his brother. He smiled crookedly. *So I will go to Gwlad Yr Haf first, brother, and greet the dead. As always, I will be ahead of you.*

Dudod nodded his attempt at a smile, almost a grimace. *Always you were first.*

And always I will be. And with that, Anieron slipped away.

THEY WATCHED, WAITING for their chance, almost unable to see it when it came because of tear-blinded eyes. Anieron ran like the wind, like Taran's Wind, away from the caves, away from the trees that hid such bitter fruit, down the sparkling sands.

And the Coranians poured from the trees, haring after the Master Bard, shouting and laughing, knowing their prey was caught. Knowing, already, who and what he was.

And as the enemy ran, intent on their quarry, a desperate band slipped from the caves, threaded their way through the rocks, and were gone, leaving their hearts behind.

Gwaithdydd, Tywyllu Wythnos—late afternoon
"ALMOST THERE, CHILD. Almost there."

Cariadas lifted her head, more because of the gentleness in Dudod's voice than because she understood his words. She followed his gaze to the smudge of emerald green, glimpsed in the distance over the low hills.

Overhead, the sun had begun to sink toward that cool green, staining the sky. She thought of how it would feel to come out of these brown, dead hills, to walk under the shadowy silence of the distant forest. She thought of how it would feel to be safe and to walk without terror of what was hiding ahead or lurking behind.

At last, after more than two weeks of running, of hiding; of traveling night after night under the light of the moon, and sleeping lightly by day; of grieving, over and over and over again for Anieron, lost to them now, maybe lost to them forever; their destination was in sight—Coed Coch, the westernmost forest in Rheged.

And so few, so pitifully few of the Y Dawnus would make it to this place. Hundreds of Dewin and Bards—men, women, and little children just beginning to feel their powers—had been captured. And then, oh, and then, the enemy had marched them in long, chained lines across Rheged. Drugged, denied food, beaten mercilessly, the weak—the very young, the very old—fell to their knees. If they did not rise, they were murdered, speared and gutted, and left to rot on the blameless earth.

Later, much later, after the ragged, starving Dewin and Bards lurched by, driven by the shouts and curses and blows of the enemy, the people of Kymru—denied the right to help those still alive—crept out to help the dead. Bodies, some so very, very small, were washed with care. Rents in tattered clothing were repaired, hair was combed and braided, blossoms of hawthorn and marigold tucked into dead hands. Fires were lit to consume and cleanse the bodies. Chants were offered to Taran, the god of the Bards, and to Nantsovelta, the goddess of the Dewin, songs to speed the dead on their way to Gwlad Yr Haf, the Land of Summer.

Cariadas knew it all, for she had seen it on the Wind-Ride during those first few horrible days, until the distance had grown too great. She did not mind not being able to see any more. She had only watched because she knew she would need the memory in the years to come. She knew she would need it for those days when the weariness of the struggle would overwhelm her. She knew she would need the memory, the rage, and the grief to keep her strong.

She trudged now behind Dudod, her head bowed, struggling to put one foot before the other. Since the new-moon phase, they had begun to travel late in the afternoon. The nights were too dark, now, for making good time. Today, knowing Coed Coch was at last so near, they had traveled since sunrise. Elstar, Llewelyn, and Cariadas took turns Wind-Riding, scouting ahead and behind for signs of the enemy. But there had been nothing.

She walked slowly, daydreaming of how it would be in Coed Coch. They would find King Owein's band of warriors. They would be taken to the camp deep in the forest. They would be warmed by the fire, be given hot food and warm blankets on which to sleep. They would hear the warriors of Owein sing gallant songs of victory, their proud heads lifted to the starry sky.

More daydreams followed. Anieron had escaped—the Master Bard had always been so clever. He would already be there in Coed Coch, waiting to welcome them. And her da, who would have heard of the taking of Allt Llwyd, would come to Coed Coch, abandoning his plans, abandoning everything just to comfort her and keep her safe.

"Stop." Llywelyn's voice, so stern, cut through her daydreams.

"What did you see?" Dudod asked, for it had been Llywelyn's turn to Wind-Ride.

"A glint of something. Behind us."

"How far?"

"Just over that last hill."

"Coed Coch is only a league away. Could it be Owein's men?"

"What would they wear to flash in the sun? I think it must be—"

A shout behind them made Cariadas jump.

"Elstar," Dudod said hurriedly. "Ride."

Elstar, her pale face smudged with dirt, her brown hair tangled and dusty, gave a nod, then was off. She stood still, her eyes closed, supported by her husband and youngest son. Then her eyelids fluttered as she returned to herself.

"A group of twenty warriors," she said tightly, "just behind that last hill. They have seen us! And more are on either side of us!"

Dudod, his eyes cutting to the hill behind them, then to the forest ahead of them, made a decision. "We run for it, then. There's no cover here. Run as if the hounds of the Lord of Chaos himself are after you! Run!"

He grabbed Cariadas and flung her forward, forcing her to lead. Looking back over her shoulder, she saw Sinend following, then

Cynfar. Elidyr grabbed his wife's hand and ran. Llywelyn hesitated, waiting for Dudod. He shouted something, pointing behind them. The hill was crested with the boar's-head helmets of the enemy. The warriors yelled gleefully and poured over the hill, laughing and shouting as they prepared to run their prey to the earth.

And they would, she understood suddenly, for there was no cover here. And the warriors came on so fast. Worse, they came pouring down from the surrounding hills, too. There were over fifty of them, rushing toward her from either side, preparing to kill her and hers—eventually. When they were done having their fun. If she were lucky, they would kill her now.

She ran, but the forest seemed no nearer than before. She risked another glance behind her. They were all there running with her, but the warriors were gaining, gaining. They'd never make it. Never.

Something flashed out of the corner of her eye, something whistled close to her ear, then flew past. Sinend, just behind her, stumbled. Cynfar grabbed for her, but missed. Sinend went down, clutching her arm where a bright red rose had blossomed. Blood poured from the wound. The spear that had grazed her buried itself in the earth, but Dudod leapt over it in the nick of time and kept to his feet. Llywelyn and Dudod picked Sinend up, hardly missing a beat, and dragged her along.

The warriors shouted, laughing, cursing. More spears flew in the air, flashing in the bloodred light of the setting sun. Ahead of her, ten warriors waited to cut them off. They were surrounded. It was over. Over.

She halted, unwilling to run to meet her death, meaning to make them come to her. That one small victory she would have. The others pressed around her, ringed by the grinning warriors.

Her short life was over. She had never even had a dream.

With a rush of wind, fire leapt up, crackling hungrily, as though sprung from the earth itself. The blue-tinged fire ringed the little band, rushing outward to hold off the ring of warriors.

Druid's Fire. How? Who?

"Sinend?" she asked, her voice shaking. But Sinend, her head drooping, held up only by the strong arms of Llywelyn and Dudod, did not reply.

"Not her, girl," Dudod said, panting. "Not her. But whom?"

Then men and women dressed in tunics of green and brown, arrows at the ready, knives gleaming, rose up from the surrounding hills. As one, arrows were loosened, cutting through the air, speeding into the backs of the Coranian warriors, shearing through the metal links of byrnies, sending the Coranians deathward.

A man with a torque around his throat of opals and gold led the Kymric warriors in their race down the hill, his short sword gleaming in his sinewy brown hand. With a wild cry, he swung the blade, severing the head of a Coranian warrior who had survived the first volley. The Kymri poured down the hills, screaming defiance, butchering the enemy as the fire raged, still ringing the little band, keeping them safe from harm.

CARIADAS SQUINTED, TRYING to see through the flames. At last the fire quieted, burned low, then was gone. Before them stood a woman with hair as black as a raven's wing, her eyes the color of a summer sky.

"Do not be afraid," the woman said kindly. "You are safe now."

"Sabrina? Sabrina ur Dadweir?" Dudod asked.

"Yes. And I know you, Dudod ap Cyvarnion."

"One thing I've been curious about," Dudod said smoothly, as though they had all the time in the world to chat together. "That day in Llwynarth, when I was there to find out about Princess Enid, I saw you in the marketplace with Bledri. Did you see me?"

"Of course, I did." She smiled. "I must say, I was surprised. You used to be better than that."

Suddenly, Dudod laughed. "Try me, Sabrina. I'll show you how good I still am."

"Dudod, for the gods' sake," a man said irritably, "act your age." The man had dark brown hair, and his green eyes flashed with annoyance. He lightly laid his hand on Sabrina's arm, then quickly removed his hand and hooked his thumbs into his belt.

"Trystan," Dudod said, nodding coolly. "Still no sense of humor,

I see. Tell me, how is Esyllt?"

Sabrina's face tightened, and her eyes flickered. But she said nothing.

"Esyllt is well," Trystan said evenly.

"A shame," Dudod said, grinning at Sabrina.

The man who had led the warriors down the hills strode up, the gold and opals of his torque flickering in the setting sun. His sword was bloody, and his face was fierce, harsh with the echoes of blood-lust momentarily stilled, lined with a pain that never slept.

"Dudod," the man said, bowing slightly. "You are all welcome in Coed Coch."

"You must not bow to me," Dudod said. "It is I who should bow to you, King Owein."

"I am King of nothing, Dudod," Owein said, his voice bitter. "However that may be, we are glad to see you alive. We were not sure of your fate. The chain of Y Dawnus is broken, and news is scanty, at best."

"Are there—are there any others who have made it here?" Cariadas asked, her voice small.

Owein turned to her. "Some," he said softly. "There are some. Not many."

"Know, then, who has come to you this day, King Owein," Dudod said formally. "This is Cariadas ur Gwydion, the heir to the Dreamer. And the Ardewin, Elstar ur Anieron, and Elidyr, my son, Anieron's heir. And here are Llywelyn and Cynfar, their sons. And this," he said, taking Sinend tenderly into this arms from Llywelyn and Cynfar's hold, "is Sinend ur Aergol, heir to the Archdruid's heir. And she is hurt."

"She will be tended," Owein said, walking forward to examine the wound. "It is not deep, and will heal well, I think. Of course, the Dewin could say better."

Elstar went to Sinend and put her hand lightly over the wound. She closed her eyes briefly as she did the Life-Reading, then opened them and turned to Owein. "You are right, Owein. We will make a doctor of you yet, I think."

Owein smiled his bitter smile. "My experiences these past years have taught me much of wounds."

A woman, fierce for all her petite size, strode up to them. "All dead, Owein," she said crisply. "Of us, only young Gwyr was wounded, and that was his own fault. We have already scavenged their rations. Enough to eat well tonight. We must go."

"Thank you, Teleri. Come, my guests. We shall not reach the main camp until tomorrow. But tonight you shall sleep safely in Coed Coch, guarded by my warriors. Come."

THE FIRE CRACKLED cheerfully, and Cariadas gratefully held out her dirty hands to the blaze. Sabrina pressed a cup of warm wine into her hands. Cariadas sipped, willing the tremors to ease off. The shakes had surprised her, coming on so suddenly, just a few moments ago when they stopped for the night beneath the spreading branches of Coed Coch.

"Drink, child," Sabrina said softly.

Cariadas drank. The brew was warm, burning like fire down her throat. She choked slightly, then, urged by Sabrina, drank some more. A warm lassitude came over her. The cup felt so heavy. Sabrina took the cup from her tired hands and set it on the ground. The Druid laid a blanket across Cariadas's shoulders. Cariadas risked a glance at the others, shamed that she had come undone. But the faces around the fire were sympathetic. Owein's warriors, alert and grave, spaced around the perimeter of the clearing, did not laugh. Dudod, Elidyr, and Cynfar gave her brief, warm smiles. Llywelyn even reached out and patted her hand. And Sinend—

"Where's Sinend?" Cariadas cried, nearly panicked. The last few moments when they had halted to camp had been a blur.

"Sinend's fine, child," Sabrina said, her voice soothing. "She's sleeping. Right over there, see?"

Cariadas strained her eyes, catching sight of Sinend bundled in blankets. Elstar's arm was around the girl's shoulders to lift her up and give her something to drink. With a tired sigh, Sinend drank. Elstar tenderly laid Sinend down, tucking the blankets around her.

Elstar rose, then came to her husband, settling down next to him. He put his arm around her, and she laid her head on his shoulder.

"We have some Dewin here in our forest," Owein said quietly. "Others have passed on to them what they saw."

"The death-march," Dudod said, his voice harsh. "We saw the beginning. Before we got too far away. Did it go on?"

"It did. All the way across Rheged they marched the Y Dawnus they had caught."

"How many dead?" Elstar asked, with a shaking voice.

"Almost half. They took over two hundred people in that raid. And at least eighty of them died before reaching their destination. Lucky them."

"Where did they take them?"

"Eiodel."

At the sound of that name, Cariadas went cold. Eiodel. That black fortress built by Havgan, the Destroyer. Eiodel, the fortress of shadows that faced Cadair Idris. Eiodel, Havgan's defiance against the mountain of Idris.

"The next day they marched them to Llyn Mwygil and ferried them on to Afalon."

"And my da?" Elstar asked hesitantly. "Is he alive?" Her tone was uncertain, as though not knowing what to really hope for.

"Anieron was alive by the time they got to Eiodel. I do not know if he still is. He was not among those taken to Afalon. Of that we are sure."

Slowly Cynfar, tears spilling down his young face, pulled something from his tunic. It glittered in his hands like a piece of sky and moonlight come to earth.

"The Master Bard's torque," Cariadas said in awe. "How did you get that?"

"Granda gave it to me," the boy said, his voice shaking. "He took it from his neck and handed it to me, as we were going down the tunnel at Allt Llwyd. He Wind-Spoke to me alone and said I should give this to my da. He said da was the Master Bard now." Cynfar held the torque out to his father. But Elidyr did not move to take it.

"No," Elidyr whispered. "It is not for me. Not yet. Anieron may be alive. We don't know."

"Alive or not," Dudod said harshly, "he cannot be the Master Bard anymore. He is not free. Take it, my son. You are the heir."

"No," Elidyr said stubbornly. "No."

"Husband," Elstar said her voice soft. "The task has passed on. Our network is broken, scattered. The children, our hope for the future, have been taken. You and I, the Master Bard and the Ardewin, we must rebuild what has been lost. Dudod is right. My da is no longer the Master Bard. You are."

Cariadas, tears spilling down her face, wept helplessly and soundlessly. Wept for Anieron, and all that had been lost with him. Wept, even more, for the look on Elidyr's face. Wept to see Elidyr's hand reach out, shaking, to touch the necklace, then hesitantly take it from his son. Wept to see Elidyr clasp it around his neck, and finger the torque as tears streamed down his drawn face.

Wept to see Dudod close his eyes and look away.

"So," Owein said quietly. "Anieron is in Eiodel, in the hands of the Warleader. How long, think you, before he talks?"

"Never," Cariadas said fiercely. "Never."

"I mean no insult. But my own sister, a lady of pride and courage, at last gave the enemy the words they longed to hear. In the end, they always do."

"My brother will never speak," Dudod said wearily.

"How can you be so sure?" Elstar asked in a voice full of tears.

"Didn't you see what he did as he ran?"

"What do you mean?" Cariadas asked fearfully. She had not seen. She hadn't been able to bear to watch as they captured him.

Dudod shook his head. "He will never speak. Never. Never sing, never tell another story, never lead another Alban Awyr, and never praise Taran with his honeyed words. Never again."

"Oh, gods, no! Dudod, he didn't! He couldn't have!" Elstar's horror spilled from her, snaking through the hearts of those who sat there, twining through their souls, leaving cold terror behind.

"He did. He cut his tongue out as he ran. He will never speak.

Unless he Speaks to us on the Wind."

The night waited in silence, broken only by the sounds of the crackling fire and Elstar's sobs. Cariadas, too stunned to cry, sat still as a stone, barely breathing. Anieron had done that to himself. He had sacrificed his beautiful voice, his chanted poems, his songs, his very being. Sacrificed it all so that they would live.

He must have known what was coming. He must have sensed it, somehow. Why else would he have given his torque to Cynfar before leaving Allt Llwyd? Anieron's last song had been sung. His voice was now stilled. How could he bear it? How could she? What would become of them all now?

NO!

The cry rang through the clearing, shattering the night, darting through the sky over Kymru, splintering the cold stars overhead.

NO!

They leapt to their feet, all of them, the warriors with their weapons ready, looking around wildly for the source of that hopeless cry.

"Who—" Cariadas began.

"Anieron. His Mind-Shout." Of them all, Dudod had not risen. "Oh, my brother," he whispered. "What are they doing to you?"

NO! NO! N—

Then all was silent.

Chapter 11

Eiodel, Gwytheryn and Caer Siddi,
Kingdom of Prydyn, Kymru
Eiddew Mis, 499

Gwaithdydd, Tywyllu Wythnos—evening

He woke up reluctantly, fighting to stay within his last attempt to forget.

Something was pulling him away from his dreams, forcing him to wake. But the dreams! They were so sweet, so pure. In them he was unfettered, running free beneath the sun, the wind blowing in his silvery hair, water playing and laughing as it wandered through the meadow, the earth at his feet sprouting rich colors. He darted through the fields as the breeze drew gentle patterns in the tall grass. And at last, at long last, he understood the meaning of those shapes born of air. He knew—at last, he knew.

Until he woke to darkness. And the knowledge was lost to him, slipping away from him along with the dream's sweetness.

"Anieron, Anieron, is it you?" That voice, remembered from some distant time, from some distant life, pulled at him until he truly woke and knew where he was—trapped in this dank, dark cell in the very bowels of Eiodel, the dark fortress of the Golden Man.

He wanted to call out to the owner of that voice. To tell the man something, anything that would help ease the fear he heard in the other's tone. But he could not speak. For he had cut his tongue out to save the others, to prevent himself from breaking. And to taunt the Golden Man with the useless prize gained.

Memories of the death-march crowded over him, overwhelming him with grief as the tears ran down his face. So many had died just in those two weeks of marching here to Gwytheryn. So many little children there had been, now dead. So many of the teachers, men and women he had known for years, some of whom had even guided his first steps.

There had been so many guards—too many for the Bards and Dewin to attempt escape, even if they hadn't been drugged with hawthorn. And the guards had been too many to allow the Cerddorian to rescue them. They would only have lost their lives, too.

The marchers had been given only drugged water, and even that in small supply. At night they had lain on the rough ground, and the nights were cold. Weakened by hunger, by exposure, the very old and the very young had died.

The Kymri had tried to help. Crowds of villagers tried to feed and soothe the captives marching by. But the guards had threatened and—in a few cases—killed those who offered aid. And so, after the first few times, the Y Dawnus had warned them off, telling their would-be rescuers to leave them to their fate, telling them not to lose their lives for this, but to save their lives for a greater task. And the people had obeyed.

"Anieron, is that you? Speak to me!"

He had it now. That was Cian's voice. Cian, Bard to King Rhoram, had been captured along with one of the testing devices. He Wind-Spoke, the only means of communication left to him now.

Cian, boyo, are you all right?

No answer. Worse still, the thought that had arrowed toward Cian seemed to bounce off again, unheard. It was like trying to speak to a foreigner in a language never learned.

He dragged himself up from the filthy straw. Blinking in the dim light of the few torches set outside the bars, he squatted on all fours, waiting out the dizziness that movement brought. A clanking sound followed his movement. Surprised, he looked down, only to discover that his hands and feet were chained.

What, he thought incoherently, was the point of that? He could not get out of here, chains or no chains. Then he understood. It was a symbol, something meant to shame him, meant to make him understand how hopeless the situation was.

But they hadn't needed to do that. He had known it already. Somehow, he had known long ago that he would not be able to see this thing through. He had known he would never see Arthur ap Uthyr sit on the High King's throne in Cadair Idris. He had known that he would never see the Coranians flung back into the sea.

Yet he had never doubted these things would happen. And he did not doubt it now.

"Anieron!" Cian's voice was terrified. His words were slurred and raspy. Why didn't the man just Wind-Speak?

Anieron shuffled on all fours to the bars of his cell, looking toward the source of that voice. Cian's cell was just across a narrow hallway. The Bard was huddled against the bars, reaching through them as though to try to touch his master. His once-plentiful brown hair was scanty and lifeless. The patches of skin that showed through the dirt and sores were a dead white. He was thin, almost skeletal.

As Anieron looked at his friend, he understood why Cian had not Wind-Spoken. The Bard wore a dull gray collar around his thin neck—an enaid-dal, a soul-catcher. Cian's birthright, the gift of telepathy, had been stolen. His very soul had been chained.

And though Anieron's tongue was gone and he could not speak, he could still laugh. And so he did, a rusty, mournful sound. He laughed because the joke was so perfect. Because he, Anieron, could not speak mundane, ordinary words. And Cian could not hear Wind-Speech. They could share nothing with each other here in the pit of shadows and hopelessness. They could not comfort each other, reach out to one another in any way. And so he laughed. Because he knew the Warleader had expected despair. Even that, Anieron would not give to Havgan.

"Anieron?" Cian whispered doubtfully. "Won't you speak to me? They took it away—they took the gift. I cannot Wind-Speak to you.

Won't you even talk to me?"

Anieron stopped laughing, opened his mouth, and showed Cian that his tongue had been cut out.

"They did that to you?" Cian cried.

Anieron shook his head, then pointed to himself.

"You did it to yourself? Why?"

Anieron looked at Cian. And the look said it all.

"So you could not talk, if they broke you," Cian whispered.

Anieron nodded his head. He pointed to the cell around him, to himself, and lifted his brows in question.

"How long have you been here? They only brought you in last night."

He pointed to Cian's cell, to Cian himself.

"After they captured me, they brought me straight here to Havgan. He questioned me, but I told him nothing. They asked and asked and asked where Rhoram and his people had gone. But I would not tell. But—but it was so strange, Anieron. Though I don't expect you to believe this, they never asked me the one question I was so sure they would ask. They never asked me where the headquarters of the Dewin and the Bards were. Never asked where the Master Bard and the Ardewin could be found. I've thought so much about that. I think I know why."

Anieron nodded. He thought he knew why now, too.

"Because they already knew," Cian whispered. "Someone had already told them I swear to you, Anieron, it was not I. They already knew. Believe me, please."

Anieron nodded, to show Cian that he was believed. And he was. Because now Anieron knew who had told them. And he wished with all his soul that he had listened to Gwydion when the Dreamer had spoken of Jonas ap Morgan. But he had been proud. Stubborn. And so many, oh, so many had paid for that. He didn't mind that he was suffering for it—it was only right. But that others had, that was on his head.

But now he understood something that must be told. The Y Dawnus who were still free must be warned about Jonas. Terrified, he now remembered where Jonas had been sent. The traitorous Bard had gone to Gwynedd, to the headquarters of the Cerddorian there. He had been sent to Cai and Morrigan, to Mynydd Tawel, to betray his people again.

He must, he must get word out somehow. If only there was a Bard close enough to hear, then there was a chance. He closed his eyes, searching, but the clang of a heavy door opening and closing distracted him. He opened his eyes, squinting in the sudden flood of torchlight.

"Set the torches and leave us be," said a voice as soft as honey, as strong as iron, a voice that barely masked the scent of blood and darkness and tears.

The light glittered off the man's golden hair, lit his amber eyes, and picked out the bloodred rubies scattered across his golden tunic. Anieron knew him. Havgan. The Warleader. The Destroyer. The Golden Man. The Slayer of Kymru.

The Warleader gestured, and one of the guards opened Anieron's cell. Anieron stood. He would not meet the Warleader on his knees. There was something about the Golden Man that was so familiar. Something in the amber eyes. Something in the line of the neck, in the set of the jaw. A memory stirred, then subsided. What was it?

A second man followed Havgan into the cell. Anieron knew him instantly by the man's black robe; by his pale, white face; by the scar that twisted away from his empty eye socket. He held a sheaf of parchment and a quill in his ivory hands.

Oh, if only Anieron still had his tongue! What he wouldn't say to the wyrce-jaga. But he could still do some things. So he pointed to Sledda's eye socket and grinned. Sledda's face went tight and still. His remaining pale eye was full of malevolence.

"Ah," Havgan said smoothly. "You find that amusing? In truth, so do I. Your eagle did that—your Arderydd. They tell me that your people seem to think that it is a sign of our final defeat."

Anieron nodded.

"Now, Master Bard, you must listen to me. We can do this hard, or we can do this easy, but we will do this. I understand that you have cut your tongue out. A gesture of defiance, I believe. But that will gain you nothing. You will simply write down for us what we want to know. One way or another, you will do this."

Anieron shook his head.

"Of course, you do not believe me. But you really should. Now, here is what I want to know. First, where is Gwydion ap Awst? Second, where are the Four Treasures? And last, who is your upstart High King, and where is he hidden?"

Sledda thrust the parchment and quill into Anieron's shackled hands.

"Master Bard, you must understand. We will know these things from you," the Golden Man said. "We will. And so I ask you again, and you will write your answer."

Anieron's eyes darted from Sledda to Havgan, from black to gold, from wyrce-jaga to Warleader. At last he scratched something on the parchment and held it up for the men to read.

"'I will tell you nothing,'" Havgan read aloud. "But you will," he went on, smiling. "Because here is what will happen if you don't. We have taken the rest of your people to the island of Afalon, not five leagues from here. There they wait to know their fate. And I can assure you, their fate will go hard if you do not answer."

Slowly Anieron shook his head. He couldn't. Not even to save his people could he answer those questions.

"If you do not answer, they will die, one by one, speared through the belly, watching as their blood runs out onto the sands. Believe me in this, Master Bard."

Anieron shook his head again. He did believe the Warleader. But there was nothing he could do.

"I expected this, of course, from a man such as you. For the last two years, Anieron, Master Bard, you and your people have defied me. You and the network you created with your daughter, the Ardewin, have caused me much trouble. You and your clever orders to the Cerddorian have cost the lives of many of my men, and the possession of many riches. But now all that is over. And now you will tell us what we want to know. Because if you do, I will not put this thing onto your neck," Havgan said, pulling something out of his tunic and dangling it in the air.

All color drained from Anieron's face. It was an enaid-dal. If they put that on him, how could he live? How could he bear it?

But how could he do what they asked of him?

He bent his head over the parchment, scribbled a few words, and held it up for Havgan to see.

"'I will tell you nothing,'" Havgan read. "And I, Master Bard, will take everything."

Quick as a snake, Sledda darted behind Anieron, grasping his arms, tightening the chains so that Anieron could barely move. And Havgan was coming toward him, the enaid-dal clutched in his hands.

NO!

Anieron's Mind-Shout rang throughout Kymru. In Coed Coch, King Owein and his men sprang to their feet. King Rhoram and his folk in Haford Bryn and Prince Lludd and his people in Coed Ddu cried out. Queen Elen in her captivity in Dinmael began to weep. In the mountains of Eyri, Queen Morrigan leapt up, her heart in her throat.

NO!

In Rheged, Rhiannon, with her daughter, Gwen, reluctantly following, stopped short, her face drained of color, tears springing to her eyes. On the fringes of Eyri in Gwynedd, Gwydion halted and bowed his head in grief.

In Dinas Emrys, Myrrdin reached out as though to plead with the young boy who heard the cry with an unmoving countenance.

And in Coed Coch, Dudod whispered, "Oh, my brother, what are they doing to you?"

NO! NO! N—

And then it was over.

Anieron fell to his knees. The silence, oh, the silence in his mind! Gone, everything he was had gone. His soul had been stolen. Who was he now? Across the dark hallway he heard Cian weeping. Anieron looked up, shaking his matted hair from his eyes. The Warleader was smiling.

"So, witch, your powers are gone. You can have them back anytime you wish. Anytime. Just tell me what I want to know."

Hands shaking, Anieron reached out for the parchment and quill. Havgan smiled wider. "You see, Sledda? It's just a matter of applying the right pressure."

Anieron slowly scratched words into the parchment. As he offered the paper to the Warleader, he smiled. He smiled even wider as Havgan read it aloud in a voice full of rage.

"'I will tell you nothing.'"

Meirigdydd, Tywyllu Wythnos—midmorning

SIGERRIC PACED THE ramparts of the fortress. Back and forth, back and forth he walked, willing himself not to think of the torment that Sledda and Havgan between them would bring to the Master Bard, who continued to defy them.

Yesterday the old man had written one thing only: "I will tell you nothing." Today he had written the same, with hands swollen and bloody, with broken fingers. "I will tell you nothing."

But Sigerric could not think of that. He would not. He willed himself not to think of the torment Havgan had already brought to Kymru; this land once so rich and fair, now so muted and barren, as though the gods of the Kymri wept and grieved over the loss.

But that was no way to think. There was only One God, only Lytir, who had blessed their efforts here. For many of the Y Dawnus had been captured, their hiding places betrayed. The network that the Master Bard and the Ardewin had created was broken and shattered. Surely they could never rebuild it.

And the Master Smiths and their families had been dispatched to Caer Siddi. So cleverly had it been done that Sigerric was sure the enemy did not know where the Smiths were held. And they would stay in Caer Siddi to mine the lead there, to make hundreds and hundreds of those collars. The Archdruid had said they were called enaid-dals, soul-catchers. The name alone was enough to send a shudder up Sigerric's spine.

But he would not think of that, either. If he did, his heart would surely break with pity for these Kymric witches, those he should hate and despise.

He shook himself, turning to stare at Cadair Idris across the plain. The jewels on the Doors flashed defiantly in the sun, glittering whole and unharmed. For despite all that Havgan could do the Doors remained closed. And Sigerric, if he ever truly had, no longer believed that they would open.

A cloud of dust across the plain snared his attention. The sun flashed on bright pennants, on metal byrnies. He squinted, trying to make out the bright banner being carried before the group of riders. It was a banner of royal purple background, with three curved lines radiating from a golden center. One line was of amber, one was of emerald and one was of sapphire, glowing richly in the sun.

The Flyflot, Sigerric thought, the device of the Emperor of Corania! Had the Emperor himself come to Kymru? Surely not! Could it be Aesc, the Emperor's brother, one of Havgan's staunchest supporters? Or perhaps it was Aescwine, the Empress's brother, one of Havgan's deadliest enemies. What was happening in Corania that one of the royal family should come here?

The cavalcade drew closer. He made out fifty warriors, all wearing the Emperor's device, dressed in white beneath byrnies chased with silver. Horses piled with baggage followed more slowly.

Then he saw a slender figure riding in the midst of the warriors. The rider wore a cloak of purest white. The sun shone on radiant blond hair. And he knew who it was, and his heart leapt, even as he told himself not to be foolish. For if it were really she, her coming here boded no good for Havgan—and even less for Sigerric himself. But he could not still the wild joy in his heart at the sight of her.

Aelfwyn, Princess of Corania, heir to the Emperor, wife to Havgan, had come to Kymru. And in spite of himself, his wounded heart sang for joy.

He hurried down the steps, calling to a guard to bring Havgan, to give him the news that his wife had come.

"The Warleader is in the dungeon, my Lord," the warriors said respectfully. "You remember that he said he is not to be disturbed."

"Go to him and tell him. You will not be punished; you do so on my orders."

"Yes, Over-general," the warrior said, clearly relieved.

Sigerric hurried out the doors, flying down the steps. Not matter what happened after, he wanted to be the first to greet her. It would mean nothing to her, he knew. But it would mean everything to him.

He stood quietly at the bottom of the steps in the courtyard. The party rode through the open gate and halted. Swiftly he made his way through the warriors who guarded her. They knew him and fell back, bowing. He reached her horse and grasped the reins as he looked up at her.

The years had not changed her. Her golden hair still glistened. Her green eyes were still haughty, still cold, and still beautiful. Her pure, white skin was unmarred, despite the long and dusty journey.

Steorra Heofan, Star of Heaven, had come to earth, to Kymru, to pierce his heart, as she had done from the beginning.

"You are welcome here, Princess Aelfwyn. Most welcome."

"Am I?" she asked, her voice cool. "Then you may help me dismount."

Swallowing, he reached up his hands and grasped her waist. Her gown was white and unstained. It clung to her body in pristine folds, outlining the perfect breasts, the slender waist, and the curve of her hips. He set her down gently, but quickly, not allowing his hands to linger on her body.

She glanced up at him, something glistening in her green eyes. For a moment she stared at him, and Sigerric was convinced that, for the first time in her life, she actually saw him. And the scrutiny he had often wished for, he now dreaded. What did she see in his face? And what would she do with what she saw?

Slowly she smiled at him. It was the first smile he had ever seen on her lovely face. Her voice softened slightly. "Well, Sigerric? No words to greet an old friend?"

"You are neither, my Lady."

Her brows raised. "Neither?"

"Neither old, nor my friend. But you are my Lady, you who will one day be Empress of Corania. And I will serve you until the day I die."

"Serve my husband, you mean, Sigerric," she said lightly, but her eyes narrowed slightly, watching him closely.

He swallowed hard. "It's one and the same, isn't it?" Oh, and what a foolish thing to say. For, of course, it wasn't. And it never had been.

She smiled again, dazzling him. "We shall see. And where is my husband? Is he uninterested that I have come? Dismayed, perhaps?"

"I have sent a warrior to bring him," he temporized.

"And where is he?"

"He is in the dungeon. We have captured the Master Bard of Kymru. Havgan and Sledda were—interviewing him."

"Then the Master Bard, at least, must be glad of my arrival."

A flash of gold caught Sigerric's eye. Havgan, dressed in a golden tunic trimmed with rubies, stood at the top of the stairs. He eyed the warriors with disfavor, then caught sight of Aelfwyn and Sigerric. He came down the steps and made his way to them.

Aelfwyn gave Havgan her hands, then slowly, but only slightly, bent her knees. Havgan turned her hands over and kissed each palm. The slowness, the sultriness of the gesture caused Aelfwyn to flush and quickly draw her hands away. She took a deep breath, then said formally, "My Lord and husband. I greet you in the name of the Emperor and Empress of Corania. And I bring their blessings on your enterprise here."

"Money would be better," Havgan said in a carrying tone.

Havgan's warriors, who were slowly filling up the courtyard, smothered smiles. Aelfwyn's forced smile stayed on her exquisite face. How she did that, Sigerric did not know. "That, too, I have brought to you." She gestured toward the heavily laden packs on the backs of the tired horses.

Havgan's brow rose. "All this for me?"

"No," Aelfwyn said shortly. "Most of this is for me."

"What are you doing, Aelfwyn?"

"I have come to support my husband in his great undertaking. And I am prepared to stay some time, until your task here is complete."

Havgan's amber eyes narrowed. "Are you?" he said flatly.

"If I am unwelcome, my Lord, I will return home."

The tone was even, but anyone could hear the threat there. To send the Princess of Corania back home would be disastrous. The Emperor and Empress would be insulted. And then only the One God himself knew what would happen.

"But, of course, you are welcome here, wife," Havgan said. Suddenly he grinned, an unpleasant, wolfish grin. "I am between bed warmers at the moment."

Aelfwyn's smile froze, her eyes widening at the insult. Her warriors stiffened, drawing closer together around their Lady. Sigerric, his face flushed, took a step forward.

With a swift glance at Sigerric, Havgan went on. "But, of course, as we both recall, such a role is distasteful to you, wife. Therefore, you will have your own apartments, well furnished with the best Kymru has to offer, which is very fine, indeed. Woolen rugs and tapestries from Gwynedd. Delicate glass from Ederynion. Fine candles from Rheged. And the best wines from Prydyn. All these I will give to you. And we will talk. And you shall tell me of home. Of many, many things." He smiled gently.

And only because Sigerric was so close to her did he see her slight shudder. Havgan had seen it, too. "Come, my lady wife," he said, taking her hands and drawing her forward. "There is much to see here in Eiodel. My steward will show you the finest rooms, and you shall choose from them. Tonight we will dine alone, you and I."

Pretending to be happy at this threat, Aelfwyn smiled and nodded at the steward who appeared at Havgan's elbow. Without another word, Havgan turned away and walked through the gates of Eiodel. Sigerric, after a glance at Aelfwyn, followed. No need to ask where Havgan was going. Sigerric already knew.

He followed Havgan across the plain. The wind whipped in his ears, keening of something lost. The wild grasses blew dead and brown, flattened by the grieving winds. The lonely, shuttered hall of the High King rose from the plain, gray and lifeless.

Still following, Sigerric mounted the eight broken steps of Cadair

Idris and halted next to Havgan, staring at the closed Doors.

Without taking his eyes from the jeweled patterns, Havgan spoke. "She thinks to defeat me, somehow."

"Yes."

"We have hated each other from the beginning. That is unchanged."

"But what can she do?"

"God only knows. But she will think of something. She must be watched most carefully, Sigerric. This task I give to you."

"It would be best, Havgan, that someone else take this task."

"What, Sigerric? Still in love with my lady wife? And she so cold, so cruel, so hungry? She will eat your heart, my friend, if you let her."

"You have never even tried to come to terms with her."

"It would be useless. If you do not know that, then I truly pity you. For you do not know her at all."

Havgan was silent for a time, staring at the bright jewels that seemed to mock him. At last he spoke, his tone absent, musing. "Do you remember, Sigerric, what I have told you of the readings I had back home? What I said of the wyrd-galdra, and how each reading was the same?"

Sigerric nodded. Even now he felt a stir of terror. The fate-magic had surely marked Havgan.

"And each time, the card for the goddess, Holda, appeared. And always she reminded me of the Woman-on-the-Rocks, the woman in my dreams. The one who never turns to face me, who never comes to me, never speaks. Her hair is like honey; the lines of her body strain with longing to come to me. But she never does."

Sigerric said nothing. In Corania, and here in Kymru, Havgan had sought women with the same color of hair. He had made love to some, had raped others. And he had killed them all, strangling them to see their eyes as they died, searching for something no one understood—least of all Havgan himself.

Havgan went on. "And do you remember what I told you of the night on Mount Baden, the place in Mierce where the Wild Hunt rides? And how Holda herself spoke to me, and told me she would see me again in Kymru?"

"I remember, Havgan."

"Where is she?" Havgan asked, his voice filled with longing. "Where is she? When the Treasures are in my hands, when these Doors open for me, when Gwydion and Rhiannon lie dead at my feet, it will mean nothing if she is not there. Where is she?"

Sigerric, unable to speak, only shook his head. Was there anyone but he who knew Havgan's inner torments? Anyone but he who did what he could to keep Havgan's soul from becoming swamped in darkness and tears? "Maybe she will come to you, Havgan. Maybe she will," he said at last, pity in his voice.

"She is here, in Kymru. I feel her. I see her in my dreams. She is here, somewhere."

"What has this to do with Aelfwyn?"

"With Aelfwyn?" Havgan asked, jarred from his dark reverie. "Nothing, I suppose. Nothing, except the sight of her reminds me that I have been cheated, saddled with a woman whose every breath hisses of her hatred."

"Cheated?" Sigerric cried, outraged. "Cheated because you have won her hand, and with it the right to rule Corania someday? Cheated because you and you alone can touch her, hold her? You call that being cheated?"

Havgan turned from the Doors, his amber eyes gleaming. "This is a woman who will not be held, my friend. And you are speaking of a woman who loathes my very touch. Which makes it all the more interesting to speculate what is so important that she would bring that horror upon herself again. And she will. Make no mistake about that." Havgan grinned. "Think on that, Sigerric, as you are thinking of all the things I have done that you despise. Think on that as you are thinking of the lies you told the Bard, Jonas, who betrayed his people. Think on that as you think of the Y Dawnus who died on the death-march. Think on that as you think of the wyrce-jaga combing Kymru for witches. Think on that as you pity the Master Bard, lying barely alive in my dungeon."

"Why do you wish me to hate you?" Sigerric whispered. "Why?"

But Havgan did not answer.

THE OLD MAN moved silently through the forest, carefully cutting to the western portion of the island, the place where the prisoners were being held. Today he was determined to find out the truth of what was happening here.

He had seen them when they first arrived just over a week ago and had recognized them instantly. Hadn't he once been a ruler himself? How, then, could he not know the Master Smiths of Kymru?

He had recognized Greid, the Master Smith of Gwynedd, first. The man's powerful shoulders were draped in chains, and his seamed face, scarred by the heat of the forge, was a mask of hopelessness. He had seen Siwan, Master Smith of Prydyn, and her children, and her children's children. He had recognized Llyenog, Master Smith of Rheged, and seen the fire in the man's eyes. He had seen Efrei, Master Smith of Ederynion, and the helplessness as the man gazed on his family.

He recalled his shock when he had first laid eyes on them. Fifteen boats from the mainland had come, docking on Caer Siddi, the small island off the coast of Prydyn, a place where no one ever came—no one except the old man himself, and he had come here to live in solitude over twenty years ago. And from these boats came the Master Smiths and their families—and a score of Coranian warriors.

The old man had watched that day, hidden in the underbrush, moving silently as he had taught himself to do long, long ago. And he had returned to the eastern shores where he had made his home, thoughtful.

Isolated as he was, he knew what had happened in Kymru. Once a year he took a boat to the mainland, a journey of half a day. There he would trade the furs he had cured for simple necessities—flour, salt, ground meal. His needs were few. And his desires were dead. Two years ago, he had gone to the mainland, as usual, and had learned the meaning of the smoke he had seen hanging like a pall over Prydyn. The Coranians had come, and had taken everything.

He had learned that his nephew, King Rhoram of Prydyn, had been wounded and, though uncaptured, was not expected to live. He had learned that his daughter, Ellirri, Queen of Rheged, and her husband, Urien, were dead. He had learned that his son, Madoc, had betrayed King Uthyr and was now the King of Gwynedd. And he had thought, then, that the twinge he felt at that last news might have been shame. But it had been so long since he had allowed himself to feel anything that he was not sure. He had returned to his island, with his necessities, and had lived calmly and quietly for another year, his mind carefully blank.

And then he had returned again the next year. He had learned that his grandson, Owein of Rheged, had gathered to him other surviving warriors and was still fighting the enemy. He had learned that his nephew, Rhoram, had lived, and was doing the same, harassing the enemy all he could. He had learned that his granddaughter, Tangwen of Gwynedd, could barely lift her head for shame of her father, Madoc, and assisted the Cerddorian as much as she was able. And he thought that the twinge he felt at that news might have been pride.

Again he had returned to his island. But then he had begun to think. And one night he had come out of his cave and stared at the shore, called by he knew not what. The waves rolled onto the sands, rimmed in silver by the moonlight. And, suddenly, his eyes had filled with tears, and he had wept for the first time in twenty-three years. He had wept for the deaths of his daughter, Ellirri, and her husband, a man who had loved her and made her happy. He had wept for the death of his grandson, Prince Elphin, who had hardly begun to live before he had died. He had even—and, oh, was it healing at last?—wept bitterly over the death of King Uthyr, the son of the man Rhodri hated more than any on this earth—the son of Awst and of Rhodri's own wife, Queen Rathtyen of Gwynedd.

The day Rathtyen died—for she would not eat after she heard what had happened to Awst—King Rhodri thought he had died, too. For he had loved his wife beyond all else. And she had not loved him as he had wished. It was then that he first repeated the triad he had

learned long ago, from his Bard, Dudod:
Three things that are worse than sorrow;
To want to die, and to die not;
To try to please, and to please not;
To wait for someone who comes not.

Had that not been the story of his life contained in that poem? Had that not been the story of his marriage? And that triad had become his litany, the only song left in his bitter, tired heart.

But on the night he had stared at the sea and begun to grieve—yes, even for that son of Awst—he had finally understood that Rathtyen had loved him as much as she could. There had been room in her generous heart to love both men who had fathered her children. And he had not seen it. He had only seen that she did not love him enough.

After twenty-three years, something was coming alive again, something he thought was dead and gone forever. And he had begun to feel. To feel pride, that some of his family had lived and fought on. To feel shame, that his son had betrayed Kymru. He had never thought to feel again. And he did not know what to do with these new feelings. And so he had waited, wondering what would come to him, what turn of the Wheel would show him the path to take.

And now he had his answer. For now the prisoners had come. And he knew he was being called again to the Wheel, called to take his place there, called back to life.

And so he stepped quietly today, coming to the fringes of the primitive camp where, after a long day of mining lead, the prisoners were allowed to rest before an open campfire. The perimeter of the camp was patrolled, but the guards were slack, having no reason to expect trouble. It was an easy matter to creep close enough to hear the Smiths talking among themselves.

It was Greid's daughter who spoke first. As her father sat wearily on the ground, she said, "Da, this must stop. You cannot do this."

"I must, child," Greid said tiredly. "Or don't you truly understand?"

"I understand, Da. You know I do. And it is because of that I am saying this. We all," she said, flinging her hand out to the other families huddled there, "we all know what I am saying. Better we should die, than you should do this thing anymore."

Greid slowly raised his grizzled head, his gray eyes piercing his daughter's drawn face. "Say you so?" he asked quietly. "Then you still do not understand. Do you think they would kill us quietly? Do you not understand the torment they would put you through? And the little ones," he went on softly, stroking the golden hair of his tiny granddaughter, a child not five years of age, who nestled on his lap. "Do you think they would be tender with them? They would not kill quickly They would make us watch those we loved suffer under their tormenting hands. No, you do not know what you say."

Greid's daughter paled, and her own hands trembled as they stroked her child's bright hair. "But, Da," she whispered, "what you make here. You know what it does."

"Yes, child. So I do. Do you think it is an easy thing to make enaid-dals and know that the necks they are bound for belong to some of our dearest friends? Do you think that easy?"

"No, Da," she whispered. And she laid her head on her father's broad shoulders, tears streaming down her white face.

"Da, perhaps the Cerddorian will come for us, will rescue us," she said, faint hope in her voice.

"Child, they do not know where we are."

"You can't know that!"

"I do know that Or didn't you understand why we traveled at night and in small groups? Didn't you understand that we were hidden from our friends' eyes? There will be no rescue. Not for us. And so we must make these soul-catchers, and only beg the gods for an easier death on the next turn of the Wheel."

Rhodri, who had first thought to speak to Greid, drew back silently. No need to take that risk now. He knew all he needed to know.

Silently he made his sure-footed way back to his cave. He knew whom he must find now—his old Bard, Dudod. He knew it would not be easy. Even in happier times, Dudod had always been on the move. But Rhodri would find him. He would find him and tell him where the Smiths were held, and how they waited for rescue.

Even more importantly, Rhodri knew he had another task concerning Madoc, his son. It was a father's duty to correct a child who had gone wrong.

As he thought this, he drew his knife and examined it, as it lay gleaming in his palm. It was a father's duty, indeed.

Chapter 12

Haford Bryn, Kingdom of Prydyn, and Dinas Emrys
Kingdom of Gwynedd, Kymru
Eiddew Mis, 499

Meirigdydd Tywyllu Wythnos—morning

The hills of Haford Bryn were brown and lifeless. Even the waters of the River Fryn, which wound slowly through the hills, were dull and gray. Rhiannon halted her mount, stooping slightly in the saddle, scanning the ground. No, there was nothing. She had not expected tracks—Rhoram and Achren were too good for that. But she scanned the ground nonetheless. If she found some sign of Rhoram's Cerddorian, it would at least be good for an opening gambit in the upcoming conversation—a conversation she suspected would be one of the most difficult of her life.

The real question was, which way would Rhoram jump? Would he support her request or stand neutral? Would he openly oppose her? Or, worse still, make a counteroffer that she must, oh, she must, refuse?

After all, she thought hesitantly, almost unwilling to even acknowledge these thoughts, after all, Rhoram's wife had deserted him. In the eyes of the Kymri, he was now unmarried. What would he do now? More to the point, what would she do?

Unbidden, Gwydion's face rose in her mind, the way he had been at the Alban Awyr celebration over two weeks ago: his silvery eyes, alight with the laughter she seldom saw, his stern mouth relaxed in a smile that had caught her unaware, his strong arms supporting her in dance after dance.

She shrugged irritably. What did it matter? What did either of these men—Rhoram and Gwydion, the two who had a hold on her heart—matter? She knew what she must do. She herself had seen the Wild Hunt, had endured the amethyst gaze of the goddess Cerridwen, the topaz stare of the god Cerrunnos, and had heard them name her one of those entrusted with the task of seeking the Treasures. The Stone of Water would be her Treasure to find. And it was her duty now to take her daughter, Gwenhwyfar, away from Haford Bryn and set the girl to her chosen task—to find the Cauldron of Earth. For that was what had been sung in the Song of the Caers. And that was what must be.

With Rhoram's help or without it, she would take her daughter from here and go. It would, of course, be so much easier if he helped. But she would not count on it. It had been many years since she had counted on a man to do anything. Once again she scanned the ground for tracks and examined the sky for telltale signs of smoke. She knew they were around here somewhere. She knew it.

"There's nothing for you to see."

The voice, long expected, did not startle her. She straightened in the saddle and turned to face the speaker with a smile. "I know," she said. "But I had to look. To be sure."

"Be sure," Achren, Rhoram's Captain, said, grinning, as she jumped from the boughs of the tree to the ground. "When I'm in charge, things are done right." Achren was dressed in black riding leathers. Her hair was braided and bound closely to her head. Her dark eyes brimmed with the welcome Rhiannon had hoped for.

Rhiannon jumped from her horse and embraced Achren. "How are they all? It is well here?"

"As well as can be expected. We lost no one in the move from Ogaf Greu. The enemy does not know where we are. But there are other things that are very ill, indeed."

"I know," Rhiannon said quietly, turning to take the reins of her horse. "Allt Llwyd was taken. The Y Dawnus are even now being death-marched across Rheged. They die. And we cannot stop it."

"No," Achren agreed soberly. "We cannot stop it. Not today. But soon, perhaps?"

Rhiannon turned, responding to Achren's underlying question. "Yes. Our vengeance begins now."

"How?"

"Gwen is to come with me. We will meet the Dreamer and one other in Ederynion. And the four of us go to claim the Treasures." She stopped and searched her friend's face. "You are pale, Achren. Are you well?"

"Well?" Achren repeated as she fell in step beside Rhiannon, motioning the way forward. Achren shrugged. "Well enough. Considering what I did to Cian."

"What you did?" Rhiannon exclaimed, shocked. "You mean what the Druid, Ellywen, did. What the enemy did. You are not to blame."

"He was in my charge," Achren said quietly. "And he was captured, and taken to Eiodel. He was my responsibility. Nothing can change that."

"Achren—"

"Of course, when I returned to Haford Bryn, I told Rhoram that I resigned my post. And he—so clever—he said that he would accept the resignation only if the Master Bard agreed, since Cian belonged to him. And the Master Bard . . ."

"Of course, Anieron would never have condemned you for what happened."

"The Master Bard said that I was, indeed, condemned—to continue to serve Rhoram." Achren's lips quirked slightly. "He said it was a fate almost worse than death, to serve such a foolish master. And Rhoram played up his outrage to the hilt. And so they all laughed, and treated it as forgotten. But I do not and never will."

"There is nothing for it, really, than to set yourself the task to hunt down Ellywen," Rhiannon said, "for her part in the betrayal of Cian."

"Yes. You do understand, don't you?"

"I do."

"Come, then. The others are waiting."

THEY FOLLOWED THE river for some leagues, as the land became wilder, the hills sharpening into cliffs, shale crunching beneath their leather boots. Scrubby bush grew on the banks, offering an occasional handhold. The way was not difficult at first, and Rhiannon's horse followed easily. Then Achren stopped, gesturing to a shadow in the rocks.

"Leave the horse here. He cannot follow from this point." Achren gave a shrill whistle, and a warrior came into sight, seeming to spring from the very stones. Achren handed the reins to the man, who took the animal, leading him over the banks and out of sight.

"We keep all the horses here. From here on in, we climb."

Rhiannon nodded, searching the surrounding cliffs. Another whistle from Achren, and a rope ladder clattered down the face of the cliff. "Hard to get into, I see," Rhiannon said briefly. "Harder still to get out?"

"Not at all," Achren replied. "There are many other trails. Rhoram would never have us hole up in a place difficult to get out of. But this is the quickest way. You first. Stop at the first ledge."

Rhiannon began to climb. As she came to the first ledge, she stepped off the ladder. Turning around, she saw the valley they had come through, her gaze following the river that twined through it. Her eyes, sharp as they were, could detect no sign of movement from the way they came.

"Very good, Achren. I see no one."

Achren grinned. "But they are there, just the same, guarding."

"I believe you."

They set off down the narrow ledge until they came to a passageway bound on either side by heavy boulders. "Welcome, Rhiannon ur Hefeydd, to Haford Bryn," Achren said, gesturing her to go first.

Rhiannon slipped between the rocks, then almost gasped. Here, in this hidden place, was a small, narrow canyon, carpeted with rich moss and grass, nestled between the forbidding cliffs. Hundreds of warriors gathered here, some drilling with bow and arrow, some practicing with dagger and spear. Snug shelters built of wood and stone were huddled against the cliff faces. Children kept close watch on herds of sheep and cows that nibbled at the scrub brush that studded the sides of the valley.

People began to turn, eyeing them as they stood at the entrance to the canyon. A warrior in the midst of those practicing with spears kept her back to the two women after one quick glance, ignoring their presence. Rhiannon had spotted her right away. She would always know her own daughter.

"Come," Achren said, "Rhoram is waiting for you."

She followed Achren down the path into the camp. One warrior, shooting arrows at a target, looked up at them, then crowed in delight. He threw down his bow and bounded up to them, catching Rhiannon up in an exuberant embrace.

"Geriant!" Rhiannon laughed. "Put me down!"

Prince Geriant, Rhoram's son, grinned down at her, setting her gently on the ground. "You are most welcome here! You are well?"

"I was," she said dryly, straightening her tunic, pretending to glare at him. "Is this how you always greet your elders?"

"And my betters," he laughed.

Before she could reply, a young woman hurled herself into Rhiannon's arms. "Sanon," Rhiannon said gently, holding the girl tightly. "Sanon."

Rhoram's daughter clung to her. Gently Rhiannon stepped back, cradling Sanon's face in her hands. So thin! And so pale. Her face, once so sweetly smooth, was sharpened into harsh angles by grief and loss. Her dark eyes were shadowed with sleeplessness. Sanon's golden hair, which spilled down her back, was the only part of her that seemed to have life.

"Sanon, my dear," she began, not knowing quite what to say.

"I know," Sanon said, trying to smile. "I don't look well."

Rhiannon knew that Sanon had been grief-stricken over the death of her betrothed, Elphin of Rheged, two years ago. But she had not, until this moment, truly understood what Elphin's death had done to the Princess of Prydyn. And, knowing this, Rhiannon's need for vengeance on the enemy grew ever hotter.

"I'm so sorry, Sanon," she said quietly, knowing it should be spoken of, acknowledged. "You loved Elphin very much, didn't you?"

"More than life," Sanon whispered. "And don't you tell me that the wound will heal. I think now it never will."

"Not if you don't wish it to," Rhiannon said firmly. "And before you get angry, remember that I know all about nursing old wounds."

Before Sanon could reply, the glint of golden hair caught Rhiannon's eye. She turned to face Rhoram.

The King of Prydyn had changed in the past few years since his wounding in the invasion. Rhoram's face was sharper, scored with lines of pain. But his sapphire blue eyes were the same. And his smile was just as warm. And Rhiannon, listening to the beat of her own heart as she gazed at him, understood that what had been between them was gone now. Gone, to be replaced by tender memories, by the warmth of friendship. When had that happened? she wondered briefly. At what point in the past four years had she truly, finally, let him go? And how was it she had not even known until this moment?

She reached out her arms and hugged him close, no longer afraid to touch him, knowing that the fire between them was gone, finding comfort in that. As he hugged her back, she felt his body relax, the tension gone from him, also. She released him and grinned up at him, to find him smiling.

"Rhiannon ur Hefeydd," Rhoram said laughter in his voice. "So kind of you to drop by."

"So it is," she agreed, smiling. "Have you some time to talk to me? The matter is urgent."

"I'll try to squeeze you in somehow."

"Gwen?"

"She is well. But she's—"

"Refusing to talk to me," Rhiannon finished. "I saw her. May I talk to you privately? Unfortunately, I haven't much time."

"You must leave today?"

"Yes. And not alone."

"Ah." He gestured for Geriant and Sanon to withdraw. She hugged them both and promised to speak to them again before she left. As Achren turned to go, Rhiannon grabbed her arm.

"No. I must speak with you, also." The three of them moved to one side of the canyon. At Rhoram's gesture, she sat on one of the nearby rocks and began. "The Dreamer has had the dream at last."

"It begins, then, our vengeance," Rhoram said eagerly.

"It does. We have found the clues to the Treasures. And we know the four who are destined to search for them. Gwydion, myself, one other whom I may not name—"

"The High King?" Achren guessed.

"Yes. If we can make him so. And Gwen."

"Mmm," Rhoram said, musing. "So you have come for her."

"I have. And we must be gone from here within the hour. We go to Ederynion, to begin the search."

"Then Gwen must go," Rhoram said firmly.

Rhiannon nodded. "I know she will not want to—"

"That is an understatement. But go, she will. You have come for her. And so she is no longer welcome here. Achren?"

It was when Rhoram turned to Achren that Rhiannon saw the truth. It was there in the way he looked at his Captain, there in the glitter in the depths of his sapphire eyes, there for anyone to see. Anyone, Rhiannon thought, except Achren herself, who appeared to see nothing.

At Rhoram's question, Achren rose and strode purposefully toward a group of warriors who had resumed their practicing with spear and shield.

After Achren was out of earshot, Rhiannon turned to Rhoram, her brows raised.

Rhoram returned her look, not even bothering to pretend that he didn't understand. "She has no idea, of course," he said ruefully. "And even if she did, she would, no doubt, not believe me."

"Is that what stops you?"

"That and the thought that she may very well carve my guts out and wear them for garters."

"Chicken," she said, grinning, as her eyes followed Achren's movements.

At Achren's sharp command, the warriors had halted their practice. Another command, and Gwen stepped up to Achren, standing stiffly at attention. Achren gestured over to Rhoram and Rhiannon, and Gwen shook her head. But no warrior ever successfully defied Achren. She snapped another command, then turned to go. Gwen hesitated briefly, then followed.

As Gwen came up to her, Rhiannon's eyes gazed hungrily at her daughter. It had been four years since she had last seen Gwen. Her daughter had grown, and they were almost of a height, now. Gwen's long, golden hair was braided and wound about her head, held in place by a band of blue. Her tunic, trousers, and boots were scuffed brown leather. Her blue eyes glittered above high cheekbones. She was beautiful. For the first time, Rhiannon wondered what young Arthur ap Uthyr would think of her daughter.

Gwen had not moved, had not even acknowledged Rhiannon's presence. But Rhiannon had been prepared for this. She rose to her feet, facing Gwen squarely.

"Hello, daughter," she said quietly, unsmiling.

Gwen's frosty blue eyes flickered over to her, hardened, looked away.

"Greet your mam," Rhoram said sharply, rising to his feet.

Gwen turned away, then found her way blocked by Achren. She turned back. "Greetings, Mam," Gwen said quickly, but without inflection.

"You are to come with me," Rhiannon said. No use in trying to be gentle and persuasive with this stubborn child.

"I will not!"

"You will. You have been named by the Dreamer, named by a song of Taliesin, named by the Wild Hunt itself. You have been named as one who will join in the task to find the Treasures, to stand at the Doors of Cadair Idris and enter there, to witness the making of a High King, and to drive the enemy from this land."

"I will not go."

"You have been named. You will."

"Da," Gwen pleaded, turning to Rhoram.

"One way or another, Gwenhwyfar, you leave here today," he said sternly. "You will either leave with your mam, or go your own way."

"Da!" Gwen cried. "You would leave me? You also?"

"You are named, child. There are no bargains to be made with that."

"Then I will go," Gwen said, turning to Rhiannon, her eyes flashing. "But not with you!"

"Your hatred makes you foolish," Achren said, her tone cold and hard. "Your place on the Wheel must be taken. Or we will all die as captives."

A cry from above made them all look up. Overhead, an eagle circled, screaming with defiance. It swooped over the camp, and the warriors ducked, not one even reaching for their weapons. For they knew what this was that had come to them.

Arderydd, the High Eagle, the sign of the High King to come, lighted on the rocks in front of Gwen. He fixed the girl with cold, gray eyes. Once again, he shrieked, spanning his wings and arching his proud neck as though to dart at Gwen. Gwen flinched, and turned to run. But Achren held her, forcing her to face the eagle.

Then, from far away, the sound of a hunting horn came to their ears. A flicker of movement at the top of the canyon caught everyone's gaze. Two riders were there on the rim. One rode a horse of pure white, and antlers gleamed from his forehead. The other rode a horse of jet-black, her shadowy hair streaming out behind her. The rider of the white horse brought a horn to his lips and blew. At the sound, the eagle shrieked again, never taking his cold eyes off of Gwen.

"Answer, Gwenhwyfar ur Rhoram," Rhiannon said quietly. "And know truly whom you answer to."

Gwen's eyes, wide and shocked, flickered from the riders to the eagle.

"The Hunt waits for your answer," Rhoram said, unmoving.

Gwen slipped from Achren's hold, and took a step toward the eagle. Then she sank to her knees and bowed her head. The bird cried out in triumph, then sprang up into the sky. It flew to the two riders, lighting on the arm of the dark-haired woman. The woman raised a thin, white arm in salute. The man nodded his antlered head. Then they flickered, topaz and amethyst, and vanished, the sound of the hunting horn still borne on the wings of the wind.

Meirwdydd, Tywyllu Wythnos—evening

GWYDION SAT ON his horse, staring at the closed door of the tiny hut. Night had gathered and descended, cloaking the village of Dinas Emrys in shadow. The village was quiet, only the occasional barking of a dog disturbing the stillness. Overhead, the cold light of the stars had begun to shine. It was tywyllu, the week of the new moon, and not even the barest sliver of the crescent could be seen in the sky tonight. The surrounding mountains could be seen only as sharp, dark outlines against the starry sky.

He dismounted, and even that effort seemed too much, for the journey had not been easy and his mind was in turmoil. His tunic and trousers were dusty and stained with leagues of travel. He had taken side roads where possible, sleeping in the brush during the day, traveling by the light of the moon when he could, knowing he was being sought relentlessly by Havgan's forces. And knowing those he loved were in danger. It had taken every ounce of his will to keep from turning back, to keep from seeking his daughter in the aftermath of the invasion of Allt Llwyd. Only the knowledge that he would be too late to prevent harm to her had kept him on his way to Dinas Emrys.

Gwydion leaned against his horse, too tired to move. Too tired to knock and enter the small hut. Too tired, in truth, to begin the battle that waited beyond the door.

Grief welled up within him. Grief for Anieron and for what Havgan must have done to wring that Mind-Shout from the Master Bard. Grief for his daughter, for he did not even know if Cariadas was alive. The network was broken, and news was scanty. And hundreds of Y Dawnus had been death-marched across Rheged, almost half of them dying on the way. The old, the small children, those too weak to endure the rough treatment, had laid their heads on the breast of Modron, the Mother, and died.

And Rhiannon—where was she? Had she made it safely to Haford Bryn? Was she even now on her way to Ederynion with Gwenhwyfar in tow, or had she, too, been taken by the enemy? If she died, would he even wish to live?

He made no move, listening to the stillness, waiting to discover the answer that was surely written on the cold stars that rode the wind tonight. Nothing. No sound. Nothing. It was over. Too late to continue this now hopeless quest. Too late.

And then he heard it, coming from some unimaginably distant place—the faint sound of a hunting horn. And at that moment, the door opened, spilling firelight and warmth over Gwydion's tired face.

"Nephew," Myrddin said, his voice tired. "Gwydion. At last you have come."

Gwydion moved forward, stumbling through the doorway, gripping Myrddin's arm. "Did you hear it?" he demanded. "Did you?"

Myrddin nodded. "I heard the horn. It is not over. It is just beginning. Arthur," he went on, speaking over his shoulder, "stable Gwydion's horse."

The boy pushed past Gwydion, averting his face, going out the door into the cold night. Myrddin, half-supporting Gwydion, settled him onto the bench before the fire.

"Cariadas?" Myrddin asked quietly. "Rhiannon?"

"I don't know," Gwydion whispered. "I don't know. You—you heard the Shout a few days ago from Anieron?"

"All of Kymru heard his Shout," Myrddin replied, thrusting a cup of warm ale into Gwydion's hands.

"Did Arthur?"

"Yes."

"Do you think it will matter?"

Myrddin did not reply, turning away to stir a pot bubbling over the fire. "I might have known you would come here at supper time."

Gwydion tried to smile, but the effort was too great. The back door of the hut slammed, and Arthur stalked back into the room. Gwydion lowered the cup, taking a long look at his nephew.

The boy was now almost a man. Sixteen years old, he would be seventeen next month. His shoulder-length auburn hair was tied with a leather thong at the base of his neck. His dark eyes avoided Gwydion's gaze. He was slender, but he did not move with the awkwardness expected in boys, but rather with the grace of a hunted thing that knows it must move quietly to survive. Gwydion saw Arthur's mother, Ygraine, clearly in the shade of the hair, in the shape and color of the eyes. He searched for some sign of Arthur's father, of Uthyr, of the brother whom Gwydion had loved so dearly, and missed so fiercely. He saw it in the shape of the face, in the set of the jaw. The firelight illuminated a clear, white line that ran down the boy's cheek.

"Where did you get that scar?" Gwydion asked, breaking the silence.

"From Arderydd," Arthur spat. "From the eagle."

"And you learned nothing from that, I see," Gwydion replied tiredly. He turned to Myrrdin. "I had the dream."

"It begins, then. Our chance to take it all back."

"It begins," Gwydion agreed gravely, cutting his eyes over to where Arthur stood. "And I have found the song, the clue to the whereabouts of the Treasures. And I know the four who must seek them."

"And they are?" Myrrdin prompted, for Arthur's benefit.

"Myself. Rhiannon ur Hefeydd. Her daughter, Gwenhwyfar ur Rhoram. And Arthur. Arthur ap Uthyr var Ygraine." Gwydion turned to the boy. "You must be ready to leave with me in the morning."

"I will go nowhere with you," Arthur said defiantly.

As though Arthur had not even spoken, Gwydion went on, turning to Myrrdin. "After we leave, I want you to go to Coed Aderyn, to the cave where Rhiannon lived those many years. Wait for us there. By Ysgawen Mis, six months from now, the four of us will return to the cave with the Treasures in our hands."

"Show me the cave so I may find it," Myrrdin said.

Gwydion reached out to Myrrdin, and they clasped hands. Both bowed their heads, and the room was silent as Gwydion sent the location into Myrrdin's mind, tracing the route that led to the cave.

"You should be safe there," Gwydion said, after it was done. "If we do not return by Ysgawen Mis, we will not be returning at all. If that happens, make your way to Haford Bryn. It's the closest place of safety. Rhoram and his people will protect you."

"If you do not return, there will be no safe place," Myrrdin said quietly. "Not for me, not for any of us. The long night will continue, not to be pushed back, ever."

Gwydion looked over at Arthur, who still stood tensely in the middle of the room, his hands balled into fists at his side. "We leave here at first light."

"You did not listen, uncle," Arthur said firmly. "You never have. I will not go."

Slowly Gwydion rose, coming to stand before his nephew. They were almost of a height, and, as they stood there, Gwydion's cool, gray eyes looking into Arthur's dark, fiery stare, Myrrdin sank down on the hearth, looking away from them both, gazing into the fire.

"You will come with me, Arthur," Gwydion said, his voice cold and level. "You will not make a mockery out of Anieron's pain. You will not make a mockery out of the Y Dawnus who died on the death-march. You will not make a mockery out of those who died in battle against the enemy."

"I will not go with you."

"You will not make a mockery out of the courage of your mother and sister, who lead the Cerddorian of Gwynedd."

"My mother! My sister!" Arthur cried. "You took them away from me and then hold them before me now? You took my da from me! You took everything! Do you think that now, when you want something from me, I will say yes?"

"You will not make a mockery out of the Protectors, out of Cerridwen and Cerrunnos, who cling to life with the barest strand of hope in you."

"I tell you, I will not—"

"You will not make a mockery out of your father's death."

Arthur flinched, and the scar on his face whitened further. His dark eyes shimmered briefly, then hardened. "When my da died, I was leagues away. I was here, unable to help him, unable to fight with him, unable to go to him, because of you. Do not speak of my da to me!"

"I found the song. The song that Taliesin, Master Bard, wrote hundreds of years ago, the song he wrote for us, to guide us to the Treasures. In the last verse are words written only for you. Here, this is Taliesin's message to you, borne across the years, for your ears alone. This is what all of Kymru says to you:

The enemy congregates like dogs in a kennel,

From contact with their superiors they acquire knowledge.

They know not the course of the wind, or the water of the sea.

They know not the spark of the fire, or the fruitfulness of the earth.

I will beg the Brenin, the High One,

That I be not wretched, a prisoner in my own land."

"I will beg the Brenin, the High One," Gwydion repeated softly. "Is that what you would have Kymru do? Is that what you would have me do? Must I get on my knees before you? If so, that is what I will do."

Gwydion sank to his knees at his nephew's feet, his head bowed. Arthur drew his breath in sharply. Myrrdin rose, making his way slowly to stand before the boy. Then he, too, sank to his knees and bowed his old head.

"I beg you, Arthur, from my knees," Myrrdin whispered, "that I be not wretched, a prisoner in my own land."

"Uncle Myrrdin, please, stand up," Arthur cried, his voice breaking with shame.

Myrrdin shook his head. "I will not rise. Not until you grant my boon. Not until you agree to take up this task, to help find the Treasures, to go to Cadair Idris bearing them in your hands. Not until you agree to become our High King, to save us."

"Please," Arthur whispered. "Please don't make me do this. All my life I have felt the chains of the Hunt waiting for me. Please, I want to be free."

"Free of your destiny, you mean," Gwydion said quietly. "But we, all of Kymru, wish to be free to fulfill out destiny, to live our lives in peace and freedom. To sing our songs, to dream our dreams, to love and be loved. This is what we wish. This is what the enemy has taken from us. This is what you can return to us. And this, this is what I have bowed my head to you for, this is what I have gone to my knees for. Do you think I would do that to you—or anyone—for anything less than that? Do you think Myrrdin would do the same for anything less?"

"Please," Arthur said, his voice breaking. "Please."

"It is not from us you should ask for release from your place on the Wheel."

At Myrrdin's words, the door rattled. The fire blazed, fed by the wind that now blew through the hut. The sound of dogs baying, the pounding of hooves, the cry of a horn, echoed in their ears.

"They come," Myrrdin said. "Those from whom you must beg for release. But I do not think they will give it to you."

The door swung open, banging against the wall with the force of the wind. Slowly, as though in a trance, Arthur walked to the door and out onto the road. Myrrdin and Gwydion got to their feet and followed.

A horse, white as snow, cantered down the road. Antlers sprang from the forehead of the rider, and topaz eyes gleamed. Another horse, black as midnight, followed, the rider's white shift gleaming, her amethyst eyes bright. They halted before Arthur, silent, looking down at him.

Gwydion spoke. "You are most welcome here, Protectors of Kymru. Welcome to Cerrunnos, Master of the Hunt. Welcome to Cerridwen, the White Lady. You are not as you were when I last saw you in my dream."

"We gather strength, Dreamer," Cerrunnos said, never taking his topaz eyes from Arthur, "as the High King prepares."

"He has not yet said he will do this thing," Gwydion warned.

Cerridwen leaned forward and lightly touched Arthur's brow, then traced the scar that the eagle had made. "We marked him long ago as the one who would lead the Hunt to take back our land. Blame not the Dreamer, Arthur ap Uthyr, that you were taken from your home, for he did as we instructed him. Do you seek revenge for those lonely years? If so, revenge yourself upon us. Now is the time for you to take up the task for which you were born. Refuse to do so, and your revenge will be complete. For we will fade away, and die, even as the Y Dawnus died from the cruelty of the enemy, even as Kymru dies beneath your feet."

"Choose now, Arthur ap Uthyr," Cerrunnos said sternly. "Choose the death of Kymru. Or choose the gamble for freedom."

"Choose," Cerridwen echoed.

Arthur stood silently, looking up into the pitiless gaze of the god and goddess. Gwydion's hands were clenched tightly, but he did not speak. Beside him, Myrrdin also stood unmoving, his head bowed.

High above in the night sky, the cry of an eagle was heard. In a rush of wings, the bird plummeted from the sky to land on the outstretched arm of Cerrunnos. The bird's cold, gray eyes gazed fiercely at Arthur. And Arthur's scar whitened almost to luminescence. Slowly, hesitantly, Arthur reached out his hand toward the eagle, and it launched itself from Cerrunnos's arm to Arthur's. The bird's claws dug into the boy's flesh, but Arthur did not flinch. The bird and the boy looked at each other for a long moment. Then Arthur nodded. The eagle shot from Arthur's arm back into the night with a victorious cry.

Cerrunnos and Cerridwen bowed their heads briefly, then turned their mounts, cantering down the road. Their forms shimmered, flickered, and then they were gone.

Arthur cradled his arm as blood welled up from the bird's claw marks. The blood dripped slowly down his arm and onto the dusty earth. He turned to Gwydion, his face tight and still. "We leave in the morning, Gwydion ap Awst, just as you wished. But do not think all is well between us, just because I do this thing you ask of me."

Gwydion looked at Arthur's white, set face, at the gleam in his dark eyes. "No," Gwydion said quietly. "I will not think that."

"Here, now, is the first of my blood shed for Kymru. It will not be the last."

Gwydion tore off the sleeve of his undershirt and quickly bound Arthur's bleeding arm, with no hint of the grief he felt. "No," he said softly, "it will not be the last."

Chapter 13

Meirigdydd, Disglair Wythnos—early afternoon

The Coranian guard watched sourly as two peddlers approached the gates of Sycharth. The older peddler wore a cloak of dull gray, patched here and there with bright, mismatched pieces of cloth. His leather boots were worn and cracked. He wore a tunic and trousers of what had once been blue wool, now faded to a drab, slate color. His hair and beard were dingy gray. He looked humbly at the guard and bowed in a move that shifted the weight of the heavy pack on his shoulders so that the man overbalanced and almost stumbled.

The guard grinned. Obviously the peddlers had little coin between them, but they might be good for some fun, after all. Guard duty in the Kymric towns was dull, for the Kymri were cowed and had little spirit.

The younger peddler's clothes were in the same worn condition as the older one, but they were of a faded brown color. His face was set in sullen, suspicious lines as he shifted the weight of the pack on his back and his dark eyes flashed. There was a scar on his face that whitened a little as he stared belligerently at the guard.

This one, the guard thought, might be interesting. "Name and business," he said in a bored tone.

The older man smiled and rubbed his hands. "Well, now, my business may very well be with you—" he began.

"Forget it, da," the younger man said shortly. "He doesn't want to buy anything from us. He just wants to take our money."

"What my son means is—"

"I know what he means," the guard said. "And he's right. There is a toll on this gate."

"A toll!" the older man exclaimed. "Since when is there a toll to enter this city?"

"Since the city belonged to us," the guard sneered. "If you Kymri don't like it, you should have fought harder to keep it."

For a moment the younger man's eyes flashed. He took a brief step forward toward the guard. But the older man stuck out his foot and the youth went sprawling. "The young," the older man sighed, "are so impulsive." The older man helped the younger one to his feet. "All right, boyo?"

"You—"

The older man tossed a small purse to the guard. "This should settle the issue of coming into the city. Is there a toll to get out?"

The guard caught the bag and opened it, then nodded. "Of course, there is," he said, gesturing them to go through the gates. "Oh, and you had best keep that boy of yours under control. Something nasty might happen to him."

"I'll remember that," the older man said, pulling his companion along.

Tight-lipped, Gwydion turned to Arthur as they made their way through the streets of the city. "You are a fool, boy."

"And you are a coward!" Arthur flashed. "Letting him talk to us like that."

Grimly, Gwydion restrained himself from delivering a well-aimed kick or two. Once again he reminded himself that Kymru needed a High King, and this sullen boy was it.

Gwydion took a deep breath. "Pay attention, or we're both dead.

Do you understand?" He waited for Arthur's rejoinder, but the boy said nothing. "Now," Gwydion went on, "we are here to meet up with the others, not to start a fight against the entire Coranian army. Have you got that?"

"You! You never fight. You just sit in the shadows and plot. And people die!"

"You know, boyo," Gwydion said in a conversational tone, "there's nothing that says the hope of Kymru has to be in perfect shape. A broken bone or two might very well teach you some manners."

"Try it, uncle," Arthur said, baring his teeth in what was supposed to be a grin, "and see what it gets you."

"How very pleased Havgan would be to meet you," Gwydion went on smoothly. "He'd love to know someone who gave me almost as much trouble as he does."

"Listen, you can't—"

"And how sorry Uthyr would be, if he could see you now."

The name of Arthur's father hung in the suddenly still air between them. Arthur looked away. Gwydion continued to scan the crowd in the marketplace, as though the name he had used hadn't even hurt him. But it had. Even now, two years later, he still missed his brother terribly. But he would not let Arthur know that. That was his business. Not the boy's.

There—he glimpsed a flash of red hair out of the corner of his eye. He did not turn his head, but slowed his steps, putting his hand on Arthur's arm to halt him. Arthur looked at Gwydion with a raised brow but, for once, asked no questions.

A red-haired woman who had been examining the glass beakers in one of the stalls turned and began to make her way through the crowd. She wore a tunic and trousers of dark green over a plain, cream-colored undershirt. Her unbound hair gleamed in the afternoon sun and cascaded down her back like a river of fire.

Without a word Gwydion followed the woman through the crowd, Arthur tagging behind. As she reached the edge of the marketplace, she turned north, making her way down quiet side streets. The houses, which had once been so fresh and bright, now seemed to huddle to one another for comfort. Occasionally they passed a man or woman sitting in their doorway. These people always looked up and then quickly looked away again when Gwydion and Arthur passed, a half smile playing on their pale faces.

Once, during the journey, they passed near the junction of two streets patrolled by Coranian guards. But, unaccountably, as the woman neared them, the guards were distracted by a howling cat that ran through their midst, chased by a panting dog, followed by four bright-eyed children, who shouted that the cat was theirs. Their attention diverted, the guards did not even notice the woman and her followers.

Finally the woman led them to the last house on the last street, nestled against the city wall. The woman entered the front door, and they followed.

The room was dim, the only light coming from the open doorway. The chamber seemed to be filled with raggedly dressed men. Gwydion did not stop to speak to any of them, but he nodded at a few. They returned his nod, but said no word. The woman disappeared through another door.

They followed her into a tiny room. A bedstead and a large, wooden chest were the only furnishings. The woman was already on her knees, pushing the chest away from the wall. There was a gaping hole in the floor. Without turning back to look at them, she jumped down the hole. Once down, she lit a candle, dropped to her knees, and crawled away from sight.

Gwydion shed his pack and helped Arthur shed his. "Down there?" Arthur asked.

"Where else?"

Arthur jumped into the hole, and Gwydion threw the packs down to him, then jumped in himself. They found themselves in a long, low tunnel. The roof of the tunnel was crisscrossed with roots, and packed with dirt. They crawled on hands and knees, following the glimmering candle that the woman held. At last the woman halted where the tunnel came to an end. She blew out the candle, then reached up over her head. A slight creak told them that a trapdoor had been opened. Light streamed down into the tunnel. The woman jumped up, catching the sides of the open door with her hands and pulling herself out. Gwydion gestured for Arthur to go next, then followed.

The late-afternoon sun felt good on Gwydion's face as he took a deep breath of fresh air. They were in a tiny clearing in the forest that began just a few feet from the city walls. He judged they had come about half a league or so. The woman gestured them away from the wooden trapdoor set in the ground. She closed the door, then set some of the loose brush over it. When she was done, she turned to them.

"The cart and the horses have been procured as you wished. And the goods, as well," she said, her eyes staring at Arthur with frank curiosity.

"Well done, Angharad," Gwydion said. "A nice little tunnel you've got there."

"We like it," Angharad said dryly. "And I will be sure to tell them it meets the Dreamer's approval. And, dare I hope, the approval of your companion?"

Arthur bowed as Myrrdin had taught him to do. "You are Angharad ur Ednyved, Captain of the Cerddorian of Ederynion."

"I am. And you are?"

"The son of an old friend of mine," Gwydion broke in before Arthur could speak.

Angharad's brows rose. "Indeed? Well, son of an old friend of the Dreamer's, have you a name?"

Arthur shot Gwydion a quick glance but did not answer, much to Gwydion's surprise. Perhaps the stakes for which they were playing had finally sunk into Arthur's brain.

"For the moment he does not," Gwydion said quietly.

"Trusting as ever," Angharad said shortly.

"The enemy is everywhere," Gwydion sighed. "You know that."

"So I do. It sounds like an interesting journey ahead of you. And it makes me wish more than ever that I could accompany you," she said thoughtfully. "You may not know this, son of an old friend, but there is no better warrior than I in all of Ederynion."

"I would like to say that she is bragging," Gwydion said to Arthur with a faint smile, "but she is not. Nonetheless, Angharad, you cannot come with us. It is only to be the four so named on this journey."

"Then let us go," Angharad said, "to the other two."

"They are both here? And well?" Gwydion asked, trying to mask his anxiety and, apparently, not succeeding, to judge by Angharad's amused look.

"Emrys is with them now. The younger one sulks a great deal."

"I'm used to that," Gwydion said, shooting a look at Arthur.

"I don't sulk," Arthur shot back, scowling.

Angharad laughed. "So, this son of an old friend causes you a little trouble. He is, then, a boy—pardon me—a young man, after my own heart."

"Somehow I knew you'd be amused," Gwydion said sourly. "Why is it that all my friends laugh at my troubles?"

"You have no friends, Gwydion ap Awst, only tools," Angharad said. "Dreamers cannot afford anything more. Come, the others are waiting."

HIS EYES WENT to her first, drawn to her as the moon draws the tides. She was thinner, and her face was more strained than when he had seen her last. Her green eyes were shadowed, but she rose when he walked through the door of the woodcutter's hut and smiled at him.

"Rhiannon," he said as he took her hands, bringing one hand to his lips without thinking. But he stopped short in surprise at himself, then lowered her hands. Unable to look at her—and yet, somehow unable to relinquish her hands—he glanced around the tiny room.

Emrys, Angharad's Lieutenant, leaned against the uncovered window, a bright dagger in his hands. He nodded at Gwydion and Arthur, then spoke to Angharad as she came in behind them, "All's quiet."

Movement in the corner of the room caught Gwydion's eye. A young woman stood up from a stool tucked away in one shadowy corner. Her long, blond hair tumbled over her shoulders. She wore a leather tunic and trousers of brown, and her blue-eyed gaze was frankly curious.

"Gwydion ap Awst," Rhiannon said, pulling her hands from his grasp, "you remember Gwenhwyfar ur Rhoram, my daughter."

"I do. It has been many years since I last saw you, Gwenhwyfar, and you've changed since then."

"I was a little girl, then," Gwen said haughtily. "But I am grown-up now."

"So you are. I would introduce you to my companion," Gwydion said, gesturing to Arthur, who stood behind him as though rooted to the floor, "but some introductions must wait a while longer."

"Why?" Gwen asked.

"Because," Rhiannon said swiftly, "some names are not to be bandied about without careful thought."

"I didn't ask you," Gwen shot back. "I asked him."

Now Gwydion knew what brought the shadow to Rhiannon's green eyes. He noticed that Arthur was now gazing at Gwen with frank dislike at her rudeness to Rhiannon.

"This, I think," Angharad said to Emrys, "is our sign that it is time to leave. Good journey to you all. May you find what you seek."

"Thank you, Angharad, and Emrys, for your help in getting us this far," Rhiannon said. "And for your company. A safe journey back to Coed Ddu to the both of you."

"Thank you, Rhiannon," Angharad said, gesturing for Emrys to follow her out the door, "and good wishes to you. With companions like these, you're going to need it." The two Cerddorian left the hut, melting silently into the shadows of the trees.

Gwydion shrugged off his pack, dumping it unceremoniously on the rough table jammed against the wall.

"I didn't think you were so old," Gwen said frankly.

"Old?" Gwydion asked in surprise. Arthur snorted, laying his own pack down on the table. "Oh," Gwydion said, gesturing to his white hair. "It's flour. It will wash out."

"I see," Gwen said, coming to stand next to him, examining his hair closely.

"How was your journey?" Gwydion asked Rhiannon as she sank down on one of the stools.

"Well enough," Rhiannon said, her eyes cutting to her daughter. "All things considered."

"Well?" Gwen asked impatiently, gesturing to Arthur. "Who is this? Or do I not get to know?"

Arthur flushed, looking at Gwen with hard, dark eyes. "I am Arthur," he said.

"Fine. Arthur what?"

Arthur took a deep breath. "Arthur ap Uthyr var Ygraine."

"The Prince of Gwynedd who was supposed to have died all those years ago?"

"The very same."

"Well, you don't look dead to me. Why the secrecy?"

"Ask my Uncle Gwydion," Arthur shot back, his eyes bright with anger. "It was his idea."

"I'm sure he had a very good reason," Gwen replied sharply.

Gwydion raised his brows, glancing over at Rhiannon. Something in Gwen's voice, in the way she defended him, surprised him.

"You are," Rhiannon murmured softly, "a very handsome man."

"Uh-oh," Gwydion murmured, eyeing Gwen. Then he did a double take, looking back at Rhiannon. "You think I'm handsome?"

She looked away, a half smile on her face. Arthur turned from Gwen and crossed the room to take Rhiannon's hand. "Rhiannon ur Hefeydd," Arthur said quietly. "I hope you are well. It is —it is good to see you again."

"And good to see you again, Arthur," Rhiannon smiled, as Arthur drew her hand to his lips and formally kissed her fingers.

Gwydion abruptly stood and, going to the door, shut it tightly. He turned, leaning against the door, to survey his companions.

"Rhiannon, you heard Anieron's cry," he said quietly.

Tears shimmered in her green eyes. "Do you think he is still alive?"

"Of course," Gwydion said, his gray eyes cold. "Havgan has no mercy."

"We heard that Cariadas is safe with Owein in Coed Coch."

Gwydion smiled. "I heard that also, thank the Shining Ones."

"The Y Dawnus who survived the march—Angharad says they were taken to Afalon."

"Where is that?" Gwen asked.

"It's the island in the center of Llyn Mwyngil, the lake west of Cadair Idris, in Gwytheryn," Arthur replied, his glance withering with contempt. "Anyone knows that."

Gwen bristled at the insult. "I meant—" she began. But Gwydion raised his hand for silence and, for a wonder, Gwen subsided.

"The Bards and the Dewin were taken," Gwydion said. "And Anieron is lost to us. The Smiths and their families have disappeared. From some hidden place they are forced to make enaid-dals, soul-catchers, collars for the Dewin and Bards that make them blind and deaf. The Coranians have captured a testing device and can now know for certain who is Y Dawnus. Havgan makes his next move, consolidating his hold on this land in his quest to defeat the Kymri utterly. And we four," he said softly, his eye traveling around the room to the three who stood there, "are going to stop him."

"How?" Gwen asked eagerly.

"By finding the Four Treasures. By finding the Stone of Water and the Spear of Fire. By finding the Cauldron of Earth and the Sword of Air. With these Treasures in our hands, we will go to Cadair Idris, and we must be there by Calan Gaef, the festival of the new year."

"And what do we do when we have these Treasures?"

"With them the Doors of Cadair Idris will open. And with them Arthur will be tested and, should he pass the test, the Tynged Mawr, he will be High King of Kymru. And he shall drive the enemy from this land."

Gwen turned to Arthur, looking him up and down doubtfully. "You? High King?"

Arthur flushed. "Yes," he said flatly. "What of it?"

Gwen shrugged. "You don't look like a High King."

"And you don't look like a Princess," Arthur shot back.

"And just what do I look like?"

"Like a spoiled brat."

"Children," Gwydion said patiently. "I'm not finished."

"I'm sorry, Gwydion," Gwen said softly. "Please go on."

Rhiannon rolled her eyes at Gwen's tone, but did not speak.

"Before any of us were born, we were marked as the four who would find these Treasures. To Rhiannon, the task to find the Stone. To me, the task to find the Spear. To Gwen, goes the Cauldron, and to Arthur, the Sword."

"Just how," Arthur said sharply, "do you intend to find these Treasures?"

"The song, a song written by Taliesin himself, has been found. And in the song are we named. And this is how they will be found. The Stone is in Ederynion, so here we look first. Next, the Spear in Rheged, then the Cauldron in Prydyn. And last, the Sword in Gwynedd. And it is by the rings that we shall find the Treasures."

"What rings?" Arthur asked.

"The rings given to each ruler hundreds of years ago by Bran the Dreamer."

"My da has his emerald ring," Gwen said. "If I had known we needed it, I could have brought it with me." She shot Rhiannon a hard look. "Why didn't you tell me?"

"Because it was not time to take it," Rhiannon said with an edge to her voice. "Each ring will come to our hands at the proper time."

"The ring of Ederynion," Arthur cut in, "who has it?"

"Queen Elen in Dinmael."

"You mean Elen who is held captive by the Coranians?" Arthur asked. "You can't be serious. We have to get to her to get the ring?"

"Too hard a task for you?" Gwen asked sweetly. "Well, I'm sure your uncle will think of something."

"Getting the ring will be my task," Rhiannon said shortly, "and I will be the one to think of something."

Gwydion sighed inwardly. "We will be disguised as merchants, a family down on their luck whose comfortable livelihood was destroyed during the war. For the last few years we have managed to eke out a living, but times are getting harder. Therefore, we have brought horses and a wagon, filled them with the goods we have left, and are now traveling to another home."

"What home?" Rhiannon asked.

"Well, the location will change, depending on where we are, of course. But it will be your brother's home. He has agreed to take us in, though I naturally foresee difficulties—your brother never did think I was good enough for you."

"And just what does this nonexistent brother of mine think you were not good enough for?" Rhiannon asked, her brows raised.

"To marry you, of course. You will be my wife. And you two," he went on hurriedly, gesturing to Arthur and Gwen, "are our children."

For a moment no one spoke as they eyed each other. From the look on Gwen and Arthur's faces, the idea held little merit. Rhiannon's eyes were fastened on Gwydion in an expression he could not read.

"And that is your plan?" Arthur asked. "The plan that you made, once again, without consulting any of us?"

"You wanted me to make sure we were all in agreement?" Gwydion asked with withering sarcasm. "Of course. How simple that would have been."

"You always tell me what I will do. You never ask. Not me, not anyone. I will not be a part of this," Arthur said, his eyes flashing, "if we must rely on you alone."

"Why not?" Gwen asked harshly, whipping around to face him.

"He can't be trusted, that's why! He'd sacrifice any of us for his precious plans!"

"How dare you say that!" Gwydion cried, moving to stand before Arthur. "I gave up almost everything I cared about to see that you were safe!"

"And made my da and mam give me up!"

"There was no other way! Do you think you would be alive right now if I hadn't?"

"Stop this," Rhiannon cried, springing to her feet. "All of you."

They were silenced, looking at each other with strained, white faces.

"From now on our lives will depend on each other," Rhiannon went on. "And unless we trust one another, we're dead. We don't have to like each other, we just have to depend on each other."

"Depend on you for what?" Gwen demanded. "To leave when you feel like it?"

"I didn't leave you because I wanted to, I left you because I had to!"

"Enough! I will tell you all this," Gwydion said evenly. "I will not spend the next months listening to everyone squabbling at each other. Gwen, you will show proper respect to your mother."

"I will do as I please!"

"You will grow up," Gwydion said shortly. "And Arthur, you will not sneer at everything I say."

"I, too, will do as I please!"

"Then I must show you both otherwise. Tonight the four of us will have a ceremony to honor the gods and goddesses whose Treasures we seek."

"Why?" Arthur asked suspiciously.

"Because," Gwydion said as his gaze traveled from Rhiannon's tense face, to Gwen's flushed cheeks, to Arthur's scornful eyes, "this group needs all the help we can get."

THE STARS GLITTERED coldly in the night sky. The beams of the full moon glided over the trees, spilling into the tiny clearing, forming a silvery pool in the center. At the perimeter of the clearing, the four of them stood silently, waiting for the signal to begin.

Arthur stood to the north, a feather in one hand and a bell in the other, his face still. Only the whitening of the scar on his face betrayed any hint of tension.

To the west stood Gwen. Her hair cascaded over her slender shoulders—gold changed to molten silver by the light of the moon. In one hand she held a smooth, white stone. A small drum hung at her waist, secured by a leather strap.

Rhiannon stood in the east, her hair flooding down her back like a shadow. In one hand she held a wooden cup of clear water. In the other she held her father's harp. The pearl of her simple Dewin's torque glowed softly at the base of her slender throat. Her face was calm, and her eyes seemed to glitter with starry light.

Gwydion stood to the south. The Dreamer's torque of opal gleamed around his neck in a fiery ring. He held a lit torch in one hand and a silver pipe in the other.

Gwydion let the silence of the night spin out around them. At last he felt a stirring in his heart, a sign that those not of this earth were watching, waiting, ready to hold sway over this night. He nodded to Rhiannon, and she stepped into the center of the clearing.

She lifted her face to the sky, the beautiful face that Gwydion held so securely, so secretly in his heart. The moonbeams carved planes of light and shadow in her countenance. She lifted her cup to the sky. "Nantsovelta of the Moon, Lady of the Waters, I bring this water to honor you. Bless me, so that I may find your Treasure. Through deepest waters will I journey, to bring your Stone back to your people, that we may be free." With that she turned the cup over, spilling the water onto the ground at her feet. The water lay like a pool of silver, bathed in the rays of the moon.

"Music I bring you," Rhiannon went on. "A dance I give to you as a sign that I am yours." She set down the cup and lightly touched the strings of the harp. The music was light, fluid, spilling into the clearing like a waterfall. Still playing the harp, she dipped and swayed with soft flowing movements, arching her back then bending forward, twirling on her feet, moving from side to side. Lit by the moon, she seemed to be as graceful, as soothing as clear water.

Gwydion felt his heart beat faster, a light sweat breaking out at his temples. He was fire, and he was called to her water, to allow her to soothe those places in his soul that were parched and barren. But he could not. He must not. He forced himself to stand where he was, even as he burned.

Another sound, the sound of water rushing in time to the harp, came to the clearing, rising from no place on this earth. The tempo of the water, like the sound of rushing rapids, sped up as Rhiannon twisted and turned, faster now, to the sound. Around and around she spun, her face lifted to the moon, her eyes closed, her fingers traveling over the harp strings so fast the movements were a blur.

With a cry, she opened her eyes, falling to her knees, pointing down to the pool of water that had formed at her feet. For Nantsovelta was there. Her face filled the pool and held a secret smile. Her alabaster forehead gleamed. Her silvery hair ebbed and flowed, swirling in the water. Her eyes changed from stormy gray, to the cool blue of quiet lakes, to the glinting green of the sea. Her voice spoke, sounding in their minds with the fierceness of a huge wave that rises from the sea, reaching for the land, carrying all along with it.

"Rhiannon ur Hefeydd, Great Queen of Taliesin's Song, marked before birth for this task: Beneath the Water, lies the Seeker. Find the Stone, find Gwyr Yr Brenin, in my name."

Then the pool vanished, soaking into the earth. Rhiannon put out a shaking, hesitant hand to the spot, but the earth was dry. She panted, taking huge mouthfuls of air as though, for a time, air had been denied her. Gwydion went to her, helping her to her feet. She clutched her harp, looking up at him with wild eyes. Gently he laid one hot hand on the cool, smooth skin of her face.

"She knows," Rhiannon whispered. "She knows."

"Knows what?" he asked gently.

But Rhiannon would not answer. Trembling, she turned away. She picked up the cup, still clutching her harp, and returned to the edge of the clearing. Gwydion stood in the center for a few more moments, looking at her, but she would not meet his eyes. With a deep breath, he began his own part of the ritual.

He lifted the torch, staring up at the dancing flame. "Mabon, King of Fire, Lord of the Sun, I bring fire to honor you. Bless me, so that I may find your Treasure. Through raging fires will I journey, to bring your Spear back to your people, that we may be free." He firmly set the end of the torch into the ground, then stepped back as the fire grew brighter.

"Music I bring to you, and dancing, to honor you." He lifted the pipe to his lips, then began to play. The music was high-pitched, sharp, and hard as the edge of flame. He began to dance, his movements rapid, blazing like the cracking fire. The fire glowed still brighter, leaping from the torch higher and higher as he danced, as sweat poured from him in the heat, as his arms, his legs, his entire body glowed brighter and brighter with a golden light. Then, with an incoherent cry, he fell to his knees, raising his sweat-soaked face to the flame.

For Mabon was there. His ruddy face glowed, and his bright hair crackled with golden fire. His amber eyes gleamed like the light of a fire so hungry it would kill anything in its path. Then he spoke, his voice blazing in their minds with the roar of hungry flames.

"Gwydion ap Awst, Knowledgable One of Taliesin's Song, marked before birth for this task: Within the Storm, lies the Blaze. Find the Spear, find Erias Yr Gwydd, in my name."

Then the face was gone and the flames died down. He knows, Gwydion thought in terror. He knows. And now Gwydion knew what Rhiannon had meant. So, she feared water the way he feared fire. The other two, they must also fear the most that which they must seek. Oh, the gods and goddesses, surely they laughed. How cruel they were. How terribly cruel.

A cool touch on his cheek made him lift his head. "He knows," Gwydion said hoarsely.

Rhiannon's face changed, softened, as she understood. "Then we will help each other, Gwydion ap Awst, to face what we must."

"Help each other?" he repeated, a question in his voice.

"Yes," she said firmly, helping his to his feet.

He looked down at her for a moment. Help each other, she had said, as though such a thing would be easy to accept. And he knew it should be, but it was not. Slowly he withdrew from her, gesturing her to return to her place. He took his own place, then stood silently for a few moments. At last he nodded to Gwen to step forward. She took her place in the center of the clearing, swallowing hard. She set the stone on the ground then stepped back.

"Modron, Great Mother, Lady of the Earth, I bring stone, the bones of the earth, to honor you. Through deepest caverns will I journey, to bring your Cauldron back to your people, that we may be free."

Then she began to beat the drum in a slow, heavy rhythm. Slowly, steadily, she danced around the stone in measured paces. The drum took on a hollow sound, as though sounding from the depths of tunnels beneath the earth. Gwen's feet dragged against the ground, digging shallow trenches as the dirt spilled over her bare feet. Her movements slowed even more, the beating of the drum growing louder and louder. At last she stood still, the earth covering her feet, a look of terror on her face. Then the earth seemed to yank her down, spilling her onto her knees, bringing her face inches from the stone. She cried out, trying to pull away, but she was held fast.

For the face of Modron was there in the stone. Her wheat-colored hair, strewn with flowers, shimmered as her eyes, the color of freshly turned earth, glowed. Her face glittered with precious stones. Her voice echoed in their minds with the power of the earth, as it shakes loose from its moorings.

"Gwenhwyfar ur Rhoram, the White One of Taliesin's Song, marked before birth for this task: Within the Center, lies the Circle. Find the Cauldron, find Buarth Y Greu, in my name."

The face faded as Gwen frantically tried to get to her feet. But she struggled in the dirt, unable to rise. Swiftly, Rhiannon reached for her, pulling her to her feet. For a moment Gwen clung to her mother, burying her face in Rhiannon's shoulder as she wept.

"She knows," Gwen sobbed. "It will be my death. Covered by the earth forever."

"No," Rhiannon soothed, stroking Gwen's hair, "for we will be with you."

"You cannot," Gwydion said quietly. "It is her task alone. But your fears are shared among us. And we will help you to face them."

After a moment Gwen stiffened in her mother's arms, then walked back to her place. Rhiannon lowered her arms slowly, then she turned away, taking her place once more, her face impassive. Gwydion stepped back, gesturing for Arthur to come forward. With a deep breath, Arthur moved to the center of the circle. Even as he lifted the eagle's feather to the sky, a slight breeze ruffled the leaves of the trees.

"Taran of the Air, King of the Winds, I bring an eagle's feather, to honor you. Through stormy skies will I journey, to bring your Sword back to your people, that we may be free." Lightly he stooped, laying the feather on the ground. But before he even straightened up, the feather lifted in the air, blown by the wind.

Arthur paled, then began to ring the bell. "Music I bring to you, and dancing." Arthur began to dance, his arms reaching overhead, cutting the air with swift movements. The bell rang with a light, airy tone. But as he rang the bell, the tone changed. It grew wild, dancing up and down the scale as though hunting for prey. The winds grew stronger, tossing the feather this way and that as Arthur tried to dance around it. The feather darted about as though looking for a way in, for a weakness. At last Arthur cried out, falling to his knees, pointing up at the sky where the feather floated. A small whirlwind had formed above their heads. And there, etched in the Wind, was his face.

Taran's gray eyes glowed fiercely like the eyes of an eagle. His sharp features seemed carved into stiff angles by the winds. His hair was formed of storm clouds, and lightning was in his eyes. His voice echoed in their minds like thunder.

"Arthur ap Uthyr, Great Bear of Taliesin's Song, marked before birth for this task: Beneath the Seeker, lies the Guardian. Find the Sword, find Meirig Yr Llech, in my name."

The winds died down, and the forest fell silent. But Arthur did not move from where he lay huddled on the ground. Gwydion went to him, taking the bell from the boy's stiff fingers, putting an arm around his shoulders and helping him to his feet. Arthur looked at Gwydion with wide, shocked eyes. "I—"

"Yes. He knows, doesn't he? Your fears. Do not let them stop you."

"How can I not?" Arthur whispered. "The winds—the storm that tried to take my life all those years ago. It waits to try again."

"Lean on us, then. For we, too, have our fears. And so we strengthen each other."

Arthur stepped back. "You offer help? You? Don't make me laugh."

"I offer help, yes."

"How much easier to offer it than to take it, Dreamer," Rhiannon said.

"It is, indeed," Gwydion replied.

Part 3
The Hunt

Cold is the night,
The rain pours down, no trifle;
A roar in which the clean wind rejoices
Howls over the sheltering wood.

> Mannawyddan ap Iweridd
> Fifth Ardewin
> Circa 265

Chapter 14

Dinmael
Kingdom of Ederynion, Kymru
Gwernan Mis, 499

Meirwdydd, Lleihau Wythnos—evening

Regan paced the ramparts of Caer Dwyr, the Queen's fortress in Dinmael. Not that the fortress truly belonged to the Queen, she thought bitterly. Nothing in Ederynion did, not anymore. For the Queen was a captive of the enemy. Regan herself was not really the Queen's Dewin anymore. She was a bond for Queen Elen's good behavior. For if Elen ever fully rebelled against her captors, Regan's life would be forfeit.

The only thing that made their lives even bearable was General Talorcan—the same man who also made Regan's life so unbearable. Because she knew, even though she had tried to run from the knowledge, that she loved Talorcan of Dere. She loved him in spite of who he was, and in spite of what he had done.

Regan sighed and leaned against the stone walls of the fortress, looking out over the silent city. It was late and the stars glittered coldly overhead. Not so very long ago Talorcan would have come to her, dismissing the guard who lurked a few feet away, taking her arm, twining his fingers around her hand.

But he would not do so anymore. He would not come to her, because he loved her. And he knew what loving him was doing to her. He knew what would happen to her heart if he took her to his bed. He knew, perhaps, what would happen to his.

She closed her eyes, willing herself to pretend the dark city before her was as it had been only a few years before. The walls would be whole and shining. This very night was the eve of Calan Llachar. There would have been singing and dancing in Nemed Aethnen, the sacred grove of aspen trees. Bright bonfires would have burned in the center of the grove. Iago, as presiding Druid, would have told the story of the death and return to life of Cerrunnos, Master of the Hunt. He would have told of Cerridwen's courage and daring, and how Cerrunnos had claimed her for his own. Silver vessels holding pieces of bread would have been passed around among laughing crowds. Those people who picked burned pieces would have jumped the flames amid cheering.

And tomorrow! Tomorrow would have been the race to the tree. The winner of the race would have been named King of the Wood and climbed the highest branches of the tree to bring down the crown of rowan and marsh marigold, and used it to crown the woman who was queen of his heart.

But nothing like that would happen here now. The Druids proclaimed the Kymric gods and goddesses to be false, insisting that the people give their allegiance to the Coranian god, Lytir. The sacred grove had been cut down, and a temple to Lytir had been built in its place. Even laughter was a thing of the past, for the Kymri no longer had cause to laugh at anything. They had been crushed utterly. No matter that some bands of warriors fought on still. It was not enough. And they all knew it. But they would never give up. Regan was no longer sure that she could do the same. Giving up sometimes seemed like the only thing left to do.

And that was when she felt it—the pull, a tug at her consciousness. Someone, a Dewin, was trying to get her attention. For a moment she thought of not answering. She had, after all, given her word that she would not Wind-Ride. Only once had she broken that word—the night she had tried to kill herself, to throw her spirit into the stars and never return. Talorcan had stopped her that night. But he was no longer here to stop her. She could do it.

Do you really think, Regan ur Corfil, that death is the only answer for you?

So, the sender was not only Dewin, she was a Bard, one who could speak from mind to mind. Which meant it had to be someone of the house of Llyr. But Regan was only Dewin and could not answer except by using the Anoeth, the secret language of hand signals, used to communicate when sight only could be obtained.

Regan stared blankly out across the city. But instead of stone walls she saw a woman she knew. It was Rhiannon ur Hefeydd who Wind-Rode to her. Rhiannon was dressed in a tunic and trousers of black leather, her hair braided on the top of her head. She was solemn and intent, but her green eyes were kind.

Regan's hands, shielded from the sight of the guard just a few feet away, moved in gestures small enough to escape his notice. *What are you doing here?*

We come to seek freedom for Kymru. The battle begins again. And the Shining Ones speak at last, demanding that their people be freed.

Regan shook her head, her fingers moving rapidly. *Too late, Rhiannon ur Hefeydd. Too late, I think.*

Do you?

The response was cool. Well, did she? She had, but now?

Listen well, Regan ur Corfil, to what I have to say. Nantsovelta herself has commanded that I find her Treasure. And to do that, I must have Elen's ring.

Her pearl ring? The one given her by Olwen?

Yes. I must have it.

Elen would surely give it to you if she had it. But . . .

Who does have it, then?

Guthlac. The Master Wyrce-Jaga. He took it from her.

You and Elen, how closely are you guarded?

Too closely for us to be of any use.

Yet I understand that tomorrow there is a special service at the temple, to distract the Kymri from remembering Calan Llachar too fondly.

Yes, and a feast here at Caer Dwyr afterward.

General Talorcan . . .

Regan stiffened. *What of him?*

Rhiannon was silent. Her image stared at Regan, her green eyes veiled. At last she spoke again to Regan's mind.

I knew him in Corania as a good man caught in something out of his control.

I care nothing for General Talorcan! Who says that I do?

We'll talk of this later. But for now I must know—does he allow you any freedom at all? Knowing him, he gives you what he can.

And just how had Rhiannon meant that? Regan wondered, her hands still.

Regan, I must go. You begin to look suspicious just standing there. In a moment the guard will jog your elbow. Listen now. I will be in Dinmael by late morning. I must be able to get into Caer Dwyr. Can you do it?

Regan thought. A name, a name whispered to her once by an innocuous-looking stable boy, came to her. Somehow, in some way, she felt less hopeless than she had only a few moments ago. Her people were still alive, still fighting. And she had been ready to give up. And now she was ashamed.

Elen needs a new dress for the feast. She has ordered material from one of the dressmakers in town. Go to the stall of Anawen in the marketplace, the third stall on the southeast side. Tell her that I sent you and ask for the cloth. You can be her assistant and bring the dress for a final fitting. Come to the fortress and ask for me.

Very good, Regan. You—who's that?

Who's what? What do you mean? I—

Someone's here. Listening to us. Another Dewin! One who may even hear Mind-Speech! Who?

Rhiannon, you must go! And don't come here now. There is no telling what he has heard.

Who? Who?

I tell you, go!

And then Rhiannon's image was gone, blown out like a candle. Regan turned to face the man she knew had been listening. But he did not come.

RHIANNON'S EYES FLUTTERED as she returned to her body. She shook her head slightly. Her gaze focused on Gwydion, who was crouched down before her, pressing a cup of ale into her hands. She opened her mouth to talk, but at Gwydion's ferocious scowl, she drank the ale instead.

"May I speak now?" she asked acidly, after swallowing the contents of the cup. "I am, after all, skilled enough to be able to Wind-Ride without becoming incapacitated."

"Charming as ever," Gwydion murmured. "But something, I think, happened there at the end."

"Someone. There was someone else in that fortress who sensed my presence. I felt it, at the last."

"Who?"

She reached out her hands and warmed them before the crackling campfire. Arthur looked at her with concern. Gwen studiously ignored the entire proceedings, poking at the fire with a stick.

"I don't know," she lied. "Whoever it was, I'm not sure how much he heard or understood."

"And Regan told you not to come."

"Regan is scared of her own shadow by now," Rhiannon said crisply. "She's been a captive for too long."

"But she may be right."

"Then I'll be careful."

"Rhiannon—"

"She said that Elen has ordered a new dress for the feast tomorrow. I am to go to the booth of Anawen the dressmaker at the marketplace and take the cloth to the fortress. There I will help with the final fitting."

"And then take the ring and leave?" Arthur asked.

"Unfortunately, the ring is no longer in Elen's possession. Guthlac, the Master-wyrce-jaga, has it."

"And so your plan is to ask him to just give it to you?" Gwydion scowled.

"I'll think of something. Tell me, Gwen, what kind of progress have you made with Shape-Moving?"

"Shape-Moving?" Gwydion interrupted before Gwen could answer. "If it's a Shape-Mover you want, I can do that. All Dreamers can, you know."

"Yes," Rhiannon said calmly. "I know. But you will stay here, safely outside of Dinmael with Arthur and the wagon."

"I will not!" Gwydion's gray eyes glinted dangerously. "And you will refrain from telling me what to do!"

"You tell me often enough!"

"You need telling," Gwydion snorted. "I do not."

"Think, Dreamer," Rhiannon said with exaggerated patience. "Something might go wrong in there. I'd be very surprised if it didn't. And if things do go wrong, you must be free to continue the quest. You are the Dreamer." She gently laid a hand on his arm, forcing him to look at her. "You know I'm right," she said softly.

He turned away from her, staring into the fire. Arthur's gaze darted from Gwydion to Rhiannon, but he did not speak. It was Gwen who broke the silence.

"I can Shape-Move," she said confidently.

"Indeed?" Rhiannon's brow rose. "Who taught you?"

Gwen shrugged. "No one. I taught myself."

"Interesting. Well, let's see you Move something, my Druid-daughter."

Gwen turned her gaze to a small rock resting at the end of the clearing, her eyes narrowed in concentration. At last the rock wobbled slightly, then was still.

"Oh, that's great," Arthur muttered.

"I'd like to see you try!" Gwen flared. "You can't even do that much, can you?"

"Someday I will!"

"But it's not someday. And you can't," she said flatly.

"Gwydion?" Rhiannon asked, willing him to understand, and to do what must be done. Willing him to help and then step back and wait.

Gwydion sighed. He stood and reached down a hand to haul Gwen to her feet. "Time for lessons," he said.

Calan Llachar—late morning

"I LOOK LIKE a fool in these clothes," Gwen said petulantly, as they passed through the southern gate of Dinmael.

Rhiannon glanced at Gwen. Her daughter wore a plain, woolen gown of light blue with a smock of unbleached linen beneath. Her hair was worn in a single braid that spilled down her back. Rhiannon was dressed much the same, but her gown was black and her long, dark hair was held back from her face with a band of forest-green cloth.

"You look," Rhiannon said crisply, "like you are supposed to. Try to remember that you're a humble serving girl."

"But I can't do anything in this dress— whoever heard of a warrior wearing one? Achren never does."

"Achren is your father's Captain, and her life can be a little more straightforward at the moment than ours. Tell me, is it possible for you to do anything without complaining? I'm just curious, because I—"

Oh, sweet Shining Ones. What had the Coranians done?

Rhiannon halted on the crowded roadway. She had heard of this. But it was different from actually seeing it. Nemed Aethnen, the sacred grove of aspen trees, the grove where the Kymri of Dinmael had once celebrated the Festivals, where they had paid homage to the Shining Ones, where they had laughed and sung and danced, where the Queens of Ederynion had gone to bear their children, was gone. In its place was a hideous temple to Lytir, the god of the Coranians. It was of plain wood, not yet adorned with the type of embellishments she had seen in the temples of Corania. The building was alien, abominable, a scar on the breast of Kymru. For a moment she wished with all her heart that she were a Fire-Weaver. She would set this building ablaze, and laugh while she did it.

"Mam?" Gwen said anxiously, nudging her. "Mam, you're staring. Come on."

Rhiannon turned away from the temple, tears in her eyes.

Strange, after so much loss, so much pain, this sight should make her weep.

Gwen tugged at her sleeve, and Rhiannon walked on. *Fool*, she thought bitterly. If anyone had been watching, they would have known her to be someone who had not been in Dinmael in recent years. She must be more careful. Gwen was certain to say something about such foolishness. But Gwen said nothing. Her hand lightly brushed Rhiannon's arm, and her touch was gentle.

A few moments later they reached the marketplace. Though it was filled with people, it was far too quiet. Gone were the laughter, the good-natured teasing, and the smiles, the spontaneous singing. Instead, people shopped quietly, mutely examining goods and giving a wide berth when possible to the numerous Coranian soldiers who patrolled the stalls endlessly.

Silently Rhiannon made her way to the dressmakers' booths, Gwen following quietly behind. She stopped at the third stall on the southeast side. A young woman, dressed in a laced kirtle of sapphire blue, looked up from her sewing. "Can I help you?"

"Yes. I'm here for the gown for Queen Elen."

"I see." The young woman eyed Rhiannon and Gwen for a moment. "I'm Anawen. And you are?"

"I am called Dwr," Rhiannon said, using the word for *water*.

"Then the dress is for you." Anawen reached beneath the counter and pulled out a pile of fine, white wool. "The seams are basted," the woman said. "Elen needs a final fitting. She—she's lost some weight in the past few weeks." The woman's gaze held Rhiannon's.

"We will do our best to fit her," Rhiannon said, taking the cloth. "And our best to see that she takes heart, and does not waste away."

Anawen smiled. "We thank you, then, the people of Dinmael. Regan will be waiting for you at the gates of Caer Dwyr."

Anawen was as good as her word. When Gwen and Rhiannon reached the gates of the Queen's fortress, Regan was, indeed, waiting for them. She was escorted closely by two Coranian guards.

"At last," Regan said sharply. "What took you so long? You know that the Queen's gown must be ready in time for the service at the temple this afternoon."

Rhiannon bent her head, surreptitiously nudging Gwen's ankle for her to do the same. "Your pardon, Lady. But we will be sure to have her ready in time."

"You had better. Come with me." Regan turned away, leading them past the stables and into the Queen's ystafell. Four guards were stationed in the front room, two on either side of the door and two more at the foot of the stairs. The Queen's chair, with its canopy of white and silver, was empty. The fireplace contained nothing but ashes and the room was dim. Regan did not pause, but brushed past the guards at the foot of the stairs. At the top of the stairs, outside of Elen's room, four more guards were posted. Again, Regan did not pay the slightest attention to these men, but walked past them as though they were not there. She opened the door and gestured them inside.

The room looked much as it had when Queen Olwen was alive. On the coverlet of the great canopied bed was a swan, stitched in silver thread, with luminescent pearls for eyes. Tall wardrobes, covered with mirrors, lined the walls. A table of white wood was covered with bottles of perfume and other delicate glass vessels spun by the famous glassworkers of Ederynion. A fire blazed in the fireplace, and white, woolen rugs were scattered on the polished floor.

Elen stood with her back to them, gazing out the window. She did not turn around when they entered the room. Quickly Regan closed the door.

"You should not have come, Rhiannon," Regan said softly. "He sensed something last night, I am sure of it."

"Perhaps. Has he said anything to you?" Rhiannon asked.

Regan shook her head. "I waited for him to come and kill me, but he never came. I haven't even seen him yet today."

"Then we must take our chances. Perhaps he didn't really catch what we were saying. He is untrained, unskilled."

"You know what he is—and who he is—then."

"The question is, does he?" Queen Elen asked, turning from the window. She was pale, and her blue eyes were shadowed with weariness. Her braided auburn hair, strung with pearls, seemed muted. She grasped Rhiannon's hands in hers.

"I sensed both gifts in him last night," Rhiannon said.

"Then it is over, before it has even begun," Regan said sadly.

"Not necessarily," Rhiannon replied.

"This thing you do, for which you need my ring," Elen began, her voice low.

Rhiannon drew a breath to speak, but Elen laid her hand over Rhiannon's lips.

"No, do not tell me you can say nothing. I know that already. But you must know we cannot help you. You have come here for nothing."

"What do you mean, you can't help us?" Gwen demanded. Rhiannon said nothing.

"Talorcan knows something is going on. And Regan's life will be forfeit. I cannot allow her to die."

"Elen," Regan said sharply, "we've been through this. My life is my own to risk. I will help them do this thing. Though I do not believe they will succeed."

"I tell you, we cannot! For two years I have done what they wished so that you will live. Do you think I will throw it all away now?" Elen demanded. She turned to Rhiannon, her face set. "You must go. I will not help you."

"Elen ur Olwen var Kilwch," Rhiannon said, the words coming unbidden to her lips, as though someone, something else was using her to speak. "I am a Dewin of Kymru. And I say this to you. The High King commands you to surrender Bran's gift."

Elen went white to the lips. Abruptly she sat, as though her legs would no longer support her.

"Elen, what is it?" Regan asked, kneeling by the chair.

"My mam's words. The night before she died. The very words she said would be used. Guard the ring, she said, for one day a Dewin will ask for it, using those exact words. And you did. Oh, Mam, Mam, you knew." Elen rocked back and forth, her head bent, tears spilling from her eyes. At last she lifted her head. "Yes. I will help you. But I, too, do not think you will succeed."

"I do not know if we will or not, Elen," Rhiannon said. "But I tell you this. The one who will be High King is alive. One day he will lead us to victory. I believe that."

"Then I must believe it, too. If only to keep my sanity here."

Rhiannon pulled Gwen forward. "This is my daughter, Gwen-hwyfar ur Rhoram. She, too, has her part to play, called by the Hunt, to win back our land."

"Then you are welcome here," Elen said, inclining her head.

Gwen flushed and gave an awkward curtsy, overwhelmed by Elen's dignity.

"Come now," Regan said, taking the cloth from Gwen. "We must begin work on the dress. And you must tell us how we can help you."

"First of all, you can start sewing," Rhiannon said with a smile. "For I cannot."

"Can't sew?" Regan stared.

"Not very well. Give me something easy to do in case someone comes in, and I will tell you what I can."

They set her to hemming the bottom of the gown—after they had pinned it up so that it would be even. Gwen was set to trimming the white, gossamer veil with silver piping. Regan set the sleeves, while Elen sewed pearls on the neck of the snowy smock.

"We will do it at the feast tonight after the service," Rhiannon said. "Gwen and I must be allowed to help serve the meal at the high table. Regan, can you arrange that?"

"Easily," Regan said, biting off the thread, then rethreading the needle for the second sleeve. "There are a number of people from the town who will be helping at the feast. I will tell the steward that I said for you to have the high table."

"Fine. Now, what does the Master-wyrce-jaga like best to drink?"

"Wine from Prydyn, of course."

"Good. You can be sure that I will keep him well supplied at the feast. I will have a special mixture just for him."

"Will you kill him?" Elen asked eagerly.

"I think not. We shall just keep him off balance a little bit. It's all we need."

"I can assure you, Guthlac will never be so drunk that you can tug that ring off his fat finger without him noticing."

Rhiannon smiled. "We'll see about that. There is more than one way to—"

She broke off as the door abruptly opened. A quick glimpse of the man standing there was enough to make her bend her head industriously to her work, even though she knew it was useless. Talorcan would recognize her no matter what she did. She had, after all, spent more than a month in his company in Corania. As her eyes focused on her work, she felt his gaze on her. He had heard it all last night, and done nothing because he had been waiting—waiting to spring the trap she had walked into. Her guess about what he would or would not do had been wrong, then.

General Talorcan walked into the room, shutting the door behind him. He stood before Elen, his green eyes shadowed in his too-thin face. Elen rose to face him, her fists clenched. Regan, pale and mute, gazed up at him.

"Queen Elen, the service at the temple begins in one hour," Talorcan said quietly. "I will escort you there. You will be ready."

"I will be ready," Elen said, her voice fierce with hatred, "to enter that abomination and pray to my gods for your deaths."

Talorcan's mouth twisted. "One day, Lady, you will have your wish, I am sure." He glanced down at Regan, then looked away. His eyes traveled indifferently over Gwen's bowed head, then came to rest on Rhiannon. As he moved to stand in front of her, Regan rose, her eyes pleading.

Slowly Talorcan reached out and took Rhiannon's chin in his hand, forcing her head up. He stared down at her for a long moment. "Once you sang 'The Lament' for my mother. Do you remember?"

"'Oh, Elmete,'" Rhiannon recited softly. "'We remember you. Bright city of our father's fathers. We remember you.' Is this what you would have me sing for Kymru, General? Shall I sing another

Lament for another country lost to the enemy?"

His grip tightened on her chin, then he withdrew his hand. "No," he said harshly. "One is enough." He went to the door and opened it. He turned around and looked at them all again. Elen's face was pale as death. Regan's eyes were hopeless. Gwen stared back in defiance, though she could not control the tremor in her hands.

But Rhiannon, knowing what he was, knowing what he had meant, knowing now what he would do, and how he would pay for it, had only pity on her face.

"Talorcan," Regan said helplessly, softly. "Oh, Talorcan, please."

"Never mind, Regan," Rhiannon said. "There will be no change of plans."

"You know me better than I do myself," Talorcan said softly. "Maybe you have since the beginning." He shut the door quietly behind him.

The revelry was at its height when Rhiannon at last made her move.

The great hall was hot and noisy, packed to overflowing with drunken Coranian soldiers. Hazy smoke from hundreds of torches, and from the fire roaring in the huge hearth, seemed to make the hall even hotter. The Coranian banner that hung over the high table showed a stylized boar, stitched in the Warleader's colors of red and gold. It seemed to shimmer in the heat, as though the boar were about to pounce on the celebrants. Rhiannon only wished it would.

From her place in the corner next to the wine barrels, she glanced up at the high table. Elen sat in the center, with Talorcan to her right and Guthlac on her left. Coolly, Elen took another sip of wine from her goblet of silver and pearls. Dressed all in white, her face frozen in an expression of stony indifference, she seemed impervious to the noise and heat.

Talorcan had not said a word throughout the feast. He looked neither at Elen, nor at Regan, who sat on his other side. He did not scan the room for Rhiannon or Gwen. He simply stared at the far wall, his thoughts obviously elsewhere.

Regan, too, had said nothing throughout the meal. She sat

pale and mute—which made Rhiannon want to kick her. For the gods' sake, the least Regan could do was act naturally. Already the Druid, Iago, who sat to Guthlac's right, was suspicious. He glanced at Regan often, and at Elen even more so. His dark eyes scanned the room continuously. But Rhiannon was careful to keep her back to him as she stood by the barrels. She and Iago had never met, but her description—as well as Gwydion's—had been sent up and down Kymru for the past two years.

She slowly filled a pitcher with rich Prydyn wine from the barrel, nudging Gwen slightly as she did so.

"It's time," she whispered to her daughter. As she passed her hand quickly over the pitcher, she emptied the contents of a small vial into the wine. Swiftly she pressed the bottle into Gwen's hands. Gwen promptly laid it out of sight behind the barrel.

"Mam, that's not enough pennyroyal," she whispered back.

"I told you, we don't want to kill him. Just put him off balance."

"Convulsions are not enough for the likes of him. Why not kill him? He's a wyrce-jaga. You know what they are."

"Because I don't want the entire army after us, that's why. It must look as natural as possible. And remember, do it quickly. Iago's at that table, and he's a Druid. He can sense what you do—unless you are quick."

"I'll be quick."

Rhiannon bore the pitcher to the table, heading for Guthlac, who sat to Elen's left. The wyrce-jaga was a huge man, and his black robe skewed ridiculously over his massive paunch. His scanty brown hair was wispy, and his jowls were greasy from the meal he had eaten. As Rhiannon moved between him and Elen to dispense the wine into his cup, she saw Elen's hand tighten on the base of her goblet.

Elen, having seen Rhiannon pour the wine and Guthlac begin to drain his cup, turned to the drunken wyrce-jaga with a sneer of disdain on her beautiful face. "Tell me, Guthlac," she said coldly. "I am curious. How does the Warleader feel about the fact that you can't capture a single Dewin or Bard, no matter how hard you try?"

Guthlac's face darkened as he swerved in his chair to face the

Queen. "What did you say?"

"I said," Elen replied, her voice patient, "how does Havgan feel about the fact that you are incompetent? Or is that last word too big for you? Do you need me to explain it to you?"

"Who are you to question me? You are nothing! We keep you alive only for our own amusement. And, believe me, that will soon pass. The moment General Talorcan gives me leave to do to you what you deserve—"

Elen's lips curved in derision. "You would not dare touch me, wyrce-jaga. One old fat man cannot frighten me."

"Why, you— " Guthlac slammed down his almost empty goblet and heaved himself to his feet. The pearl ring he wore on his greasy hand shone in the light of the torches as he swung his hand toward Elen's upturned face.

Iago, who had been closely listening, leapt to his feet, interposing himself between Elen and the enraged Guthlac. It was then that Guthlac's convulsions began. With a cry, his body jerked, his hand flying out. And as his right hand jerked, the ring flew off, as though impelled by the force of his convulsions, arching through the air and across the table, to land with a splash in the nearly empty jug of wine Gwen held in her hands. Yet no one seemed to notice, their attention held by the wyrce-jaga's now helpless movements—and, more importantly, by Elen's calculated scream.

Iago caught at Guthlac's flailing hands, forcing the man to the floor. "Regan!" he cried. Regan hurried over to him, kneeling on the floor. "What's wrong with him?" the Druid panted. "He's convulsing."

"Too much wine," Regan said crisply. "He's wearing out his body with his appetites. It will pass."

Slowly Talorcan stood, staring at Guthlac's now-bare ring finger. Yet the General did not move. Nor did he seem to mark that Rhiannon had now joined Gwen, surreptitiously reaching into the pitcher.

The men in the hall were now on their feet, straining to see what was happening to Guthlac. The wyrce-jaga continued to flail as Iago snatched up a part of his robe to put between the convulsing man's lips.

"Where's the ring?" Iago cried.

"Why worry about that now?" Regan asked sharply, trying to help Iago still Guthlac's flailing limbs. "No doubt it flew off. We'll find it in a minute."

Iago, his suspicions already alerted, leapt to his feet. His eyes scanned the crowd. As ill luck would have it, he looked Rhiannon full in the face as she turned at the door to be sure Gwen was behind her before slipping out into the night.

Their eyes met—cool green to fiery black—and Iago shouted, pointing to Rhiannon and Gwen. "Don't let them get away!"

One of the soldiers, less drunk than most, reached out and grabbed Gwen's skirt. Rhiannon snatched up a nearby platter and brought it down on the man's head. His eyes rolled up as he fell. Another soldier lashed out with his fist, catching Rhiannon with a glancing blow on her temple. She staggered, her hand going to her head. She could feel blood streaming down her face. She tried to regain her balance as Gwen grabbed her arm and dragged her through the doors and down the steps of the hall.

The doors of the hall slammed behind them, impelled by the force of Gwen's Shape-Moving. "Hurry," Gwen panted, "I can't hold them very long."

Stumbling, partially supported by Gwen, they made for the still-opened doors of the fortress, when the sound of the alarm made her heart sink. The gates began to close. Behind them, soldiers spilled through the doors of the hall as Gwen's power weakened. She looked around wildly, trying to make out the buildings in the darkness. Where to go? How to get out of there? They turned, now making for Elen's ystafell.

A hand shot out of the darkness, closing on her wrist with bruising force, bringing her up sharply.

"This way," Talorcan said. "Hurry."

"Mam, no! It's a trap!"

"You have no choice but to trust me if you want to get out of here alive," Talorcan said grimly. "It's up to you."

Rhiannon's eyes flickered back to the hall. Soldiers with torches leapt into the courtyard. Any moment now they would be seen. She turned to Talorcan and nodded. "Get us out of here."

Without another word he spun around, herding them into the ystafell and shutting the door behind them. The room was dark, and Talorcan lit no candles. He rustled behind the canopied throne that stood against the east wall. They heard a click, and the throne swung outward, revealing a trapdoor beneath.

"How did you know—" Rhiannon began.

"Any good soldier thoroughly investigates the enemy."

"Why haven't Elen and Regan used this to flee?"

"There is a lock at the door on the other end. I put it there, and only I have the key. Come on." He dropped down through the door, helping Gwen and Rhiannon to descend. Then he pulled the trapdoor shut and pushed some kind of lever. They heard a scraping above, as the wooden throne returned to its previous position.

"Put your hand on my shoulder, Rhiannon. And you—" he turned to Gwen, "whoever you are, put your hand on her shoulder. We can't risk a light."

They did as they were told, following Talorcan into the darkness. It seemed to go on forever. Rhiannon, through her dizziness, was acutely aware of Gwen's trembling hand on her shoulder. Gwen did not like dark, underground places.

They were slowing now. At last Talorcan halted. He stood silently for a moment, then nodded, as though satisfied. The sound of a key fitting into a lock, another click, and above them, the barest glimmer of starlight could be seen. Talorcan leapt up, grasping either side of the trapdoor, pulling himself out. He reached down, searching for Rhiannon's hand. His hand was cold and much too thin, but strong. He pulled her out, and she saw they were on the edge of the forest just outside the town walls. She crouched down beside him on her knees, cradling her head in her hands. So dizzy. And so much blood. She could feel it, sticky and wet on her face.

Talorcan pulled Gwen out of the tunnel, then spun on his knees to face them. In the faint starlight, his face was no more than a shadow.

"I called Gwydion," he said quietly. "I think he heard me. He should be here soon."

"Talorcan," Rhiannon began, "how can I, how can we—"

"Don't thank me," he said coldly. "That is the last thing I want to hear. Or don't you understand what I have become?"

"I know what you have become. You have become what you were meant to be from the beginning. You are one of us."

From far off, drifting over the night sky, the faint sound of a hunting horn could be heard. A tinkling of silver bells, the barest hint of a hoofbeat, and the sounds were gone, the night still again.

"The Wild Hunt," Rhiannon said softly. "It's Calan Llachar. Of course, they would come."

"Farewell, Rhiannon ur Hefeydd, and farewell to your companion. I must go. Tell Gwydion ap Awst that, if I should see him again, I will kill him, as is my duty."

"I understand," Rhiannon said.

"Do you?"

"Yes. Keep Elen and Regan safe, against the day when they will be free again. And the day when you, too, will be free."

"That day will be never. I am a fool, but not such a fool as to believe I could ever be free." He melted away in the shadows, without even waiting for her answer.

And then she felt strong, warm hands, cradling her head, a soft cloth mopping her face, the sound of his voice, whispering that she would be all right. And she knew that was true, for Gwydion had come.

Chapter 15

Llyn Wiber
Kingdom of Ederynion, Kymru
Celynnen Mis, 499

Suldydd, Disglair Wythnos—late morning

Gwydion observed Rhiannon closely out of the corner of his eye as she sat next to him on the wagon box. By now she was fully recovered from the blow to the head she had received in Dinmael thirteen days ago, but Gwydion continued to be anxious.

Not anxious, really—enraged would be more like it.

He was enraged because someone had dared to harm her, enraged because she had come so close to being captured and the thought of that still twisted his heart with cold, harsh fear. He was enraged because she had been determined to take such a terrible chance and he had not known how to stop her—indeed, he had known from the beginning that he could not. And that powerlessness alone was enough to infuriate him.

"You're doing it again, Gwydion," Rhiannon said crisply. "And I feel fine. Or did you just want to yell at me some more? You haven't done that yet today, so you're long overdue."

He looked away from her without replying and glanced over at Gwen and Arthur, who rode their horses on either side of the wagon. Sometimes he thought he saw something in their eyes that told him they knew exactly why he was so angry. But, if so, neither one of them had said a word about it. Gwen had continued to treat her mother as if Rhiannon didn't exist. And Arthur continued to treat Gwydion as less than the dirt beneath his feet.

The wagon creaked as they made their way to the lake of Llyn Wiber in northern Ederynion. They had been drawn here by the power and the pull from the pearl ring Rhiannon wore. She had guided them here all the way from Dinmael, from the moment she had put on Elen's ring and it had begun to glow. North, she had said then, the blood still dripping down her face. North. The Stone was there.

So in the last two weeks, north was where they had gone. Just a few days ago they had passed into the cantref of Dinan, into the commote of Mawddwy. And there they had again reviewed the clues from the song.

"Under the gravestone
In the land of glass
The serpent lies coiled.
Beneath the water lies the seeker."

"The serpent lies coiled," Gwydion had mused, "beneath the water."

"I know where it is. And you do, too," Rhiannon had answered. "Isn't Llyn Wiber, Lake of the Serpent, just a day away? 'Under the gravestone,' the song says. In the center of the lake is the cairn of Carreg Fedd, the Gravestone. It's there. The Stone is there."

He felt her shiver slightly as the lake came into view. Overhead the sky was a clear, cool blue. The forest, which gave way at the water's edge, stood silent guard over the lake. The water had an emerald cast to it, as though the serpent still slept beneath.

Gravestone, indeed. It would not be Rhiannon's, he vowed silently. And he knew that he would willingly leave the Stone in this lake rather than see her harmed. He wondered at himself, because he knew that was the truth.

Slightly ahead of them, he saw Gwen and Arthur on their horses, cantering up to the water's edge. The horses dipped their heads and drank noisily. Gwydion halted the wagon, set the brake, and climbed down. Rhiannon stayed where she was, absently fingering the ring she wore.

"Hold," a powerful voice boomed from the trees.

At these words thirty men and women melted from the forest to surround their tiny band. Arthur and Gwen leapt from their horses, their hands flying to loosen their weapons. Rhiannon sat unmoving on the wagon box, calmly eyeing the newcomers.

The man who had spoken stepped from the trees and came to stand before Gwydion, his sword drawn and his face grim. The man was huge, his powerful shoulders straining against the brown leather of his tunic. His hair was iron gray, and his blue eyes were bright in his tanned face. Two women closely flanked him. One had fierce dark eyes and her dark hair was braided and wound around her head. The other had light brown hair and cool gray eyes. Both had arrows nocked and ready as they watched Arthur and Gwen narrowly.

"Have the cubs put up their weapons," the huge man said, gesturing to Arthur and Gwen, who had both pulled short spears from their packs.

"Arthur, Gwen," Gwydion said from beside the wagon. "Put your spears down."

"But, Gwydion," Gwen began in protest. The woman with the dark hair shifted slightly so she was aiming directly at Gwen.

"Do as I say," Gwydion said calmly. He turned to the huge man. "Well-met, Drwys Iron-Fist."

The huge man smiled as he put up his sword. "Well-met, Gwydion ap Awst, Dreamer of Kymru. The Cerddorian of Penbcullt are here, as you have Wind-Spoken for us to be. How may we serve you?"

"You might help me down," Rhiannon said, as she extended her hand to the huge man. "And then introductions are probably in order."

"Ah, you are Rhiannon ur Hefeydd, and every bit as beautiful as I have heard."

Gwen and Arthur put up their weapons and came to stand beside Gwydion as Drwys helped Rhiannon down from the wagon.

"If only the Dreamer had thought to tell us he had called you,"

Arthur said with a cold glance at Gwydion, "you might have found a warmer welcome from us."

"It is of no matter," Drwys said. "We would not have harmed you."

"I was thinking of the harm we might have done to you."

Drwys grinned, and the Cerddorian tried to hide their smiles. "I do not think we would have come to harm from you, boyo," he said.

"Do you not?" Arthur asked belligerently, his hand going to his dagger.

Gwydion said hastily, "Let me introduce to you the Lord of Dinan. He is not called Iron-Fist for nothing, and I urge you to treat him respectfully. In his day even Queen Olwen's father, King Custennin, always trod lightly around Drwys."

"Ah, well," Drwys boomed. "I was a hothead then."

"And so different now," the woman with the dark hair murmured, a hint of laughter in her dark eyes.

"And this is Sima ur Naw, the Gwarda of Is Fechyn. Her brother, Emrys, is Lieutenant to Prince Lludd in Coed Ddu."

"We met your brother," Rhiannon said. "He was very kind."

"Unlike his sister," the other woman with light brown hair put in.

"And this is Caras ur Saidi, the Gwarda of Mawddwy," Drwys went on.

Before anyone else could speak, Caras said, "My sister is Ellywen, she who was once Druid to King Rhoram of Prydyn, she who betrayed Cian the Bard into the hands of the Coranians. Know this before you greet me."

"Caras ur Saidi," Rhiannon said, "there are some of us who are related to those who have betrayed Kymru. The shame is theirs, not ours."

Caras lowered her bow. "People must know who I am before they give me greetings. It is only right."

"The honor of your family is whole, because of you," Rhiannon said. "There is no dishonor here."

Drwys gestured to Gwen and Arthur. "And these children are?"

"This is my daughter, Gwenhwyfar ur Rhoram," Rhiannon said as Gwen sketched a curtsy.

"And the boy is the son of an old friend," Gwydion broke in before Rhiannon could continue.

"Ah," Drwys said. His bright blue eyes gazed knowingly on Arthur, but he did not say what he was thinking. "Tell us now what you wish."

"The first few days we were dogged by a contingent of Coranian solders."

"Led by Iago," Gwen put in.

"Druids," Caras said, snorting in contempt. But she fooled no one, for the sheen of angry tears was in her gray eyes.

"We lost them by the time we reached the commote of Elfael," Gwydion went on. "By the time we crossed into Cydewain, we were sure the pursuit was over."

"Both the Dreamer and I Wind-Ride each day, and we have seen only lone Coranian messengers and a few soldiers here and there," Rhiannon said.

"And?" Drwys asked.

"And we don't for one moment believe that we lost the pursuit," Gwydion said. "Havgan wants us too badly. We think they have gotten word to a contingent up here. We need you to guard our back as we do now what we must do."

"And that is?" Drwys asked.

"That is something we may not name."

"I see. Well, then, Dreamer, you shall have what you wish. My Cerddorian will fan out, and we will be sure you do what you must do undisturbed."

"You simply do as he asks?" Arthur asked indignantly. "No questions?"

"We do not question the Dreamer, boyo," the Lord of Dinan said with finality. "You would do well to follow our example." Before Arthur could answer, Drwys and his people melted back into the forest and the quiet descended, as though the Cerddorian had never even been there.

"You might have told us," Arthur began fiercely.

But Gwydion ignored the boy and turned to Rhiannon, taking

her cold hands in his own. His mind was now made up. "You're not going into that water," he said firmly.

She turned to him in surprise. "The Stone is mine to find."

"You can't swim," he said. "Or did you forget that?"

She flushed. "Of course. Throw that up to my face."

"I'm not throwing that up to you! I'm telling you that I will go. You will not risk your life for this."

"If not for this, then for what?"

"Not for anything. You're not going," he said flatly. "And that is that."

"I am going. Find me a log."

"A what?"

"A log," she said patiently. "A piece of wood. Something that floats."

"No."

"Yes. You cannot find the Stone and you know it. The ring is for my finger alone, and it alone can guide the way to the Stone. Without that Stone Arthur will not be High King. And without that, we are lost. Now get me that log. Now."

He stared at her, his anger at fever pitch. Why would she never do what he asked her to do?

"Now, Gwydion. I will not be cheated of what is my rightful task."

"Rhiannon," Arthur said hesitantly. "I don't think Uncle Gwydion's trying to cheat you. I think he's trying to help."

"Fine," Rhiannon replied between gritted teeth. "He can help by getting that log."

Gwydion turned away, thrashing through the bushes at the edge of the forest. He found a short log on the forest floor and brought it back to her, flinging it at her feet.

"There," he said tightly. "Anything else?"

Anything else? She wanted to say *yes*. She wanted to say, *go in my place. Call the Stone and waft it into my hands.* But she said none of these things.

"You can have a blanket handy," she said, "for when I come

back."

She knew what Gwydion had been trying to do. As always, he thought he was the only one who could do things right. He thought he should be the one to get the Stone, because he didn't trust her to do it. She knew what he thought of her.

She turned to face the lake. In the middle was a pinnacle of rocks jutting up like jagged teeth. The water rippled against it, as though begging to be let in.

Yes, the Stone was there, in Carreg Fedd. In the center of the lake, of course. It was too much to expect it to be at the edge. And she would have said that out loud, but she seemed to have trouble breathing.

She also seemed to be shaking. She had to stop. It was water. Only water. If she kept her head above it, held on to the log, propelled herself to those rocks, she'd find a way in. Get the Stone. Come back. And they'd be on their way. That's the way it would happen. It would be all right.

With a silent prayer to Nantsovelta, Queen of the Waters, Lady of the Moon, she unlaced her kirtle and stepped out of her wool dress. Her cream-colored linen smock hung to just past her thighs. She unlaced her boots and took them off. She checked that her hair was still tightly braided and bound.

Trembling in every limb, her breath constricted in fear, she picked up the log, walked past Gwydion, Arthur, and Gwen without even acknowledging they were there, and stepped into the water. When the water reached her waist, she positioned the log in front of her, putting her hands on it to help keep afloat.

She turned her head to look at them for what might be the last time.

Gwen was kneeling by the water's edge, leaning forward slightly as though trying to help Rhiannon begin. Their eyes met, and Gwen smiled in encouragement. And then Gwen dropped her eyes as though realizing she had been too kind.

Arthur smiled at her and nodded, though his smile was strained and his shoulders were tense. His eyes searched the lake warily.

And then she turned to Gwydion. He stood stiffly, his hands clenched into fists, the knuckles white. And as she looked at him, he slowly released his fist and held his hand out to her, as though longing to bring her back. She reached out her hand in farewell and then turned to go.

She took another few breaths to try to calm herself and then launched herself into the water, clinging to the log in front of her. She set her sights on the promontory, and propelled herself toward it, willing herself to do that which she had feared for years beyond counting.

And willing herself to live through it. To come back to those who waited, with the Stone in her hands.

GWYDION WATCHED HER go without a word. His body was taut with anxiety, his knuckles white with tension. He never took his eyes off of her as she made for the rocks in the center of the lake. She traveled steadily and did not falter. His heart felt as though it would burst with pride—and fear.

And then he felt it. Something was wrong. Where? He wrenched his attention away from Rhiannon's journey to Ride the Wind, to try to discover what was happening. But before he could even do so, Caras appeared before him as if from thin air.

"Drwys says you were right. The soldiers are here."

"Where?"

"Over the last hill to the south. There are twenty of them. They carry the banner of Havgan—the white boar on a field of red and gold. Drwys says for you to go, that we will hold them off."

"We cannot go," Gwydion said, shaking his head. "Rhiannon is still in the lake."

"You must go! They will see you."

"I won't go without her. Arthur!" he barked. "Take the wagon and move it far back into the forest. Gwen, take your horse and Arthur's and follow the wagon. The two of you go with Caras. Caras, can your people lead them off?"

"We will do what you wish."

Arthur, for once not questioning Gwydion's judgment, climbed into the wagon and grabbed the horses' reins.

"What about you?" Gwen called out to Gwydion as the wagon

lurched forward.

"I'll stay here," Gwydion replied as he turned back to the lake to see Rhiannon. "I'll Wind-Speak to Rhiannon, tell her to—"

But he did not finish what he was going to say. For, as he looked to the rocks, Rhiannon had disappeared, and the log was floating alone.

As SHE DREW closer to the rocks, Rhiannon tried to still her breathing, telling herself to be calm. The water was cold, and she tried to stop herself from wondering what lay beneath the surface. Perhaps the serpent wasn't dead. Perhaps it was just waiting in the dark below for the chance to pull her down, to fill her lungs with water, to tear her apart, to devour her . . .

Stop it, she told herself fiercely. *Stop.*

She needed something else to think about. Riddles, that was it. What is whiter than snow? Truth. What is sharper than the sword? Understanding. What is blacker than the raven? Death. No, that was the last thing she should think about.

Nantsovelta, help me, she cried deep inside. *Help me. I'm so afraid.*

She remembered a prayer to the goddess, which she had been taught long ago, and she recited it in a low voice, her breath coming short and hard with fear.

"O vessel bearing the light,
O great brightness outshining the sun,
Draw me ashore,
Under your protection,
From the shortlived ship of the world."

But not now, Nantsovelta, she thought. *Do not take me now. Help me to live. Help me to bring back your Treasure to the use of the High King, for whom it was made.*

Don't let me be taken by the serpent, she pleaded.

Stop. There was no serpent. It was only water. Water was good. It gave life. It did not mean to kill.

Aunt Llawen, why did you die? Why did the water take you from me when I needed you so much? You left me alone, and I was alone for so very long. Then Rhoram came to me, and loved me, and I wasn't alone anymore. But he did not stay. No one ever stays. They leave and leave and leave, and I am so alone.

Da. Da, why did you never love me? What had I done? What was I that you loathed the sight of me? Why was I nothing in your eyes?

No, that was no way to think. She had forgiven him, years ago, when she had finally understood. She would not travel that path again. Her da would have loved her, if his spirit had not died the day she was born, the day her mother died.

But her daughter hated her. Her former lover was nothing to her now. And Gwydion was dangerous. She had no one but herself. And it must, it would be enough. She would do this thing and maybe learn to think better of life and her place in it.

But she was so afraid.

At last she reached the rocks, her thoughts incoherent, her body cold and shivering, her spirit shriveled with fear.

She saw and understood then that the path she must travel was beyond her power to take. She could never do this thing. Never. There were no openings above the water. And the Stone must be inside. And to get inside she would have to dive down, try to find a way in before her breath ran out. Oh, and if there was a tunnel, how could she stand to swim into it? How could she know how long the tunnel was? She would be trapped under there, unable to surface, and she would die.

Gwydion's face came to her, as she remembered his outstretched hand as she left him on the edge of the lake. She wanted to go to him and lay her fear in his hands. She wanted to feel his strong arms around her, to shelter beside him.

And it was that thought that spurred her. What had she been thinking—that she would find shelter in Gwydion? That was the thought of a fool. She would not return to the shore without that Stone. That would show Gwydion what she could do.

She released the log, keeping her head above water for a few moments. Then she took a deep breath, and dove.

GWYDION CROUCHED WITHIN the shelter of the trees, his eyes fixed on the promontory in the center of the lake. The log she had been holding floated alone and she was gone. He tried to Ride out to her, but he could sense nothing, could see nothing. It was as though she had never been there, as though the rocks were a wall that could not be climbed, could not be brought down, could not be lessened in any way.

She was dead. Drowned. And all because of him. All because of his dreams. All because he had found her that day and forced her to stand with him in his fight for Kymru to be free. He had not valued her as he should have. He had never told her the truth. He had been too afraid.

As the Coranian warriors poured down the hill and to the shores of the lake, he did not move. They must have killed the Cerddorian, for he saw no sign of them. He hoped vaguely that Gwen and Arthur had gotten away, but he could not make himself care too much. He knew the soldiers would eventually find him, but that thought had no meaning. She was dead.

And everything was over.

And so, as they came closer, Gwydion did not move from his place.

He merely waited. And wondered that the heart he thought dead could give him so much pain.

IT WAS DARK BENEATH the water. Above her she could see glimmers of light shining through the surface of the lake. But the light died quickly. She put her hands out to the rocks, feeling for a way in. She would always remember that she found it within seconds, as though it had been waiting for her. Perhaps it had.

Knowing that if she stopped to think she would never move, she grasped the rough edges of the tunnel and propelled herself inside. She used her hands to push herself along, shooting through the water as fast as she could. Her lungs were burning, and she could feel a scream building inside her throat.

No. She would not cry out. She would live through this. And she would bring the Stone back. She would do this thing because that was what Nantsovelta required, and for too long she had run from all the things she should have done.

Her hands, feeling the way along the roof of the water-filled tunnel, suddenly grasped nothing. She shot up, knowing that if she did not break the surface she would die. If there was no surface . . .

But there was. She came up inside the mound of rocks into darkness. She could tell by the sound of the water that slapped at the walls that she was in a narrow cave and the ceiling was low.

She reached out and grabbed hold of the rocks, and rested in the water for a moment. So dark. How could she find the Stone?

But then she saw a glimmer of light and saw that it was coming from the pearl ring she wore. The light grew stronger, a bright, shimmering light, like the path of moonlight dancing on water.

The cave was small. The pool of water where she had surfaced was directly in the center of it. A ledge ran around the water, rough and uneven. Shadows capered and menaced throughout.

Where? Where was the Stone? Surely it was not at the bottom of the lake. Surely it was here somewhere. And then she saw an answering glimmer from the ledge. And she saw Nantsovelta's treasure, Gwyr Yr Brenin, Seeker of the King.

The Stone was square, each side no more than a foot long. The surface appeared to be granite or something like it, shot through with a lattice of bright threads of silver. At each silvery junction a pearl rested, as though formed by the stone itself. At the center on the top of the Stone was a figure eight, the symbol of Annwyn, Lord of Chaos. The symbol was studded with shining onyx, black as night. She reached out a trembling hand to trace that figure. There was a cavity at the center, a narrow slot where something must go. But what?

That did not matter now. The Stone glowed even brighter in response to her touch. She seemed to hear a harp, playing a sweet melody. "Nantsovelta," she breathed, and bowed her head until it rested against the Stone. "Daughter of Chaos and the Weaver, Bride of the Sun, Lady of the Waters, Queen of the Moon, to you I bend my spirit. Do with me as you will."

"So you have come at last," a man's voice said, low and gentle.

Her head shot up, and she looked wildly around. Who was in here with her?

A slight shimmer next to the Stone solidified and became the figure of a man dressed in a robe of silver trimmed in sea green. His blue eyes were mild and sad, yet something in the set of his fine, drawn mouth spoke of a deeper joy, come from the wisdom that grows from suffering. Around his neck was the glow of ghostly pearls.

"Who are you?" she demanded, her heart in her throat.

"I am Mannawyddan ap Iweridd var Fabel," he replied.

Her breath caught in her throat. Mannawyddan, the Fifth Ardewin of Kymru, one of the Great Ones of Lleu Lawrient, the last High King! But Lleu had been murdered over two hundred years ago.

"Why are you here?" she whispered.

"To guard the Stone. To ensure that no one but you ever found it."

"All this time?" she asked, shocked.

"All this time," he replied gravely. "My spirit has been bound here, denied its rest in Gwlad Yr Haf, the Land of Summer, where the spirits of my love, Queen Siwan of Prydyn, and our son, Merfryn, dwell. Where the spirit of Lleu himself rests—or did," Mannawyddan said, with a faint smile. "For Lleu has returned."

"You recognized him."

"I did. His spirit is strong within young Arthur. The High King does, indeed, return."

"Oh, Mannawyddan," she breathed. "I am sorry that you waited so long."

"It is of no matter. This is what I agreed to when my brother, Bran the Dreamer, gave me this task. And I was glad to do it, as one last gift I could give to my murdered High King."

"And now that I am here, now that I have come, your spirit may go to its rest?"

"Indeed, it may, Rhiannon ur Hefeydd var Indeg. For you have come, and faced your fears and conquered them. The fear of water chains you no more. Though you have others that do."

"What—"

"You know of what I speak. And his fear is even greater

than yours. Try to remember that, my Dewin-daughter. Now, take the Treasure and go. But go carefully, for the enemy is near." The shimmer faded, and she was truly alone.

The enemy! Instantly she was on the Wind-Ride, searching. Mannawyddan had spoken truly. Twenty Coranian warriors were on the shore, searching for her and her companions. But surely Gwydion and the others had gone. Where were the Cerddorian?

Even as she thought that, she saw the warriors' heads go up and turn as one to the north. She followed their gaze and saw Gwen and Arthur on their horses, shouting taunts at the warriors.

"Fools!" Arthur shouted. "You couldn't find the sun in the sky on a clear day!"

"Idiots!" Gwen called out, laughing. "You'll never catch us!"

The warriors leapt to their horses as Gwen and Arthur turned their mounts. And then the chase was on. She saw them disappear over the hill, Arthur and Gwen far ahead of the warriors, leading them into the forest where, surely, the Cerddorian waited.

But where was Gwydion? She scanned the trees, but there was no sign of him. Perhaps something had already happened to him. Perhaps he was hurt, dead, dying.

The thought spurred her on. She grabbed the Stone from the ledge, and as she hauled it into the water, she had a moment of horror. Suppose it sank? Suppose she couldn't carry it? She couldn't even swim. How could she—

But the moment the Stone touched the water, she saw her fears were groundless, for the Stone floated. She could easily hold on to it and keep herself afloat.

And then she had another horrible thought. If it floated, how would she get it down into the water-filled tunnel and out again? Tentatively, she tried to force the Stone under the water. It went easily, as though sensing what must be done and eager to do it.

Taking a deep breath, she once again submerged into the water, holding the Stone in front of her as though holding on to life itself.

Gwen and Arthur drew up their sweating horses. Hidden from

the warriors by the endless trees, they watched the contingent gallop past them and down the path. The Cerddorian waited for the soldiers around the bend, hidden in the trees. They would slaughter the Coranians, down to the last man, Arthur knew. He had seen it in Iron-Fist's cold blue eyes when they had planned this.

"They really are fools," Gwen whispered.

"They know nothing of the Kymri," Arthur said. "And that, in the end, is what will kill them."

"Yes," Gwen said firmly. "It will."

"And besides," Arthur said absently, his thoughts elsewhere, "they would never have been able to catch me. I'm very good at this."

"At what? Running away?" Gwen countered, stung that he was taking all the credit. It had, after all, been partially her idea to be the bait.

"I've been doing it all my life," Arthur said bleakly. "And so, my girl, have you."

"I'm not your girl!"

"Thank the gods for that."

"You—"

"Hush," he said firmly. "Let's get back to the lake. We need to find Gwydion. And I hope to the gods that your mother has returned, safe and sound."

"And with the Stone."

He turned to look at her, and there was contempt in his eyes. "Just safe and sound would be enough for me. But not for you, I see."

"What do you mean by that?"

"I mean that you are cruel to her. And she doesn't deserve it."

"You don't know anything about it. And you're a fine one to talk of cruelty to others, the way you treat your uncle."

"That is something you know nothing about. Come on."

GWYDION HUDDLED NEXT to the tree, his head resting on his drawn-up knees. She was dead. And everything was over. Now what would he do?

The snap of a branch, the sound of steps, did not make him raise his head. The warriors had returned for him. Now would be his turn to die. And everything was ash, dust, everything was gone, and he did not care that life was over.

"What kind of welcome is this?"

Her voice. Her voice from the dead. He raised his head and saw her.

Her shift clung to her body like a second skin. Her feet were bare. Her braided hair was slicked against her head. In her arms she cradled the Stone. Her green eyes shone with triumph.

He leapt up, grabbed the Stone, and set it down, as though it was nothing. He took her in his arms and held her close. He closed his eyes and breathed in the scent of her, reveling in the feel of her body against his, feeling the beat of her heart against his own, knowing that this was always how it had been meant to be.

He looked down at her, and she raised her face to his. Her green eyes were soft, and her lips parted as he bent his mouth to hers.

And before their lips touched he felt that he was at last at peace, having surrendered to the truth of his heart.

But his peace lasted only for a moment.

For he remembered everything about who he was, then. He remembered that he was the Dreamer and he had almost given up, all because he had despaired of losing her.

He remembered that the things he had done, that the things he must do, were tasks given him by the gods, and he must not fail.

He remembered what would happen to Kymru if he weakened.

And he knew he must not.

So he withdrew from her, dropping his arms, stepping away, standing in the forest by Llyn Wiber and feeling so cold as he saw the shock, then the humiliation, then the anger, in her emerald eyes.

Chapter 16

Coed Coch and Llwynarth
Kingdom of Rheged, Kymru
Celynnen and Draenenwen Mis, 499

Gwyntdydd, Cynyddu Wythnos—early afternoon

Twenty-five days later, Gwydion, Rhiannon, Arthur, and Gwen silently made their way through the dense forest of Coed Coch in southern Rheged. They were on foot, having left the wagon behind in the trees a few leagues back, unable to further penetrate the woods with it in tow.

They walked in single file, waiting for the forces of King Owein to contact them. Owein and his people knew they were here, for Gwydion had contacted his daughter, through Wind-Speech. But the forest of Coed Coch was huge, and it would take some time for Owein's people to reach them and guide them to the hidden camp; Cariadas had explained that Owein had forbidden knowledge of that location to anyone, including to the Dreamer and his party. Gwydion's daughter had apparently expected outrage from him about this, but Gwydion had not felt any anger. Owein was right—such behavior was their only safety from traitors within. He did not forget that one of their own—whomever that might have been—had betrayed the location of the Y Dawnus at Allt Llwyd. And Owein's own sister had, in the end, betrayed her brother's presence in his previous hiding place in Coed Addien.

Thoughts of Enid, Owein's sister, continued to irritate Gwydion. The stupid girl had stolen her brother's ring and journeyed to Llwynarth to persuade Bledri, King Morcant's Dewin, to repent of his collusion with the enemy and return to Owein. Bledri had promptly turned her over to Morcant Whledig. And Morcant was now determined to make Enid his wife, and, in so doing, claim the ring of the House of PenMarch for his own. It would be Gwydion's task to get the ring back from beneath the watchful eyes of Morcant, Bledri, and Baldred, Havgan's General in Rheged.

Gwydion glanced behind him at the others who followed. Gwen was right behind him, as she often was. It seemed as though whenever he turned around, she was there. Rhiannon trudged behind Gwen, looking, as was always the case now, at anything and everything except at Gwydion. Her eyes had not met his since that day at Llyn Wiber. She had barely spoken two words to him since then.

Why wouldn't she understand? Because, he thought bitterly, she was a woman. And they never understood anything beyond their own desires. Higher concepts of honor and responsibility meant nothing to them. It was because of his responsibilities that he had withdrawn from her that day by the lake. His was the task of ensuring the return of the High King to Kymru, the task of driving the enemy from their land. And he could not be, would not be, fettered in any way in the pursuit of that task.

It was true that what had almost happened between them had been Gwydion's fault. At the sight of her safe and sound, his heart had leapt and he had, momentarily, lacked the ability to check his impulses. But since then he had been in full control.

Behind Gwen, Rhiannon almost stumbled, for the balance of the Stone she was carrying in the pack on her back made her footing awkward. Arthur, the last in line, put his hand beneath her elbow to steady her. She smiled her thanks, and Arthur's returning smile and slight flush told its own tale of how the boy felt about Rhiannon.

A violent rustling in the bushes halted the party. Gwydion, his walking staff raised, immediately placed himself between the source of the sound and Rhiannon. Arthur leapt forward, drawing his knife, to stand next to Gwydion, while Gwen guarded Rhiannon's back, for the Stone Rhiannon carried was precious beyond price.

Then a slight figure, her red gold hair curling around her shoulders in its usual disarray, burst from the bushes and hurled herself into Gwydion's arms.

"Da!" she cried, hugging him fiercely.

Gwydion dropped his staff and held his daughter close. He kissed her forehead, then tilted her chin up to meet his gaze. She was thinner than when he had last seen her. There was a line above her brows now for all that she was smiling. He remembered she had been in Allt Llwyd when the caves had been invaded. He remembered that she had journeyed with the few survivors across Rheged to take refuge with Owein. He remembered that she had barely escaped with her life. Tears came to his eyes, and he held her close to him. Should anything ever happen to Cariadas, his heart—touched by so few that many claimed it didn't even exist—would break.

"Daughter," he murmured softly into her hair. "Cariadas, my very dear."

Three more people came from the forest to stand beside them. He gently disentangled Cariadas's arms from his neck to greet them.

"Trystan ap Naf," he said to the Captain of Owein's forces. "Well-met." He grasped Trystan's hand, and the man's green eyes lit with welcome.

"Teleri ur Brysethach," he went on to Trystan's petite but fierce Lieutenant. "What is your count of the enemy dead now?"

"Forty-two, including three wyrce-jaga," Teleri replied with a grin. "Ah, the day I got the wyrce-jaga was a fine day, indeed."

"It must have been," Gwydion agreed. "And Sabrina ur Dadweir," he went on. "I hope that you are well?" he said, for Sabrina's blue eyes were shadowed.

"I am well, Dreamer. As well as anyone in Rheged can be with Princess Enid's wedding to come so soon."

"You were not at fault, Sabrina," Trystan said, with the air of a man who has said the same thing dozens of times before. "You did all you could to save her that day in Llwynarth. Enid did this to herself."

Trystan turned to Gwydion. "We rejoice that you have come. Owein has asked us to convey you safely to his nearest refuge. Elidyr, the Master Bard, and his wife, the Ardewin, have asked me to tell you that the new network is building apace and they expect to have it all repaired by the festival of Calan Gaef. They are in the southern part of Coed Coch and cannot come to greet you. But they will be listening for your Wind-Speech to them tonight and will give you all the details."

Gwydion shook his head. "It is not enough. They must have the network repaired sooner than Calan Gaef. By Ysgawen Mis, at least."

"They have done a great deal in a short time," Trystan pointed out stiffly.

"I think much of their work, Trystan," Gwydion said coolly. "But on Calan Gaef, truly momentous things will happen. This Kymric new-year festival will be like no other. And our network of Y Dawnus must be functioning before then."

"Do you know my companions?" he went on smoothly, for he was not going to argue with—or be judged by—Trystan. "This," he said, gesturing airily to Gwen, "is Gwenhwyfar ur Rhoram var Rhiannon, Princess of Prydyn and apprentice Druid. And this is the son of an old friend." The lack of any further identification of the boy was not lost on those present. After a moment of silence, when it became clear that Gwydion was not going to add any other information, Sabrina greeted these two formally in the name of King Owein.

"I think you know Rhiannon ur Hefeydd," Gwydion went on.

Trystan bowed to Rhiannon. "We have never met, but I know of you."

"And I you, Captain Trystan," Rhiannon replied. "But I must ask you about another matter. Is my Uncle Dudod here with you? Or with Elidyr and Elstar?"

"Neither, Lady. Dudod is on his way to Llwynarth, to prepare for your coming to that city."

Rhiannon turned to Gwydion, accusation in her green eyes. "Why didn't you tell me you sent him there?"

"You didn't want to talk," Gwydion replied innocently, picking up his staff. "Remember?"

"You—" Rhiannon began, then stopped as she noticed that Cariadas was looking from Rhiannon to Gwydion, bewildered. The girl seemed close to tears. Whatever Rhiannon had been about to say—and Gwydion was pretty sure what the general import would have been—remained unsaid. He knew that it was only a momentary respite. Rhiannon would not very easily forgive Gwydion for dispatching her uncle to Llwynarth. But Gwydion had no choice—someone had to set up the arrival in Llwynarth, and Dudod was the obvious choice.

"Take us to Owein," Gwydion said. "There is much to talk about."

THE JOURNEY TO Owein's hidden camp was accomplished in cool silence for the most part—the one notable exception was Cariadas. Gwydion's daughter chatted almost without stop to everyone, and while no one initiated conversation, no one was unkind enough not to respond to her overtures. Gwen, in particular, was taken with Cariadas and so, in another way, was Arthur. But the elders in the party were mute. Sabrina was subdued. Rhiannon was furious. Trystan covertly watched Sabrina, but his face was unreadable. Only Teleri seemed unaffected by the general atmosphere, but she often ranged ahead of the group, scouting for potential trouble.

Cariadas, at the news that Gwen was a Druid, chatted about her friend Sinend. She was sure that the future Archdruid could help Gwen with further lessons, if Gwen wished. And she was very curious about Arthur. She spoke to him about general subjects, but questions were in her eyes. Secretly Gwydion was amazed that Cariadas had learned enough restraint not to try to worm Arthur's identity out of them.

They reached the camp after a few hours. Sentries melted out of the forest to greet them and escort them into the camp proper. The camp was small, for it was not King Owein's main camp. There were forty Cerddorian practicing their archery, wrestling, staging mock knife fights, and the like. Gwydion and the rest were led to a brown-colored tent erected within the shelter of a copse. The tent was large, and Gwydion barely had to duck his head to enter. The rest followed, all except Teleri, who stationed herself outside the tent flap.

In the dim light Gwydion recognized King Owein, his younger brother, Prince Rhiwallon, and Sinend, the daughter of the Archdruid's heir.

Owein uncoiled his thin, wiry frame from where he sat and formally embraced Gwydion. "Dreamer," Owein said, "you are very welcome here. The things you have asked for have been done. Tell me what else you need from us, and it is yours."

"Such deference is bad for him, Owein," Rhiannon said tartly.

Owein's face relaxed slightly as he greeted her. "You are more lovely today than those years ago when I followed you and the Dreamer to meet the Wild Hunt and hear of our fate."

"And you have become very well spoken. I am pleased."

Before Owein could reply, Gwydion said, "This is Gwenhwyfar ur Rhoram."

"The Princess and I have met before," Owein said, his smile forced.

"Yes," Gwen replied. "When you and Enid came to visit us on Ogaf Greu—" Gwen stopped abruptly, her face red. Everyone present knew the time she meant—when Owein had offered his hand to Gwen's half sister, Princess Sanon, and had been refused. And when Geriant, Gwen's half brother, had offered his hand to Enid and been accepted. But that marriage had not taken place, and a new marriage loomed for Enid.

"This is the son of an old friend," Gwydion said quietly, gesturing to Arthur.

Owein looked at Arthur curiously, but merely said, "You are welcome here." Arthur bowed his head to Owein but did not speak.

"We have fulfilled the first task given to us by the Shining Ones," Gwydion said formally. "The first Treasure has been found." He nodded to Rhiannon. She opened her pack and brought forth the Stone. The pearls gleamed and the silver veins shimmered in the dim light.

Inside the tent they all gasped. "A mighty task, indeed, Dreamer," Owein breathed. "And it is for the further completion of this task that you are here, is it not?"

"It is," Gwydion nodded. "For I have come to claim the ring of the House of PenMarch, as foretold by Bran the Dreamer."

"But, to my sorrow, I do not have the ring."

"We know. We have come for help to retrieve it from Princess Enid."

"This is great news!" Owein exclaimed. "For if the Dreamer is to help us rescue Enid, how can we lose?"

But Gwydion shook his head. "We do not go to Llwynarth to rescue Enid, but to rescue the ring. I can do nothing about Enid's fate."

"You must!"

"I tell you, I cannot," Gwydion said harshly. "The ring is to be used to find the Spear, and I do not know where it lies. Do you think it can be easily found in a country seething with the enemy over Enid's escape? That will endanger everything, and I cannot allow it."

He expected them to attack him, and they did. Owein protested angrily, and his brother, Rhiwallon, backed him up. Trystan was enraged. Sabrina demanded that he help rescue the Princess, saying that, if he did not, she herself would burn Llwynarth to the ground. Gwen and Arthur added their protests, for it seemed monstrous that they not help Enid. Even Cariadas and gentle Sinend argued for the rescue.

Of them all, only Rhiannon said nothing, until the argument reached a fever pitch. At this she rose, and there was something in her stance, something in her face, that made everyone fall silent.

"The Dreamer is right," she said quietly, to Gwydion's astonishment.

"King Owein," she continued in the shocked silence, "Prince Rhiwallon, truly do we understand your feelings and your love for your sister. But understand this. There is nothing we can do. We have all sacrificed for our country, haven't we? Sinend, you ran away from your home to throw in your lot with those who had been outlawed. Cariadas, you have not seen your father for years at a time, and have lost the Master Bard, whom you loved, to the enemy. Sabrina, you have endured shame for being a Druid, and for being powerless to save Enid from her folly. Trystan, you, too, have endured shame—the shame of surviving your King and Queen. Owein and

Rhiwallon, you have lost your mother and father. And your eldest brother, too, has died at the hands of the Coranians.

"All this—these heartaches, these tragedies—are lamented by the Kymri. But there is more at stake here than Enid's future. Kymru is at stake. What Enid did, she did of her own free will, hard as that is to accept. And though you love her, you must leave her to the consequences of her actions."

Rhiannon's cool, smooth voice rippled through the tent. At her words the Stone beneath her hand seemed to glow brighter. Her pearl ring gleamed. "I do not speak for myself in this," she went on wryly. "Left to myself, I would, as we all know, oppose the Dreamer's wishes to my last breath."

She glanced at Gwydion, and he abruptly shut his mouth, which had been hanging open in shock. "But remember," she went on, "that the Shining Ones knew that this would happen. For listen now to the line of a song that was left to guide us in our darkest hour: 'Fast was the trap of the woman in Caer Erias.' And Caer Erias, the fortress in Llwynarth, is where Enid now waits the day of her marriage. Her trap is unbreakable. We cannot help her. We can only pity her. And, if we can, get from her the ring of PenMarch, to make our last hope come to fruition."

After she was done, the silence in the tent lengthened. At last, Owein looked up, his blue eyes lined with tears. "I have sent Dudod to Llwynarth as the Dreamer wished. I will leave my sister in captivity, if this is what I must do. But you must take Trystan with you. And Trystan will be guided by this wish—that if there is any way to rescue my sister, he will do it. And if there is not, he will give her my love and my hope for a better life to come the next turn of the Wheel."

Suldydd, Lleihau Wythnos—early morning
THE DAY OF Princess Enid's wedding to Morcant the Pretender dawned bright and clear. The morning was cool, but there was a hint of afternoon heat to come. The capital city of Llwynarth was crowded, for today was both market day and the day when the people of Rheged would see their Princess given to the enemy.

Gwydion, Rhiannon, Trystan, Gwen, and Arthur, all plainly dressed as became a farmer's family, made their way through the crowded streets to the marketplace. They did not falter when they passed what had been Nemed Draenenwen, the sacred grove of hawthorn trees, now destroyed to make way for a temple to the Coranian god.

Gwydion led the way confidently, armed with the information that Dudod had given him via Wind-Speech the night before. Without halting he led them to the stall of Menestyr, one of the most important cloth merchants in Rheged. It had been this man, Gwydion had been told, who had first tried to warn Enid when she had come to Llwynarth many months ago.

Gwydion halted at the back of the stall, motioning for the rest to precede him. The interior was dim, and bales of cloth teetered precariously, stacked one on top of the other. They could hear good-natured bickering from the merchant and his customers up in front of the stall, but little light penetrated to the back, due to a curtain placed between the front counter and the back of the stall.

"Care to buy something?" a man's voice inquired at Gwydion's elbow.

Before Gwydion could answer, Rhiannon launched herself at the man and hugged him tight. Keeping her voice down, she began to scold him. "Uncle Dudod! How dare you leave for Llwynarth without telling me? After all I have done for you, how could you treat me so shabbily?" She smiled as she said it and kissed him soundly.

"Well, my dear," Dudod replied airily, "you know the life of a traveling man. Here one day, gone the next. You are not the first woman to be displeased by such habits."

"And I won't be the last, I'm sure."

"Thank you, Dudod, for your efforts," Gwydion said. "We have had a slight change of plans, as you can see by Trystan's presence."

"Owein wasn't happy with your plans, I see," Dudod replied, grasping Trystan's arm in greeting.

"Not quite. But you will be happy to know that your niece stood up for me. If it hadn't been for that, we'd still be with Owein, arguing."

"Did you now?" Dudod asked, turning back to Rhiannon. "That must have hurt."

"Ha, ha," Rhiannon said flatly.

"I wasn't joking. And the rest of your party?"

"This is Gwenhwyfar. You saw her last some time ago when we found Rhiannon in Coed Aderyn."

"You've changed a great deal, dearest Princess," Dudod said, kissing her hand.

"Remember her age, uncle, and yours," Rhiannon said dryly.

"And this is the son of an old friend," Gwydion went on. He knew that Dudod was fully aware of Arthur's identity. But he was not yet ready for Trystan to know it.

Dudod understood instantly. "Greetings, son of an old friend. Now, we have fine clothes to make you all very important people, indeed—important enough to get into the temple for the ceremony. Our good merchant, Menestyr, has already gotten places for you—some in the back and some in the middle, as requested. Gwydion and Rhiannon, General Baldred will surely recognize you if you are too much in his eye. And Gwydion, Trystan and I have the same problem with Bledri and Morcant. Whatever contact must be done with Enid, it will be done by Gwen and this young man."

"It would be better, I think, if only those two went to the temple," Trystan said.

"But not as safe. They will need your protection if anything goes wrong," Gwydion replied. "Between you, I, Rhiannon, and Dudod, we can get them out in case their task does not come off as easily as I expect. We will be sure to sit well away from them as Dudod has arranged."

"Then on with the clothes and off to the wedding," Dudod said, "on this, one of the saddest days in the history of Kymru."

"Poor Enid," Gwen said, to no one in particular.

GWYDION, TRYSTAN, AND Rhiannon sat in the very back of the temple, close to the doors. Inside it did not look much different from the temples Gwydion had seen during his time in Corania. A drinking horn rested on the left of the stone altar. The bowl to hold the bull's blood was on the right, and the ritual knife gleamed wickedly in the light of four white candles placed in the corners of the altar. Above the altar was the banner with the symbol of Lytir worked in gold on white cloth. The pit where the bull was usually housed was covered over, for there would be no sacrifice today—not of a bull, at any rate, Gwydion thought.

Gwydion glanced at Rhiannon to his right and at Trystan, on Rhiannon's other side. The three of them were dressed richly. Rhiannon's dark hair was covered with a veil of misty blue, secured to her head with a circlet of silver. She wore a kirtle of dark blue over a white smock. Trystan's hair was secured at the nape of his neck with a band of gold and emeralds, and his tunic and trousers were green. Gwydion was dressed in a black tunic and breeches, and his hair was secured at his neck with a band of rubies.

Gwen and Arthur were halfway down the aisle, toward the middle of the temple. Gwen was in a gown of white (which she had protested against, saying she preferred her breeches and boots). Arthur's tunic and trousers of saffron drew Gwydion's eyes like a lodestone. Of them all, Arthur was the most important, and Gwydion watched him like a hawk.

Once again, though surely no one would believe it, Gwydion tried to think of some way to rescue Enid. Though he had said it was impossible, he tried again to think of a way. Much as he despised her for her foolishness, that was all it had been—foolishness. She had not thought to betray her brother, had not thought to put herself into this slavery. She had not really thought of anything at all except for her infatuation with Bledri. And she would soon pay full price for that. But even as his thoughts went round and round, he knew it could not be done. They would be more than lucky to leave Llwynarth with the ring. They would surely have no chance of getting Enid out, too.

The noise outside the temple alerted him that the ceremony was about to begin, and he wrenched his thoughts away from rescuing Enid, knowing it to be useless.

The doors of the temple opened, and as the procession entered, the crowd rose to its feet. The first two men to enter, Gwydion knew by reputation. They were Oswy, the Coranian Byshop of Rheged, dressed in a robe of green, and Saebald, the Master-wyrce-jaga, his black robe relieved by a stole of green. Behind them walked General Baldred, resplendent in a golden tunic trimmed with rubies. Next to him came Bledri, the renegade Dewin who had thrown in his lot with the enemy—and Princess Enid to the wolves. Bledri wore the traditional silvery robe of the Dewin with his pearl torque around his neck. At the sight of him in those garments, which he had no right to wear, Rhiannon gave an angry hiss—lost, of course, in the noise.

Behind them came Morcant, he who had once been a Lord of the murdered King Urien and was now the self-styled King of Rheged. His dark eyes were gleeful as he looked down at the woman whose thin hand rested on his arm. It was Morcant's lecherous look at the Princess that almost made Gwydion throw everything to the winds and kill the traitorous King.

Princess Enid did not look to the left or the right but straight ahead as she walked down the aisle on Morcant's arm. The opal ring of the House of PenMarch glittered on her hand. Little was to be seen of Enid's face beneath her veil, but her stiff shoulders, her rigid bearing, told its own tale.

At the sight of their Princess dressed in the Coranian manner, in a gown of red with a golden veil cast over her head and shoulders, the crowd murmured sharply in dismay. But the whispers were quickly halted at the sight of the Coranian guards that poured in behind the couple.

As Morcant and Enid reached the altar, four guards grasped the poles of a square canopy and held the red cloth over the couple. Byshop Oswy lifted his hands for silence.

This was no traditional Kymric wedding. This couple would not stand before a Druid in a green grove surrounded by joyous friends and family. The groom would not carry an alder branch and the bride would not carry ivy, those symbols of Cerrunnos and Cerridwen, the Protectors of Kymru. There would be no talk of the Great Wheel, of rebirth and beginnings, of finding the heart's love for this turn of the Wheel. There would be none of that, for this was a Coranian wedding, built on treachery and greed.

At the Byshop's signal, Morcant, his voice gloating, pulled a simple band of gold from his little finger, which he put on Enid's trembling hand. "With this ring, I thee wed, and this gold and silver I give thee; and with my body, I thee worship; and with all my worldly chattels, I thee honor."

Then Enid replied, her voice low and hopeless. "I take thee to be my wedded husband; to have and to hold; for fairer, for fouler; for better, for worse; for richer, for poorer; in sickness and in health; to be bonny and buxom in bed and at board; till death us depart."

Then she slowly pulled the opal ring off her finger. She bowed her head and blindly held out the ring to Morcant. He snatched it from her and put it on his finger. Then he triumphantly tore the veil from her head and pulled her to him, crushing his mouth upon hers.

The crowd was frozen, plainly horrified. Out of the corner of his eye, Gwydion saw Trystan's hands clench into fists. He almost remonstrated, when he realized his own hands were clenched, as well.

General Baldred stepped forward, grabbing one of Morcant's arms, thus effectively ending the embrace. Baldred raised Morcant's hand, the hand where the opal ring glittered, and called out, "This is your true King! Today has he received the ring from the hand of King Urien's daughter. Today has he wed her, and let none now dispute—he is your King!"

ALONG WITH THE rest of the spectators, Gwen rose as the wedding party retraced their steps up the aisle. The sight of Enid's face unnerved her. Enid was pale, and there were tears in her eyes. Her mouth was swollen and red from Morcant's kiss. But the Princess held her head high, not looking directly at anyone. Yet Gwen knew Enid would recognize her when the moment came. They had gotten to know each other well when Enid and her brother had come to visit Ogaf Greu; the time when Gwen's brother, Geriant, had looked on Enid and loved her and begged her to marry him. Gwen contrasted the dark, hideous Morcant with Geriant, who was so golden, so beautiful, so brave, and so kind. She thought that perhaps Enid was remembering that, too.

"Ready?" Gwen whispered to Arthur as Enid neared them.

"Of course," Arthur replied. "Don't be a fool." Arthur craned his neck and looked down at his feet as though noticing something wrong with his boots. He tsked in exasperation and bent to pull them up tighter. His elbow jabbed her sharply in the ribs, and she yelped, jumping away from him and, somehow, falling to her knees in the center aisle—directly in front of Princess Enid herself. Gwen clutched at the Princess's red gown to steady herself and looked up into Enid's eyes.

"You there, what are you doing?" Morcant demanded.

"She fell," Enid replied, holding out her hand to help Gwen to her feet.

As Gwen rose, her palm brushed against Enid's. And the note smoothly passed from one girl to the other.

Arthur yanked Gwen back to her place, and the wedding party continued up the aisle.

"Did she get it?" Arthur whispered.

Gwen nodded, too overcome by the glimpse of torment she had seen in Enid's eyes to speak.

RHIANNON WAITED WITH the others in the bathhouse at Caer Erias, listening for the sound of Enid's arrival. Getting into the fortress had been easy, for the doors were opened in expectation of the guests for the wedding feast.

Rhiannon reached out and laid a gentle hand on Gwen's hair, searching for some way to comfort her daughter. For Gwen had been pale and had not spoken a word since the wedding. Rhiannon expected Gwen to jerk her head away, but the girl did not. Instead, Gwen turned to her, her blue eyes filled with tears. Blindly Gwen reached out and Rhiannon was there, pulling her daughter into her arms, softly stroking her hair and whispering words of comfort. After a moment Gwen stiffened and drew away, shifting to the far side of the bench on which they sat.

Rhiannon said nothing, for she had long since recognized that the hatred her daughter felt was fair. She had done the same to her father years ago. Myrrdin had tried to tell her, to warn her that the

Wheel turned around.

Rhiannon settled back onto the bench and waited. She looked up and Arthur caught her eyes as he stood near the doorway with Trystan, Dudod, and Gwydion. He left them and came over to her, settling himself on the bench between Rhiannon and Gwen. He ignored Gwen's taut back and turned to Rhiannon.

"She will not be much longer, we think. It should not be too difficult for her to excuse herself from the feast. She need only say that she wishes to bathe in order to be presentable to the King tonight."

Rhiannon smiled. Arthur was not saying anything she didn't already know, but he was trying to help. She glanced over at the men in the doorway and Gwydion returned her gaze, then quickly looked away.

"My uncle is a fool," Arthur said quietly.

"So he is," she replied. "And I have learned to let fools be fools and not to be bothered with them."

"No, you haven't."

Before she could reply, they heard the sounds of movement outside the bathhouse. Gwydion, Trystan, and Dudod moved away from the inner door, motioning for the others to hide themselves.

The outer door opened and shut, and they heard footsteps nearing the chamber. The second door opened, and Enid stood framed alone in the doorway. She quickly shut the door behind her and flew into Trystan's arms.

"Trystan, oh, Trystan," she cried, weeping in the shelter of his arms. "My brother has sent you to save me after all! Oh, how I have begged the gods for this!"

Trystan closed his eyes in agony and bowed his head over hers. For a moment the only sound was of Enid weeping. Then she raised her head. "Let's be gone from here," she said eagerly. "How do we go?"

"We don't," Gwydion said coldly, moving to stand next to Trystan. Dudod and Arthur took their places on either side of Gwydion while Rhiannon and Gwen went to stand in front of the door.

"What do you mean, we don't?" Enid cried, not looking at Gwydion, but rather at Trystan.

"I—I'm sorry, Enid. We can't," Trystan said, his voice breaking.

"Can't?" Enid stepped away, searching their faces wildly. She spun for the door, but Rhiannon and Gwen were in her way. "What are you doing here if not to come for me? Why won't you help me? Why?"

"We did not come here for you because there is nothing we can do for you," Gwydion said. Only the tautness of his shoulders betrayed how hard those cold words were for him to say. "We have come for the ring."

"The ring?"

"The ring you stole from your brother, its rightful owner."

"I didn't steal it!" Enid flared. "I—I borrowed it."

"Then the time has come for you to return it. For we have need of it. The land wakes to fight for freedom. The Protectors are come back to us. The Treasures must be found. Even now we have one in our possession. And the Treasures will be used to make a High King, one who will drive the enemy from this land. And to find the next Treasure, we need the ring."

"You can't have it!" Enid cried. "Not without taking me with you. That is my price!"

"Your price?" Gwydion hissed, stepping closer to her. Enid looked around, but the rest of them only stared at her, appalled at what she was saying.

"Your price?" Gwydion asked again, his voice cold and deadly. "How dare you talk to us of price. For all of us have paid—and will continue to pay—in heart's blood for what has been done, for what will be done. We have lost those we have loved. We have lost our country, our freedom, our way of life. And you—you who placed yourself in your own prison—demand help. You who have caused suffering to your brothers, to Sabrina and Trystan because they could not save you, to Prince Geriant who loved you, to the Cerddorian who had to flee for their lives from Coed Addien when you betrayed their hiding place—you set a price. You sicken me. We stand at the brink of destruction, and all you can think of is to be rescued from what you have done to yourself."

"Get me out of here!" Enid screamed. "Get me away from Morcant.

Away from Bledri and the things that they do to me! Get me out and you will have your ring!"

"Enid ur Urien var Ellirri, I know you have listened to your brother speak of your father's last message to him. And so I say this to you now, in the words foretold by Bran the Dreamer, the words passed down from ruler to ruler, 'The High King commands you to surrender Bran's gift.' Know that I am the Dreamer who was born to give you this command. Know that to ignore this command is to betray Kymru herself."

The chamber was silent as Enid and Gwydion faced each other. The color drained from Enid's face at Gwydion's words. At last her eyes filled with tears, and she dropped her head. "Forgive me," she whispered. "Please forgive me."

Trystan stepped forward and again took Enid in his arms. She clung to him and her tears fell, but she was silent. At last she raised her head and turned to face Gwydion. "I do not have the ring. I gave it to Morcant in the ceremony today. But I can get it for you. When he takes me tonight, he will be thinking of nothing but my humiliation and of inflicting pain. I can get it for you then, for he wears it on his finger."

Gwen choked back a sob at Enid's words. Enid turned to Gwen. "Give your brother a message from me. Please."

Gwen nodded but could not speak.

"Tell Geriant that I wish with all my heart that I had known what I had in him. Tell him that I wish he were the man I married today. I would have spent the rest of my life with him and been content. But that will never be now."

"Enid," Gwen wept. "If we win Kymru back, Geriant can be yours. He will never suffer Morcant to live."

"No," Enid said quietly. "It is too late for that. The woman he would find then would be very different from the girl he loved. They do things to me here that change me. Tell him I am sorry. Tell him that, in the end, I paid for my foolishness, paid full price, as the Dreamer would say."

Enid turned away from Gwen and went to stand before Gwydion.

Rhiannon was not surprised to see the torment in Gwydion's eyes as the girl looked up at him, her face set. "Dreamer, I will do as you ask. Stand beneath the window of the bedchamber in the Queen's ystafell in an hour's time. Then will I give back what I have stolen.

"Trystan," she went on, turning to her brother's Captain, "there is only one more thing you can do, if you will. I ask you to do all you can to release a captive from Caer Erias."

"Enid, I can't—"

"No, not me," Enid smiled faintly. "I know that. But there is someone else here who has suffered longer than I have. March Y Meirchion, my father's huntsman, Esyllt's husband, is here.

Trystan paled and swallowed hard. "You ask this of me? To rescue the man whose wife I have loved for so many years?"

"He does not deserve to be imprisoned here. No matter what you feel for his wife."

"A great gift you give me, Enid," Trystan said, his face working. "A great gift. The chance to save him and return him to his wife, the chance to make up to him, in some small measure, for the pain I have caused him."

"The pain Esyllt has caused him, too. For would she not be happy to have him back again?" Enid grinned wickedly.

"What a lovely gift for Esyllt," Dudod grinned back. "Come, Trystan," he said, slapping his friend on the back, "let us take this man back to his loving wife."

"How did you know, Enid, that I would give my soul to do this?" Trystan asked.

"The look in your eyes. You are changed. March is held in the cellars beneath the kitchen. It will not be easy."

"Don't be foolish, girl," Dudod said smoothly. "There is no kitchen in the world that doesn't have a wine barrel I can't take with me."

"I STILL SAY it's foolish," Gwydion whispered to Rhiannon for what seemed like the hundredth time as they waited, crouched down next to the walls of the ystafell hidden from casual sight by the barrels stacked there.

Rhiannon sighed. "Yes, I know you do. You have said so, over and over. But this is something Trystan must do. And what better man to help him than Dudod?"

"Once we get back to Menestyr's stall and join Gwen and Arthur there, we will not wait one minute past midnight for them," Gwydion threatened. "They are on their own."

"There is no need to wait for them at all, Gwydion," Rhiannon said serenely. "They won't be coming with us on our journey. They will be returning to Coed Coch."

Gwydion muttered something under his breath.

"What did you say?" she asked sweetly, turning to him.

He did not reply, but searched her face for a moment. "Rhiannon," he began. "About that day by the lake. I'm sorry. I—"

"Best not to talk about it, Dreamer. Let's just say you were overcome at the joy of seeing the Stone. After all, think of the years you dreamed of it. You would, of course, be momentarily grateful to anyone who had retrieved it for you. I understand."

And she did. She knew Gwydion ap Awst through and through. He cared nothing for her, and never had. It had been the Stone, the fact that she had done his bidding like the puppet she was, that had almost made him kiss her in gratitude.

"You don't understand," Gwydion whispered harshly. "You—"

"Hush," she breathed, putting her hand on his arm to silence him, nodding to the upper window. Gwydion's eyes followed her gaze. The curtains that hung over the window rustled slightly. A thin, white hand pushed the window open. For a moment they saw her. Her hair was disheveled. Her robe, open at the neck, revealed red welts on her chest. Her eyes were swollen from weeping, and her mouth was torn and bleeding.

But she smiled as she tossed the ring down to them as it turned end over end, the opals flashing fire under the pale light of the stars.

Chapter 17

Coed Sarrug
Kingdom of Rheged, Kymru
Draenenwen Mis, 499

Meriwdydd, Tywyllu Wythnos—early afternoon

South," Gwydion had said when he put on the opal ring. "South." So they had gone south, traveling Sarn Halen, the great north/south road that bisected Rheged.

Rhiannon remembered, from the time she had worn the pearl ring of Nantsovelta, the pull she had felt, the relentless pull toward the place where the Treasure was hidden, the pull that never lessened until the Treasure had been found. So she was not surprised that Gwydion did not sleep well during the ten days of their journey. And not surprised when he was restless and uncommunicative. It had been the same for her.

And there was another similarity—the fear. She had been afraid of what she had known was coming as they neared the Stone. And she knew Gwydion's fear.

It was something she had never taunted him with. She could—and did—taunt him with the things that everyone already knew about him. That he was cold, that he cared nothing for others, that he used people. But she had never shown that she knew his secret fear. She had never said to anyone that the great Dreamer, that cold, impervious man, feared Mabon's Fire.

He would have been appalled that she had known the truth. But she had known it for years. Hadn't she traveled with him more leagues than could be counted? And every night he had Fire-Started their campfire using different ways to shape the blaze—blossoming roses and roaring lions, jeweled necklaces dripping with flames, swords that slashed through the air trailing fire. No one put on such a display of mastery except for one reason—because they were secretly afraid. This she had understood a long, long time ago, but had kept that knowledge to herself. Strange that she could hate him, but she would not humiliate him.

They had left Llwynarth ten nights ago, soon after returning to Menestyr's stall. Only a few moments after they had arrived there, Dudod and Trystan had returned with a wine barrel and had hauled March Y Meirchion out of it. Poor March had been almost nothing but skin and bones after two years of captivity.

March had said little as they helped clean his scars and filthy body. He merely kept staring up at Trystan in disbelief. As well he might, for Trystan had cuckolded March for years. Rhiannon smiled, visualizing Esyllt's horror when they brought her husband back to her.

Trystan, Dudod, and March had also left Llwynarth that night. They would make their way back to Coed Coch in easy stages, giving March time to recover his strength.

"By the time you reach Coed Coch," Gwydion had said, "I hope we will be right behind you."

"How long for you to recover the Spear?" Trystan had asked.

Gwydion shook his head. "No telling. But we are in a hurry, and so I hope it will not be long. The ring tells me that we go south. But I don't know how far we must go."

"Take the location of Owein's main camp from me," Dudod had said.

"I'm not sure Owein would like that."

"I am quite sure he would not. But take it just the same. You will need it."

"Rhiannon," Gwydion had said, eyeing Dudod. "Take it from

your uncle."

"You think I would take this opportunity to take things from you when your guard is down, Dreamer?" Dudod had asked, his voice hard.

"Dudod, you can take anything you want from anyone, any time you want. Did you think I didn't know that? But I thought it might be easier for you to be read by your niece."

Dudod had looked Gwydion up and down. "Kindness ill becomes you, Dreamer."

"So it does," he had agreed mildly. "Rhiannon?"

And so she had been the one to place her hands on her uncle's head. She had been the one to read the forest of Coed Coch, to learn the signposts, the location of Owein's main camp.

"Be sure that Owein himself is there when we come," Gwydion had said when it was done. "And also be sure that Elidyr and Elstar are there. I must speak to them about the network of Y Dawnus."

"Yes, O Great One," Dudod had replied, grinning. "Anything else?"

"Yes. Find yourself a nice, warm widow. You deserve it for your work today."

"Your wish is my command, Dreamer."

"Good. At least someone thinks so," Gwydion had said, with a withering look at Rhiannon.

March had asked only one question as they had cleaned his wounds and fed him, trying to help him gain some strength for his journey. "Why?" he had whispered to Trystan. "Why?"

And Trystan had laid down the cloth and looked down at March. "Because I owe it to you. And you know that."

"You owe me nothing. You never took anything from me that I really had."

"She liked it the way it was—having both of us."

"And now she has only me?"

"Yes," Trystan had said evenly. "Only you."

March smiled faintly. "She won't like that."

"Then find another who will."

"I just might do that, my friend. I just might."

Rhiannon smiled as she remembered the conversation. Then the wagon slowed, and she looked up. "What's ahead?" she asked.

Gwydion nodded toward the town of Margam, which was half a league away. "We will leave the road soon, after we pass through the town."

"Which way?"

"Northeast."

She mused on the verse from the song of the Caers. "Within the dark forest / In the land of honey / The hill of oak stands."

"Yes, I think we go to Bryn Duir, the hill of the oak."

Standing within Coed Sarrug, the Grim Forest, the hill was bare of trees but one—a storm-blasted oak that had stood there for years beyond counting. Often struck by lightning in storms, the oak was never fully destroyed. She glanced up at the sky, where storm clouds threatened. Poor Gwydion—lightning meant fire. And they both knew it.

"Yes," Gwydion said to her unspoken comment. "A storm. And a tree that draws lightning. The gods laugh at me, I think."

Impulsively, she put her hand on his. "We will be with you. Don't be afraid."

He turned to her, and his gray eyes were alight with something she did not understand. "You know."

"I always have."

"And have never said."

"You have never said anything to me of water. Why would I say anything to you of fire?"

"You are generous, Rhiannon ur Hefeydd. More generous than I deserve."

"Ah. You noticed."

Arthur rode up next to the wagon box. He nodded toward the town. "There is a checkpoint up ahead," he said quietly.

Gwydion glanced up at the road ahead. "We will leave the road after we go through the town."

"Why not now?" Arthur asked.

307

"Because the path we want does not branch off until after the town, of course. And because they have already seen us."

"Of course," Arthur said sourly. "How kind of you to explain."

"Patience," Gwydion said airily, "is a virtue."

"And so is treating your companions like people—not puppets."

Gwydion's brows shot up. "Are you sure that's a virtue? I don't recall that one."

Gwen drew up her horse on the other side of the wagon box. "Shall we go on?" she inquired in a polite tone. "Or does Arthur wish to argue some more about nothing of any importance whatsoever?"

"Why don't you keep your questions to yourself!" Arthur snarled.

"And why don't you get off that horse, bend over, and—" Gwen began.

"Gwenhwyfar," Rhiannon said sternly. "Hush."

"You can't tell me what to do! I—"

"We are nearing the soldiers, if anyone cares," Gwydion interrupted. "Now would be a good time to show some of that family unity we do so well."

"Brothers and sisters always bicker," Arthur said with a forced smile. "Or so they tell me. I would not know."

"Of course, you would throw that up to my face," Gwydion said. "And at such an opportune time, too. Thank you, my son."

"Da," Gwen said sweetly, "I believe those soldiers want us to stop. I hope it's not for very long—I want to get to Uncle Bryndan's house and take a bath."

"You are always complaining about being dirty," Arthur said sourly, as Gwydion slowed the wagon to a halt in front of the soldiers that fanned across the road. "Mam, can't you tell her to shut up about that?"

"Your sister has her little ways," Rhiannon replied serenely, as though the soldiers were not there. "And it wouldn't hurt you to take a bath yourself."

"He likes smelling like horses," Gwen put in with a sniff of disdain. "He's little better than an animal himself."

There were other Kymri clustered around the soldiers, waiting for their turn to get through the checkpoint and into the town. They smiled appreciatively at the squabbling. The Coranian soldiers, on the other hand, began to look impatient as they waited to be noticed.

"Ha! At least I don't have to go around smelling like a perfume bottle. As though any boy would look twice at a scrawny girl like you—no matter what you smell like."

"I'm not scrawny," Gwen flared. "I'm slender."

"No meat on those bones," Arthur scoffed. "What man would want that?"

"You—"

"I—"

"Children," Gwydion said sternly, "This is not the time."

Gwen and Arthur looked around and appeared to notice for the first time that there were soldiers about.

"Captain," Gwydion said, standing up in the box and bowing with a flourish. "You see before you an honest merchant, down on his luck. Care to buy something? Pots and pans? Cloth?"

"Two children?" Rhiannon asked sweetly.

The Kymri waiting their turn laughed. The Captain, his blond hair flaring in the afternoon sun, continued to look impatient. There were twenty soldiers at the checkpoint, all armed to the teeth. Standing in the dust all day did not seem to agree with them.

Rhiannon, though she did not show it, was nervous. This was a lot of soldiers for such a small town. It was obvious that word had gone out from Llwynarth about the ring. She knew that her and Gwydion's descriptions had been sent about Kymru ever since Havgan had taken this land. Havgan would have been told about the ring disappearing from Llwynarth. Perhaps he had guessed who had done it and stepped up all the checkpoints in Rheged. If so, there might be trouble.

"If there is anything we want in Kymru," the Captain said sourly, "we take it. Not buy it. And I do believe there might be something we want." The Captain eyed Rhiannon and grinned.

Gwen bristled, and her hand crept to the knife at her side. But

Arthur nudged his horse forward into Gwen's, making her horse dance sideways. Rhiannon barely heard his whisper to her daughter.

"Let them handle it," Arthur said quietly.

Gwen did not reply, but she gave Arthur a look that said she would have plenty to say later. She took her hand from her belt and laid it across the pommel of the saddle.

Frantically, though it did not show in her face, Rhiannon called out in Wind-Speech for the flock of ravens she knew was only a short distance away.

"Captain," Gwydion said in a pained tone, "you are uncivil. I am a merchant down on his luck, and you serve me with this kind of talk. Life is hard enough as it is, for we are going to my wife's brother's holding in Coed Sarrug. And you know they don't call it the Grim Forest for nothing."

Some of the Kymri smiled, and even the Captain's stance relaxed somewhat.

"And my brother-in-law! Well, that's another story. Never did he think I was good enough for his sister. And now he can't wait for his chance to be proven right. We lost everything in the war, you see. And now we must throw ourselves on his charity. Worse than that, he raises pigs! Can you see me helping in the pigsty? Have mercy, sir, isn't life hard enough? Imagine what he would do to me if I showed up without his sister!"

"There speaks the brave man I married," Rhiannon said sourly. "I think a turn with the pigs would do you a world of good."

"Then perhaps you would like to come with us," the Captain said. "We could show you a better time." As he said that, his eyes widened. Slowly he moved forward, grabbing the bridle of one of the wagon horses. For a moment everything was quiet. And Rhiannon clearly saw the recognition in the Captain's eyes. So, their descriptions had, indeed, reached all the way to Gwent.

"Hey, Captain," one of the burly farmers said. "Can't you move it along? Find your women on your own time. It's market day, and I have food to sell!"

The other Kymri began to clamor for the Captain to move them along. Just then, a flock of ravens flew overhead. Cawing and calling to one another, they set up another clamor, enough to hurt the eardrums.

"All right!" the Captain shouted. "All right!" He jerked his head at the wagon, stepping away from the horses. "Go on through."

But Rhiannon was not fooled. She had seen the Captain's eyes, and had guessed his orders. Let them through, and follow them where they go.

They passed through the town, riding slowly, for the streets were crowded. The people of Margam did not seem to pay them any attention, but Rhiannon knew better. They were being watched very closely, indeed. The crowd seemed to part like water to let them through, then closed in behind them. It was not enough to stop the pursuit, but it gave them a little time.

When they reached the other end of town, they were not being visibly followed. They left the Sarn Halen road, turning northeast toward Coed Sarrug. As they neared the wood, Rhiannon Wind-Rode back along the trail and saw what she had expected to see. "All twenty soldiers following us," she said crisply.

"Only twenty?" Gwydion replied. "I'm insulted."

"Indeed," Rhiannon said.

DUSK WAS FALLING by the time they reached the outskirts of Coed Sarrug and halted the wagon. Gwydion climbed down and unhitched the horses. As Rhiannon mounted one of them, the black cloth of her dress hiked up to her knees, exposing the sheath strapped to her calf, which held a long, sharp knife. As she waited for the others to be ready, she quickly braided her hair to get it out of her way.

ARTHUR AND GWEN were also armed, both carrying short spears as well as knives at their belts. Only Gwydion was not armed. He mounted the other wagon horse, his black tunic and trousers blending with the shadows cast by the trees. A sudden flash of lightning illuminated his set, taut face. Thunder rumbled in the distance, and the horses moved skittishly about.

"A storm," Gwydion muttered. "Of course. 'Within the storm

lies the blaze.'"

"The Song of the Caers?" Gwen asked.

"The Song of the Caers," Rhiannon agreed. "We will find what we seek at the top of Bryn Duir. There lies Tymestl Pren, the Storm Tree, an ancient oak. And that is where we go."

"Storm Tree? I have heard of it," Gwen said softly. "It is always hit by lightning in a storm. It burns, but it never dies."

"Shouldn't you take the Stone with you?" Arthur asked Rhiannon. "Surely it is unwise to leave it here, unguarded."

"It will not be unguarded, boyo," a woman's voice said from the dark shelter of the trees.

As one, Arthur and Gwen leapt from their horses and spun to face the voice, their hands on their weapons.

"A likely pair," a deeper, masculine voice said.

"So they are," Rhiannon agreed. "Please, come and greet them."

At her words fifteen men and women melted from the shadowy forest. Their tunics of dark green and brown blended in with the forest so perfectly that it was difficult to make them out. The wind whipped the trees, rippling the cloaks of the Cerddorian who stood there.

The man and woman who had spoken approached the wagon. The woman carried a drawn sword in her fist. She bowed to Gwydion, who inclined his head. Her long, dark brown hair was braided tightly, and her emerald green eyes were fierce. The man had flaming red hair and a short-cropped beard. His brown eyes were sharp and fiery. He, too, bowed to Gwydion.

"Children," Gwydion said quietly, "this is Atlantas ur Naf, the Lady of Maelienydd, and the sister of King Owein's Captain, Trystan. And this is Tyrnon Twrf Liant, the Lord of Gwent. They are the leaders of the Cerddorian in southern Rheged."

Arthur and Gwen took their hands from their weapons and bowed to the two Cerddorian.

"We are sorry we were not prepared to greet friends," Arthur said, shooting a venomous glance at Gwydion. "But, as usual, we were not told to expect your arrival."

"Why should you have been?" Atlantas said, with a palpable lack of sympathy. "The Dreamer's business is his own."

"You have called us, Dreamer, and we are here," Tyrnon said swiftly, before anyone could reply. "How may we serve you?"

"I fear the Coranians recognized us at the checkpoint today. I ask that you prevent them from following us."

"Where do you go?" Tyrnon asked.

"To the Storm Tree."

"Ah," Atlantas said. "Then Mabon's Fire calls to you."

In the uncertain light only Rhiannon noticed Gwydion's involuntary shiver. "It does," she agreed. "And the Coranians follow us."

"How many?" Tyrnon asked.

"Twenty," Rhiannon replied.

"The entire guard, then," Atlantas said to Tyrnon. "I will enjoy this."

"Be careful, Atlantas," Gwydion warned. "If you massacre the guard the entire Coranian army will descend on Gwent."

"We are not fools, Gwydion ap Awst," Tyrnon said quietly. "We will merely—ah, misdirect them."

"And if a few of them get hurt along the way," Atlantas said grimly, "well, accidents will happen."

"So they will," Tyrnon agreed dryly. At his gesture a third figure detached from the group within the shelter of the trees and came to stand by the wagon.

"This is Cimin ap Cof, the Gwarda of Gwent Uchcoed. He will see to it that your wagon and its contents are here when you return," Tyrnon said.

The man had black hair and dark eyes. His expression was set as he spoke to Gwydion. "You must know, Dreamer, who I am."

"I do know you, Cimin ap Cof. There is no need. And no shame."

"Then the others must know." The man turned to Rhiannon, Gwen, and Arthur. "My brother is Iago, he who was once the Druid to Queen Olwen of Ederynion, he who now aids the enemy in imprisoning Queen Elen. It is right that you should know this before you leave the guarding of your possessions to me."

Surprisingly, it was Arthur who answered. "Cimin ap Cof, the Dreamer is right when he says there is no shame. You serve your rightful Lord, and do your part to reclaim Kymru. For this your family will be honored."

Arthur spoke with such conviction, and with authority well beyond his years, that even Rhiannon was surprised by the underlying power they all sensed in him.

"You honor me," Cimin said quietly, bowing to Arthur. His brow was furrowed as he tried to sort out who Arthur might be, but, wisely, he asked no questions.

"Fear not, Dreamer," Atlantas said, her tone fierce. "The Cerddorian of Coed Sarrug will not fail you."

"I did not think you would," Gwydion said. "Come," he continued, speaking to Rhiannon, Arthur, and Gwen. "It is time." He turned his horse to the forest and disappeared into the shadows.

Rhiannon, Arthur, and Gwen mounted their horses and followed. Before entering the forest, Rhiannon turned to look back at Atlantas, Tyrnon, and Cimin. She raised her hand in farewell, in case she never saw them again.

THE FOREST WAS dark, so dark she could see nothing but the tail of Gwen's horse in front of her.

"How long before we reach Bryn Duir?" Gwen asked, turning in the saddle.

"At least two leagues."

"Then we had better go faster. There is no telling how many soldiers might make it through the Cerddorian."

"We will go no faster than the Dreamer rides, Gwen," Rhiannon replied shortly. "The Spear is his to find, and the pace is his to set."

"But, mam—"

"It is his to set."

GWYDION RODE THROUGH the forest as if in a trance. Lightning began to play across the sky, faster and faster. The light flashed through the dense forest, sometimes making their path seem as bright as day.

Soon they would reach Tymestl Pren, the Storm Tree. And there, he knew, he would find the Spear. And he knew, too, what he would have to face to get it.

Fire.

Lightning flashed again and again. Gwydion found it hard to breathe, so great was his fear. The fire, the fire. He knew what fire could do. It burned. It burned and burned and burned and would not stop.

Fire. Mabon's Fire. Mabon, King of the Sun, did not make gentle fires. No, Mabon's fires were hungry. And they waited for him, waited for their chance to devour him. And he was afraid. So afraid.

And so he neared Bryn Duir, the lonely hill that rose up on the middle of the forest. And there, at the top of the hill, was a mighty oak tree. The middle of its huge trunk was split, but the tree still stood. Here and there he could see old scars from previous storms. Yet the tree had not died. The fire had attacked the tree again and again, but the tree still stood.

He dismounted, no longer aware of the others with him. Slowly he walked up the hill, with eyes only for the blasted oak.

When he was halfway up the hill, lightning laced over the tree itself, enclosing it with bright, bony fingers. Then the lightning withdrew, spent. And the tree still stood. But it was burning.

Burning. The tree was burning. Flames licked hungrily at the wood. It was burning, just like the tree in Coed Dulas had done years ago, when he and Uthyr were children. That tree had burned and the fire had tried to kill him. But it had not, because Uthyr had been there to protect him.

But Uthyr was not here now. Uthyr was dead.

When the time had come, Gwydion had been unable to save his brother. He had been far away when Uthyr died on the field before Tegeingl. He had been in Coed Aderyn, waiting to confront Havgan at Cadair Idris. He had not been there for his brother, and so his brother was no longer here for him.

"Uthyr," he whispered as he approached the now-burning tree.

"Uthyr, I am sorry. So sorry."

But there was no answer, other than the crackling of the fire. And that was answer enough.

In Gwydion's mind he was back again in Coed Dulas, trapped within the branches of a burning tree, and Uthyr was not there this time. This time, the fire would take him.

He shook with fear as he faced the tree, feeling the heat on his face, knowing that there was no Uthyr to save him. His brother was dead.

He saw nothing, heard nothing, felt nothing, but the flames as he stood there, transfixed, gazing at what he knew was his death.

So when the four Coranian soldiers burst out from the surrounding forest and sped up the hill toward him, he did not even know they were there.

"GWYDION!" RHIANNON SCREAMED from the bottom of the hill where they had halted. But Gwydion did not even move, did not seem to even be aware of anything but the burning tree as the soldiers who had somehow eluded the Cerddorians' trap went straight up the hill toward him, their weapons drawn.

Rhiannon hiked up her skirt and pulled out her knife. She threw it in an overhand cast and it sped up the hill, plunging through the back of one of the soldiers. The man went down in a welter of blood. Beside her Arthur's spear shot true, finding its mark in the back of another soldier. But the two remaining soldiers were gaining on Gwydion, and she leapt up after them. Arthur was right beside her, with Gwen already ahead.

Rhiannon screamed Gwydion's name again. But only the soldiers seemed to hear her. One of them turned at her cry, while the other one continued on, closing swiftly on Gwydion.

Gwen, who had sprinted up the hill, shot across the path of the remaining soldier, bringing him down by rolling in front of him. The soldier fell facedown, and Gwen drew her knife and stabbed him in the back.

But the last soldier was still on his feet; his short spear in his hand, only a few feet now from Gwydion's unprotected back.

Knowing she would be too late, Rhiannon hared after him, still screaming Gwydion's name.

WITHIN THE DIM reaches of his consciousness, Gwydion heard Rhiannon call out to him. But even that had no power to bring him back from where he was—the past.

Close to dying, again.

The flames licked at the tree; the heat seared his face. Sweat ran down his body.

The burning. It burned. It burned.

And then he saw it—the gleam of opal in the heart of the tree. His eyes traced the pattern, and he marveled at what he saw.

For there, in the very center of the oak, stood the Spear. The shaft was made of twined silver and gold. The base was circled with fiery opals. Where the shaft joined with the gleaming tip was another grouping of the shining gems. And set into the tip of the Spear itself, black onyx, formed in the figure eight of Annwyn, Lord of Chaos, gleamed like hungry night.

He had never really thought that the Spear, that the Sign of Fire belonging to Mabon of the Sun, that Erias Yr Gwydd, Blaze of Knowledge, would be so beautiful. He had thought only of his fear.

"Take it, my son," a voice from within the fire called to him. "It is yours."

"Who calls me?" Gwydion whispered.

"It is I, Dreamer. Bran ap Iweridd var Fabel."

Bran, Dreamer to murdered High King Lleu Silver-Hand. Bran, who had guided Gwydion in the search for Caladfwlch. Bran, whose spirit was still not at rest.

A flicker within the flame, and the dead Dreamer showed himself. He was dressed in the Dreamer's robe of black trimmed with red. The ghost of the Dreamer's opal torque gleamed at his neck. His dark hair hung to his broad shoulders, and Bran's gray eyes—so like Gwydion's own—bore into Gwydion's.

"Why?" Gwydion whispered. "Why did you do this thing?" he asked, understanding the sacrifice Bran had made.

"To guard the Spear. To ensure that no one but you would claim it. When you take it, my task is done and I may rest, at last, in the

Land of Summer with those I love. Take it. Set me free."

Gwydion swallowed hard. "But the fire," he whispered help-lessly. "It burns."

"It does. And still you must reach through your fear to take what you must. Do what you were born to do."

"Will the fire burn me if I do?"

"All fire burns, Gwydion ap Awst. All. For that is its nature."

Gwydion gritted his teeth. This was not the past. This was now. Uthyr was dead and could not save him. But Bran had given even his soul to give Gwydion this chance. He would not fail. If he was brave, if he was quick, he might live.

And so, heedless of the Coranian warrior at his back, he reached through the flames. And the fire burned.

WITH A CRY Rhiannon leapt for the last soldier. His spear was set to throw at Gwydion's back, but one second before the spear left his hands, Rhiannon barreled into him with both feet, pushing him to the ground. The spear cast was wild, far off the mark. The soldier came to his feet, pulling out his sword from its sheath, and leapt for her with death in his eyes.

She tried to rise, but he was too quick. She grabbed his sword arm, deflecting his blow just enough so that he cut her shoulder.

She cried out. Gwen and Arthur were too far away, and the man was raising his sword for his next blow.

At least, she thought, as she prepared to die, the Dreamer would live. Her part was done, for the Stone was retrieved. Gwydion would see to it that the other two did their duty and then all the Treasures would be in their possession. Arthur would go to Cadair Idris with the Treasures in his hands and face the Tynged Mawr, the Great Test. He would survive this and be High King. And the powers that he would have then would drive the enemy from their land.

And Kymru would be at peace. And she would be dead. But her life would have meant something.

And that, at the last, was enough.

THE SOLDIER RAISED his sword, his blue eyes glittering with hate. He brought it down toward her unprotected face, and her green eyes held his, for she would not flinch from this.

And so she saw the moment when the sword halted in midair, clanging against the Spear of Fire, breaking the sword in two.

And she saw clearly when the fiery Spear caught the man full in the chest, and fire blossomed where his heart had been.

The soldier fell back, dead before he hit the ground.

She looked up to see Gwydion standing there, holding the burning Spear, the skin of his hands blackened and smoking, the sleeves of his tunic in flames.

She leapt up and pushed him to the ground, making him drop the Spear. She smothered the flames with her body, then drew back, bending over him, her hands on his chest to see if he still breathed.

He opened his eyes and looked up at her, his gaze filled with pain. And yet a strange peace was in his gray eyes. And she knew that look—the look of fear faced and mastered.

"And so you save my life," he rasped.

"And so you save mine," she replied. "Again."

"Rhiannon ur Hefeydd," he murmured, "you are wounded. What am I to do with you?"

Gwen and Arthur helped them both to their feet. For a moment Gwydion faced the burning tree. Then he straightened his shoulders and turned to her, cradling his burned hands. His eyes were suddenly cold as he stared at her, the tenderness of a moment ago quenched.

"You will never do that again," he said harshly.

"Never do what again?" she asked in surprise.

"Interfere."

"He was going to kill you!"

"The Spear was mine to find, mine to take."

"You bastard," she spat at him. "I risked my life for you."

"And I am telling you not to. Ever."

She turned from him, too furious to speak. And there, on the forest floor, the Spear gleamed, its physical fire spent. Yet the opals burned still, blossoming with a fire of their own.

Chapter 18

Suldydd, Disglair Wythnos—early afternoon

Ten days, Arthur thought tiredly, was a very long time for two people not to exchange one word. He had not thought it would last this long. It was not that he had underestimated his uncle's stubbornness—far from it. It was something else he had underestimated—just how much Gwydion ap Awst loved Rhiannon ur Hefeydd. And how frightened Gwydion was at the thought of harm coming to her.

The two of them walked in front of Arthur in single file, for the woods of Coed Coch were too dense to allow the passage of a wagon. Rhiannon insisted on carrying the Stone in a sling across her un-wounded shoulder. The weight of it did not seem to bother her. And Gwydion had rolled the Spear into an innocuous-looking blanket and carried it across his shoulders.

Gwydion's hands were still bandaged, for they had been badly burned. Every night Gwen would smear on the salve Rhiannon had told her how to make from mallow, then rebandage Gwydion's hands. Gwen had been the one to do that, since Rhiannon flatly refused to. Nor would Gwydion have allowed it, in any case.

The sword cut in Rhiannon's shoulder was healing the way it should, and she should be able to take the bandage off by tomorrow.

Every night it had been Arthur who would smear on the salve of rosemary and sage at Rhiannon's direction—under Gwydion's fierce gaze, as though his uncle was daring Arthur to make a false move. But Arthur knew better, and he was very careful.

Arthur sighed inwardly as he scanned the path through the woods. He knew that any moment now, King Owein and his Cerddorian would greet them. Arthur found himself actually looking forward to seeing other people again—ten days of silence from one half of the party was ten days too long.

Gwen quickened her pace behind him to walk alongside. "How much longer, do you think?" she asked in a low voice.

"To get to the camp?" Arthur asked.

"No, until they start speaking to each other again."

Arthur shrugged. "However long it takes for Rhiannon to understand."

"Don't you mean, however long it takes for Gwydion to stop being a fool?"

"Oh, so at last my uncle does something you don't approve of. That's a change."

"At last, you see my mother is not perfect. That's a change, too."

There was no one else, Arthur thought, who could irritate him like Gwenhwyfar ur Rhoram. "You don't understand," he said loftily. "I don't think you ever will."

"Oh, I understand all right. I understand them, and I understand you."

"What about me?"

"Yes, what about you? My thoughts exactly. You come on this journey with us, against your will, to help retrieve the Treasures. But never, not even once, have you said you will be High King. So, what are you doing here?"

"I am here," he said, raising his voice, "because the Lord and Lady of the Hunt gave me no choice. For Kymru I will help find the Treasures. But as for being High King, that I tell you I will not do. Let them find another. All I wish is to be left alone!"

"Then Kymru dies," Gwydion said as he halted and turned to face Arthur.

"Kymru will still have you to fight for her," Arthur retorted. "That is enough."

"It is not enough," Gwydion said quietly, "and you know it. Do you hate me so much that you will see Kymru beaten forever just to spite me? Is that why you will not take your true place at the Wheel? Or are you just a coward?"

Before Arthur could answer, a rustle in the underbrush heralded the arrival of Owein and his people. As Arthur expected, the first person he saw was Cariadas, Gwydion's daughter. She came running up to her father, but stopped at the sight of Gwydion's bandaged hands.

"Oh, Da," she whispered. "You are hurt."

"I am better now," Gwydion said as he gently took his daughter in his arms, careful not to use his hands, "just at the sight of you."

The forest now seemed full of people. There was King Owein, looking tired and grim. Captain Trystan and Sabrina the Druid carefully supported March, who had recently been freed from Llwynarth. March's bardic wife, Esyllt, stood a little off to one side, her face cold. Elidyr and Elstar, the Master Bard and the Ardewin, were there, as was Sinend, the Archdruid's heir, and Dudod, Rhiannon's uncle.

"Did you get it?" Cariadas asked, with tears in her eyes, nodding toward the pack across Gwydion's shoulders. "Did you get the Spear? Is that why your hands are burned?"

"Yes, we have the Spear of Fire," Gwydion answered. "And, yes, that is how my hands were burned."

"Rhiannon," Dudod said, as he came up to his niece. "You are hurt."

"It is much better than it was," she replied. "In a few more days, I will hardly notice it anymore."

"How were you wounded?"

"Interfering," Gwydion snapped.

"She was saving the Dreamer's life," Gwen said coldly, coming up to stand by her mother. "I suppose that could be called interfering, now that I think of it."

They all seemed to freeze for a moment. Then Dudod slowly walked up to Gwydion, his face impassive. "My niece risked her life for you? And was wounded because of that? And all you can think to say about it is that she was interfering? Have I got that right?"

"You have got it right," Gwydion agreed, turning away to greet Elidyr and Elstar.

"Dudod, no!" Cariadas cried, as Dudod cocked his fist back to swing.

Gwydion spun around to face Dudod. For a moment the two men looked at one another. Then Dudod seemed to see something. The same thing, Arthur thought, that he himself had seen.

"Fool," Dudod said quietly, dropping his arm.

"Yes," Gwydion agreed. "But I have no choice."

"Fool again. Because you do."

Owein crossed over to Gwydion. "Trystan has told me all that happened in Llwynarth. We thank you for bringing March back to us."

Gwydion faced the King. Owein's face was drawn, his eyes filled with anguish. "Believe me, Owein, I wish I could have brought her out, too."

"I don't believe you, Dreamer. But then, you did not think I would."

"No, I did not. There are many things that people don't believe about me. But here is one thing you will believe." He gestured to where Arthur stood. "This is my nephew, Arthur ap Uthyr var Ygralne, the Prince of Gwynedd."

"Arthur?" Owein asked, astonished. "The Prince we all thought dead years ago?"

"The same," Gwydion answered. "The man who will be our High King."

Instantly Owein was on his knees. Every last one of them there followed suit. Arthur stared at them as they knelt. They should not do that, he thought incoherently. They must not.

"I will not be High King," Arthur rasped. "Do not kneel to me. I am not the one who will save you."

"If not you," Dudod asked quietly, "then who?"

"Get up!" Arthur shouted in frustration and anger. "Get up! I am not the one."

"You mean, you will not be the one," Dudod went on. "A shame. When I first saw you, I saw Uthyr and Ygraine in you. But there are not enough of them inside you after all. You must be more like your Uncle Madoc, the traitor."

For a moment Arthur could not speak. The contempt in Dudod's eyes hit him like a blow. To be compared to Madoc! To be likened to the man who had betrayed Arthur's father! It was not to be borne.

"Get up," Arthur said once again, his voice cold and distant. "Find another man to save you. It will not be me."

ALL THIS TIME, Cariadas thought, as she knelt down next to Gwydion, all this time, all her life, she had known what her father was. And it was only now that she was angry, only now, when she truly saw what he was capable of.

The tent Owein had given the Dreamer and Arthur was small and snug. Gwydion sat on his bedroll as Cariadas unbandaged his hands. She did not look at him.

"Where are Prince Rhiwallon and Lieutenant Teleri?" Gwydion asked.

"Owein put them in charge of a raid in Clwyd. Rhiwallon could not bear to be doing nothing while Enid was—was getting married."

"Do you believe that I would not save Enid? Or do you believe that I could not?"

"I believe that you could not, Da."

"Then, what is wrong?"

She shook her head and gently smeared the salve onto his hands. He was silent while she bandaged them. Done at last, she sat back on her heels and looked up at him.

"What is it?" he asked again.

"I despise you," she said quietly, her eyes full of tears.

"Cariadas—"

"No. Not for Enid. For Rhiannon. For what you are doing to

her—after what she did for you."

"You don't understand."

"I do. And let me tell you something, Da." She rose to her feet. "You are worse than a fool. You are cruel. And you say I don't understand and you know I do. How could you do this to her? How could you turn love away like that? Do you think it is so cheap? So easily had that you could throw it away?"

"Cariadas—"

"I love you, Da. But I can't watch you do this and say nothing. All my life I have loved you. And I know you have loved me. And nothing is ever going to change that. Not even this. Not even what you have become. But, Da, you are wrong to run from love. You can give any reason you want why you do that. Duty, you say, no doubt. But you are only afraid."

"Daughter—"

"Only afraid. And that is all."

ANIERON, ONE-TIME Master Bard of Kymru, stirred in his bed of filthy straw. He slept often now, for when he was sleeping, he dreamed. And when he dreamed, he did not know that he lay in the dungeon of Eiodel, Havgan's fortress. He did not see the slimy walls, hear the rats, feel the cold. He did not remember what they had done to him.

In his dreams he was young and free again. In his dreams he spent busy days in the Bards' College of Neuadd Gorsedd, surrounded by fellow Bards, singing songs, chanting poetry. In his dreams he walked the fields of Gwytheryn, and the wind flew down to make patterns in the grass, patterns he could almost understand. In his dreams the air was fresh and clean and Taran of the Winds was at his back. In his dreams he Wind-Spoke to his brother, to his colleagues, to his daughter, to his grandsons.

But then, as was happening now, he would wake. And he would remember that he was not free, that he could no longer Wind-Speak, that he, since he had cut out his own tongue, could no longer speak or sing at all.

And he would remember that he no longer had fingers left to pluck a harp string, to play the pipe, to make music. For they had cut them off, one by one, when he would not tell them what they wanted to know.

The same questions over and over as they cut him. Who was the man the Kymri believed to be the High King? Where had the Ardewin and her husband gone? What did he know of the Treasures?

But that was why Anieron had cut out his tongue—so he could not answer their questions. They gave him paper and ink and told him to hold the pen between his palms and write the answer.

But he had not. He had only screamed.

And when they left him alone, he had his dreams. And his hope of death.

But now something had awakened him. He painfully drew himself up from the straw as far as he could. It was not far, for they had shackled his wrists to the wall and the best he could do was rise to his knees.

"Anieron?" whispered Cian, his fellow Bard. His fellow prisoner. "Did you hear it? Someone's coming."

Anieron could not answer, so he grunted.

"So you are awake," Cian said. Anieron heard a rustle in the cell across from him. There was no light, but he could tell from the sounds that Cian was rising to his feet.

"They come again," Cian said, his voice little more than a whisper. "Why don't they just kill us? You will not answer their questions, and I have no answers. Why do they keep doing this?"

Anieron knew why. When Sledda would come to question him, Havgan would come, too. In the light of the torches, Havgan would sit before Anieron, gleaming in gold and rubies. His handsome face would betray nothing—no anger, no joy. He would simply look at Anieron as the Master Bard screamed.

Only one time had Havgan showed anything. That was the time when Anieron had finally recognized him. Anieron would never forget that moment. Sledda had been bending over him like a night crow, cutting off Anieron's forefinger. And he had cried out, and turned his gaze to Havgan. And he had seen what he should have seen long ago.

He had seen that, except for his honey-blond hair, except for his amber eyes, Havgan was enough like Gwydion to be his twin. And Anieron had known then, who Havgan was: the brother of Arianrod; the son of Arianllyn, Rhiannon's aunt; the son of Brychan, Gwydion's uncle; the son of a Bard and a Dewin who had been sent to Corania years ago as a result of a dream. And this was what had come of that dream—a nightmare. A nightmare for Kymru.

Havgan had risen, for he had seen the recognition in Anieron's eyes. He had stood before Anieron, gleaming golden in the torchlight.

"The Ardewin at Y Ty Dewin had such a look in his eyes when he saw me," Havgan said gently. "I killed him, before he could speak. But you cannot speak. And to kill you would be a boon to you. And so I will not. You will live here in Eiodel a long, long time. And I will bring you a gift, Master Bard. A gift to help you while away the hours." Havgan had turned and opened the cell door. "Cut off all his fingers," he had said carelessly to Sledda. "He will never write anything for us."

That had been two nights ago. The thought of a gift from Havgan made Anieron's heart pound with dread.

Someone was coming down the steps. The growing light of a torch made him blink as his eyes burned from the light.

It was Sledda, along with a band of soldiers. The Master-wyrce-jaga's sharp features wavered in the light as he gestured to the guards to open Cian's cell.

"Where are you taking me?" Cian demanded weakly as they hauled him out into the corridor.

"To join your friends," Sledda answered with a cruel smile. His remaining gray eye gleamed. The empty socket, twisted with scar tissue, was like a pit of darkness in his pale face. "To join the Y Dawnus on the isle of Afalon."

"Why?"

"Their fate has been decided since the Master Bard will not give us the information we seek. They are to be collared."

"Why don't you just kill them now?" Cian asked.

"Ah, that would be too easy a death. This will be much worse. We have noticed that those who are collared sicken, but take a very, very long time to die. The children seem to go first."

Anieron closed his eyes briefly. The children. Oh, the children.

"You needn't act as though you care, Master Bard," Sledda hissed. "If you did, you would have saved them. You would have told us what we want to know."

Anieron looked back at Sledda, his gaze steady, full of contempt. The warriors began to march Cian away.

"Anieron!" Cian called as they hauled him up the steps. "I will tell them of your bravery. We will live as long as we can, to honor you. We will live for that day when we will be freed. Anieron! Anieron, may Taran be with you!"

The door clanged shut. Anieron knew he would never see Cian again. He would die alone in this cell, with no friend to comfort him.

Sledda, now alone, unlocked Anieron's cell and entered. He carried a bag, which he set down in the straw. "I have your gift from Havgan." Sledda smiled as he lifted the thing from the bag.

Anieron's breath caught in his throat at what he saw.

His harp. His harp, brought here from the sack of Allt Llwyd. The harp gleamed in the torchlight. The wooden frame was carved in the likeness of Queen Ethyllt of Rheged, the mother of Anieron's child. Her beautiful smile sent a barb of grief into his heart. The frame was inlaid with silver, and the sapphires scattered across it glowed. He had made that harp in memory of the woman he had loved so long ago. The strings shimmered softly as Sledda placed it at Anieron's feet.

"I have put it where you can play it when you like," Sledda mocked. "Or, perhaps I should say that you could, if you only had fingers. What a pity you don't. I will leave the torch so you may see and truly appreciate Havgan's magnificent gift." Sledda smiled again and left the cell. The clang of the upper door convinced Anieron that he was alone.

He strained forward to take the harp in his bloody palms. He ran the back of his hand over the strings, but the jangle of chords made him wince. He laid his head on the frame and wept, as he had not done since coming to Eiodel. He could not sing with his tongue cut out. He could not play with his fingers gone. He could not Wind-Speak with the collar around his neck.

It was all gone. Everything he had. Everything he was. Everything he had hoped to be. Now he waited only for death, a death it seemed would never come. Oh, if only he could have one boon, one gift from Taran before he died. If he could have that, death would be so sweet. He would ask for the harp to play. He would sing one last song—a song to be heard by all those in Kymru, Kymri and Coranian alike, a song like no other, a song of freedom and hope.

Taran, King of the Winds, he began in his mind, *I beg*—but there here stopped. He could not ask for such a thing. Who was he to have such a gift? No, he could only wait for that blessed moment when his spirit would leave this world for Gwlad Yr Haf, the Land of Summer. And there he would meet the friends who had gone before. And there he would wait his chance to be reborn. And maybe, while he waited for rebirth, he could play his harp and sing. He could never do those things now.

The touch of a cool breeze on his face made him raise his head in bewilderment. A breeze in the dungeons of Eiodel? That was not possible. But it was true.

The breeze caught the straw, sending it floating gently. The torch sputtered, then burned brighter still. And, oh, the wind brought with it the scents of Kymru. He smelled the cool mountain air of Gwynedd and the fresh clean lakes and rivers of Ederynion. He breathed in the scent of the sun-baked wheat fields of Rheged and the rich vineyards of Prydyn. He even knew the scent of the meadows and plains of Gwytheryn and a hint of the mountain of Cadair Idris that reached from the meadows to the sky.

His collar dropped off into the straw. His mind drew in the breath of Taran, and his Wind-Speech returned. The shackles around his wrists fell away. Most wondrous of all, the harp began to play the melody that he had crafted night after pain-filled night in this cell.

His heart bursting with joy, he began to sing the words in his mind.

And I am manacled
In the earthen house,
An iron chain
Over my two legs;
Yet of magic and bravery,
And the Kymri,
I, Anieron, will sing.

Shall there not be a song of freedom
Before the dawn of the fair day?
Shall this not be the fair day of freedom?

You of Corania
After your joyful cry,
Silence will be your portion.
And you will taste death
Far from your native home.

Shall there not be a song of freedom
Before the dawn of the fair day?
Shall this not be the fair day of freedom?

And as he sang, he knew that everyone who was in the land of Kymru could hear him. Every man, woman, and child was listening to his song of hope.

He sang, and he knew a joy like no other he had ever known.

GWYDION TURNED TO Rhiannon as they sat by the great campfire in Owein's hidden camp. They were all there —Arthur and Gwen, Elstar and Elidyr, Owein and Trystan and Sabrina, Cariadas and Sinend, Dudod and Esyllt and March. In front of them all he would beg Rhiannon's pardon for his treatment of her.

He would never tell her why he had treated her so coldly. He would never tell her of his hideous fear that she would die. He would never, ever tell her that he loved her so. But he would say that he was sorry for his cruelty. Never had Cariadas spoken to him that way before. And he could not even be angry with her, because everything she had said was true. And so he turned to Rhiannon and opened his mouth to say those words. But he did not.

For just then a breeze began, a wind that seemed to swoop down from the stars themselves. And with the wind came a song.

And I am manacled
In the earthen house,
An iron chain
Over my two legs;
Yet of magic and bravery,
And the Kymri,
I, Anieron, will sing.

Elstar leapt to her feet, her arms reaching up to the sky. "Da!" she screamed. "Da!"

Dudod sank to his knees, stunned, his face awash with tears. "Brother," he whispered. "Oh, my brother."

And as Gwydion listened to the song, he reached out and took Rhiannon's hand, the hand that was already reaching out for him. And he began to weep, as he had not done for many years, and Rhiannon held him, rocking him in her arms as she, too, cried.

For they knew that this night, one way or another, the song would end.

IN LLWYNARTH, QUEEN Enid taunted her new husband as Bledri and General Baldred looked on. "The ring of the House of PenMarch has been in my family's hands for hundreds and hundreds of years! I give it to you and you lose it in less than a day!"

King Morcant reached out and grabbed Enid by the hair. "Do you think I am a fool? You took it from me!"

"How could I?" Enid screamed. "I am no better than a prisoner here. What could I have done with it?"

"I don't know, but you have done something. And I swear to

you—"

The song came to them on the wings of the wind that rushed through Caer Erias, overturning chairs and tearing tapestries from the walls.

Shall there not be a song of freedom
Before the dawn of the fair day?
Shall this not be the fair day of freedom?

And Enid, her clothing torn, her hair disheveled, her lower lip bruised and bleeding, smiled as Morcant, Bledri, and Baldred froze in dread.

IN DINMAEL, QUEEN Elen of Ederynion halted with her cup halfway to her lips. In the great hall a wind began to blow. It tossed the tapestries back and forth, and the torches guttered wildly. General Talorcan rose from the table, his sword in hand.

You of Corania
After your joyful cry,
Silence will be your portion.
And you will taste death
Far from your native home.

REGAN JUMPED TO her feet, her face pale as death as she laid her hand on Talorcan's arm.

"Put up your sword, General," Elen said coldly. "The singer is not one that you can kill this night."

Talorcan looked down at Regan. "My love," he whispered, "silence will be my portion. When I am dead, then you will be free."

"No," Regan whispered back. "When you are dead, then I will be also."

"Anieron," the Druid Iago moaned, his dark eyes full of fear. "Taran's Wind brings him."

"He does," Elen smiled. "Your new god cannot stop Taran of the Winds."

Talhearn the Bard sat by the fire in the depths of the forest of Coed Ddu. He sighed. Prince Lludd was at it again.

"I tell you that I will wait no longer!" the Prince cried. "My sister has been captive long enough!"

"And what," Angharad asked, her green eyes flashing, "might your brilliant plan be to rescue her? Do you have thousands of men up your sleeve, perhaps? Enough to storm Dinmael and bring her out?"

"I will find a way! I am tired of waiting, I tell you—"

The wind rose in the forest, hurtling through the trees, bringing with it the song of the Master Bard.

Shall there not be a song of freedom
Before the dawn of the fair day?
Shall this not be the fair day of freedom?

"Oh, Anieron," Talhearn whispered to his old friend, as the rest of the Cerddorian leapt to their feet. "Oh, Anieron. Brave you are. Brave you have always been. Farewell, my friend."

PRINCESS TANGWEN SAT quietly in the great hall, looking down at her plate. She refused to look at her father, King Madoc, for fear he would see contempt for him in her eyes. She refused to look at General Catha, for fear she would see the lust in his eyes. She would not look at Arday because anything she saw in the eyes of her father's mistress only confused her more.

"Tangwen," Catha said as he flicked her cheek carelessly with one finger. Startled, she lifted her head. Catha's handsome face was inches from her own. "Come, Princess, you must not be so glum. Just think of what I could do for you—"

But his words were abruptly cut off as a strange wind whistled through the hall, darting back and forth, throwing down the tapestries and almost smothering the fire.

You of Corania
After your joyful cry,
Silence will be your portion.

And you will taste death
Far from your native home.

"You will taste death," Tangwen whispered, staring up at Catha. "Far from your native home."

Out of the corner of her eye, she saw Arday lift her hand to hide a smile.

HIGH IN THE mountains of Mynydd Tawel, Dinaswyn, the former Dreamer of Kymru, sat down by the fire. Her joints ached, as they always did these days. It was not fair to live so far beyond the time of usefulness. For the thousandth time, she wished she had died the day the dreams had passed to Gwydion.

She looked around at her companions. Ygraine sat stiffly, her eyes staring into the flames as though conjuring visions of her dead husband, Uthyr. Morrigan sat next to her mother's knee, and she, too, was staring into the flames. But if she knew Morrigan, the girl was not seeing the faces of those she loved—she was seeing visions of weapons and war.

Arianrod did not stare at the fire. Her head back, she scanned the stars. The firelight played on her amber eyes and honey-blond hair. What was the child looking for? Dinaswyn wondered. What had she always been looking for?

"Some apples, my lady?" the Bard asked.

Dinaswyn turned and gave Jonas a smile. He was always so helpful, so kind. He had come to them recently, sent by Anieron, just before Allt Llwyd had been taken.

But the smile faded from Jonas's pale face as the wind whipped down the mountains, thundering into the camp, bringing with it a song.

And I am manacled
In the earthen house,
An iron chain
Over my two legs;
Yet of magic and bravery,

And the Kymri,
I, Anieron, will sing.

Jonas cried out at the words, and huddled on the ground, his face hidden in his hands. Dinaswyn rose and went to him, patting his shoulders.

"Never fear, boyo," Dinaswyn said as the tears streamed down her face. "It is the voice of the Master Bard. It is the voice of Kymru herself this night. Never fear."

GENERAL PENDA GLANCED around the high table. King Erfin, brother-in-law of the dispossessed King Rhoram, was tearing into his meal as though it was his last. Efa, Erfin's sister and formerly Rhoram's wife, daintily dipped her hands in a basin of rosewater. Her sensual smile as she looked at Penda was only annoying—he had long since discovered that what Efa had to offer was not much different from any other woman. Ellywen sat stiffly at her place. The woman did everything that way. Penda wasn't even sure she didn't sleep standing up. It would be like her.

How much longer must he be here in Kymru? He longed to be back home in Mierce with his father and son. If only he could convince Havgan to let him go. But it was an idle thought. Havgan would never let any of his band go. Penda and Catha, Talorcan and Baldred, Sigerric and Sledda—they were here in Kymru to stay, for as long as Havgan was here.

Somehow, from somewhere, wind whipped through the great hall. Penda leapt up, sword in hand, though he did not know what he could do with it.

You of Corania
After your joyful cry,
Silence will be your portion.
And you will taste death
Far from your native home.

"Ellywen," Penda whispered. "What does this mean?"

The Druid was pale as death, and her lips trembled as she answered. "Anieron. Taran of the Winds grants him a boon. Oh, Anieron, what have I done?"

IN THE HIDDEN vale of Haford Bryn, Rhoram squatted down next to his son, putting a hand on the young man's shoulder. Geriant did not say a word, and Rhoram sat next to him on the ground, waiting.

At last, Geriant spoke. "Poor Enid."

"Yes," Rhoram agreed. "You loved her."

"No, I love her. Not loved. Love. And when we battle again to take Kymru back, she will be a widow by my hand."

"She may not be the girl you love by then."

"That does not matter. I will make her free. Free to be with whomever she will. I know it won't be with me."

Rhoram's brows raised. "And why not?"

"Da, if she had loved me, she never would have gone to Llwynarth to find Bledri in the first place. She would have been content with me. But she was not. She will never love me. She never has. But that doesn't matter. I love her, and I will free her."

"My son –" Rhoram began. But there he stopped.

For a wind whistled over Haford Bryn, and it brought with it a song like no other he had ever heard.

Shall there not be a song of freedom
Before the dawn of the fair day?
Shall this not be the fair day of freedom?

"Anieron," Rhoram whispered, knowing what this wind meant, knowing that the enemy would not suffer Anieron to live. "Oh, you are brave."

"Shall this not be the fair day of freedom?" Geriant asked slowly, his eyes gleaming. "Will we not make it so?"

IN THE ARCHDRUID's chambers at Caer Duir, Aergol sat quietly across from Cathbad. Cathbad could not see it, but then the Archdruid had always seen only what he wanted to. But Aergol knew. Soon, very soon, their Coranian allies would come to Caer Duir with enaid-dals in their hands. The Coranians no longer needed the help of the Druids, and they would soon realize it, if they hadn't already.

Cathbad drank deeply from his golden cup. "Soon the Dreamer will be in our hands. The word is out across Kymru to find him and Rhiannon ur Hefeydd."

"The word has been out to find those two for years, but they have never been found," Aergol replied shortly.

Cathbad waved his hand. "No matter. They will be found. And when they are, we will make them tell us where your daughter is. Sinend will be brought back to Caer Duir, to be trained the way she should be."

"My daughter is safe enough wherever she is," Aergol snapped. "And you can just leave her be."

"Leave her be! Are you mad?"

"Are you?"

And that was when Taran's Wind came whistling down the corridors of Caer Duir. Cathbad leapt to his feet, but Aergol remained seated and bowed his head.

And I am manacled
In the earthen house,
An iron chain
Over my two legs;
Yet of magic and bravery,
And the Kymri,
I, Anieron, will sing.

Oh, yes. Of bravery and the Kymri, Anieron would sing, Aergol thought. Would that he could be that—brave, a man of the Kymri. Maybe he could. Yes, maybe he still could.

HAVGAN'S ROOMS IN Eiodel were glorious. Tapestries sewn with precious stones adorned the walls. The stone floor was covered with carpets woven by the Master Weavers of Gwynedd. Delicately etched goblets and glass pitchers blown by the glassmakers of Ederynion were scattered on tables. The finest Prydyn wines filled the pitchers. Fine candles from Rheged cast a soft light. A fire roared in the hearth, illuminating Havgan's huge bed.

The woman on the bed was naked, and her hands clawed uselessly for Havgan's face. His huge, battle-scarred hands were wrapped around her throat. He stared down at her, watching her die, watching her eyes for that thing he had been looking for all his life. Her honey-blond hair flowed over the bedspread as she fought to breathe. He had already forgotten her name. She was only a woman of the Kymri, one who had been brought to him because of the color of her hair, because that was the color of the hair of the Woman-on-the-Rocks, the one who was always turned away from him.

Slowly, her struggles ceased. Her eyes remained open as she died. And still they had not shown him anything. Nothing at all. Another waste of his time.

He rose from the bed. The light of the fire crawled greedily over his naked body. He reached for a robe and wrapped it around him. He would have Sledda take care of the body. Sledda would like that. He went to the door and opened it. Both Sigerric and Sledda were sitting in the outer chamber.

"Ah, you have finished, my Lord," Sledda said, licking his pale lips.

"Take care of her, wyrce-jaga," Havgan said shortly.

Sigerric turned away from Havgan, looking down into his wine cup.

"Sigerric, my friend," Havgan smiled. "Is something wrong?"

Sigerric shook his head, but still would not meet Havgan's eyes. "Come, come," Havgan went on. "The girl was not anyone you knew."

"Havgan," Sigerric whispered. "Why?"

"You know why. But once again I am cheated."

And then the winds came. They howled through the halls of Eiodel, slashing and tearing. The glass bottles smashed into pieces. The tapestries flew from the walls. The fire roared up. And the song came.

And I am manacled
In the earthen house,

An iron chain
Over my two legs;
Yet of magic and bravery,
And the Kymri,
I, Anieron, will sing.

"The Master Bard," Sigerric breathed. "He is free."

"He is not free," Sledda gasped. "I left him in his cell. My Lord, I swear it!"

"Kill him!" Havgan screamed. "Kill him!"

You of Corania
After your joyful cry,
Silence will be your portion,
And you will taste death
Far from your native home.

"Far from our home, Havgan," Sigerric said quietly. "Death far from our native home."

"I said, kill him!" Havgan screamed to Sledda, who stood frozen in the doorway. Without another word, Sledda turned and ran from the room.

THE WIND BLEW. The harp played. And Anieron sang and sang. From all across Kymru they heard him. Some wept as they listened. Some hearts leapt for joy at the promise of freedom. Some were afraid. But they all heard him. Anieron closed his eyes as he sang, overcome with this last blessing of Taran.

He heard the cell door open, but he did not stop his song.

He stopped only when he felt the knife enter his heart. He opened his eyes as he fell to his knees. Sledda stood there, panting, Anieron's blood splashed over his black robe. The wind quieted. The harp stopped playing.

Anieron was dying. But he had one last thing to say to everyone in Kymru before his spirit left this world. *Sledda of Corania, I say this to you, for it is true. For the murder you do to me today, you will die at the hands of the High King himself.*

Good-bye, my brother, Anieron whispered as the darkness took him. *Good-bye.*

"GOOD-BYE, MY brother," Dudod whispered, as he knelt by the fire in Coed Coch. "Oh, good-bye."

Arthur sat unmoving while all those around him wept. Then, slowly, he rose. They quieted as he stood. Even Dudod lifted his head, watching.

"I, Arthur ap Uthyr var Ygraine, vow today that Anieron's last words will be true. One day I will take vengeance on Sledda for the murder of the Master Bard. I, who will be High King of Kymru, swear this. You do not need to find another. It shall be me."

Chapter 19

Arberth and Haford Bryn
Kingdom of Prydyn, Kymru
Cerdinen Mis, 499

Suldydd, Lleihau Wythnos—late afternoon

Aidan ap Camber, Lieutenant to King Rhoram, knew that he was going to die. He didn't mind dying so much—it happened to everyone, sooner or later. But he did mind the fact that his death was sure to be painfully slow. And, no doubt, extremely messy.

Aidan tensed as the Coranian soldiers moved in closer. He put a comforting hand on Cadell's shoulder as the Dewin swallowed hard. It was dark in the back of the smithy, and he could barely make out Cadell's face, but he was quite sure his friend was just as on edge as he was. The punishment set aside for Cadell would be even worse than what Aidan would endure. Cadell would be collared with an enaid-dal and sent to the isle of Afalon in Gwytheryn. And, once there, there would be no escape. The collar would slowly kill him, if the Coranian guards at the isle didn't kill him first as they played their sick games on the prisoners.

For the hundredth time that afternoon, Aidan turned over possible escape plans in his mind. And, for the hundredth time, he concluded that it was not possible. Their only hope, since they had no weapons, was to break cover from the smithy and be killed instantly.

Cadell knew this as well as Aidan did.

Ah, well, Aidan thought, it had been a good life. Even after the Coranians had invaded, life had been good. He had served King Rhoram faithfully and well and had no regrets on that score. He would very much regret having to leave Lluched, the Gwarda of Crueddyn and Cadell's sister. He thought it was very possible that he was in love with that fierce Cerddorian. And he was sorry that he would not be here to see the High King return and take back Kymru from the invaders. That was a fight he wished he could be a part of.

The irony was that he and Cadell had been all set to leave enemy-occupied Arberth today. Their mission had been accomplished, and they had been heading home, after being here for five days. Cadell's mission had been to set up portions of the network of Y Dawnus, broken when Anieron and the rest of those in Allt Llwyd had been taken. Now spies were again set in the fortress and in the city. Elidyr and Elstar, the Master Bard and the Ardewin, would be pleased. The last link was now reforged, and the network in western Prydyn was once again in place.

If only Aidan had not been recognized, they would have left the city by now. How Queen Efa could recognize him from a quarter of a league away when he had his back to her was something he could not fathom. Never, he thought wryly, underestimate the capacity for vengeance of a woman scorned.

For it had been Aidan who, at King Rhoram's orders, had tricked Efa into leaving the caves of Ogaf Greu, enabling Rhoram and his people to disappear to a new location without the risk of being betrayed. Aidan had tricked her into abandoning the King by making her believe he was in love with her and he would follow her to Arberth to join the Coranian cause. The part where he had to pretend to be in love with her had not been as pleasant as he had anticipated. Efa, though she was beautiful and sensual, had made Aidan's skin crawl. The fact that she was selfish, faithless, and rotten had been harder to ignore then he had first thought.

When Efa had cried out his name in the marketplace, Aidan had not even turned around. He knew the voice, and he knew what it meant. He had grabbed Cadell's arm, and they had melted into the crowd. They had almost made the east gate when the guards shouted for them to stop. So they had run through the streets of Arberth, not daring to approach the spies they had just installed. The work they had completed was far too important to risk.

They had done their best to throw off pursuit by creating havoc in the marketplace as they ran. The people of Arberth had helped. Goods had somehow gone flying into the paths of the Coranians, dogs had yipped at the guards' heels, and stalls had unaccountably collapsed on the soldiers. The help of the people had been just enough to enable them to reach the smithy, just outside the marketplace. There the Smith had urged them in, hustled them into the back, then returned to the open front to continue forging horseshoes.

The guards were now searching the marketplace from stall to stall. Every moment brought them closer to the smithy. The city gates were shut tight. Even if they could somehow sneak away from the smithy, they had nowhere to go.

"They've reached the last row," the Smith said from the front, his voice low. "They'll be here next."

The Smith of Arberth was a burly, taciturn man, one of the Master Smith's assistants. The Master Smith and her family had disappeared out of Arberth months ago, taken by the Coranians.

Aidan looked at Cadell. "Shall we make it quick, my friend?" he whispered.

Cadell nodded, then shuddered. "Better than the collar. Anything would be better than that."

The two men rose. The plan was simple. Run out of the smithy and right into the spears of the soldiers.

But before they could even begin, the sound of horses' hooves stopped them. Someone, they could not see whom, had halted in front of the smithy.

"Smith, I demand that you look at this horse's shoe. I tell you, there is something wrong with it."

Aidan froze. He knew that voice. It was Ellywen, King Rhoram's former Druid. Cold, callous, and controlled, Ellywen had been a special protégé of the Archdruid and had been hand in glove with all his schemes for years.

"I assure you," the Smith growled, "there is nothing wrong with that shoe. I put it on just two days ago. It is your imagination."

"My imagination? Perhaps you forget who I am. I will have you dancing in the air with a sword at your throat before you can even blink."

That was true, Aidan thought. Druids were Shape-Movers, and such a thing was very well within her power. The Smith had better not be foolish. But if he were, Aidan and Cadell would have to help him.

"Very well," the Smith said, still surly. "I will look at it. But you are not going to be able to go anywhere."

"Nonsense. I wish to ride out to the vineyards today."

"The gates are closed. They won't let you through."

"I know the gates are closed. And they will let me through. I see no reason why I should be inconvenienced because these soldiers are so incompetent that they couldn't find water in the middle of the sea."

"Well, if they do let you through, you shouldn't go alone."

"I won't be alone. I will take two guards with me. Does that satisfy you?"

The Smith's reply was too low to hear. Aidan strained to make out the words, but he could not. But he did make out Ellywen's equally low-voiced reply. "Where?"

Aidan heard the clink of metal, then Ellywen's footsteps coming to the back of the smithy. They had been betrayed! He had no weapons, so he flexed his hands, ready to break Ellywen's neck. Might as well take this opportunity to rid the world of one more Druid before he died.

The curtain that separated the back from the front of the smithy was suddenly drawn. A little light spilled in, illuminating Ellywen's pale face, her braided brown hair, and her cold, gray eyes. She held a sack in her hand. Tossing it to the floor, she said sharply, "Put those on."

For a moment Aidan and Cadell could only stare at her. "Hurry up," she hissed. "We haven't much time."

"What's in the sack?" Cadell asked in astonishment.

"Coranian chain mail, helmets, and some weapons. Didn't you hear me? I said I would take two guards."

Still they did not move. How could they possibly trust her? On the other hand, Aidan thought, their choices were a bit limited at the moment. And she had not raised the alarm. Why would she trick them out of hiding when she could just call the soldiers right now and it would be all over?

"Why?" Aidan asked as he reached for the sack, not really expecting an answer.

"Because of Anieron," she said, surprising him. "I felt him die three days ago. When he sang the song."

Aidan raised his brows. "Since when do you care what the enemy does to the Kymri!"

"And because I helped capture Cian, and sent him to prison," Ellywen went on, as though Aidan had not spoken. "And Achren would not kill me, even though I begged her to. And so I must live, for now. And do what I can to undo what I have done, until death takes me, as it ought."

"Cian was your friend," Cadell said quietly. "You and I and Cian served Rhoram for years together. How could you do what you did?"

"I am a Druid," Ellywen said. "And I learned to do what I was told, as I was taught. But that is finished. Hurry up. Do you think we have all day to talk about this?"

Aidan and Cadell put on the Coranian byrnies; shirts made of interwoven metal that reached to just above their knees. They picked up their shields, and donned the helmets with the figure of a boar carved at the top. Each held a short spear.

"You'll do," Ellywen said shortly. "But not by much. For Modron's sake, keep your heads down."

Cadell laughed sharply. "For Modron's sake? What right do you have to call on the Great Mother? You are a Druid, and have turned from her to the Coranian god."

"Mock me, then," Ellywen said between gritted teeth. "It is just what I would expect of a Dewin."

"Cadell," Aidan said quietly, "enough. Ellywen, if you get us through, you had best come with us. They will find you out."

Ellywen shook her head. "No. I can't. I must stay here. My duty now is to pass on any information I can to the network. Tell me whom to speak to."

"So that's it," Cadell said flatly. "This is how you think to trick us into revealing them. It won't work, Ellywen. You might as well kill us now."

Ellywen's gray eyes flashed, then subsided. "You are right to be suspicious. Very well, then, have your people contact me when they think things over. And let's leave it at that. Now, hurry. We have spent too much time here as it is. Follow me."

Ellywen turned and led the way to the front of the smithy. The Smith held her stirrup as she mounted her horse. For a moment Aidan hesitated. But they had no choice except to trust her. If she betrayed them, they might be able to die quickly, now that they were armed. He nodded at Cadell to follow, then marched to Ellywen's side. Cadell took a place on the other side of her horse.

"How did you know about us?" Aidan asked.

"She saw you in the city and recognized you a few days ago," the Smith replied, before Ellywen could answer. "She came to me and we thought of this, just in case."

"Thank you," Aidan said gratefully, though he knew better than to shake the Smith's hand now that others could see them.

"I am glad to serve King Rhoram," the Smith said quietly. "And I dream of the day when I can do so in the open again."

"That day will come, my friend," Aidan said. "It will come."

"Shall this not be the fair day of freedom?" the Smith replied, a light in his eyes.

"As the song said," Aidan agreed. "So it shall be."

Ellywen clucked to her horse, and they moved off toward the east gate. They skirted the marketplace that was still in disarray. They saw squads of soldiers still searching the stalls, but they casually walked on by.

As they neared the east gate, Aidan saw that it was, indeed, closed, and guarded by thirty men at least. The Coranians were taking no chances. Ellywen rode up to the gate as though the men were not there. Finally, just as she was only a few feet away from the closed doors, she halted her horse. She sat there, looking down her nose at the Coranian Captain who had come up to them.

"May I help you, Druid Ellywen?"

"Open the gate."

"I am sorry, my Lady. That is not possible."

"Surely it is not impossible. I have seen your men do it hundreds of times," Ellywen said with cool disdain.

The Captain flushed but held his ground. "We have orders to keep the gates closed until the men we are searching for are found."

"But, Captain, your men are so inept that by the time they have found them, this day will be long over. And I am not going to wait until tomorrow."

"I have my orders," the Captain said shortly.

Ellywen leaned down in the saddle until she was just inches away from the Captain's face. The hood of her brown Druid's robe fell back. "Captain, do you know—really know—what Druids can do?"

The Captain paled and swallowed hard. "I—"

"No, don't talk. Save your voice for screaming. Men do scream so when they are on fire."

"I—"

"But don't worry. I don't take offense. I know you are just doing your job. So I will make it easy for you. I am going to open that gate. And you are going to stand there and let me go through. Then no one has to die today. Understood?"

The Captain nodded.

"Good." Ellywen gestured with her hand to the gate. The bar shot up into the air, then floated down gently to rest against the wall. The gates slowly swung open.

"That is called Shape-Moving," Ellywen said to the Captain. "It is another one of the things we can do. Don't forget that, will you?"

The Captain nodded, but did not speak. Smiling pleasantly, Ellywen rode forward out of the gate, with Aidan and Cadell following.

Ellywen rode on for nearly a league before she halted her horse.

"Ellywen," Aidan said earnestly, "if you talk to the guards like that all the time, I am surprised they have not yet taken matters into their own hands and burned you for a witch."

"They fear their leaders more than me," Ellywen said. "And General Penda would not let them harm me."

"For now," Aidan warned.

"Do you think I don't know that? I don't think Penda lets me live because he likes me. He lets me live because the Archdruid wills it so."

"And Cathbad's wishes will cease to matter to the enemy very soon."

"Another thing you think I do not know." She nodded toward the people who were laboring in the vineyards to the north. "I will return to the city when they do, and by the north gate. In the crowd it will not be so obvious that I return alone. Now go."

"Ellywen," Aidan said as he grasped the horse's bridle. "Come with us."

"I have told you, I can't. It will take me many years to even begin to undo what I have done. I must start here."

"You must go—"

"I must stay. The better to view Rhoram's eventual triumphant return to his city. If I am lucky, he will kill me." She gave a tiny smile, one of the few Aidan had ever seen on her face, and he had known her for years. "Tell him that, incredible as it sounds, I miss him."

"He won't believe it," Cadell warned.

"Oh, I think he will," Aidan said. "He always did know us better than we knew ourselves."

"Would that I had understood myself better before," Ellywen said bitterly. "Then maybe Anieron would not have died."

"But his death was triumphant, Ellywen," Cadell pointed out. "Before he died, Taran of the Winds gave him a great boon. And he gave us a great song."

"Yes," Ellywen said quietly. "Shall this not be the fair day of freedom?' Is there anyone in Kymru who could hear his song and believe that freedom is not far behind?"

"Yes," Aidan said. "Freedom is at hand."

"Not for me, Aidan ap Camber. Not for me."

Suldydd, Tywyllu Wythnos—midmorning

KING RHORAM EXITED his tent, sitting down on a rock to wait for his guests. As he sat, he absently twisted the emerald ring on his finger. If he were right, the ring would leave his hand today.

Tonight, he and his people who were hidden here in the valley of Haford Bryn would celebrate Calan Olau, one of the eight yearly festivals of the Kymri. He remembered years past when this festival of the harvest had been celebrated. In those years there had been a harvest to celebrate. These days he and his people lived off the enemy caravans they had been able to capture, off the game and edible plants they could forage, off the dreams of a future when the land would be theirs again.

At Calan Olau they celebrated the tale of Mabon of the Sun, when the god returned from Gwlad Yr Haf, the Land of Summer, with the harvest in his hands. On this night the moon would not be seen in the sky, for his wife, Nantsovelta, Lady of the Waters, had come to earth to greet him. In the past there would have been a great fair and horse races by the dozen. In those days he had always entered the races, and had always won. He smiled wryly to himself—perhaps he was getting old, reliving glorious moments of his past. He remembered how he always chose a woman to help him celebrate, even after he had married Efa. By then he had truly understood whom he had married, but it had been too late to undo what he had done. The only years he had not chosen a woman were the few years he was with Rhiannon. Then he had not wanted anyone else but her.

His son, Geriant, and his daughter, Sanon, joined him, sitting on either side of him on the large rock.

"How much longer, Da?" Sanon asked quietly.

Sanon always spoke quietly, when she spoke at all, and that was rarely. Ever since the death of Prince Elphin of Rheged, she had been that way. Sometimes, when Rhoram remembered the bright, openhearted, merry girl his daughter had been, he would feel a need to kill every Coranian he could get his hands on.

"Not much longer, daughter," Rhoram replied, when he realized he had been silent too long. "Achren has gone to lead them in."

"I do so want to see Rhiannon and Gwen again," Sanon said. "I really do."

For the first time in years, Sanon's voice held a hint of anticipation. It was a small step, Rhoram knew, but it was a step nonetheless.

Geriant rose from the rock, looking toward the rim of the valley, shading his eyes with his hand. "They are here."

Rhoram and Sanon rose, and the three of them made their way through the other Cerddorian who had stopped their work to greet the guests.

Rhoram watched as Achren led the party down the rocky path to the floor of the hidden valley. Rhiannon wore a leather tunic and trousers dyed forest green, and her hair was braided and wound around her head. She carried a pack on her back. Gwen was next, and she, too, wore a leather tunic and trousers, but hers were dyed a soft brown. Her golden hair spilled down her back, glistening in the sun. Next came a young man Rhoram did not know. He was tall and thin and his shoulder-length brown hair was secured at his neck with a strip of leather. He had a bow slung across his shoulder and a quiver over the other. Gwydion was behind him. He wore leather gloves on his hands and carried a rolled-up blanket across his shoulder.

When the party reached the valley floor, like a bird, Gwen shot away from them and into Rhoram's waiting arms. "Da! Da, I'm home!" she cried.

He held her, stroking her hair. He closed his eyes briefly in gratitude that his youngest daughter was indeed home—for a time. "Yes, you are home. Welcome. Oh, welcome, my Gwen," he whispered.

Then he held her at arm's length to look at her. "My, you have grown," he went on with a wink. "I had best interview the young man you are with and let him know the consequences should he play fast and loose with you."

"Oh," Gwen shrugged, "that's just Arthur. And we don't like

each other at all."

Rhoram grinned. "It often starts that way."

"Da," Gwen admonished, "don't be ridiculous." She hugged Geriant, then Sanon, with tears of joy streaming down her fresh face. Her brother and sister could not seem to let her go, and they, too, were weeping.

Rhoram looked away to find Rhiannon. She was coming toward him, slinging the pack off her back and laying it gently down. She grinned at him, her green eyes shining like emeralds. He held out his arms, and she came to him with no hesitation, no confusion, and no fears, for their past had been set to rest between them some time ago. He held her for a moment, raising his eyes over her shoulder to glance at Gwydion.

The Dreamer stood stiffly, clutching the leather strap of his bundle, and the look on his face could have burned water. Rhoram smiled, then let Rhiannon go. He walked up to Gwydion, grasping the man's arms. "You are welcome here, Gwydion ap Awst. Most welcome."

"Really," Gwydion said flatly.

Rhoram smiled even wider, then turned to the young man who stood next to the Dreamer. He clasped the man's hand. "I am Rhoram ap Rhydderch. You are welcome to Haford Bryn. And you are?"

The young man glanced at Gwydion. At the Dreamer's nod, he answered, "I am Arthur ap Uthyr var Ygraine, Prince of Gwynedd."

Rhoram's eyes widened. The boy thought to have died all those years ago had not. Rhoram's quick mind pieced together why. "Then you are even more welcome, High King," Rhoram said quietly, sinking to his knees.

Arthur gestured frantically for Rhoram to get up, but Rhoram stayed where he was. The other Cerddorian, seeing that Rhoram was kneeling, sank to their knees also, though they did not know why.

"Who are you that my father bows to you?" Geriant asked as he came near.

"This is Arthur ap Uthyr," Gwydion replied, his voice carrying over the valley. "Your High King."

Instantly Geriant and Sanon were on their knees. Rhiannon walked over to Arthur and gently put a hand on his shoulder.

"If you don't wish them to bow to you, Arthur," she said gently, "tell them to stand up."

"Please," Arthur said hoarsely. "Stand up."

"See how easy that was?" Rhoram teased as they rose to their feet. "Practice. Practice, boyo, is the key to success."

Arthur smiled tentatively.

"Where did you travel from?" Sanon asked.

"We came from Coed Coch, leaving there ten days ago," Gwen replied.

"Oh." Sanon said nothing for a moment. Then she went on, her voice hesitant. "Were they all well there?"

"Yes," Gwen said, obviously mystified at the question.

"Everyone? Even—even Owein?"

Gwen's brows shot up in surprise. "Um, yes. Even Owein."

It was Gwydion who stepped into the momentary silence, taking pity, apparently, on Sanon's bright red face. "Gwenhwyfar," he said sternly. "I believe you have something to ask your da."

Gwen jumped slightly at Gwydion's tone, then she, too, reddened, clearly telling Rhoram that his daughter had a crush on the Dreamer . . . Oh, well, he thought, she'll grow out of it. Young girls fell in and out of love all the time. He wondered how Rhiannon felt about the situation. Her face was impassive, but he thought there was a hint of exasperation in her eyes. What a time these four must be having, he thought, and struggled not to laugh.

"Behold, King Rhoram, one of the House of PenBlaid comes to you with a request, as was foretold by Bran the Dreamer," Gwydion intoned.

"Da, I need—" Gwen stopped. She was silent for a moment, her head cocked as though she heard something that others could not. Then she continued, her words steady and sure. "In the name of the High King to come, surrender your ring to me."

The words. The exact words foretold so many years ago. Without hesitation he pulled the ring from his finger and laid it in Gwen's open palm. Gently he closed her fingers over the ring.

"My daughter has spoken the words foretold. The ring of the House of PenBlaid is now hers to do with as she will."

Slowly, Gwen uncurled her fingers, looking down at the ring.

"Put it on," Gwydion said quietly.

Gwen put the ring on her forefinger. Instantly the emerald began to glow. "West," she said.

"We must go," Gwydion said, shouldering his bundle.

"What?" Rhiannon exclaimed. "We just got here. Don't be ridiculous."

"Uncle Gwydion," Arthur jumped in. "One night here isn't going to hurt us."

"I want to spend some time with my family," Gwen said, a mulish look around her mouth.

Again, Rhoram struggled not to laugh. Surely Gwydion was the most foolish man alive. Did he think that if they spent the night, Rhiannon would come to Rhoram's bed? "Dreamer," he said solemnly, "you must stay. Tonight is Calan Olau. You must celebrate with us. We have no Druid, and so the Dreamer must help us honor Mabon of the Sun. What better homage for you to give the one whose Treasure you carry?"

"You are clever, Rhoram ap Rhydderch," Gwydion said. "Yes, we have the Spear. And we have the Stone." Gwydion took off his gloves and showed Rhoram the red, angry flesh of his hands. "This is what the Spear did to me. I have been burned by Mabon's Fire. And you are right, for that gift it is only right to honor him. And I will honor him for another reason. Because Rhiannon ur Hefeydd was gravely wounded protecting me, but she did not die. And that is a greater gift than the Spear itself."

Rhiannon's shocked face told its own tale. Never had Rhoram seen two such foolish people. But it would come out right. He hoped.

Before anyone could say a word, one of Rhoram's Dewin came running up to him. The woman panted out her message without preamble. "Word from Aidan and Cadell. They were almost captured in Arberth, but they got away."

"Thank the gods," Rhoram breathed.

"They are free now only because of Ellywen ur Saidi."

Achren's face went white as she put a hand on the Dewin's arm, whipping the woman around to face her. "Ellywen the Druid?" she demanded.

The woman nodded. "Please, Achren, you're hurting me."

Achren slowly released the woman's arm. "You are sure of this message?"

"I am sure. Cadell himself passed it on. They escaped from Arberth three days ago and are making their way here."

Achren shook her head. "I can't believe it. Ellywen of all people. After what she did to capture Cian, she lets Aidan and Cadell go? There must be a trick in it somewhere. Are they sure they are not being followed?"

"Aidan is sure. He said to tell you this specifically."

"Aidan would know," Rhoram said thoughtfully. "Then we must believe them. It is lucky, after all, that you did not kill her those months ago, Achren."

"I did not kill her because it seemed the worst thing I could do to her," Achren replied shortly. "It was not mercy."

"Cadell said she spoke of Anieron's death," the woman said, her eyes filling with tears. "And that Ellywen said she would spend the rest of her life in penance for that."

"Then it will be the only valuable thing she has ever done," Achren said shortly. "My King, I reserve the right to kill Ellywen should she be lying."

"Done, Achren."

THE STARS GLITTERED coldly overhead as Gwydion stepped up to the stone altar. He wore a robe of black, and the Dreamer's torque of fiery opals gleamed around his neck.

The grove of hazel trees was small, barely enabling Rhoram's Cerddorian to gather there. The greenish tree trunks twisted around each other in clumps, and the dark green leaves were still in the calm night.

Eight unlit torches were placed around the rough-hewn stone altar. A small bowl on the surface of the stone held wild grain, and next to it lay a loaf of bread. In the center of the grove, rowan wood was piled high in a circle.

Arthur stood next to Rhiannon. He had been uneasy since this afternoon when they had all bowed to him. That was something he thought he would never get used to. When he had declared he would avenge the Master Bard, he had not thought of all that his declaration had meant.

He had sworn to see it done, in the name of the High King. And he had named himself as that man. And now, though his thirst for vengeance had not cooled, his instincts to run had once again returned. It had not been that long ago when he had understood that to refuse his task meant punishment for Gwydion. And he had so wanted Gwydion to suffer, as a way to pay back his uncle for Arthur's own suffering.

Because of Gwydion, he had been taken from his mother and father when just a little boy. He could not even clearly remember his mother's face, retaining only a blurred image of beauty, of dark eyes and auburn hair. Once, and once only, his father had visited him. They had only spent a few hours together, but the bond between them had been strong. And then, soon after, his father had died, and Arthur had grieved for so very long, was still grieving for that loss. *Da*, he thought, *oh Da, I can't do what they ask of me.*

As though she understood his thoughts, Rhiannon, who stood on his right, put her arm across his shoulders and whispered to him. "Never mind all that now, Arthur. Tonight we honor Mabon of the Sun."

King Rhoram, who stood on Rhiannon's other side, gave Arthur a searching look, then smiled. "It's not so terrible, lad. The hardest part is picking the right people to do your job for you."

Gwen, who stood on Rhoram's other side with Geriant and Sanon close by, shushed them. Achren, who stood behind these three, her dark eyes alert for any sign of danger, grinned at Gwen's insistence that they all give Gwydion the kind of attention Gwen gave him. Dafydd Penfro, Rhoram's counselor, coughed to hide his laughter.

"This is the Wheel of the Year before us," Gwydion began. "One torch for each of the eight festivals when we honor the Shining Ones." As he named each festival, he gestured, and, one by one, the torches burst into flames. "Alban Elved, Calan Gaef, Alban Nos, Calan Morynion, Alban Eiler, Calan Llachar, Alban Heruin, and Calan Olau, which we celebrate tonight."

"We honor him," the crowd murmured softly, the sound of hushed voices like that of a gentle breeze.

Gwydion continued, "Let the Shining Ones be honored as they gather to honor the bringer of the harvest. Taran, King of the Winds. Modron, Great Mother of All. Nantsovelta, Lady of the Waters. Annwyn, Lord of Chaos. Aertan, Weaver of Fate. Cerridwen, Queen of the Wood. Cerrunnos, Master of the Hunt. Y Rhyfelwr, Agrona and Camulos, the Warrior Twins. Sirona, Lady of the Stars. Grannos, Star of the North and Healer."

"We honor the Shining Ones," the folk in the grove said in unison.

Then Gwen spoke the ritual question. "Why do we gather here?"

"We gather to honor Mabon," Gwydion replied. "For behold, he has gone to the depths of Gwlad Yr Haf and returns with the harvest in his hands. In the long night of the year—"

The Cerddorian replied, "All the land was bare and cold."

"In the dawn of the year," Gwydion continued.

"Buds burst on the trees, shoots sprouted from the ground."

"In the noon of the year," he intoned.

"Flowers bloomed, grain grew, the land was fruitful."

"Now is the time of harvest," Gwydion continued. "Ripened fruit falls into our hands. The golden wheat falls beneath the scythe. For Mabon has returned victorious. Behold, the grain Mabon has given." Gwydion picked up the bowl and threw the grains into the pile of rowan wood. As he did so, the wood burst into flames. And, within the flames, they saw fantastic shapes. Fiery horses galloped across bright fields. Honey dripped from golden honeycomb. Warriors brandished burnished spears in triumph. Flowers blossomed from fiery buds into flame-colored roses.

Arthur saw Gwydion look at Rhiannon out of the corner of his eye. Rhiannon smiled at the Dreamer. Arthur was shocked to see Gwydion smile in return.

Gwydion then picked up the loaf on the altar, gesturing for some of the warriors to begin passing baskets of broken loaves among the crowd. When everyone had a piece, he held up the loaf, saying, "The light of Mabon, King of Fire, shines on us at night. The light of Mabon, Lord of the Sun, shines on us by day. From him comes our bread."

"All hail Mabon!" the people cried as they began to eat the bread. Then they sang the celebration song.

"Greetings to you, sun of the season,
As you travel the skies on high,
With your strong steps on the wing of the heights,
Victorious hero, bringer of harvest.
Sweet acorns cover the woods,
The hard ground is covered with heavy fruit.
Grain has ripened golden.
Greetings to Mabon, bringer of harvest."

Within the grove people began to dance. Gwen ignored Arthur and made directly for Gwydion. But Arthur saw his uncle hold out his gloved hands and excuse himself from dancing. Rhoram gestured for Rhiannon to join him in the circle and she did so.

Arthur stepped to the fringes of the grove. He did not know how to dance very well and hoped he would not be asked. Gwydion made his way to him. Without preamble the Dreamer said quietly, "I had a dream of you, the day before you were born."

"I am not interested in your dreams, uncle," Arthur sneered. He did not think he wanted to hear what Gwydion had to say.

"I was in a forest," Gwydion went on, as though Arthur had not spoken. "I heard the sounds of the Wild Hunt. And the young eagle they were chasing came to take refuge on my shoulder. I promised the eagle I would save him. When the Hunt found us, Cerrunnos and Cerridwen demanded that I give the eagle to them. But I said no, he wanted to be free."

"Then what?" Arthur asked in spite of himself, as Gwydion paused.

"Cerridwen said that all men wish to be free, but that in this world it cannot be. And I recognized the truth of that. I, myself, was not free. And never have been."

Gwydion paused. "Then I asked them, will the eagle be happy in the chains they brought for him? And they said it was not for him to be happy. It was for him to be who he was born to be . . . They said that the only way to save Kymru was to give the eagle to them."

"And you did," Arthur said flatly.

"I did," Gwydion agreed, turning his silvery gaze onto his nephew. "And they said that I must protect you from the traitors in our midst. They said that they would see to it that, when the time came, the eagle would lead Kymru to take back its own. Then they said one last thing. They said that no man can keep another from the pain of his destiny. No man can keep another from his truth."

Gwydion took a deep breath and said the words Arthur thought he would never hear. "I'm sorry."

"For what you did?"

"No. For what must be."

Chapter 20

Maen and Ogaf Greu
Kingdom of Prydyn, Kymru
Gwinwydden Mis, 499

Llundydd, Disglair Wythnos—afternoon

Eight days out of Haford Bryn, in the city of Maen, Gwen's nerve broke.

She knew with every fiber in her shaking body that she could not do this thing they asked of her. She could not go into Ogaf Greu, to the caves where she had stayed with her father's people. She could not go back. She could not go beneath the earth. Not again.

And Ogaf Greu is where they said she must go. It was in the song, they said:

Down the cavern's twilight road
In the land of wine.
The maze of blood awaits.

In Ogaf Greu—the caves of blood—had long been rumored a path, Cyfnos Heol, the Twilight Road. It was said that those who took that path beneath the earth never returned to the light of day.

It did not matter how often she reminded herself that there had been no one within memory who had found that path. No one she had ever known had disappeared in Ogaf Greu during those days she and her father's Cerddorian had lived there. It did not matter

359

that the path itself was unknown, only rumor of it was whispered. Because she knew it did exist. And she knew that she was expected to find and take that road. And she knew that she could not do it.

She could not. For, if she did, she would never return.

The others could say what they liked—that the Song of the Caers spoke of the White One who took the Twilight Road. And they could point out that her name, Gwenhwyfar, meant White One. They could say that she had been named by the Wild Hunt as the one to take Cyfnos Heol. They could say that none but she could retrieve Modron's Cauldron from the depths of the earth and take it up into the bright world.

They could say all these things, but it made no difference. Because she could not do it. She could not.

"DONE, THEN," GWYDION said to the man in the stall. "Two pots to you for the bread, the cheese, and the ale. It was a pleasure doing business with you."

"And with you, boyo," the older man said with a grin. "Always a pleasure to help a fellow countryman."

At Gwydion's signal, Arthur unloaded the pots from his pack and handed them over to the man.

"Have much trouble with the local soldiers?" Gwydion asked casually.

"Oh, there are checkpoints whichever way you take to leave town. On market days, like today, they make everyone go through the same checkpoint and they are extra careful. Though what they think they will find here in Maen, I don't know," the man replied. "It's usually pretty quiet here."

"Is it?" Gwydion asked, his brows raised. "That's not what I have heard."

"Well," the merchant said with a smile, "by Kymric standards it is pretty quiet. Of course, sometimes things do happen to the Coranians here."

"A shame, that," Gwydion said with a grin.

"So it is," the man agreed, handing Arthur the supplies. "Take good care, though, at the checkpoint today. Seems one of those wyrce-jaga is here. And things seem to get out of hand when they are around."

"Thanks for the information, friend," Gwydion said, his face serious. "And we will be careful. Come, boyo, let's be on our way."

Arthur, his hands full, hurried to catch up to Gwydion. "What's so awful about a wyrce-jaga being here?" he asked, taking in Gwydion's frown.

"Don't ask foolish questions, boy," Gwydion replied in a distracted tone as they neared the center of the marketplace. A wyrce-jaga here in Maen! That was all they needed, he thought. Things were going to be more difficult than he had anticipated.

"At last!" Rhiannon called out in a shrewish tone as she saw them coming. She folded her arms and scowled. "I thought you'd never be done fussing over your trading. Every place we stop you absolutely have to take forever. Once a merchant, always a merchant. I remember my da used to say that you were so cheap—"

"It's important to get the best deal possible, I always say," Gwydion replied absently, his thoughts still focused on the wyrce-jaga. He laid a hand on Rhiannon's arm and said, in a low tone, "There is a wyrce-jaga here, at the checkpoint."

Rhiannon sucked in her breath sharply.

"But what makes you think we couldn't pass right through?" Arthur asked again. "We look all right. We act right. Just a merchant family down on their luck. This wyrce-jaga has no way of telling that we are anything other than that."

"I wouldn't be too sure of that," Rhiannon said darkly.

"I think you two are losing your nerve, letting a thing like this bother you," Arthur went on. "Besides, we don't even have the Treasures with us. That's why we left them with the wagon in the north wood."

Gwydion and Rhiannon exchanged a look. "What, then, you foolish boy, do you think a wyrce-jaga is doing here?" Gwydion asked in a honeyed tone. "Picking wildflowers, perhaps?"

Arthur scowled and opened his mouth to reply, but Gwydion hushed him with a sharp gesture. Ignoring Arthur, Gwydion spoke to Rhiannon. "What do you think?"

"No choice, really," she said. "We must go on."

"So we must. Where's Gwen?"

"Where's Gwen?" Rhiannon repeated blankly. "Didn't you see her?"

"No."

"She said she was going to catch up to you," Rhiannon said, her face stricken.

"We never saw her," Gwydion said, frowning. "Now where—"

"She's run away," Arthur said abruptly. "Gone back to her father."

"How can you know that?" Gwydion demanded.

"Oh, for the gods' sakes," Arthur said sharply, "didn't you understand how frightened she's been of going to the caves? Didn't you two know that?"

"She never said—" Rhiannon began.

"She didn't have to," Arthur interrupted. "At least, not to me."

"Rhiannon," Gwydion said quietly, "find her. Now."

Rhiannon immediately lowered her eyes to the ground. With Arthur and Gwydion surreptitiously holding her arms to keep her on her feet, her spirit rose above Maen and she began to Wind-Ride.

After a moment she stiffened in their arms and shuddered. She moaned and her knees buckled. She would have fallen if Gwydion and Arthur had not been holding her.

"You know better than to come back so fast and hard," Gwydion said calmly. "You'll have a headache for that. What did you see that frightened you so?"

She raised her head and her green eyes, dilated with fear, stared at Gwydion. "Gwen," Rhiannon whispered. "At the gate. They were taking her to the wyrce-jaga."

"She has a pretty good chance of talking herself out of any problem," Arthur said. "Her description has not been published, not like you two."

"Arthur's right," Gwydion said, his tone soothing. "Why are you—"

"Because the wyrce-jaga has a testing device," she said fiercely.

"He will know. He is testing them all. Gwen will show as a Druid, and then she is lost. And so are we."

Gwydion dropped Rhiannon's arm and grabbed the reins of his horse, his hand digging into his saddlebag. He found the item he was looking for and deftly tucked it up his sleeve.

"What was that?" Arthur asked. "What are you doing?"

"Saving Gwen," Gwydion answered simply. "Let's go."

GWEN HAD LEFT RHIANNON in the center of the marketplace, telling her mother that she wished to follow Gwydion and Arthur.

"They can gather supplies without your help," Rhiannon had said sharply.

"I just want to look at the stalls," Gwen had said impatiently. "Just for a few moments. Then I'll find them and come right back." She had walked away quickly, not waiting for her mother's reply.

This was her chance, and she wasn't going to let anyone stop her. She would leave Maen today, and make her way back to her father in Haford Bryn. Let them find another to take the Twilight Road in the Cave of Blood.

She lost herself in the market-day crowd, surreptitiously making her way to the checkpoint. She had taken a few coins from Gwydion's hoard that morning. It should be enough to pay the toll to the soldiers and get her out of town.

As she neared the gate, she saw there was a small crowd of people waiting to get out. Why was it taking so long, she wondered? As she joined them she craned her neck to see past them to what was happening at the gate.

By the time she saw what was happening, it was far too late to run. For there was a wyrce-jaga at the gate holding a testing device in his thin, bony fingers. To Gwen he seemed like a night crow with his obsidian eyes and clawed hands. Soldiers who held their weapons at the ready surrounded the people who were waiting.

An old woman, her scanty hair bound with a black kerchief, stepped forward and proudly held out her hand.

The silvery material of the box in the wyrce-jaga's hands glittered in the sun. The top of the box was decorated with jewels. In the very center was a group of onyx stones, for Annwyn, the Lord of Chaos, arranged in a figure-eight pattern around the bloodstone for Aertan, Weaver of Fate. Grouped around the onyx were four large stones: pearl for Nantsovelta of the Waters, opal for Mabon of the Sun, sapphire for Taran of the Winds, emerald for Modron the Mother. More stones rested in each corner. One held an amethyst for Cerridwen and another a topaz for Cerrunnos, the Protectors. Diamond for Sirona of the Stars, alongside garnet for Grannos the Healer. A ruby, for Camulos and Agrona, the Warrior twins, nestled in the last corner.

"Put your finger in the hole here," the wyrce-jaga said, pointing to the opening of the device.

"I know how to do it," the woman said with a sniff. "I was tested when I was a little girl. Wasn't Y Dawnus then, and I'm not now. But I wish I was. I'd know what to do with the likes of you."

"Just do it, old woman," the wyrce-jaga said, coldly. "And be grateful that you are not any of those things—if, indeed, that is the truth. For if you were, you would be dead."

"Brave words from such a little boy," the woman sneered as she inserted her finger into the opening. The amethyst and the topaz began to glow. As the woman removed her finger, the glow faded.

"So, you are Kymri, nothing more," the wyrce-jaga said.

"And nothing less," the woman said proudly.

The crowd was grinning now as the wyrce-jaga waved the woman on her way.

"Next," the wyrce-jaga called.

She checked around, meaning to return to the marketplace and find another way out of the city. If she should be tested, the emerald on the device would glow and they would know her for a Druid. She would be collared with one of the hateful enaid-dals and taken to the isle of Afalon. And, once there, she would die.

But her movement to leave had been too abrupt, and the guards were too quick.

"What have we here?" one of the guards asked. "Not anxious to be tested? Now, I wonder why."

"Leave me be," Gwen said in a breathless tone. "I—I forgot something. I must go back for it."

"Forgot something!" the guard laughed. "Forgot that you must not be tested? Here, wyrce-jaga," the guard called out, "this one needs to be next!" Two guards grabbed her by the arms and fairly dragged her past the waiting townsfolk, depositing her in front of the wyrce-jaga.

Just at that moment, Gwen saw Gwydion, Rhiannon, and Arthur making their way through the crowd, leading their horses. As they neared, people let them pass, melting away before them.

"Gwenhwyfar," Gwydion said sternly as he came to stand before her. "I told you to wait for us."

"I—I'm sorry, Da," she said, her voice trembling. "I thought to go on ahead and wait for you all outside. Then I changed my mind, but they wouldn't let me go."

"I should hope you changed your mind," Rhiannon said sharply. "We've been all over looking for you."

"Females," Gwydion said to the wyrce-jaga in a confidential tone, "always have a mind of their own. Always."

"Just who do you think you are?" the wyrce-jaga demanded.

"Ah, a merchant, good sir. And who are you?"

"I am Hild of Winburnan," the wyrce-jaga said. "And you are impertinent."

"No, just a traveling merchant. But at one time, I was one of the richest men in all of Kymru."

"Were you," the wyrce-jaga said flatly.

"Indeed, I was. But the war," Gwydion shook his head, "changed things."

"Don't listen to him, sir," Rhiannon called out as she came to stand by Gwydion, leaving Arthur to hold their horses. "He was never the richest man—never even close. Why, many was the time I had to take in a little sewing to make ends meet the best I could."

"And who are you?"

"I have the misfortune to be his wife," Rhiannon said. "And a very hard lot that is, too."

"Thank you, my dear, for your support," Gwydion said, baring his teeth in a smile. "But I believe that I can dispense with it."

"My father always said—"

"Yes, I know what your father always said about me. How could I forget, the way you remind me every day?"

"He said you would never amount to anything. He said—"

"Enough, woman!" Gwydion exclaimed.

The wyrce-jaga watched them both, his head swiveling from one to the other, Gwen momentarily forgotten. Gwydion walked directly up to the wyrce-jaga, flailing his arms.

"I tell you, wyrce-jaga, this woman is too much! Here I am, just trying to make a decent living, but does she ever shut up? No! Day in, day out—" As he gestured, somewhat dramatically, his hand hit the wyrce-jaga's arm and the testing device went flying, landing in the dust. With a gasp, Gwydion leapt to it, picking it up and trying to dust it off with his sleeve. "Good sir, my apologies," he stuttered.

The wyrce-jaga, his face red with rage, snatched the device back. "You fool!" he shouted. "If you have harmed it—"

"Oh, no one can harm one of those. They are indestructible. Didn't you know that?" Gwydion asked in surprise.

"You—"

"I am ready to take your test," Gwydion said bowing. "And then I can assure you we will be on our way."

"Good," the wyrce-jaga said briefly. "You are lucky that I don't have one of those soldiers run you through."

"I do, indeed, feel lucky, good sir. Perhaps a pot or two might make up to you for the inconvenience. At, say, half-price?"

"Put your finger in the device and then get out of my sight!" Hild raged.

With another bow and a flourish, Gwydion did as he was told. He noticed Rhiannon's still face and he longed to reassure her, but he could not.

The amethyst and the topaz glowed. And that was all.

Hild nodded to Rhiannon. "Now you."

With a look that seemed to say to the Coranians that this was all a waste of time, Rhiannon inserted her finger into the box. And the amethyst and the topaz glowed. And that was all.

"Our children wait, good sir," Gwydion said. "Perhaps you could test them now also? Then we can be on our way."

With a scowl Hild motioned for Arthur and Gwen to step forward. At the wyrce-jaga's command, they each inserted their fingers into the box. Again, the amethyst and the topaz glowed. And that was all.

"On your way," the wyrce-jaga said sharply.

"My thanks, good sir," Gwydion said jauntily as they mounted their horses and rode off through the gate.

No one spoke until they had returned to the wagon hidden deep in the wood. Rhiannon loaded the supplies into the wagon while Gwydion and Arthur hitched up two of the horses. Gwen sat her horse, unmoving, watching them. At last Arthur mounted his horse while Gwydion and Rhiannon climbed into the wagon box.

"All right," Rhiannon asked, turning to Gwydion. "How did you do that?"

"Did you know that once, when Arthur was four years old, he was publicly tested?"

"I suppose that I did."

"Remember that, Arthur?"

"Yes. You tested me in private, with my mam and da and Susanna the Bard. And I remember that every single jewel on the device lit up. But this time—"

"This time was like when I tested you on public. Only the amethyst and the topaz glowed. And that's all that device will ever do. I had it specially made for that purpose."

"Then where is the real device?"

With a flourish, Gwydion pulled the device from his sleeve. "I couldn't let them keep it, now could I?"

"That is the one they took from Cian?" Arthur asked.

"The very same."

"By the gods," Rhiannon breathed. "And now they don't have a real device any more. Very clever, Dreamer."

"Yes, I thought so, too."

"It does make me wonder what that wyrce-jaga was doing here, though," Rhiannon went on. "Why was he here in Maen, such a small place? And with the only testing device the Coranians have?"

Gwydion shook his head. "I couldn't say. But I wonder—" he trailed off, frowning.

"You wonder what?" Arthur asked.

"Some months ago I had a dream of the Protectors. And Havgan was in that dream. Indeed, he was so real that I have wondered ever since if he didn't dream the same thing."

"Havgan is a Dreamer?" Rhiannon asked in an appalled tone.

"Perhaps. Perhaps not. But I wonder if he didn't know somehow that Maen was an important place for the testing device to be, though he did not, perhaps, know why."

They were silent for a moment, contemplating that thought. Then Gwydion, with a shrug, picked up the reins.

"Wait," Gwen said in a low voice.

The three of them stared at her, waiting as she had asked them to do.

"I'm sorry," she said at last, her head bowed so she would not need to see their eyes. No one spoke, so she forced herself to go on. "I was afraid. I was going back to my da." Again, they made no answer. "I was afraid," she said again. She steeled herself to see the contempt in their eyes as she raised her head to look at them.

But their eyes did not hold contempt. Wonder of wonders, there was kindness there. And understanding. And pity for her in her agony.

"Of course, you were afraid, Gwen," Gwydion said quietly. "Rhiannon and I, when we came close to our Treasures, we were afraid."

"So we were," her mother agreed, her voice kind.

"And I am afraid, Gwen," Arthur said suddenly.

"But you two did what you must do," Gwen said slowly. "And you, Arthur, you will go on."

"So I will," Arthur replied.

"Then so must I," she said.

Meirwdydd, Disglair Wythnos—early morning

RHIANNON NEVER TOOK her eyes from her daughter's pale, tight face. The fear she saw there almost broke her heart. But Rhiannon knew better than to show that—Gwen neither wanted nor needed her mother's understanding. And so Rhiannon's own countenance was unmoving. Only the pity in her eyes betrayed her.

Gwen stood stiffly just outside the entrance to the caves of Ogaf Greu. The rushing of the sea as it crept up and down the sandy beach hissed in their ears. The sun was just beginning to lighten the sky as the stars winked out. The morning was cool—but that was not why Gwen shivered.

Today Gwenhwyfar ur Rhoram var Rhiannon would enter the cave and search for the Cauldron, the Treasure belonging to Modron, the great Mother. Gwen would go alone. The task was hers, and no one could take it from her.

Rhiannon well remembered that day, years ago, when Gwen had been lost in the caves that branched out from their hiding place in Coed Aderyn. She remembered at last finding her daughter, sobbing, at the bottom of a pit into which she had fallen. After that Gwen had a horror of being beneath the surface of the earth.

True, Gwen had lived here in the caves of Ogaf Greu with Rhoram and his people for years. But she had been sure, she told them, to never be alone there, always having people within call. But today, Gwen would go alone.

Gwydion stood on one side of Gwen. His usual stonelike expression was unmoving as he surveyed the surrounding beach. Arthur stood on Gwen's other side. He had spoken little in the past few days as they journeyed from Maen to the caves. And he said nothing now. But there was pity in his dark eyes. The scar on his face whitened a little as he looked down at Gwen.

Gwen was dressed in a tunic and trousers of soft, brown leather. Her blond hair was braided tightly to her head. Her jaw was clenched so tightly that the cords on her neck stood out. She twisted the emerald ring of the House of PenBlaid around and around her finger.

At Gwydion's nod Arthur handed Gwen a length of rope. She shrugged it over her shoulder, still fingering the ring. Gwydion held two torches in his hands. He stared at one, and the end of it burst into flame. He handed them both to her and she took them with trembling hands.

"Remember, Gwen," Gwydion said sternly, "what I taught you about Fire-Weaving. Don't lose your concentration, and you can do it. If the first torch should go out, light the other one in that way."

Gwen nodded. Before she could turn to go, Rhiannon reached out and touched her arm. But at Gwen's flinch, Rhiannon dropped her hand and stepped back.

Rhiannon ducked her head, staring at the ground, so the others would not see the pain in her eyes. She would not watch Gwen go—Gwen did not need even that from her.

She heard the sound of Gwen's boots, taking her first, hesitant steps toward the wide, dark mouth of Ogaf Greu, the Caves of Blood. The footsteps halted, then came back in a rush. Gwen threw her arms around Rhiannon. Before Rhiannon even had time to hug her back, Gwen was gone, vanished into the caves.

Rhiannon took a deep breath, trying to surreptitiously wipe away the tears that had come to her eyes. She turned away from Gwydion and Arthur. Then Gwydion's strong, scarred hands gently grasped her shoulders. Standing behind her, he said nothing, merely pulling her back against him, letting her feel the warm strength of his body.

Without even thinking about it, she twisted in his arms to face him as she burst into tears. Her sobs seemed to go on and on as Gwydion stroked her hair and held her tight. He said nothing, just let her be what she was—a wounded woman, crying out in her pain.

GWEN STOOD WITHIN the shallow entrance to the caves, waiting for her eyes to adjust to the darkness. Behind her the morning light streamed in, gathering in a pool at her feet, leaving the rest of the cave in shadow.

She glanced down at the ring on her finger. It seemed to glow slightly, pulsing on her finger in time with the beat of her heart. Taking a deep breath, she made her way to the first entrance. Ducking slightly, she began down the familiar passageways. The light from the torch shifted over the cave walls that glittered in the wavering flames.

Not knowing exactly what she was doing, she found herself moving toward the chamber where she used to sleep when she had lived here. But as she did, the glow from the ring faded. So, she thought, so even the familiar ways, which held enough terrors for her were not right. It was not enough that she was, once again, beneath the earth. It was not enough that she was alone. It was not enough that all she could think of was that the walls would collapse and cover her.

Taking a deep breath, she retraced her steps and took an unused passageway at random. The light of the ring strengthened slightly. She followed the passageway down for what seemed like hours. The passageway abruptly ended into a junction. Here there were three more passageways, three pools of darkness, and three more ways to die.

And she knew that she had come to it at last—Cyfnos Heol, the Twilight Road; the path from which no one was said to ever return.

"Stop that," she muttered, as she stood still, trying to decide which way to take. Her words seemed to be swallowed up instantly, smothered, left lifeless. Like she would be soon. The walls would collapse and she would—

She would start screaming in a minute if she didn't stop this. She moved to stand before the east passage and looked down at the ring on her shaking hand. It seemed as though the glow had lessened. She moved to the north passage, but the glow did not change. West, she thought to herself as she came to stand before the last passage. Of course, west for Modron the Great Mother. And, indeed, as she stood before the west passage the ring began to glow with a greater intensity. Taking a deep breath, she hitched the coil of rope more firmly over her shoulder, griped the lit torch and the unlit one tightly, and began to walk down the passageway.

It was narrow to begin with, but it seemed to narrow even more as she went. In some places her shoulders brushed both walls. Only the thought of what the others would say if she came back empty-handed prevented her from turning around and running away.

Longer and longer the passage ran. There were no other exits, no openings, nothing but this narrow passageway. Truly she was on the Twilight Road. She was finding it hard to breathe now. She had no idea how long she had been down here. She glanced at the flaring torch and was startled to see how far it had burned down. She would need to light the other torch, soon. But if she did that, how would she make it back before the second torch went out? She should have brought more. Gwydion should have seen to it.

She continued down, following the twisting, serpentine, narrow way. Down she went to the center of the earth, to the realm of the Mother. Twisting and turning, turning and twisting, spiraling through this maze of passageways, traveling the Twilight Road.

The torch guttered. Shocked, she realized that it had almost burned down. She would have to light the second torch. She stopped and, remembering what Gwydion had taught her, took a deep breath to calm herself. She stared at the tip of the unlit torch and willed Fire to come to it. But nothing happened. No, this was wrong. She was trying too hard. Another deep breath, a moment to find and feel the inner balance. A moment to reach for the flames. But still, nothing happened.

Fool, she thought to herself fiercely. You cannot do what every Druid in Kymru could do. Oh, gods, if only her mother had not hidden her away all those years she might have learned how to do this. If only her mother had sent her to Caer Duir to learn, she might be able to bring fire now.

No, these thoughts would not help her now. "Modron," she whispered. "Great Mother, Giver of Harvests, Queen of the Earth, please help me to call fire." But nothing happened. Her other torch had nearly burned down. She could not do it. Quickly she touched the lit torch to the unlit one. The new torch blazed up, and she set the old torch on the ground.

Please, Modron, she thought, *please don't let it be much farther. Or else I will never get out of here.* But, no, Modron had not answered her earlier plea. Modron cared nothing for her. She felt a pull, a faint tug, something—but what? She stopped, wanting to understand. The ring on her finger lost some of its glow. Had she missed something? Some turning? But how? There were no other ways out.

The glow of the ring became fainter still. The pull she had felt became stronger. And then she realized what she had to do, why Modron had not answered her prayer for fire. Fire would not do for the Great Mother. Fire belonged to Mabon of the Sun. But the Mother was different. Abruptly she threw the torch on the ground and extinguished the flame. Total darkness surrounded her.

No, there was light. The light from the emerald began to glow stronger. Modron was here, guiding her. She started forward, and the rocky ground became smooth as glass beneath her feet. The passageway began to widen.

Somehow her fear was gone. She almost ran down the passage lit by the verdant glow of the ring. There, not far now, an opening. A pit of blackness far, far beneath the earth. And she was not afraid.

She burst into the cavern, and the ring flared up even brighter than before. The chamber was perfectly round, the walls smooth and glittering with gems. In the center a green light glowed, pulsing, ever-changing. She walked slowly toward the light that came from the pit.

The pit. One much like the pit she had fallen into so many years ago. But this time she was not afraid. The ring on her hand, the glow from the pit, the beat of her heart pulsed in the same rhythm. She squatted by the hole and leaned over to look.

And there it was. Y Pair, the Cauldron of Modron. Buarth Y Greu, the Circle of Blood. The shallow bowl was made of glittering gold with a dizzying array of spirals etched on all sides. The lip of the bowl was covered with emeralds. In the center of the inside of the bowl was a figure eight, etched in onyx, the sign of Annwyn, Lord of Chaos.

She shrugged the rope from her shoulders. There was nothing to tie it to anyway, and she knew she would not need it. Not now. Not now that Modron had given her access, at last, to that place within her, that place that had always been there, but she had never been able to reach easily or consistently. Because now she could Shape-Move whenever she wanted. She could feel other things inside her that she could now do. She could Fire-Weave, calling fire when needed. These things denied her for so long, were hers now.

"They have always been yours." The low, musical voice that seemed to come from everywhere, from nowhere, from the pit, from her heart, was warm and kind.

"Who is here?" Gwen asked. "Who are you?"

"I am Arywen ur Cadwy var Isabyr. I was the Fifth Archdruid of Kymru."

Her heart in her throat, Gwen whispered. "The Archdruid to Lleu Lawrient, the last High King."

"Yes," Arywen agreed with a sigh.

A flicker of green and brown shimmered at the end of the pit, then the shade of Arywen coalesced in the emerald light. She had long, black hair, held back from her beautiful face with a band of gold and emeralds. Her Archdruid's robe was forest green, trimmed in brown at the hem and throat. Around her slender neck hung the ghost of the Archdruid's torque, shimmering emeralds set in a circle within a circle.

"You—you are here? Have been here all this time?" Gwen asked.

"I have," Arywen's shade said.

"How you must have loved him," Gwen said in awe.

"We all loved Lleu Silver-Hand. Bran and Mannawyddan, Taliesin and I, his four Great Ones, loved him with such a love that death itself could not sunder it. I am glad you have come, White One, so that I may now complete my journey to the Land of Summer and see again those I have loved." Her green catlike eyes glowed emerald in the shifting verdant glow from the pit.

"I thank you, Archdruid," Gwen said formally, "that I have been led here. And I thank you, most of all, that Modron's gifts have at last been given to me."

"They were always yours, but you would never take them."

"I was afraid. The caves—"

"Are Modron's places. The warm, dark places of the earth. Her places just as much as the crops that grow above, the wheat that reaches toward the sun, the apple trees, the wildflowers. To embrace that which she has to give you must embrace all that she is. And this you have never done. Look to yourself, Gwenhwyfar ur Rhoram var Rhiannon, for that reason."

"My mother—" she began.

"Loves you. And left you for the good of Kymru. Your fears, White One, are your own."

At last, after so many years, she understood. She knew, now, why her druidic gifts had been so hard to reach. For what gifts could have made their way through a heart so hard?

At last, she said, "I am the White One, the one who comes to take the Cauldron back to the land above, so that we may reclaim Kymru. Joyfully I have come. May I take it?"

"It is yours, daughter. Take it."

Gwen stretched out her hands toward the bottom of the pit, and the bowl began to rise.

THEY WAITED BY the mouth of the caves as they had waited all day and into the night, rarely speaking, but comforted, nonetheless, by each other's presence.

Gwydion absently fed another piece of wood to the small fire. Overhead the sky was just beginning to brighten as morning crept over the horizon. He looked over the campfire at Rhiannon. She had not slept—none of them had slept—as they waited. There were dark circles beneath her eyes. Her fears for Gwen were etched in the tight lines bracketing her mouth.

"I truly do believe she will come back," Gwydion said quietly.

Arthur rose from his place next to Rhiannon and went to stand by the mouth of the cave. He stared into the entrance and did not bother to answer.

"I have not been able to Wind-Ride after her at all," Rhiannon said softly. "I can see nothing. Why?"

"Modron," Gwydion replied. "It is her doing. I have not been able to track her, either."

Arthur started, then peered even more intently into the cave mouth. "I thought I heard something."

Rhiannon leapt to her feet and grabbed Arthur's arm. "Are you sure?"

"No, but I—"

From the mouth of the cave came a faint, emerald glow. The light grew stronger. Gwydion came to stand beside Rhiannon and Arthur.

Gwen walked from the cave to stand before them. In her hands she held the golden Cauldron of Modron. The emeralds on the bowl were glowing, pulsing in time to the emerald on her hand.

Gwen smiled.

"It is done," Gwydion said.

Part 4
The Return

Three things are worse than sorrow;
To wait to die, and to die not;
To try to please, and to please not;
To wait for someone who comes not.

A Kymric proverb

Chapter 21

Mynydd Tawel
Kingdom of Gwynedd, Kymru
Gwinwydden Mis, 499

Gwyntdydd, Tywyllu Wythnos—early afternoon

Arthur gazed at the purple mountains that rose sharply before him, their stark edges outlined against the deep blue sky. Jagged peaks pierced the skyline, still dusted with snow, even at this time of year. He took a deep breath of clean, cool air. Home. At last, he was coming back, to the only home he could remember, Dinas Emrys, the little village where Great-Uncle Myrrdin had raised him.

This portion of Sarn Gwyddelin, the main road through Gwynedd, wound up and down through the mountains. In front of him the wagon creaked along. Gwydion drove slowly here, trying to avoid the worst of the rocks on the road. In a few days they would have to abandon the wagon, as they made their way closer to Mynydd Tawel, the hiding place that Arthur's father, King Uthyr, had prepared for his people. And there, they would meet Arthur's sister, Morrigan, who had the ring of King Uthyr in her keeping. At last he would meet the sister he had been too young to remember.

And there, too, would be Ygraine, the mother Arthur barely remembered, for he had not seen her since he was four years old. All because of Gwydion. All because of the Dreamer's plots. All because his uncle had plans. His hatred of Gwydion, a hatred that sometimes slept but never fully departed, blossomed again in his heart like a deadly rose.

Suddenly Arthur was filled with a longing to go to Dinas Emrys. Of course, Myrrdin was not there. But he so desperately wanted to see again the only home he had ever known. After all, it was on the way to Mynydd Tawel. No reason that they could not take the time. No reason at all. Taking another deep breath, he urged his horse forward next to the wagon box.

"Uncle," Arthur said sharply.

Gwydion, never taking his gaze from the road, replied quietly, "You are to call me da, boyo. Remember that."

"There isn't anyone else around," Arthur exclaimed, "and you know it."

"And how would I know that?"

"Because Rhiannon has been Wind-Riding this whole time, looking to be sure we are alone here."

Rhiannon, in her place next to Gwydion in the wagon box, did not even turn her head. Her gaze was blank, as her spirit roamed the mountainsides, looking for signs of trouble.

Gwen urged her horse up next to Arthur's. "What are you arguing about now?" she asked.

"What makes you think I'm arguing?"

"You're talking to Gwydion. And that means you are arguing," she said smugly.

He flashed her a distinctly unfriendly look. It did not seem to faze her.

"Uncle," he began again, "we are going to Dinas Emrys."

"We are not," Gwydion replied. "We don't have time."

"I want to go," Arthur insisted.

"No," Gwydion said again.

"Why? Because you know how much I want to?"

Gwydion took his eyes from the road and turned to face Arthur. His cold, gray gaze held a hint of contempt. "There are always reasons for what I do, Arthur. And none of them have to do with pleasing or displeasing you."

"So I noticed," Arthur flared, "years ago."

"Then remember it. And remember, too, what we are doing here and where we are going. And remember that we must be at the Doors of Cadair Idris with the Treasures in our hands by Calan Gaef."

"Why must we be there at the New Year?" Gwen asked.

"Because that is the time when the nights are the longest, and when the veil between the worlds is the thinnest. If Arthur is to succeed there, he will need all the help he can get."

"Thank you, uncle," Arthur spat, "for your great faith in me."

"I will have faith in you when you are a man."

"I am a man now!"

"No, you are a boy, one who thinks of yourself first. When you begin to think of Kymru instead, then you will be a man."

"You—" Arthur began.

But at that moment, Rhiannon stirred by Gwydion's side. Her lids flickered rapidly over her green eyes, and then her gaze came into focus.

"What is it?" Gwydion asked, one hand still holding the reins, the other on Rhiannon's arm.

"A wyrce-jaga," she said quietly. "And some soldiers. And—and some prisoners."

"Prisoners? Who?" Gwydion asked.

"Dewin," she whispered. "And Bards. I know them, and so must you. And they are coming this way, down the road. They are wearing enaid-dals. Even if they wanted to Wind-Speak with us, even if we wanted to offer some word of comfort, we could not. We can give them nothing."

"They wear collars," Gwydion said flatly. "Collars that the Smiths are making."

"So they do, and will, until the Smiths can be found and freed," Rhiannon said.

"The Smiths should never, ever be doing such a thing," Gwen said fiercely. "They should have died first."

"The Coranians have the Smith's families, Gwen." Rhiannon pointed out. "Their wives and husbands, their children and grandchildren. And so they make the collars."

"They are cowards!" Gwen insisted.

"And you know all about cowardice, don't you, Gwen?" Arthur said coldly.

Gwen's face turned bright red. "You would throw that up to me."

"Hush," Gwydion said. "Enough of that. The Smiths know that one day we will find them and rescue them. Until then, they wait. As all Kymru waits."

"Here they come," Rhiannon said tightly. "Just around the bend."

"Will any of them say anything to us?" Arthur asked. "Give us away?"

Rhiannon turned her green eyes on Arthur, then turned away. "No," she said coldly.

"I was just asking—"

"It was a foolish question. Now hush, boy," Gwydion said.

The wagon rounded the bend, then halted, as Gwydion pulled the horses to the side of the road to allow the other party to pass. There were ten Coranian soldiers, five in the front and five in the back, surrounding the prisoners. They carried spears and shields carved with the boar's head, symbol of the Warleader. They wore shirts of woven mail that reached to their thighs. Behind the first five soldiers walked a wyrce-jaga. He was dressed in the customary robe of black, moving like a shadow in the sunlight. Following him were two men, two women, and a young girl, their hands bound behind them, collars of dull, gray metal clasped around their throats. The skin on their necks that bordered the collars was red and blistered.

"Clear the way," one of the soldiers barked as they neared the wagon.

"We have," Gwydion said shortly. "There is plenty of room to get by."

Arthur saw Rhiannon rest her hand on Gwydion's arm, as though restraining him. A muscle worked in Gwydion's jaw as he looked at the prisoners.

Slowly, the prisoners raised their heads and gazed back at them. None of them made a sign, but Arthur thought he saw the glint of recognition in the eyes of the four adults. Then, as though they might have feared someone else would see it, too, they lowered their gazes back to the ground.

The wyrce-jaga strode up to them. "You are rude, peasant," the man sneered. "We will have to teach you manners."

Arthur tensed, then urged his horse a little closer to the wyrce-jaga. Next to him, Gwen did the same. For a few moments, everyone was quiet as they waited for the next act that would set everything in motion. Arthur's hand crept closer to his knife.

But just then, one of the women moaned low in her throat, then fainted, dropping heavily to the ground. The other woman and the girl knelt down next to her, but could not help her as their hands were bound.

"You see?" the woman cried as she knelt, "I told you that we were trying to go too far today. Now she's fainted. I told you that would happen. But, no, you wouldn't listen to me. We need more water, I said, more food."

"Coranians always think they know best," one of the male prisoners agreed. "You can't convince them of anything they don't want to hear. Why, just this morning I was trying to explain to that wyrce-jaga what a pig he was, and he didn't believe me."

"They never do," the other man said in a confidential tone. "The more obvious a thing is, the harder time they have understanding it."

The wyrce-jaga turned from Gwydion, his face red with rage. "The prisoners will be quiet!" he shrieked. "Captain, I insist that you shut them up."

"You want them killed, wyrce-jaga?" the Captain inquired contemptuously. "Is that what you want?"

The woman who had fainted moaned again, then struggled to sit up. One of the soldiers knelt beside her, then helped her to her feet.

"I—I'm sorry," the woman whispered. "The heat, the collar, it was too much." For someone who had fainted, the woman's color was surprisingly good.

"Of course, it was too much!" the other woman exclaimed. "Captain, how much farther until the next town?"

"You know that as well as I do," the Captain said shortly. "It's your country."

"It is our country now!" the wyrce-jaga exclaimed.

One of the male prisoners gave a short laugh. "Enjoy it while you can, pig."

The Captain stepped between the prisoners and the wyrce-jaga, as the wyrce-jaga raised his hand to strike. The Captain did not speak, but the witch-hunter lowered his hand. The Captain turned away, and, ignoring the wyrce-jaga, shouted the order to march. The witch-hunter fell in behind the Captain, and the party moved on. The prisoners did not look up as they passed.

Arthur sat on his horse, unmoving, looking after them. No one spoke. Finally, Arthur turned to Gwydion and Rhiannon.

"Who was the one who fainted?" he asked quietly.

"Morwen," Rhiannon said. "She was one of the teachers at Y Ty Dewin. And one of the least likely women in the world to really faint."

"And the other woman?" Arthur asked again.

"Elivri. One of the most accomplished harpists at Neuadd Gorsedd," Gwydion replied.

"And the others?"

"Maredudd," Rhiannon said, "is a Bard. A friend of my Uncle Dudod's for many years. When I was a little girl, he taught me how to play the pipe."

"Trephin," Gwydion said, "is Dewin. And the finest doctor I ever met. I do not know the girl."

"Where were they being taken?" Gwen asked.

"To Afalon, the island in Llyn Mwyngil in Gwytheryn."

"To die there."

"If they are not rescued soon, yes."

Arthur was quiet again, still gazing at the place where the prisoners had been. "Someone should help them."

"Someone will," Gwydion said. "They shall be rescued."

"How?" Gwen asked.

"The High King will see to it," Gwydion said, holding Arthur's gaze.

For a long time, uncle and nephew stared at one another. At the last it was Arthur who looked away.

Suldydd, Cynyddu Wythnos—afternoon

THE AIR WAS clean and cold near the peak of Mynydd Tawel. Beneath Arthur's feet, clover sprang, green and fresh. As he moved steadily up the mountain, he heard the sounds of rushing water, coming from the myriad of tiny brooks that laced the hillside. Overhead hawks wheeled and soared, crying out as they rode the wind.

Ahead of him Gwydion, Rhiannon, and Gwen halted. Rhiannon, dressed in a tunic and breeches of dark green, adjusted the pack on her back that held the Stone of Nantsovelta. Gwen, wearing riding leathers of dark brown, also had a pack, in which she carried the Cauldron of Modron. And Gwydion, in a tunic and breeches of black, had the Spear of Mabon wrapped in a blanket, and slung over his shoulder with a leather strap.

They had their Treasures. But Arthur did not. The only thing left to gather now, the Sword of Taran, had not been found. And that would be his task. And to do that, he needed his father's ring. And so they were here, in Mynydd Tawel. Today, at last, Arthur would meet his mother and his sister.

"Why are we stopping?" Gwen asked.

"For Arthur," Gwydion replied. "He should lead us now, not I."

Arthur gazed up at Gwydion, who stood ahead of him on the mountain. Without a word, Arthur passed by Gwen, then Rhiannon, then Gwydion, until he stood in the front. And then he led them up the mountain.

They had almost reached the top, and had still seen no one, when a faint whistle was heard. Arthur halted, and looked over in the direction the whistle had come from. Just slightly to the east of them was a narrow fissure. Arthur turned toward it, and the other three followed.

Before they reached it, a man appeared from the gap in the rocks. His hair was brown, sprinkled lightly with gray. His brown eyes were steady and fearless, even as they shimmered with unshed tears. And as Arthur halted before him, the man's firm mouth widened in a smile. The man knelt on the rocks, his head bowed, and reached for Arthur's hand.

"Son of my king," the man murmured, "you are welcome here. The Cerddorian of Gwynedd, who work to take back your father's land from the enemy, are honored that you return to us."

"Arthur," Gwydion said, "this is Cai ap Cynyr. Your father's Captain, now the Captain to your sister, Morrigan."

"Cai ap Cynyr," Arthur said, as he raised the man to his feet. "I thank you for your welcome. But you must not kneel to me. Not you, who was one of my father's dearest friends."

"The Captain who outlived his King," Cai said bitterly, his face shadowed.

"The Captain whom my father trusted with the lives of those he loved," Arthur said gently. "Is there any greater trust than that? Or any other man worthy of such a trust?"

Cai cleared his throat but did not answer, though he squared his shoulders as though a weight had fallen from him. Then two more men came through the fissure and bowed to Arthur. One had golden hair and light brown eyes, and his wide mouth was quirked in a grin. The other had sandy brown hair and fierce eyes of piercing gray. The man with the golden hair spoke.

"Arthur ap Uthyr var Ygraine, you are most welcome here to the mountain home of the PenHebogs, the true rulers of Gwynedd. Long have we awaited your coming. Long have we awaited the sight of you. Long have we—"

"That's enough, Duach," Gwydion said dryly. "I see you haven't changed a bit. Arthur, this is Duach ap Seithfed, once your father's doorkeeper. Now a Cerddorian and the Lord of Dunoding."

Arthur bowed briefly to Duach. "I thank you for your kind words, Duach."

"Don't encourage him, my Lord," Cai said with a smile. "He will only go on." Cai gestured to the other man. "This is Dywel ap Gwyn, the Gwarda of Ardudwy."

Dywel dropped to his knees and bowed his head. Before Arthur could even ask the man to stand, Dywel spoke. "My Lord, it is only right that you know who I really am before you greet me. My brother is Bledri, the Dewin in Rheged who betrayed King Urien and Queen Ellirri, he who now sits at the right hand of the false King, Morcant. I am sworn to kill him if I can."

Suddenly the knowledge came on Arthur. From where, and how, he did not know. "It is not for you to kill your brother," he said, his words sure and firm. "Instead he shall be exiled Beyond the Ninth Wave to pay for his crimes."

Before any of them could reply, a young woman darted from the gap in the rocks. She hurled herself into Arthur's arms. Startled, he could only put his arms around her to keep their balance.

"Arthur, it's you. It's really you, isn't it?" she asked as she released her hold at last and gazed up at him, her hands grasping his arms tightly.

She had auburn hair that glowed in the sunlight and dark eyes that sparkled with the sheen of tears. She had high cheekbones and a pointed, determined chin. She wore a woolen tunic and trousers of blue and a sapphire ring around her finger. Something about the auburn hair, the eyes, the face, something he seemed to remember from long, long ago, held him.

"Morrigan?" he whispered.

"Yes! You knew me. You did! See, Cai, I told you he would, even though we have never met."

"So he did, my Queen," Cai agreed with a laugh.

"I remember you, a little," Morrigan went on, her eyes shining.

"And then Gwydion took me away," Arthur said, bitterness in his tone.

"For a reason." The woman who spoke slipped through the rocks like a ghost. Her auburn hair was touched with frost. Her dark eyes were cool and watchful. She stood proudly, dressed in a plain kirtle of gray with a linen undertunic of white. Her smooth hands were clasped by her side as she moved to stand before him.

"Yes," Arthur agreed gravely, "for a reason." He moved forward, past Morrigan, to stand in front of the woman. "Mam," he said softly. "Mam, I am home."

"You look like your da," she said, as they faced each other, unmoving.

"Your son is returned to you, Ygraine ur Custennin var Elwen," Gwydion said solemnly. "As I promised would happen one day."

"So you did, Dreamer," Ygraine replied, still not taking her eyes from her son. She reached up and touched his face. "So like your father," she murmured. "So like."

Arthur reached out and gently gathered Ygraine to him. "Mam," he said softly. "Mam." They stood there, holding each other gently, saying nothing for some time.

At last, Ygraine withdrew from him. "You are welcome here, my son. Your father charged me to do all I could to see to it that you became what you were born to be. Ask, now, then, what we can do for you."

"Before my father died, he gave away his ring, the ring of the House of PenHebog." Arthur turned to Morrigan. "He gave this ring to you, his daughter, the day he sent you from Tegeingl."

Morrigan nodded, her eyes filling with tears.

"And so I ask for it now, in the words that were foretold by Bran the Dreamer, the words I know my father said you must wait for. These, then, are the words: In the name of the High King to be, surrender Bran's gift to me."

"Those are the words," Morrigan agreed, her voice shaking. "The very words he said to me the day he sent me away." Slowly, Morrigan pulled the sapphire ring from her finger. The sunlight glinted off the stone in a flash of blue as though a piece of the sky itself had fallen to her palm as she passed the ring to him.

Arthur kissed Morrigan, then put the ring on his finger. The sapphire glowed as he stared down at it, pulsing in time with the beat of his heart.

"Which way?" Rhiannon asked gently. "Which way to the Sword of Taran?"

"North," Arthur said. "North."

GWYDION SAT BY the fire that night, listening to Cai and Susanna tell Arthur of Uthyr's last days. He tried not to listen. But he had to, because they were all listening to Cai. No one else spoke to divert him from Cai's words.

Arthur listened eagerly, his dark eyes flashing. Morrigan sat beside Arthur, holding his hand, listening just as avidly. Ygraine sat a little apart from them, with a countenance carved of stone. But Gwydion knew that she was hanging on every word.

Susanna sat next to Cai, her hand resting on the shoulder of her son, Gwyhar. She, too, was listening closely. And every time Cai mentioned Griffi, the man who had been Uthyr's Druid, Susanna's lover, and the father of her child, her mouth curved in a reminiscent smile. There was sadness, still, but she had moved beyond the grief. How she had done it, Gwydion did not know. He himself could not seem to be able to. Thoughts of both his brothers could still pierce his heart and tighten his throat, could still bring the grief, fresh and raw, rising relentlessly to flood his mind with memories.

Gwyhar listened with shining eyes when anyone spoke of his father. For Griffi had bravely stood fast against the Archdruid's order and had stayed by his King.

Neuad, Morrigan's Dewin, her golden hair flowing down her shoulders, also listened intently. Next to Neuad sat Jonas, the Bard whom Anieron had sent to Gwynedd.

Dinaswyn sat next to Gwydion. The firelight played over the frosty hair of the former Dreamer. Her gray eyes seemed far away. Whatever she was contemplating, it was not pleasant. She had greeted Gwydion as warmly as she ever greeted anyone, which was to say not at all. But she had kept him by her side since they had arrived. Yet she had barely spoken. Gwydion knew her well enough to know she had something on her mind.

Finally, Arianrod sat on the other side of Dinaswyn. His greeting to her had been awkward at best. She had emerged from the gap in the rocks as though she were a Queen deigning to greet a servant. She had elaborately braided her beautiful, honey-colored hair. She wore a shift of amber, barely covered by a low-cut kirtle of topaz. Amber earrings dangled from her delicate ears, and an amber necklace nestled in the curve of her firm bosom. Every breath she took set the amber dancing, drawing the eye to where it rested. She had not greeted anyone with warmth, but the degree of coldness with which she had greeted Rhiannon defied description.

But Rhiannon, now sitting across the circle with Gwen, had not seemed to notice, or to be affected by the cool greeting. Instead, she had smiled, and complimented Arianrod on her pretty dress, then mentioned how chest colds were so difficult to get rid of. Gwydion had almost smiled but had managed to keep his face impassive.

Bedwyr, Morrigan's Lieutenant, was not here, having been sent on a mission to Tegeingl a week before. Apparently Tangwen, King Madoc's daughter, was now a trusted contact for the Cerddorian, and Bedwyr had been sent to meet with her.

"He spat, over the wall, directly into Madoc's face," Cai was saying.

"And Madoc nearly fainted with rage," Susanna put in.

"'Pit your seven hundred against my warriors, brother,' Uthyr said that day. 'And you shall see how true warriors of Gwynedd fight. Come against me, then. We are ready for you.' And we were. We fought Madoc's armies that day, and by the time the day was over, the city was still ours," Cai went on.

Why did they have to do this? Gwydion wondered. Why did they have to talk of Uthyr? He remembered begging Uthyr to leave Tegeingl, long before the enemy came. He had known that Uthyr would die if he fought the enemy. Uthyr had known it, too. And he had stayed in Tegeingl just the same.

"Griffi was horrified to get that letter from the Archdruid," Susanna said. "He could scarcely believe that he was being ordered to fight for Madoc, not against him."

"What did he do?" Arthur asked eagerly.

Susanna smiled. "Uthyr crushed the letter into a ball and threw it in the air. Griffi set it on fire and burned it to ashes. The ashes dropped on Madoc's head."

Arthur, Morrigan, and Gwyhar laughed, delighted with the tale of Madoc's discomfiture.

"Tell them," Ygraine said harshly, breaking through the laughter. "Tell them, Neuad, of what you saw on your Wind-Ride on that last day of Uthyr's life."

Susanna fell silent. Cai's smile faded, and his eyes became dull and lifeless.

"Ygraine," Neuad began hesitantly.

"No. Tell them. Tell Arthur of that last day. And what you saw."

Neuad bowed her golden head and was silent for a time. At last, she raised her face to Arthur. "I was Wind-Riding toward Tegeingl. I knew that this would be the final battle. The enemy, over a thousand strong, marched over the hill. Uthyr, with Griffi and all his warriors behind him, sat on his horse just outside the city, and waited. Madoc was in the forefront of the Coranian army, next to General Catha. When Uthyr saw him, he raised the horn of Gwynedd, and blew the charge."

No one spoke. No one moved. The crackling of the fire seemed very loud in the now-still night.

"The battle began. Our warriors fought bravely, but they were outnumbered. They knew that they rode to their deaths. But they sang as they rode to meet the enemy. I could see the fear on Madoc's face as Uthyr came straight for him. General Catha made a signal, and the Coranians let Uthyr ride through, with Griffi behind him.

"Griffi rose in his saddle, pointing to the Coranian commander, preparing to Fire-Weave. But the General threw his ax into Griffi's chest, and he fell from his horse. His lips moved, once, shaped Susanna's name. And then he died."

Gwyhar's blue eyes filled with tears, and he swallowed hard. Susanna bowed her head. She closed her eyes, and so did not see Cai's swift, abortive movement toward her.

"Catha spoke to Uthyr, demanding his surrender, no doubt. And Uthyr laughed as he dismounted his horse. He took a dagger from his boot, and the two of them spoke. I could not tell what they said, but in the end, Uthyr gestured to Madoc, and Catha stepped back. Madoc was frightened. He knew he was no match for his brother. They fought with daggers, for a time. Then Madoc stumbled, and Uthyr raised his knife to finish it. But then Catha threw his ax again, and it buried itself in Uthyr's back. He fell, and Catha wrenched the ax from Uthyr's body, and turned him over with his foot, so the King lay faceup on the ground."

Morrigan had bowed her head, and tears streamed from her eyes and dropped to the ground. Arthur put his arm around her, and she leaned into his shoulder. His own eyes were filled with tears, but they did not fall. He stared at his mother, as Neuad continued to speak. And Ygraine continued to listen with no expression on her face.

"Catha said something to him, but Uthyr did not answer. He closed his eyes, then he smiled. Then he died."

They were silent as Neuad finished. Tears streamed down the Dewin's face, but her recitation had been steady.

"Why, Ygraine?" Gwydion rasped, breaking the silence at last. "Why?"

"Arthur needs to know," Ygraine said steadily. "He needs to re-member this story for those nights when it seems his task is too hard. For those times when he thinks he has reason to not perform it. For those times when he looks at you, and thinks to spite you by not be-coming what he was born to be."

Arthur looked at his mother with astonishment, then bowed his head over Morrigan's. Ygraine brushed her hand over his hair lightly, then clasped her hands in her lap again.

Gwydion stood. He stared down at Ygraine, but could not speak. She had known. And she had done what she could. Never, in all his life, had Ygraine given him anything but her hatred. Until tonight, when she gave him the way to be sure that Arthur ap Uthyr var Ygraine would do what he must do to take Kymru back from the enemy.

A gift like that, of such value, given at such a high cost was some-thing he had never expected from one who hated him so. Because she still did. He could see it. But she put Kymru first tonight. As he had always done.

He turned, and walked into the night.

IN THE DARKNESS, Gwydion scaled the sides of the hidden valley, making for the peak of Mynydd Tawel. Halfway up, he stopped, out of breath and weeping. He turned and sat down on the clover-studded ground, gazing back at the valley. Campfires dotted the valley floor. There were over five hundred Cerddorian here. They lived in rough huts built on the valley sides. So well hidden was the valley, however, that the presence of hundreds of campfires would make no difference. No one who did not know the way in would ever find it.

Uthyr had chosen well.

Gwydion dashed his sleeve across his eyes, pulling his black cloak closer around him. It was quiet up here, away from the others. He glanced up at the night sky. Overhead, the constellation of Arderydd wheeled above him. Arderydd, the High Eagle, was bright and cold, the stars piercing in their brilliance. The High Eagle, the sign of the High King. And there would be a High King. There would. Uthyr's son. But Uthyr was dead.

Gwydion.

For a moment, Gwydion considered not answering Dinaswyn's Mind-Call. But he could not. *Yes, aunt?*

There are many of us, Gwydion, who loved Uthyr. And who miss him now, and will miss him until the day we die. You are not alone in this.

He was my brother. I loved him.

Yes.

For a moment, she was quiet. Gwydion hoped that she would not speak again. But she did.

When do you leave?

At first light.

Do you know where you are to go?

Yes.

But you will, of course, not tell me.

Dinaswyn—

It does not matter. It used to, but not anymore. Listen to me. I speak to you now to remind you of your promise to me.

My promise?

That, when the fires of testing are upon us, you will use me. You have not forgotten that promise, even though you pretend to. And I have not forgotten that promise. Your word has been given. See to it that you keep it.

At that, Dinaswyn's Mind-Touch was gone. Gwydion sighed. He had, on occasion, thought his aunt had forgotten that promise. But deep down, he had always known better. And he had promised. But he did not want to use her. No matter what she might think, he loved her dearly, and did not want to see her hurt.

He heard the sounds of someone coming up the mountain after him. The scent of perfume wafted up to him. Ah, of course. Arianrod. Who else? Just when he most wanted to be alone. It would not be the first time she knew that and came to him anyway. He hoped this would be the last. But he did not count on it.

"Gwydion," she purred, as she came to him and sat next to him on the cold ground. "You have not spoken to me but a handful of words all day."

"True."

"So, you have the Treasures. All but one."

"All but one."

"And tomorrow you leave again. Where will you go?"

"To another place."

She laughed. "Sometimes, *cariad*, I think you do not trust me."

"Arianrod, I have never trusted you. And I have known you all my life. Why would I start now?"

"Tell me, Gwydion, does Rhiannon make love as well as I?"

"I wouldn't know."

"Never bothered to find out? Well, who could blame you? Why waste your time on someone like her?"

"I think her beautiful."

She stiffened. "You do?"

"Yes. Very."

"You disgust me, Gwydion ap Awst. You really do." She stood and looked down at him. "When next we meet, you will treat me with more respect."

"Arianrod, I have also never respected you. Why would I ever start?"

"Because when I see you again, you will do so, or you will die."

"Another empty promise, like all of your promises, *cariad.*"

Without another word, she left him.

ARIANROD STORMED DOWN the mountain, back to the hovel where she lived with Dinaswyn. Fools. They were all fools. Huddled here in cold and near starvation. No comforts of life. Fighting an enemy they could never defeat. Never.

Well, she had tried. She had tried to live this way for years. But no more. She had tried, one last time, to seduce and hold the Dreamer. But no more. Never again. Now she would do what she should have done long ago.

Meirigelydd, Cynyddu Wythnos—early morning

EARLY-MORNING FOG touched the peak of Mynydd Tawel as the party slipped out of the valley and through the narrow gap in the rocks. Rhiannon halted just outside the fissure, waiting for the others to come through. Poor Arthur was pale and silent. Gwen, for once, was quiet herself, taking none of her usual opportunities to bait the boy.

Gwydion was his usual impassive self. Rhiannon had seen Arianrod leave the fire last night, and had known exactly where the woman had gone. Rhiannon and Gwen had spent the night with Ygraine and Morrigan, and so she had not known when Gwydion or Arianrod had come back down the mountain. She could have Wind-Rode after him, but she disdained that kind of subterfuge. And, besides, he might have sensed her. He did not look tired, but that meant nothing. Viciously she hoped that Arianrod had caught the world's worst cold.

Morrigan and Ygraine followed Arthur through the gap, then halted. Arthur opened his mouth to speak, but shut it again.

Morrigan stepped forward and hugged him. "Take care, brother," she said softly. "Come back to us as soon as you can."

Arthur smiled down at her, and smoothed her hair with a trembling hand. "I will." He turned to Ygraine.

She took his face in both her hands and kissed his brow. "Go, now, my son. Go and do what you were born to do. We shall wait for you."

"Good-bye," Arthur said, then turned and led the way down the mountain. The sapphire ring on his hand pulsed in the light. For a time, no one spoke. The morning was slightly chill, but the sky was clear. It would be hot by midday. As they crossed one of the brooks that cut through the slopes of Mynydd Tawel, Gwydion called a halt. He stood over a small bush, about one foot tall. The leathery leaves were bright green, and tiny yellow flowers clustered around them.

"Penduran's Rose," Rhiannon said as Gwydion pulled off some of the leaves. "Why are you harvesting it?"

"Because we will need it," Gwydion replied, as he stowed the leaves in the pouch at his belt.

"That's you," she said sourly. "Forthcoming with information, as always."

"Are you sure it was wise to leave the Treasures back there?" Gwen asked. That was as close to a criticism as Gwen ever got of Gwydion's plans.

"Dinaswyn will see to it that they are safe. There are few I would trust with such a task. Do not underestimate her."

"Where are we going?" Gwen asked. "Besides north, I mean?"

"Do you know, Rhiannon?" Gwydion asked, a smile lurking in his eyes.

"Of course, I do."

Gwydion waited for her to be more specific. If he thought, after all this time, she was a fool, he would know better.

"The song says, 'Down the dark path/In the land of mountains the black stone looms. / Beneath the seeker lies the guardian.' The dark path is Tywyll Llwybr. And the Path is said to lead through Mynydd Gwyr, Seeker Mountain."

"And the black stone?"

"Is obviously Ddu Llech, the Stone that Llyr himself raised in the memory of his mother, Lady Don of Lyonesse."

"Then, Arthur ap Uthyr," Gwydion said, turning to the boy. "You must take us there."

"Yes," Arthur said quietly. "I will."

Mynydd Gwyr and Mynydd Tawel
Kingdom of Gwynedd, Kymru
Ysgawen Mis, 499

Llundydd, Disglair Wythnos—dawn

Four days later Arthur raised his eyes to the heights of Mynydd Gwyr, Seeker Mountain, highest mountain in Gwynedd. It would take him half a day, at least, to reach the peak, had that been his destination. But he didn't think he would need to go that far.

The azure depths of his sapphire ring pulsed on his finger as he looked down at the path at his feet. He carried no pack, no food, and no water. He would go to the mountain, with the ring as his guide, with the path at his feet. And with an aching in his heart. For the last person to wear this ring besides Morrigan had been his father.

He fingered the ring, remembering when he had last seen his father, so many years ago, on the day when Gwydion had brought Uthyr to see him. A single day was all they had. And he remembered his father's parting words—that an eagle cannot fly with broken wings, that Arthur must be what he was born to be.

Oh, but he didn't want to. He didn't. Sometimes, when he saw what the Coranians were doing to his country; when he saw Y Dawnus with enaid-dals around their necks; when he saw his mother and sister in hiding; when he heard the dying song of the Master Bard; then he wanted to take his country back and see to it that his

397

people lived in peace. But when he looked at the uncle whom he hated, when he thought of the peaceful days he had spent herding his flock, then he wanted nothing more than to be left alone.

Even now, with the ring on his finger and his feet on the path, he wanted to turn and run. Run, far away, back to Dinas Emrys, back to the life he had led. But he could not. He never could. All that was ended the day Gwydion had returned to take Arthur back into the world.

The wind rippled through the dawn, stirring the hair on the back of his neck with light fingers. He shivered.

"It's Taran's Wind," Gwydion said softly. "He seeks to know you."

Arthur turned to glance at Gwydion, who stood just behind him. His uncle's gray eyes were alight as he stared up at Mynydd Gwyr.

"You are to seek the Black Stone of Don, Ddu Llech, raised by Llyr, the First Dreamer, in memory of his mother. Legend has it that it rests in a hidden valley. And the only way to the valley is Tywyll Llwybr, the Dark Path, that which lies at your feet."

"Why has no one else ever found that valley, if all they have to do is follow the path?" Gwen asked, as she stood by Arthur's side.

"Because the Winds of Taran prevent it. There have been some who have tried to follow the path. But the winds defeat them, blowing as soon as they set foot on the road," Rhiannon said softly. She laid a gentle hand on the back of Arthur's neck, stilling the hairs that had been raised by the wind. "Do not fight the winds," she said quietly. "Let them take you where you must go."

Oh, he didn't want this. Didn't want any of it. He wanted to be left in peace. Yet, in spite of that, somehow, he was putting his foot forward. He was taking the Dark Path. And in spite of that, the wind was not blowing. Not for him. He had the feeling that when he returned, if he returned, he would be a different man than he was now.

"Tell me, uncle," he said, looking over his shoulder to Gwydion. "Could I die up there? Dashed against the rocks by the winds?"

"It has happened to the others, Arthur," Gwydion said impassively.

"It could happen to you."

"But your dreams. Have you seen us come to Cadair Idris with the Treasures in our hands in your dreams?"

"I have seen nothing. I have had no dream since the one at the beginning of this year, the one that said it was time to seek the Treasures."

"Why no dreams, uncle? Are you not the Dreamer?"

"I have been given no dreams, because everything hangs in the balance. The gods have nothing to say. They only wait. As we all do."

"Then, uncle, if I should not return, what will you do?"

"We will hide the Treasures again, and wait for another."

"And another will come."

"I think not, boyo. I think not."

Arthur turned away and gazed up at the mountain again. And began to climb.

HE ONLY LOOKED BACK once. Many hours later, as he was halfway up the mountain, and the path curved to the west, he looked back. Far below, he saw the tiny figures of the three whom he had traveled with for so many months. He halted, out of breath, and wiped his brow with his sleeve. The three raised their hands, and the rings flashed light from their fingers—the opal on Gwydion's hand blazed fire, the pearl on Rhiannon's hand glimmered whitely, the emerald on Gwen's finger flickered. He raised his own hand, and the sapphire gave out an azure glow. Then he turned away, and followed the path, out of their sight, around the mountain.

THE SOUND OF trickling water caught his ear. It would be good to drink; he was hot and dusty from his climb. He stepped off the path, to follow the sound to the stream, and the winds drove at him fiercely, tumbling him to his knees. Crawling, the wind roaring in his ears, he regained the path and the winds died down.

"I just wanted a drink of water," he croaked, his throat dry and dusty. He rose to his feet. "That's all I wanted," he muttered, as he continued up the path. The day was hot and the air was thin. His breath labored in his chest. But he stumbled on, keeping his eyes on his feet as they dragged him up the path.

The path led to a narrow fissure. He slipped between the rocks, through an opening so narrow that he left much of the skin on his arms behind him. He wriggled through as best he could, and the path continued. He glanced up at the sky. It was late afternoon now. Soon it would be dark. He had a torch thrust into his belt, and flint and tinder in his pouch. That would help, providing, of course, that the winds would let him light a fire. Somehow, he didn't think they would. Water had been denied him. Fire would probably be denied him, too.

He followed the path, which now led through a narrow canyon. His scraped and bleeding shoulders touched either side of the rocks that rose sheer from each side of the path. How many, he wondered, had made it this far? Not many, he thought. Because for the others, the winds would have blown when they stepped onto the path. But, for him, the winds blew only if he stepped off of it. So far, anyway. That could change at any moment. And probably would.

As if the winds heard him, they began. They swooped from the sky, down the sheer rocky face, and began to pound him. He fell to his knees, the wind roaring in his ears. Grit and dust blew into his eyes, blinding him. He crawled forward, unwilling to stop, unable to go back without the Sword.

The winds pushed at him, thrusting him back. Doggedly, he continued forward, leaning into the wind, gasping for breath.

Suddenly, as if the memory lay waiting only a hand span away, he remembered the day he almost died, the day Taran's storm had come to Dinas Emrys, so many years ago. He had been on the mountain that day, herding the sheep back to the byre. But one ewe had gone astray, and he had gone back up to look for her. He had found her, caught in a bush, struggling to get free. And then the storm had broken. Not a storm, really. Because the sky was clear and there was no rain. But the winds had tried to kill him, to push him off the mountain. And they had. Only at the last moment he had grabbed onto the branch of a low bush. He had dropped the ewe, and she had gone tumbling down the sheer cliff face. And he had hung on, grimly, knowing that if he could hold on long enough, Myrrdin would find him.

He remembered how his strength had ebbed that day, just as it was ebbing now. He remembered that he felt his grip loosening, and he knew that he would die. And he remembered how his hand had slipped from the branch, how, just at that last moment, he felt a hand on his wrist, and had opened his eyes to see Myrrdin above him, hanging on to him, pulling him to safety.

But today Myrrdin was not here. And the winds were going to kill him. Taran's Winds. Taran did not want the Sword to be found. Taran wanted to kill him. And he would. For the winds were pushing him against the rock faces, tearing more skin from his body. Blinding him. Pushing him back.

From far, far away, he heard the sound of an eagle's cry. Fierce, proud, the sound came down to him, carried by the winds.

The eagle called out to him. Somewhere, high overhead, an eagle rode the winds, going where they led. Soaring on the wings of the wind. Not fighting against them. Using them, to get to his prey.

And he knew what he had to do. He stopped trying to go forward. He halted on his hands and knees as the winds rushed about him. Slowly, he stood up. For a moment he fought to stay on his feet. But then he let go. He let the winds push him to the ground. He let the winds tumble him back. He rolled with the winds, going where they wanted him to go.

And so he returned to the narrow fissure, fetching up hard against the rocks. Then the winds died. He rubbed the grit and dust from his eyes, blinking tears to wash them away. He stood up, bleeding and bruised. And he waited in the suddenly still air.

A slight breeze tugged at him. He turned with it, and saw, just next to the fissure, a thin, dark gap in the rocks. He stepped forward and released his hold on the rocks, confident that the winds would let him go.

And they did.

He reached the gap and squeezed through. He found himself

in a peaceful glade. There was thick, green clover beneath his feet. A gentle stream meandered through this unlikely glade, surrounded on all sides by sheer cliffs. Trees lined the perimeter—and he knew them, and why they were there. The long, drooping branches of the white birch trees were studded with tiny yellow flowers and light green catkins. The rowan trees with their rounded crowns spread their branches to the sky. They were covered with white flowers and studded with tiny red berries. The ash trees with their low hanging branches were covered with clusters of long, purplish flowers. And the gnarled oak trees with their thick trunks hung heavy with acorns. A single yew tree wept evergreen needles over the huge, black stone that lay in the center of the clearing.

Of course, for who else would guard the resting place of the Lady Don but the gods themselves? Birch for Taran of the Winds. Rowan for Mabon of the Sun. Ash for Nantsovelta of the Waters. Oak for Modron, the Great Mother. And, finally, yew, for Annwyn, the Lord of Chaos.

Llyr, the First Dreamer, would have planted these trees here, long ago, when his people had first come to Kymru, fleeing the destruction of Lyonesse, that proud island that had sunk beneath the sea twelve generations ago. The Lady Don had died in that terrible time, her body lost in the vast ocean. But Llyr had raised this stone in memory of her.

The mirrored obsidian of the stone seemed to wink at him in the fading light. The ring on his finger pulsed brightly, bathing the glade in an azure glow. Slowly, Arthur approached the rock, and he sank to his knees beside it. He reached out and touched the stone. It was so cold. He thought for a moment of the Lady Don, and her fight against the Druids who had killed her husband. He thought of the legend that her youngest child, Llyr, had been created a whole man outside of her body, in a fashion that no one now understood, aided by the magic of the Danaans who had sheltered her.

The Sword of Taran was in this glade for Arthur to find. The ring on his finger told him that. It was here, but where?

There was not a breath of wind. Nothing to guide him. Nothing except the glow of the ring on his finger. He rose to his feet, and reached out to the yew tree. But the ring's glow faded slightly when he did so. Ah, the stone itself, then. Once again, he touched the cool stone, and the ring glowed so brightly that he had to squint through the glare to see.

He braced his feet, pushed his fingers beneath the stone, and pulled. But the stone did not move. The Sword was there, beneath the stone. He knew it. But how could he get to it if the stone would not move?

And then the winds came.

They hurled down the rocky cliffs, and the branches on the trees began to dance. The air filled with the tiny flowers that flew from the branches in the violent wind. Arthur was pushed to his knees, gasping. The wind seemed to cut his skin from his bones. And he cried out, then.

"Taran!" he shouted. "Taran of the Winds, help me!"

The winds pushed at him, flattening him to the ground. And then he saw it. The winds had made their way beneath the stone, lifting one end of it. A few inches from his face, he saw a bright glitter. His hand shot out beneath the stone, and he grabbed for the bright twinkle of metal. With the rasp of metal on rock, he pulled out the object and the winds died. The stone sank back into its place.

In the silence, Arthur rose to his feet, the Sword of Air in his hands. He held the blade upright before his eyes. He had it. Y Cleddyf, the Sword. Meirig Yr Llech, Guardian of the Stone. The handgrip was made of silver mesh, chased with gold. The hilt of silver was fashioned like a hawk with widespread wings and sapphire eyes. The hawk's claws held the knob at the end, on which was the figure eight, the symbol of infinity, studded with onyx. The scabbard was gold, etched with a dizzying array of silver circles and chased with sapphires. Slowly, he pulled the Sword from the scabbard. The blade itself shown brightly, images of a serpent etched on either side of the blade.

He lifted the Sword to the sky, and whirled it over his head. Once, twice, three times. "Taran," he called, laughing. "I have found it!"

"So you have, boyo." The voice was rich and musical. "You have at last."

"Who—?" Arthur began. And then he knew as a shimmer of light condensed beside the Stone and he saw the shade of a man long dead.

The man wore a robe of blue trimmed in white. Around his neck was the ghost of shimmering sapphires.

"Taliesin," Arthur breathed. "Fifth Master Bard of Kymru."

"Yes," the ghost said gently. "I am Taliesin ap Arthen var Diadwa. And I greet you in the name of Lleu Lawrient, my High King."

"But why are you here? Have you come from Gwlad Yr Haf just to greet me?"

The ghost's green eyes, full of joy and sorrow, glinted, and his white-blond hair gleamed. "No, for my spirit has never journeyed to the Land of Summer. I have waited here for you for over two hundred years. Glad I am you have come, so that I may, at last, go home."

"How could you have done this thing?" Arthur asked, awed.

"Bran the Dreamer asked it of me in the name of Lleu. He asked all of us to hide and guard the Treasures until the time they would be needed again. He asked this in the name of Kymru. How, then, could we refuse?"

And Arthur was ashamed then, for he had, in one way or another, refused in his heart to do the one thing for Kymru that he knew she needed.

"Yes," Taliesin said gently, reading his thoughts, "but you will do it nonetheless. And that is all that is asked of you. Is it too much?"

"No," Arthur whispered. "No." He sank to his knees, the sword held upright before him. "I pledge to you that I will carry this Sword for Kymru."

And Taliesin sang, his rich voice a balm to Arthur's shame.
"SHALL THERE NOT be a song of freedom
Before the dawn of the fair day?
Shall this not be the fair day of freedom?"

"Anieron's song," Arthur whispered. "The one he sang before he died. Taran's last gift to him."

"Mourn not Anieron, Master Bard. He dwells with those he loves in the Land of Summer, where I will soon end my journey. He waits, and watches for the fair day of freedom, which is at hand. You will avenge his death," Taliesin said, his voice stern.

"I will," Arthur replied, his head bowed.

"Then go from this place. Your friends need you." Then Taliesin was gone.

ARTHUR MADE ITS way through the narrow gap in the rocks, turning one last time to look at the peaceful glade. The clover was studded with the flowers that had blown from the trees. As he looked, the wind stirred the trees gently, as though the branches themselves were bowing to him.

As he wriggled through the gap, and his feet touched the Dark Path, he heard a voice in his head, urgent but controlled. Gwydion.

Arthur, I know you can hear me, but can't answer.

He stood stock-still, his heart beating uncomfortably. He had never heard the undertone of terror in his uncle's voice before.

When you find the sword, you must return to Mynydd Tawel with it immediately. Take the other Treasures and go to Myrrdin in Coed Aderyn. He will help you.

What was he saying? What had gone wrong?

We were captured as we waited for you. They come at us now with enaid-dals. Somehow they knew we would be here. You must go. Now.

How could he? How could he leave them?

I know you will not want to. But you must remember that you, alone, are the important one. Rhiannon, Gwen, and I have done what we set out to do, and the Treasures are yours now. Return to Mynydd Tawel and reclaim them from Dinaswyn. Go now and—

Gwydion's Mind-Speech was cut off. For a panicked moment, Arthur thought the Dreamer was dead. Strange how, after so many years of wishing for just that, his heart was filled with sorrow and dread. No, Gwydion was not dead. He had been collared, along with Rhiannon, and Gwen. They were to be taken, no doubt, to the island of Afalon to die.

Then he realized that, no, they would not be so lucky as all that. Instead they would be taken to Havgan, the Golden Man. Havgan would kill them, but he would take his time. Again and again Havgan had announced that Gwydion and Rhiannon would be found and would die. And Gwen would not be spared.

Suddenly, his eyes filled with tears. Gwydion would die in as great an agony as Havgan could devise. Rhiannon, with her flashing green eyes and lovely smile, would be gone. And Gwen, she who argued with him and exasperated him, whose golden hair he thought so beautiful, would be dead.

He had not known, until now, that he found Gwen beautiful.

He would not let that happen. No matter what Gwydion said, he could not leave them in the hands of the enemy.

And as he made his way down the Dark Path, down the Seeker Mountain, to the place where they had waited for him, he remembered one thing—he did not know how to use a sword.

But that did not matter. Because Taran did.

Suldydd, Lleihau Wythnos—Alban Nerth, dusk

DINASWYN UR MORVYN, the former Dreamer of Kymru, walked calmly into the now-silent glade within the hidden camp in Mynydd Tawel. The Cerddorian of Gwynedd gathered here, waiting to celebrate Alban Nerth, the festival in honor of Y Rhyfelwr, Camulos and Agrona, the Warrior Twins.

The warriors that lined the perimeter of the alder grove held lit torches. The stone altar in the north quadrant of the grove was heaped with vines—grapevines, barberry vines, blackberry vines, elderberry vines. Scattered throughout the vines were juicy, red apples. Eight unlit torches were set in brackets around the stone.

Dinaswyn surveyed the men and women gathered there. Morrigan, dressed in a fine gown of dark blue, with a kirtle of light blue beneath, stood quietly, for once. Her auburn hair was bound in a single braid and wrapped around her head and scattered with sapphires. Around her neck she wore the sapphire and silver torque of the House of PenHebog. Beside her, Ygraine stood in her customary white, her expression unreadable, her eyes cool. Yet Ygraine could not fool Dinaswyn, for she saw the slight tightening around her eyes that spoke of fear for her son.

Cai and Susanna stood together, not quite touching. Always Cai was close to Susanna, but never did he reach for her. Dinaswyn almost sighed in irritation. Men were such fools. Cai's face spoke of his fears, too. For his Lieutenant and nephew, Bedwyr, had not yet returned from Tegeingl. He had been due back yesterday, and there had been no message to explain the delay. Neuad, Morrigan's Dewin, stood with Junao, the Bard who had been sent to them by Anieron before he died.

She lifted her hands, and pointing at the eight torches, lit them with Druid's Fire, one by one. "This is the Wheel of the year before us. One torch for each of the eight festivals when we honor the Shining Ones: Calan Gaef, Alban Nos, Calan Morynion, Alban Awyr, Calan Llachar, Alban Haf, Calan Olau, and Alban Nerth, which we celebrate tonight.

"We gather here," she went on, "to honor Camulos and Agrona, Y Rhyfelwr, the Warrior Twins."

"We honor you," the crowd responded.

"Let the Shining Ones be honored as they gather to watch the content. Taran, King of the Winds, Modron, Great Mother of All. Mabon, King of Fire. Nantsovelta, Lady of the Waters. Annwyn, Lord of Chaos. Aertan, Weaver of Fate. Cerridwen, Queen of the Wood. Cerrunnos, Master of the Hunt. Sirona, Lady of the Stars. Grannos, Star of the North and Healer."

"We honor the Shining Ones," the warriors intoned.

Cai stepped forward, and began. "Why do we gather here?"

"We gather," Dinaswyn answered, "to honor Camulos and Agrona, the Warrior Twins, son and daughter of Aertan, Weaver of Fate, and Annwyn, Lord of Chaos."

"Why do we honor them?" Cai went on.

"Behold, they have braved the depths of Bro Yr Hud, Land of

Mystery, and the monsters that guard it, and have returned victorious, laden with gifts."

"What gifts do they bring?"

"They have returned with the vine harvest, the gift of wine do they bring. And, most wondrous, do they bring the apple tree to us." So saying, Dinaswyn held up an apple and cut it in half. She raised both halves above her head, turning the inside of the fruit to the crowd. "See, then, the seeds of the apple. Within this fruit is the sign of the Wheel."

"Today," Cai said, "we celebrated the strength of our warriors. The strongest and bravest stand before us now." Cai gestured, and those who had won the archery contests throughout the day stepped forward. There was Morrigan and Cai himself, as well as Duach ap Seithfed, Cynwas Cwryfager, and Dywel ap Gwyn.

"How can we choose Y Rhyfelwr from these fine warriors?" Cai asked.

"The warrior blessed by Camulos and Agrona will be the one who impales the apple. Warriors, stand forth!" Dinaswyn called. The five of them stood apart from the crowd in front of the altar. Each carried a bow and an arrow, fletched in their own colors.

"The one whose arrow pierces the apple first in the air will be honored as the greatest warrior on this Alban Nerth," Dinaswyn said.

The men and women in the grove fell completely silent. In the stillness only the sound of the fire that wavered from the torches could be heard.

Dinaswyn threw the apple into the night sky. Higher and higher it arched, controlled by Dinaswyn's Shape-Moving ability, until it reached its apex over the grove and began its descent. Moving swiftly now, it fell toward the earth. As one, the five winners of the contests shot their arrows, which sped toward the moving target overhead.

But the apple jerked sideways, impelled by another force, sidestepping the five arrows. The crowd gasped. Before anyone could even put another arrow to bow, the apple arced over the heads of the crowd, toward the fringes of the grove. Suddenly, from the trees, a shining blade appeared in a brown hand, and cut the apple cleanly in half.

Morrigan threw down her bow and cried out with joy. "Arthur!"
For the hand that held the sword did indeed belong to Arthur ap
Uthyr var Ygraine. Arthur stood quietly at the edge of the grove, the
point of the sword pressed to the earth, his hands clasped on the hilt.
The sapphire eyes of the hawk at the sword's hilt seemed to glow. The
scar on Arthur's face whitened as he put out a hand to stop Morrigan
from launching herself at him. And Morrigan stopped where she
was, and, taking in Arthur's sword, Arthur's stance, Arthur's gaze,
she sank to her knees and bowed her head.

"Behold," Gwydion said, walking out of the shadows of the
grove followed by Rhiannon and Gwen, "Behold, Taran's Warrior.
He who carries the Sword of Air. He who saved us from our enemies,
and brought us out of bondage."

Dinaswyn looked closely at Gwydion, Rhiannon, and Gwen.
Their necks were blistered and red. "You have been wearing enaid-
dals," Dinaswyn said flatly.

"We have," Gwydion agreed. "For we were captured by the
Coranians while Arthur walked Seeker Mountain. But Arthur came
for us, and not one enemy soldier now remains alive."

"He cut the collars from our necks with the Sword of Taran,"
Rhiannon said, solemnly. "And the Wind itself carried them away,
far up to the sky, to do no one further harm."

"He saved our lives with the Sword of Taran," Gwen said, her blue
eyes shining, "And called the Wind itself to confound his enemies."

By now, the entire crowd was on their knees, bowing to Arthur.
Dinaswyn, after a moment's hesitation, having only to do with the
nature of her astonishment rather than any false pride, at last sank to
her knees also.

Arthur's dark eyes scanned the crowd, resting for a few moments
on the bowed heads of his mother and sister.

"Where is Arianrod?" Gwydion asked quietly.

"Arianrod is not here," Dinaswyn answered. "She has gone to
Carnavon to take the place of the Dewin there who was captured."

"She has not," Gwydion said. "She has gone to him."

Dinaswyn's breath caught in her throat. "To Havgan?" she asked, her mouth suddenly dry with fear.

"To the Golden Man," Gwydion agreed.

"You know this to be true?" Dinaswyn asked.

"From my dream last night," Gwydion said. "You must all go south, to Cemais. Begin to leave at first light in groups of no more than five or six. The camp must be cleared within ten days."

"So long?" Cai asked in astonishment. "Arianrod is Dewin, and could send a message to the soldiers in a matter of moments."

"But she will not. She will carry her message to Havgan himself, and will entrust her information to no other. She will bargain with him before she reveals where we are," Gwydion said with calm certainty.

Dinaswyn nodded. Yes, they would have that time, for Gwydion was right. Arianrod would never give the information to any but Havgan himself. And would not give it even to him, until she was sure she would receive what she wished for. They would not be undone by Arianrod's greed. Instead, her greed would save them.

A rustle in the trees caught their ears. And from the alders burst Bedwyr, Cai's nephew. He was travel-stained and unshaven. His brown eyes were wild and fierce, and his brown hair was tangled and wet with sweat. His chest heaved, as though he had run all the way from Tegeingl. And perhaps he had, Dinaswyn thought. Perhaps he had.

Without a word he dove through the crowd and with a cry of rage, he launched himself at the throat of Jonas. The two men went down, rolling over and over on the ground, with Bedwyr's hands locked on the Bard's throat. At Arthur's quick gesture, six warriors pulled the two men apart and held them. Bedwyr was gasping in fury at being held back from his prey. And Jonas was clutching at his throat, trying to get air into his heaving lungs, his head hanging down as he was held upright between two warriors.

Arthur strode through the grove, and the crowd parted for him like water. He came to stand before both men, and planted his sword on the ground, crossing both hands on the hilt. His dark eyes bore down on Bedwyr, demanding answers without a word.

"Who are you who carries such a sword?" Bedwyr gasped out.

"I am Arthur ap Uthyr var Ygraine, High King to be of Kymru. This is the Sword of Air. And you are Bedwyr ap Bedrawd, returned from a mission to Tegeingl. Where, I think, you have learned something of great value."

"I have," Bedwyr said shortly. "In Tegeingl we have a spy, very highly placed in King Madoc's confidence, his daughter, Princess Tangwen."

"And what information has she given you about Jonas?"

"He is a traitor," Bedwyr spat. "A traitor to us all. It was he who was responsible for the capture of the Y Dawnus at Allt Llwyd. He who was responsible for the prisoners taken, for the people killed in the death-march across Kymru, for the death of Anieron, Master Bard, himself. 'Shall this not be a fair day of freedom,' Jonas ap Morgan?" Bedwyr asked, his voice dripping with rage as he recited the refrain from Anieron's Death-Song.

"You lie, Bedwyr," Jonas snarled. "You have always hated me. And now you use this false story to be rid of me."

"How did you come by this knowledge?" Arthur asked Bedwyr.

"Princess Tangwen overheard Madoc and General Catha discussing it. They said that, within the next few days, Jonas was due to come to them in Tegeingl, to bring them news of the whereabouts of the Dreamer and his friends, to give them all the locations of the Cerrddorian camps."

Dinaswyn came to stand before Bedwyr. "Jonas was due to leave tomorrow," she said, "to take the place of the Bard in Gwynedd, who had been captured just a few weeks ago." Dinaswyn turned her gray eyes on Jonas. "He volunteered to go."

"He sent the message to the soldiers who captured us," Rhiannon said, her voice harsh and cold. "Or else how did they know we were there?"

"He followed us, the first hour after we left," Gwen said, her face hard. "He must have, to overhear where we were going, but still not be missed."

"It was Arianrod who Wind-Rode behind you," Jonas said, as he bowed his head. "It was she who sent the message where you were. An introduction, she called it, to Havgan."

"And you, Jonas ap Morgan, who betrayed the location of Allt Llwyd, as you would soon have betrayed those here in Mynydd Tawel," Gwydion said with certainty. "It was you."

"It was," Jonas said, his voice breaking. "But not by my choice. I had to."

"Your wife and child are dead, Jonas ap Morgan," Bedwyr said. "They were dead by the hand of Sledda, the Arch-wyrce-jaga, before you even betrayed Anieron and his people."

"No," Jonas sobbed. "No."

"Yes. I heard Catha and Madoc say so," Bedwyr went on, relentless. "They laughed about it. It was all for nothing, even from the beginning."

"I see Anieron in my dreams," Jonas sobbed. "His fingers are cut off, his tongue cut out, an enaid-dal hangs around his neck. He stares at his harp, but has no fingers to play. Then the wind begins. And his song. I hear his song waking or sleeping. He will not leave me. He stares at me with pity in his green eyes. He will not let me go! Let me go!" Jonas screamed, his head thrown up to the sky. "Let me go!"

Taran's Sword whistled through the air. The shining blade sliced through Jonas's body, cutting the man cleanly in half. Arthur swung the sword over his head, once, twice, three times, and the blood sheeted off the blade, until it was once again clean and shining.

"You have your wish, Jonas ap Morgan," Arthur said coldly to the corpse that lay at his feet, as he thrust the now-clean sword into its scabbard. "You are free."

Chapter 23

Llundydd, Disglair Wythnos—afternoon

Arianrod ur Brychan var Arianllyn rode up to the gates of Eiodel with her head held high. She wore a silken shift of soft primrose beneath a kirtle of amber. The shift was cut low, showing off the deep cleavage between her round, high breasts. She wore an amber necklace around her slim throat, and amber earrings. Her honey-blond hair was worn loose, flowing freely down to her slender waist.

She rode proudly, but she was afraid. Yet she was determined to let none of her fear show on her beautiful face. Instinctively she knew that to show fear to the Golden Man was to find oneself in bondage to him forever.

And being in bondage to another person was something she would never do. All her life she had been free from others. And she had done that by caring for no one. Perhaps it might have been different if her parents had lived. But they had been sent away when she was just a child to the land of Corania. And they had never returned.

When she was just a little girl, she had hoped every day, prayed to the gods every night, that they would return. But they had not. And by the time she had been sent away to school at Y Ty Dewin, she had known that they never would.

Only two years old when they went away, she could not really remember them. Just snatches of long-ago memories—the whisper of honey-blond hair that had belonged to her mother, the brightness of amber eyes that had belonged to her father. These things they had given her. And nothing else, for they had deserted her.

And so she had learned that hard lesson —to never love another person. And she never had. She never would. She would do as she had always done—seek out those with power. Hold them to her with her body until she moved on to another, making sure that she left them before they could leave her.

And never, never, let anyone touch her heart.

The gates of the Golden Man's fortress were open. The fortress itself was grim, built of dark stone, standing bleak and harsh, facing the closed, jeweled Doors of Cadair Idris, the empty hall of the High King. She wondered if he understood that the Doors would never open for him. Or did he think that they would, someday?

Perhaps she could promise him a way that they would. After all, she did know where the Treasures were. Or, at least, she knew who had them, and that was enough. She would show him how to get these Treasures, show him how to find Gwydion, Rhiannon, Gwen, and Arthur. With the Treasures in his hands, the Doors would open for Havgan. And he would not know until it was too late that the Treasures would kill him. For the gift of getting into Cadair Idris, Arianrod could demand many, many things.

The wild grasses and flowers of the plain swayed before her, disturbed by the faint breeze. Taran's Wind. *Stop me now, Taran, if you can*, she thought. But the god could not. No one could. She laughed, and spurred her mount toward the gate.

As she neared the gate, a troop of soldiers barred her way. They wore byrnies of woven metal, which reached to their knees. They carried spears and bright shields, blazoned with the sign of the boar's head. They were hard-eyed and watchful as she slowed her horse to a walk and drew up before them. She eyed them disdainfully.

"I wish to see your master," she said haughtily. "Show me to him."

From their midst a man pushed his way through. He had light brown hair, and haunted, dark eyes. He was tall and thin, as though wasting away with a fever from wounds that no one could see. He came to stand before her, holding her horse's bridle.

"You are not the Golden Man," she said with certainty.

"I am not," he agreed, "thanks be to God. I am Sigerric, Overgeneral of Kymru. And you are?"

"My name, for the moment, is my own. I wish to see Havgan, Bana of Corania."

"Conqueror of Kymru," he finished for her.

"Not yet," she said with a twist of her lips. "But I can help to make him so."

"I see. Then, you of no name, you may dismount, and I will see if Lord Havgan will consent to see you."

"He will," she promised.

HE KEPT HER waiting for some hours. But she had known that he would and was neither angered nor frightened. She waited in an antechamber, small but comfortable. There was a fire in the hearth. Two chairs were set before the fire, but she disdained them, wishing to be on her feet when he arrived. A beaker of wine and two goblets were placed on a small table between the chairs. She had drunk a glass some hours ago when she had first been shown this room, and had no more, for she would need all her wits for the coming encounter.

She was standing at the window, her back to the doors, looking out at Cadair Idris and watching the shadows begin to gather, when he came to her.

The opening door made no sound, and so she only turned when she heard his whisper, a whisper that made no sense.

"The Woman-on-the-Rocks."

She turned around then, startled, and looked into the face of the Golden Man. And she saw that she had disturbed him in some way. But how, she did not know.

He was tall, and strong. The muscles of his shoulders swelled against the sleeves of the undershirt he wore beneath his golden tunic. The tunic was embroidered with hundreds of tiny rubies. His breeches were black, and his calf-length black boots were trimmed with gold. His honey-blond locks reached his shoulders. His face was tanned and smooth. And his amber eyes devoured her.

And something in her, something she did not even know was there leapt at the sight of him.

"I want your name, among other things," he said.

"My name is Arianrod ur Brychan var Arianllyn."

"Ah. Cousin of the Dreamer, through your father's brother."

"Yes."

"And cousin to Rhiannon ur Hefeydd, through your mother's sister."

"You know us well. Anierion, Master Bard, whom you killed, was an uncle of mine. And so was Cynan, the Ardewin whom you killed when you first came to Y Ty Dewin."

"But you do not care, do you?" he asked, a faint smile on his handsome face.

"You do not know me well enough to know what I do and don't care about. And you never will."

"You think not?" He laughed. "We will see about that, Arianrod ur Brychan."

His nonchalant air, as he strode into the room and seated himself before the fire, did not fool her. She had seen the lust in his eyes.

She, too, took a seat before the fire. He poured out a goblet of wine and handed it to her. For a brief moment their fingers touched. And that moment was like nothing she had ever known. She felt scorched by him. Her pulse quickened. Her heart pounded. She took a deep breath to steady herself, then looked over at him.

And there she saw the telltale beat of his heart at the base of his throat. She saw the fire in his eyes, in eyes that matched her own, even to the shape, even to the amber light. Where in the name of the gods had he come from? From where had sprung this man who was so like her?

"Your soldiers had the Dreamer and his companions in their hands, thanks to me," she said disdainfully. "But they failed to hold them. They were fools and died because of it. Are all your people so inept?"

"Witch, I would not be too proud here in the depths of Eiodel, were I you," Havgan replied smoothly, but the undertone clearly held menace. "I would ask you to tell me the location of the hidden camp where Morrigan and the Cerddorian were hiding, but I fear they are no longer there."

"I am sure they are not."

"You waited too long, witch, to tell me."

Arianrod shrugged. "I had to wait, to see if we could deal."

"And you believe we can?"

Arianrod smiled. "I am sure of it."

"You are unwise to be so sure." Havgan's smile was wolfish, and the naked hunger there made her shiver for a moment.

"If you still seek the Treasures, I know where they can be found," she said, taking a sip of wine.

"In the hands of Gwydion the Dreamer. This much I know. Surely you don't think I will let you live if you give me only information I already have?"

"Oh, you will let me live, Havgan of Corania. For many reasons," she said, letting him see the fire in her eyes, drinking in the heat of him.

He smiled and, dashing the cup from her hands, grabbed her hair, dragging her from her chair to her knees, bending over her.

"Do not tell me what I will or will not do, Arianrod," he said softly. "And do not make me tell you that again."

"And do not tell me what I may or may not say, Havgan," she replied fiercely. "Or I will tell you nothing."

Their amber eyes locked, testing each other, taking each other's measure. Slowly he released her, trailing his hands through her hair, then lightly over her breasts as she did so. He sat back in his chair, studying her thoughtfully.

Calmly she rose from her knees, then took her place once again in her chair. She smoothed the front of her dress as though she had not a care in the world. But, in truth, she felt like laughing. She had him. She could see that in his eyes. She did not think, at that moment, that he might have her, too.

"The spy you placed in the camp in Gwynedd is dead," she said steadily. "The Bard, Jonas."

"Ah. Which would be why we have not had a message from him all week."

"Yes. Arthur ap Uthyr, son of the dead King of Gwynedd, killed him."

Havgan's amber eyes flickered. "I had been given to understand that Arthur had died in childhood."

"We had all thought that," Arianrod said. "Thanks to Gwydion."

"Who must have spirited the boy away, knowing what he was."

"The High King of Kymru."

"Not yet," Havgan said coldly.

"Arthur killed the Bard with the Sword of Taran, the last of the Treasures to be found," Arianrod said.

"You were there?"

"In a manner of speaking. I Wind-Rode to the camp that night and saw it all. I am Dewin."

"Yes. I knew that when I knew who you were."

"Then you know that I may be of use to you. You know that, among other things, I can find where Gwydion and his friends are now. And I can guide you to them. They have all the Treasures—the Stone of Water, the Cauldron of Earth, the Spear of Fire, the Sword of Air."

"If it is true that you can do these things, then is it true that you will?"

"I might try. For a price."

"Yes. Your price. I knew we would come to that. Speak it, then."

"I will help you, Lord Havgan, if it is truly your wish to be master of Kymru. And my price is that you will keep me with you for as long as I wish to stay. And you will let me go when I wish to leave."

"But I will not let you go, nor will you wish to leave, Arianrod ur Brychan," he said, as he stood and reached down to pull her up to him. He ran his hands through her honey-blond hair. "The Woman-on-the-Rocks has come to me at last," he said, and there was a hunger, a longing, in his voice she did not understand. "I dreamt of this, again just last night."

"Who is the Woman-on-the-Rocks?" she whispered, as she ran her hands across his chest, over his shoulders, down his arms.

"A dream," he murmured against her lips. "Just a dream from long ago."

His lips fastened hungrily on hers. His tongue darted in and out of her mouth, tasting her. He kissed her lips, her throat, her breasts, until they were both breathless. With a cruel smile he grabbed the neckline of her gown and tore it, baring her body to his amber gaze. His lips burned, and the rough touch of his hands made her moan in pleasure and fear. He pushed her to the floor and took her slowly, in passion, in lust, in some other longing that she could not name, and she matched him with a fire of her own. They were burning, spiraling up and up, harder and harder, faster and faster. At last they cried out together in an ecstasy so intense that it seemed like agony.

She had found him. The one she had waited for so long. And she would never let him go.

HAVGAN ROLLED OFF of her, and they lay side by side on the cold floor, sweat-soaked and gasping for air.

The Woman-on-the-Rocks, he thought to himself, incoherently. At last, the woman in his dreams who only turned and turned toward him but never faced him. She was here. She was the one who had haunted his dreams since he was a child. She was the one whom the cards of the wyrce-galdra had spoken of. She was the one whom the goddess Holda had told him would be here for him. The other half of himself, the one he would find in Kymru.

At last, she had come to him.

At last, he could kill her.

Kill her—not just the pale shadows of her he had taken and murdered throughout the long years. At last, he would read the mystery of who she was, and what she meant, in her dying, amber eyes. At last he could punish her for all those years when she never turned to face him. At last.

When he mounted her again, she gave a satisfied laugh, which was cut off abruptly when his hands encircled her neck and he began to squeeze.

Her eyes flew open, and she stared up at him. But she did not struggle. She did not try to scream. She did not make a sound. Instead, she smiled up at him as he began to murder her.

For she knew, somehow, that he could not do it.

And he could not. Her smile was the answer. It always had been. The Woman-on-the-Rocks had turned to him and faced him at last. And he knew that he would be in bondage to her from now until the day he died. And he knew that he should kill her now. He knew that to leave her alive might solve the mystery of his life—a mystery to which he never wanted to know the answer.

But he could not. And he did not understand why.

His hands dropped away from her neck. Still straddling her naked body, he looked down at her, then leaned forward and kissed her mouth in violence, in passion, in the knowledge that she was his. And the fire began to build again, coursing through his body and hers.

He knew he would let her live.

For now.

Gwyntdydd, Tywyllu Wythnos—afternoon

GWEN SIGHED TO herself as Gwydion called a halt just outside the gates of Degannwy. Though she loved Gwydion with all her young heart, there were times when he could be just a bit tiresome. She could tell from the expression on his handsome face that he was going to give them the same warning he gave before they entered any village, town, or city. He said it every time, as though they were mental defectives who could not possibly be expected to retain complex information. She could see by Arthur's expression that he, too, was feeling the customary warning to be a bit worn.

Gwydion's gray eyes flickered over them; to Gwen, her golden hair bound in a long braid, wearing a brown leather tunic and trousers, the pack on her back hiding the Cauldron of Earth; to Rhiannon, dressed in a tunic and trousers of hunter green, her dark hair pulled back from her face with a leather band, the pack on her back carrying the Stone of Water; to Arthur, whose dark eyes traveled restlessly over the walls of the town, and whose bedroll tossed over his shoulders contained the Sword of Taran.

Gwydion himself, his gray eyes demanding their attention, dressed in a tunic and trousers of black leather, the bedroll on his back containing the Spear of Fire, said sternly, "Remember, we are a poor family down on our luck, and we—"

"—are not to draw any attention to ourselves," Arthur said in a bored tone, completing Gwydion's customary sentence.

"Correct," Gwydion said sternly. "You must remember—"

"—that our descriptions are circulating through all of Kymru," Gwen finished.

"There may be wyrce-jaga here—" Gwydion went on.

"—as well as soldiers. Be careful. Do your business quietly," Arthur interjected, with a solemn wink at Gwen.

"And keep your hands on your packs at all times. That is most important," Gwen said. "We did not go through all this to get the Treasures to lose them now." She grinned impudently at Arthur as she continued reciting Gwydion's customary speech. Arthur grinned back. Rhiannon smothered her smile by turning it into a cough.

Gwydion frowned, but for a moment, she thought she saw a gleam of laughter in his eyes. "It is especially dangerous," he said coldly, "now that Arianrod has reached Eiodel. She has surely told them that we carry all the Treasures and she will have guessed that we are making our way toward Cadair Idris."

"So," Gwen interjected, finishing Gwydion's usual warning, "you must be very careful."

Gwydion did not answer, but turned on his heel and stalked through the gate, making for the marketplace in the middle of town. Gwen followed and Arthur came next, with Rhiannon behind them. Rhiannon's low laughter floated through the late-morning air. In spite of the stiffness in his stride, Gwen was sure that if she could see

Gwydion's face, he would be smiling.

At the marketplace they made their purchases of foodstuffs without incident. As always, Gwen was puzzled by the behavior of the townsfolk. There was no way they could possibly know who the four travelers were who had entered their town. Yet, as the folk of Kymru always did, they somehow seemed to know that Gwen and her companions were on a matter of urgency. Customers ahead of them at the booths seemed to melt out of the way as they approached. But they were always surrounded by the people, and kept from the prying eyes of Havgan's solders who were stationed throughout the square.

Everything went smoothly until they began to leave the marketplace. And then it all seemed to fall apart at once as a group of soldiers blocked their way.

"Hold there," the soldiers barked. "Hold for the preosts of Lytir!"

Gwydion stopped in his tracks and motioned for the others to do the same as two preosts made their way across the road, dressed in robes of bright yellow, and the wooden amulets of Lytir hanging around their necks on chains of gold. The two men were solemn and haughty, their plump hands tucked inside their flowing sleeves, their faces set in determined piety.

The preosts had almost passed them when Gwen saw Gwydion's shoulders stiffen slightly. She glanced around to see what had alarmed him, and met the eyes of the Captain of the guard. The man's blue eyes were narrowed in suspicion, as he looked at the four of them as if ticking off in his brain the descriptions he had surely received—descriptions of them all, from Arianrod herself.

She watched in dismay as the Captain's suspicions reached a certainty. The man opened his mouth, and then her view of the Captain was cut off, replaced by the sight of a dozen burly backs belonging to the men of Degannwy.

"Ho, preost!" one of the older men shouted good-naturedly. "Tell me, boyo, why does your god seem to hate for you to work?"

The crowd laughed as more and more people began to edge in front of Gwen and the others, pushing them back to the rear.

"Holy Lytir," one of the preosts began, his voice haughty, "does not disdain work. It is for the thralls to work the earth, for the Lords to work the thralls, and for our mighty King to work the Lords. But the preosts of Lytir do the most glorious work of all—to praise the name of God."

"Hard work, indeed, preost," one of the other men called out.

"Very hard!" a woman shouted. "Hard to praise your god when your mouth is full of our food!"

The crowd murmured agreement, and, as one, took another few steps toward the preosts. The Captain, still searching the crowd for the four people he thought he had seen and recognized, made no sign to his soldiers. The preosts began to look frightened, but continued to stand their ground.

"It is written, people of Degannwy," the second preost announced, "that 'great is the fear of Lytir; the earth trembles before him.'"

"Someone trembles now," another townsman said with a grin, "but I don't think it is Lytir. Tell me, preost, is it true that your god welcomes martyrs?"

"Captain!" the first preost barked. "Are you going to let these folk threaten us?"

For a moment, it looked as though the Captain would do just that. His eyes scanned the crowd, and he was clearly considering abandoning the preosts to go after Gwen and her companions.

"Of course, he is," a woman called out. "Why risk his neck for the likes of you?"

At this the Captain gave the crowd a startled look, as though seeing them for the first time. So busy had he been trying to look through them, that he had not really noticed them. In that moment he realized that practically the entire population of Degannwy was staring at him, surrounding him and the preosts, bent on doing more, perhaps, than distracting him. The Captain decided to deal with the more obvious threat. "Stand back!" he barked. "Stand back and let the preosts through to their duties."

The townsfolk stared sullenly at the Captain and the preosts, and for a moment all was still. Then Gwen and her companions were at the fringes of the back of the crowd, just moments from the gate. One man murmured to them quietly, "Go now. We will take care of this."

Gwydion grasped the man's forearm in gratitude. "How can we repay you?"

"Remember the people of Degannwy when Kymru is free again. Now, go."

As they made their way through the gate, Gwydion grasped Rhiannon's arm to pull her along. "Go see what's happening," he hissed.

Rhiannon's eyes took on a glazed look as Gwydion hurried her along while she Wind-Rode back to the center of town. Just as they reached the trees a quarter of a league outside the gates, Rhiannon halted. Her eyelids fluttered for a moment as she shook her head as though to clear it.

"The crowd backed off," she said with a tiny smile. "But the preosts are still a little pale. The Captain has begun searching the town."

"But won't, as we know, find anything," Gwydion said.

"How did they know who we were?" Gwen asked. "The townspeople, I mean?"

"They didn't, Gwen," Rhiannon said absently as she settled her pack more firmly on her back.

"Then why?"

"The Kymri guard their own," Arthur said, his dark eyes quiet. "They always have."

Suldydd, Cynuddu Wythnos—late afternoon

RHIANNON WALKED THROUGH the woods of Coed Aderyn silently. There, she remembered, was the spot where she had snared the rabbit on Calan Morynion, the year that Gwydion had come to her. And there was the place where she had killed her first deer, and skinned it. It had taken her many hours to do that, for, when she first came to these woods, she was inexperienced. But she had learned. She had learned to live here, to feed herself and her child, to exist in a sort of shadow-life, cut off from the world.

And there, in front of her at last, was the clearing she had first noted when just a little girl. And there was the pond, fed by the waterfall that played over the rocks. And behind the waterfall, she knew, was the cave. Her cave. The place she had come to so many years ago to nurse her child and her wounds.

She stopped by the pool, staring down into it, seeing her wavering reflection. Without a word to the others, she set down her pack and loosened her hair from its braid. The others—Gwydion, Arthur, and Gwen—did not speak. She ran her fingers through her now-loosened hair, then knelt down beside the pond. Though the day was somewhat cool, she rolled up the sleeves of her linen shirt, and plunged her hands into the cold water.

She murmured the prayer to Nantsovelta beneath her breath,

"O vessel bearing the light,
O great brightness
Outshining the sun,
Draw me ashore,
Under your protection,
From the shortlived ship of the world."

How glorious it was, she thought, to fear water no more. How wonderful to like to plunge her hands into the coolness, to want to dive in and discover the depths and the mysteries that lay there. How magnificent it was to know this freedom from fear. And how sad it was to think of the years wasted. But she would not be sad. Not today.

She rose from the pond and faced the others. And she smiled, as she had not smiled in some time. "Home," she said, drinking in the forest, the water, the warm sunlight that dappled the clearing, and the quickening air.

"Yes," Gwydion agreed, gravely, as he reached out and laid a light hand on her hair. "You are home."

And for a moment she ached for him, for she knew that he was thinking of his own home, of Caer Dathyl, closed and shuttered, surrounded by Coranian soldiers. They had passed near Caer Dathyl on their way back to Mynydd Tawel after Arthur had retrieved the

Sword of Taran and rescued them from the Coranian soldiers. And Arthur, whose hatred of Gwydion had been so intense for so long, had offered to go just a little way out of their path, so that Gwydion might look on his home. But Gwydion had refused, saying only that they did not have the time. Yet Rhiannon had seen the telltale beat of the pulse at his throat when he had said it. And she had known how much he had longed to return to Caer Dathyl.

So now she reached out and tentatively laid her hand on his arm. "You will return to your home, one day. I swear it."

Unexpectedly, Gwydion smiled. "You will see to it, of course. I would back you against a contingent of Coranian soldiers any day."

"As well you should," she said, relieved that he had not seen fit to leap away from her touch. Maybe they could be friends. Even though he did not, had never, wanted her for a lover, they had been partners, working together for some years now for the freedom of Kymru. And if that partnership were all she had ever had from him, all she would ever have, well, her life then would be well spent. Better, she knew, than it would have been if he had never found her, if she had continued to hide away, fearing to be hurt again.

She caught the flicker of movement out of the corner of her eye, and turned to face the waterfall.

"He's here," she said with a smile, and nodded at Arthur.

Arthur did not move at first as the old man stepped out from the cave behind the waterfall. It was only when the man stepped over the rocks and stood within the clearing, his arms spreads wide, that Arthur dropped his pack and ran into Myrrdin's arms.

WHEN RHIANNON STEPPED inside the cave, the first thing she did was to sink to the ground in front of the hearth, holding her chilled hands out to the crackling fire. A pot of stew bubbled over the flames, as well as a smaller pot that steamed fragrantly. *Chamomile tea*, she thought as she went to the familiar cupboard and pulled out five clay mugs. Wrapping a rag around the handle of the pot, she poured the tea into the mugs and set them down in front of the others as they gathered around the rough, wooden table.

She noticed that Myrrdin's trunk, the one carved for him by his father many, many years ago, sat against one wall. Fresh rushes covered the floor. The light of the fire played off the walls, which glittered with rock crystal. Rough, wooden shelves held books and a few pieces of crockery.

Myrrdin, his white beard clipped short, smiled. His dark eyes were kind as he gestured for her to sit on the bench next to him. "You are looking well, child," he said gently.

"As are you, uncle," she replied with a fond smile. "By the way, Neuad especially charged me to remember you to her when next I saw you."

"Did she now?" Myrrdin said dryly. "I had hoped she would have forgotten me."

"Not in the least," Rhiannon said. "Why, when she spoke of you her whole face lit up."

"Wonderful," Myrrdin said sourly.

"Come, uncle, you don't fool me. You are not as displeased as you let on."

"You are wrong," Myrrdin said, a little too sharply. "Why, the girl is less than half my age!"

"She is not a girl, Myrrdin," Rhiannon pointed out. "She is a woman."

"To me she will always be a girl."

"We'll see about that soon enough, won't we?"

"What do you mean by that?" Arthur broke in. "Is Neuad coming here?"

"They are all coming here, Arthur," Gwydion said. "And, much as I am enjoying this beautiful moment discussing Neuad and her foolishness, I think this is the time for Myrrdin to give us all the news."

"Who do you mean? Who is coming here?" Arthur demanded fiercely.

Gwydion turned to Arthur and studied the young man for a few moments. At last, he said quietly, "I am sorry, Arthur, that I have not taken the time to discuss our next moves with you."

Rhiannon was astonished. Never had she heard Gwydion apologize to Arthur for his high-handed way of doing things. It underlined to her, once again, how the power had shifted, since that night when Arthur had returned to Mynydd Tawel with the Sword of Taran in his hands.

"Apology accepted, uncle," Arthur said firmly, but without rancor. "Now, tell me."

"I have sent for the key leaders of the Cerddorian to join us here in Coed Aderyn. King Rhoram and his people from Haford Bryn in Prydyn; Prince Lludd and his folk from Coed Ddu in Ederynion; King Owein and the rest from Coed Coch; and your sister, Queen Morrigan, and the folk formerly in Mynydd Tawel. They are journeying here now, in small groups, and will begin to arrive in a few weeks."

"Why?"

"We must get into Cadair Idris. To do that, we must bring the Treasures to the Doors and use them to gain entry. And to do that, we must distract Havgan and the Coranians. Havgan's fortress of Eiodel is just a few steps away from Cadair Idris. Cadair Idris is always guarded."

"And is even more so now," Myrrdin said quietly. "The guard has been doubled in the last week."

"Arianrod," Rhiannon said bitterly.

"Yes," Myrrdin said. "She came to Havgan's fortress last week. And offered her help to him."

"In return for what, exactly?" Arthur asked.

"For what she had always wanted—power," Rhiannon said, studiously not looking at Gwydion.

"I refused her, you see," Gwydion said quietly to Myrrdin, "at Mynydd Tawel. And she was determined not to be left behind there anymore."

So, Gwydion had refused Arianrod after all. Rhiannon thought that very strange. A fact that Gwydion was apparently aware of, since he looked at her so pointedly.

"Yes," Gwydion said, answering her unspoken question. "I did, indeed. I take it you did not think so?"

"I didn't think about it at all," Rhiannon lied airily. "Who you sleep with is your business."

"So it is," Gwydion agreed. "So it is."

Llundydd, Cynyddu Wythnos—early evening

DUDOD WALKED AWAY from the marketplace with a casual air. After many years of serving his now-dead brother, Anieron, Dudod was well schooled in the ways of deviousness. For he was not casual at all, now. He was fully aware that he was being followed.

The man who followed Dudod was, for the moment, unidentifiable. He wore a cloak with the hood well pushed down over his forehead, his features left in shadow. The man's hands were those of an old man, but the man's walk was vigorous. He had been following Dudod for the last hour as the Bard had made his way through the marketplace in the center of Brecon, one of the most important cities in the cantref of Ceredigion in Prydyn.

As Dudod had done for his brother, now he did for his son, Elidyr, who was now the Master Bard of Kymru and faced with the backbreaking task of knitting together the broken network of Dewin and Bards that had spanned the country. The network had been broken almost beyond repair earlier this year, when the Coranians had raided Allt Llwyd. Many key men and women had been captured then. And much damage had resulted to internal communications.

It was this damage that Dudod had come to Brecon to repair. He had done his job well. Now all of Prydyn was once again functional, and Elidyr would again receive messages at his refuge with King Owein in Coed Coch.

As Dudod always did when he thought of the damage done, he thought of his dead brother, who had cut out his own tongue rather than betray secrets to the enemy. Anieron had died at the hands of the Arch-wyrce-jaga, Sledda, not many months ago. As he always did, Dudod swore to himself that he would exact revenge from that one-eyed night crow. He would see to it that Sledda suffered mightily before he died.

But now was not the time to brood over his future plans for vengeance. Brecon was his last stop, and, from here, he was to go to Coed Aderyn. It was to that forest, on the border between Prydyn and Gwytheryn, that the others were to make their way. It would be from there that the Cerddorian of Kymru would receive their orders to create the diversion necessary for the others to get into Cadair Idris. And Dudod would be there to see it all. He would kill this man who followed him as soon as he had the chance. And then he would leave Brecon as quickly as he could.

Casually, he made his way down one of the busy streets, whistling, stopping occasionally to make an infinitesimal correction to the folds of his cloak, to his boots, to the lacing of his tunic. He didn't want to go too fast for his follower. And he did not. For every time he contrived to glance behind him, the man was there, not bothering to mask that he was following. Bad sign, that. A sign that Dudod must take this man out as soon as possible, for when those who followed did not mind being spotted, things were very bad, indeed.

Dudod turned down a narrow side street, still whistling. The man who followed him was just a few paces behind. Now was the time to act.

He slipped into the constricted opening of an alleyway. The alley was narrow and dark, nestled between the two houses on either side. As he pressed himself against the wall, he drew his knife from the top of his boot and waited quietly, barely breathing.

The slight light that drifted past the opening was blocked off as the hooded man halted in the narrow passageway. The man's hands were empty of weapons, but that meant nothing. Silently, the man slipped into the alley, and faced Dudod from just inches away.

"If you kill me, old friend, I hope you will do a quick, clean job. I am sick of long, drawn-out deaths."

That voice! Something about it was familiar, but even Dudod, who had perfect pitch and a memory that had never before failed, could not place it. Someone he had known, he thought, from the time he had been Bard to the court of Gwynedd, long ago, when Queen Rathtyen was alive.

The man removed the hood of his cloak. In the dim light, Dudod could make out gray hair, which still held a glint of reddish-gold, like a treasured memory. He had an aquiline, commanding nose, and his skin stretched tightly over a face that was little more than a skull. And blue eyes, eyes that Dudod now remembered had often been cold and distant, but which now sparkled with life and purpose.

"You are a hard man to find, Dudod," the man said softly. "I have been looking for you for many, many months."

"Rhodri! Rhodri ap Erddufyl! By the gods, man, I thought you were dead!"

"I was, Dudod," Rhodri agreed softly. "I was, when I left Tegeingl after Rathtyen died, and left Gwynedd in the hands of her son, Uthyr. I was when I left my own son, Madoc, and hid myself away."

"And in the years since?"

"Living a half life on the island of Caer Siddi. Dead, really, for all those years."

"Until?" Dudod prompted.

"Until now, since the enemy has come. I have heard, Dudod, of the death of my daughter, Ellirri, once Queen of Rheged, and the death of her husband and oldest son in battle with the enemy. I have heard of my son, how Madoc betrayed Uthyr and threw in his lot with the Coranians. And I have seen—"

"What?" Dudod asked as Rhodri paused. "What have you seen?"

"I have seen the Smiths of Kymru in bondage. I have seen them make those collars meant for our own Y Dawnus. I have seen them die inside as they do this."

"You know where they are being held?"

"I do. And it is for that which I have found you. I will give this information to the man who desires it most. You must take me to him."

"And that is?"

"To the Dreamer."

"To Awst's son," Dudod pointed out.

431

"That he is the son of my one-time rival means nothing to me anymore. If it did, I would still be residing in Caer Siddi, empty inside."

"Then I will take you to him, Rhodri. As you wish."

"Good," Rhodri said. "And then I must go, for I have another task."

"And that is?"

"Madoc." Rhodri spoke the name of his son as though he had ashes in his mouth.

"And what will you do, Rhodri ap Erddufyl, once-time King of Gwynedd, when you see your son?"

"What must be done, Dudod ap Cyvarnion. What must be done."

Chapter 24

Coed Aderyn, Kingdom of Prydyn,
and Eiodel, Gwytheryn, Kymru
Colleen Mis, 499

Suldydd, Cynyddu Wythnos—late afternoon

They were all assembled and waiting when Gwydion entered the enormous cavern. Rock crystal, set in the rough walls of the huge cave, shimmered in the light of the hundreds of torches set in brackets around the chamber.

As he entered he paused for a moment, scanning the faces of the folk who stood around the walls.

The party from Rheged was led by King Owein, who stood unmoving, his cool blue eyes surveying Gwydion as intently as he himself was being surveyed. Around his neck he wore the opal-studded torque of Rheged. His red trousers were tucked into calf-length boots of brown leather, the cuffs studded with opals. Opals shimmered from the brooch that fastened his red cloak over his left shoulder.

Trystan, Owein's Captain and Teleri, his Lieutenant, stood closely on either side of the King, both dressed in red breeches and white tunics. The badge of Rheged, a white horse rearing on a field of red, glittered on the front of their tunics. Trystan's green eyes were steady as he returned Gwydion's gaze. Teleri fingered the dagger tucked into the belt at her waist and nodded briefly to Gwydion.

Owein's younger brother, Rhiwallon, stood just behind and to the right of Owein, his reddish-gold hair glinting in the light of the torches, his stance wary, as though even here, danger might threaten his brother. Next to Rhiwallon stood Esyllt, Owein's Bard, dressed in a robe of bardic blue fastened at the waist with a fine chain of silver. Around her neck she wore a torque of silver with a triangle in which a sapphire dangled. Sabrina, one of the few Druids who had not followed the Archdruid down the road of betrayal, wore the Druid's robe of brown with green trim at the sleeves and hem. Around her neck she wore the Druid's torque of gold, from which flashed an emerald set inside a circle and a square. The two women stood as far apart from each other, yet as close to Trystan, as they could.

Gwydion's eyes lighted on the rest of the band from Coed Coch. There was Cariadas, his daughter, the next Dreamer. She wore a gown of black with an undershift of red, and her red-gold hair was braided and bound to the crown of her head with ribbons of red and black. He smiled at her, and she smiled back. Her smile was less sunny than it had been some months ago, but it was even more beautiful for all of that, for she always seemed now to be touched with just a hint of sadness, ever since the death of Anieron, Master Bard. Sinend, she who would one day be Archdruid, stood quietly, with her eyes downcast, as she always did. She wore the customary Druid's robe of green and brown and the Druid's torque set with an emerald.

Elstar, the Ardewin, and Elidyr, her husband, the new Master Bard, stood closely together. Elstar wore a robe of silver-gray, the pentagonal badge of the Dewin, a silver dragon on a field of green, over her heart. Around her neck she wore the Ardewin's torque, a collar of silver set with pearls. Elidyr wore his robe of white trimmed in blue. The badge of the Bards, a white nightingale on a field of blue, was fastened to a belt of silver around his waist. Around his neck he wore the torque of the Master Bard, which shimmered with sapphires. The fine lines around Elstar's eyes, the tired droop of Elidyr's mouth, told their tale of long nights and days as they struggled to reconnect the broken chain of Y Dawnus. Yet they gazed triumphantly at Gwydion, for this task was now complete, as Gwydion had told them it must be by this time.

The couple's sons, Llewelyn, who would be the next Ardewin, and Cynfar, who would one day be the Master Bard, stood on either side of their parents. Cynfar, the younger, possessed the green eyes of his granda, Anieron. Llewelyn had the sandy hair and brown eyes of his father. The faces of the two young men were fierce and eager.

The folk from Ederynion clustered around Prince Lludd. Lludd stood stolidly, his thumbs tucked into the belt around his waist. He wore a tunic and trousers of sea green. His boots were of white leather, studded with pearls. He did not wear the torque of Ederynion, for that was around his sister's neck. He was, every moment of every day, Gwydion knew, anxious to rescue Queen Elen from the hands of the Coranians. But the boy was now a man, and had learned to wait, and his impatience could be seen only in the tight set of his jaw, and in the flicker of fire in his brown eyes.

Angharad, his Captain, her flaming red hair braided tightly to her head, surveyed Gwydion with her keen, green eyes. She wore white breeches and a tunic of sea green. The badge of Ederynion, a white swan on a field of sea green, glittered on her shoulder. The gaze of Emrys, her Lieutenant, danced over to Angharad, then quickly away. Angharad did not seem to notice. Talhearn, Lludd's Bard, stood to one side of the Prince in his robe of bardic blue, his wise blue eyes calm and patient.

Queen Morrigan stood at the front of her party from Gwynedd. She wore a gown of brown with an undertunic of blue. The slight, mulish set of her mouth indicated that getting her into a dress had been a struggle. But, apparently, in the end, the solemnity of the occasion had won out. Around her neck she wore the silver torque of Gwynedd, studded with sapphires. The girl's auburn hair and dark eyes were echoes of her mother, Ygraine, who stood behind her daughter, stiff and cool in white trimmed with pearls. Yet Gwydion saw much of his dead brother, Uthyr, in Morrigan, too, in the way she tilted her head, in the set of her fine mouth.

Cai, Morrigan's Captain, and Bedwyr, her Lieutenant, stood on either side of the Queen, their identical brown gazes steady. Both wore blue tunics with brown breeches, and the badge of Gwynedd, a brown hawk on a field of blue, was buckled around their waists.

Susanna, Morrigan's Bard, and Neuad, her Dewin, stood, each on either side of Cai and Bedwyr. Susanna's red-gold hair glinted in the torchlight, and her generous mouth was curved into a smile as she waited. She wore the Bard's torque of sapphire around her neck. Gwyhar, Susanna's son, stood next to his mother, garbed in a robe of bardic blue. His freckled face was eager. Neuad, breathtakingly beautiful, stood as still as a statue, her robe of sea green barely moving with her breath, her eyes never leaving Myrrdin, who stood just at the entrance of the cave.

Just a little apart from them stood Gwydion's aunt, Dinaswyn. She wore a gown of black and an undertunic of red. Her frosty hair spilled down her back, and her gray eyes gazed back at Gwydion without expression.

King Rhoram stood at the forefront of the party from Prydyn. The torchlight played over his golden hair and shifted over the deep lines of pain that cut clefts around his mouth. He wore a tunic and trousers of dark green. His boots were black, and the cuffs were studded with emeralds. Around his neck he wore the gold and emerald torque of Prydyn. In spite of the lines of pain in his face, he was smiling, his blue eyes glowing.

Achren, Rhoram's Captain, and Aidan, his Lieutenant, stood on either side of Rhoram. Achren's dark eyes danced, and Aidan's easy grin came to his face as Gwydion surveyed them. They both wore the badge of Prydyn, a black wolf on a green field, stitched over their hearts on their green tunics.

Geriant and Sanon, Rhoram's son and daughter, stood just behind their father, their golden hair glowing. Sanon was pale, as she always was; yet she stood proudly in her gown of black and undertunic of dark green. She was not looking at Gwydion, but at Owein, who seemed to be unaware of her gaze. Geriant was dressed like his father and bore a great resemblance to him, for he, too, had lines on his face—but his were lines of sorrow, put there, Gwydion knew, by Owein's sister, Enid, now the captive wife of Morcant, the traitorous King of Rheged. Cadell, Rhoram's Dewin, wore the

Dewin's robe of sea green trimmed with silver and the Dewin's torque of silver and pearl. He gazed at Gwydion steadily. Dafydd Penfro, Rhoram's counselor and Gwydion's old friend, stood quietly, his dark eyes watchful.

Near the entrance to the cavern, Myrrdin stood, his dark eyes calm. He wore the sea-green robe of the Dewin and a simple Dewin's torque around his neck. If he regretted that he was not wearing the Ardewin's torque, which glittered around Elstar's neck, he gave no sign. And Gwydion, knowing his uncle, knowing that Myrrdin, in his wisdom, did nothing that he would later regret, knew he had come to terms with his sacrifice of long ago.

Next to Myrrdin stood Arthur. He wore a tunic and trousers of black, tucked into plain, black boots. He wore no badge, no torque. The Sword of Taran rested in its scabbard around his waist. His left hand was clasped on the hilt, and his gaze was steady as he calmly waited for Gwydion to begin.

Gwen wore the brown and green robe of the Druids. She wore no torque around her neck, for she had never gone to Caer Duir to receive one. Her golden hair was braided and wound around her head like a crown. In her hands she held the golden Cauldron of Modron, and she looked at Gwydion with infatuation in her blue eyes.

And then, saving the best for last, his gaze met Rhiannon's. Rhiannon, her dark hair falling down her shoulders like a shadow, was dressed in the Dewin's robe of sea green. Around her neck she wore the Dewin's torque of silver and a single pearl. At her feet rested the pearl-studded Stone of Nantsovelta.

For a long moment, he simply gazed at her and she returned his gaze with her emerald green eyes. He said nothing, not because there were things he could not say, but because he did not think he needed to. He could read in her eyes that she knew how much this moment meant to him. She knew that he had been working toward it for so many years. She knew how he had struggled and fought and even, sometimes, wept, waiting and working and dreaming toward it.

And yet, perhaps he was wrong about not needing to say any words to her now. For she had been a part of the struggle for years, and had never given up. She had never left his side in those dark years, no matter how much she might have wished to. And she might have, for he had not been easy to live with and he knew it. Perhaps, then, he did need to say something to her before he began. The torchlight played over the shadows of his black robe trimmed in red. The opal torque around his throat glittered as he left the center of the chamber to stand before her.

"Many times I would have given up," he said quietly, for her ears alone, "had you not been there."

"Not you, Gwydion," she said. "Never."

"You are wrong, Rhiannon ur Hefeydd. Had you not been there, this would not be happening now."

A smile, beautiful as the dawn, came to her lovely face. Her green eyes glowed. He clasped her hand and lifted it to his lips, and kissed her palm, never taking his eyes from her.

"Thank you," he said simply.

"You're welcome," she replied, just as simply.

He let go of her hand and again strode to the center of the chamber. His eyes sought and found King Rhoram's. And Rhoram was smiling, without the faintest shadow in his eyes.

"We begin our gathering here," Gwydion intoned, "with the Oath of our people."

As one, they recited the oath.

"If I break faith with you,
May the skies fall upon me,
May the seas drown me,
May the earth rise and swallow me."

"You are here today," Gwydion began, in a solemn, powerful voice, "to play your part in freeing our land from the enemy. We welcome King Owein; his heir and brother, Prince Rhiwallon; and his people from Rheged. We welcome King Rhoram; his heir and son, Prince Geriant; and his folk from Prydyn. We welcome Prince Lludd, heir to Queen Elen, and his people from Ederynion. We welcome Queen Morrigan and her folk from Gwynedd." As he said this, Gwydion bowed to each ruler, and Owein, Rhoram, Lludd, and Morrigan gravely bowed back to the Dreamer.

"We welcome the Dewin—Elstar, Ardewin; Myrrdin of Gwynedd; Neuad of Gwynedd; and Cadell of Prydyn. We welcome the Bards—Elidyr, Master Bard; Talhearn of Ederynion; Esyllt of Rheged; Susanna and Gwyhar of Gwynedd. We welcome the Druids —Sabrina of Rheged and Sinend of Gwytheryn. We welcome the Dreamers—Dinaswyn and Cariadas of Gwynedd." Again, Gwydion bowed in turn as he named them, and each one returned his bow.

"And we welcome those who have returned to Coed Aderyn bearing the Four Treasures, hidden away in the days of the last High King, Lleu Lawrient. We welcome Gwenhwyfar ur Rhoram var Rhiannon, who bears the Cauldron of Earth." At this, Gwen stepped forward, holding the Cauldron high. She placed it gently on the floor of the cavern in front of Gwydion. The golden Cauldron glowed, and the emeralds set within its rim gleamed. From those watching came an intake of breath, a murmur, for the beauty of the bowl, and reverence for Modron, the Great Mother.

"We welcome Rhiannon ur Hefeydd var Indeg, who brings the Stone of Water." Rhiannon stepped forward, carrying the Stone, and set it next to the Cauldron. Streaks of silver shot through the Stone. At each silvery junction the pearls that rested there glowed softly. Elstar, the Ardewin, whispered the name of Nantsovelta in awe.

"I beg you to welcome my humble self," Gwydion began with a grin as he bowed.

"Humble!" snorted Myrrdin. "I beg to differ."

The people laughed, just as Gwydion had intended. "I, Gwydion ap Awst var Celemon, have come bearing the Spear of Fire." Gwydion flourished the Spear, and laid it on the floor, next to the Cauldron and the Stone. The twined silver and gold of the shaft of the Spear glowed in the torchlight. The opals at the base and top flickered with fire.

"And now, I most earnestly beg your welcome to the one who bears the Sword of Taran. Arthur ap Uthyr var Ygraine. The next High King of Kymru!"

Arthur strode up to Gwydion, removed the Sword from his belt, and held it over his head. The sapphires on the scabbard of gold and silver shimmered as Arthur stood, holding the Sword. With a bell-like ring that reverberated throughout the cavern, he drew the Sword from its scabbard. The hawk's hilt seemed to writhe for a moment, its sapphire eyes glowing. Arthur raised the Sword high, then plunged it, point down, into the earth.

The people gathered there began to cheer. Arthur bowed to them and nodded, acknowledging their welcome. But they would not quiet. The heartfelt relief, the hope they now felt, could not be suppressed. The cheering grew louder. Some of the people had tears spilling down their faces. They hugged one another in joy and hope.

Gwydion held up his arms and, at last, they quieted. "You have all been called here to take up your various tasks—tasks necessary to our freedom. Bands of Cerddorian from Prydyn and Rheged, from Ederynion and Gwynedd, are now secreted throughout Coed Aderyn. These warriors have been brought here to create a diversion. The purpose of this diversion is to draw Havgan and his warriors from his fortress of Eiodel, leaving the way open for us to approach the Doors of Cadair Idris. The Doors will open for us, for we have the Treasures in our hands. Once inside, we will make for the throne room, and Arthur will undergo the Tynged Mawr. And, if he passes the test, he will be our High King. With the powers of the High King, Arthur will lead us and take back our land!"

Again, the people could not contain themselves, and they erupted into more cheers. Arthur flushed, but did not look down.

"Now, each country has provided two hundred warriors for this diversion," Gwydion went on. "The diversions will be led by the Captains and the Lieutenants of each country."

"What?" Prince Lludd protested. "I lead my warriors!"

King Owein and Queen Morrigan vigorously agreed, but King Rhoram, wiser than they, held his silence.

"The rulers of the four countries may not be a part of this battle," Gwydion said sternly. "For they have a different task. They must witness the making of the High King. This is the law."

"But I am not a ruler," Prince Lludd protested. "My sister rules

Ederynion. I lead our people only against the day when Elen herself is freed."

"Prince Lludd," Arthur said quietly, "there is no one here who thinks that you seek to take your sister's place as ruler of your country. But her place you must take, nonetheless, in this matter."

For a moment Lludd did not speak. The two young men stared at each other, Lludd with defiance and Arthur with authority. Finally, Lludd nodded, and spoke. "It will be as you wish, High King. I am yours to command." The Prince bowed to Arthur and stepped back.

After a moment, Gwydion continued. "It is also the law that the Ardewin, the Master Bard, the Dreamer, and the Archdruid witness this event. Elstar, Flidyr, and I stand ready. But Cathbad, the Archdruid, will be unable to attend." There was some laughter at this, though Sinend lowered her gaze in shame.

Dinaswyn, Sinend's grandmother, went to the girl and put her arm around her shoulders, for the traitorous actions of Aergol, Sinend's father and Dinaswyn's son, shamed them both.

"Sinend ur Aergol var Eurgain," Gwydion said gently, as the girl lifted her startled eyes to the Dreamer. "Will you honor the ceremony as the heir of the Archdruid's heir?"

Sinend blushed, and tears filmed her fine, gray eyes. But she held her head proudly, for, perhaps, the first time, and answered clearly. "I will."

"In one week's time, on Calan Gaef, the ceremony where we honor Annwyn, Lord of Chaos, and his mate, Aertan, Weaver of Fate, we will enter Cadair Idris.

"Four days from now, our warriors will move out of Coed Aderyn in small groups, moving at night, hiding during the day. It will take them three days to be ready and in position at the crossroads of Sarn Ermyn and Sarn Achmaen, south of Cadair Idris. At the same time, those who are to go to Cadair Idris will also leave Coed Aderyn, using the network of caves we have discovered. We will then wait, well hidden, less than a league away, for the challenge to be delivered. The day before Calan Gaef, Rhiannon and I will Wind-Ride to Havgan and deliver our challenge. Be assured that he will meet our warriors at those crossroads on Calan Gaef. Captains, remember," Gwydion said sternly, looking at Trystan, Achren, Angharad, and Cai, "that this is a diversion only. Your purpose is to draw off the Coranians, allowing the rest of us to get into Cadair Idris. Your purpose is not to attempt to defeat the Golden Man and his warriors. We do not seek to sacrifice the lives of the Kymri. Later, you will lead and fight battles for that purpose. Is that understood?"

"If we meet the Golden Man," Achren said, her dark eyes sparkling, "do we have to be nice to him?" The others laughed.

"You may damage him slightly, Achren ur Canhustyr, if you must," Arthur said fiercely. "But he is mine, understood?"

"It is understood, High King," Achren replied gravely.

"Now," Gwydion went on. "I must—"

"You must welcome your late-coming guests!" a new voice called out.

As one, those gathered there turned to the entrance. Dudod stood there, travel-stained and weary. Yet his tone was jaunty as he continued. "Welcome two more wanderers, ready to take part in this bid for freedom! For we have news!"

"And who is 'we,' Dudod?" Gwydion inquired, gesturing to the man who stood next to the Bard. The man's hood was up and his features unidentifiable.

"Welcome," Dudod went on, "to Rhodri ap Erddufyl, one-time King of Gwynedd!"

The silence was complete as Rhodri removed the hood of his cloak. The old man stood quietly, his keen blue eyes surveying those gathered there. King Rhoram walked slowly up to him. "Uncle?" Rhoram asked hesitantly.

"It is truly I, Rhoram," Rhodri said gravely.

"Uncle," Rhoram repeated, then threw his arms around Rhodri. "You are most welcome here."

King Owein, too, walked up to the old man, followed by his brother, Rhiwallon. "Granda?" Owein whispered.

"I saw you last when you were just a tiny lad," Rhodri said softly. "You have the eyes of your mother."

"My mam loved you," Owein said slowly. "She said that you

loved us all, even though you went away."

"I was grieved to hear of Ellirri's death," Rhodri said softly. "And of your father's. He was good to her."

"They loved each other very much. Elphin, my oldest brother, died, too."

"Those are deaths that will be avenged, Owein. We will see to it, you and I and Rhiwallon."

"Rhodri has news for us," Dudod said to the company. "News that, I am sure, will be welcome." Dudod nodded at Rhodri.

"I know where the Smiths are being held," Rhodri said mildly.

"What?" Arthur leapt in front of the old man. "Where are they?" he demanded.

"In Caer Siddi, the island off the coast of Prydyn."

"I vow to rescue them," Arthur said. "It shall be the second thing I do."

"And what is the first thing?" Rhodri asked.

"The first thing is to kill Sledda, the Arch-wyrce-jaga. For he killed Anieron, Master Bard, and I have sworn to see him pay for that."

"I felt it when Anieron died," Rhodri said. "As did all of Kymru. And I heard his song. Together, we will make this a new day of freedom, as Anieron wished."

"We shall," Arthur agreed.

"Then," Gwydion said, lifting his hands to the company, "we are ready. Our tasks are before us. From here we will go to Cadair Idris, and take back that which was once ours. For this task, we ask for the blessing.

"*The peace of lights,*
The peace of joys,
The peace of souls,
Be with you."

"*And with you,*" the crowd sang out.

"*Owein!*"

Owein knew, as he knew nothing else so surely, whose voice it was that called him. Heart pounding, he stopped and turned on his way back up the passage from the cavern. He had been, he thought, the last to leave. She must have been hiding in the shadows, and he had passed her by.

Owein found himself thinking of the song by Gwyn ap Nudd, the Fourth Ardewin of Kymru, father of the last High King,

My golden girl, with the brow like the lily,
Under your web of golden hair,
I have loved you.
Is there any help for me?

Is there any help for me? he thought again. But, no, how could there be? For she did not love him. She, who was to have been the wife of his older brother. She, whom he had loved from the very first moment he saw her. She, who had never loved him.

"Princess Sanon," he said, somewhat stiffly, for he did not know what to say.

Sanon ur Rhoram, Princess of Prydyn, gazed up at him with her dark eyes. Her golden hair flowed down over her shoulders to her slender waist, held back from her face by a black band sparkling with emeralds.

"Owein, I—" she began. But she could not seem to finish.

Fool! Owein thought. *She stands before me and I can say nothing!* If she turned away now, he would have only himself to blame. Whatever she wanted to say to him, and he did not think he could bear to hear it, she was his love, and he must help her.

"Sanon," he said softly. "I . . . I am glad to see you. Are you well?"

Her pale face took on a rosy hue as she lowered her gaze. "Yes. Yes, I am well. And you? How do you and your people fare in Coed Coch?"

"We do the best we can, Sanon. We waylay caravans; we steal our own food back from the enemy. We take back our gold and silver. We harry them, and we kill them when we can. But it is not enough."

"Da says the same. But, today! Oh, Owein, today we have seen the Treasures! We have seen the High King. The one to lead us back to freedom."

So, that was it. Arthur ap Uthyr. He who had lost Sanon first to his own brother, then to his brother's memory, would now lose her to the High King. "Arthur will surely lead us back into freedom, Sanon," he said stiffly. "But if you are looking for an introduction to him, you must look elsewhere. I do not know him any more than you do."

"An introduction?" Sanon asked, puzzled. But then she understood Her eyes flashed. "Owein ap Urien," she said sternly, "you are a fool!"

"As I was just telling myself, Princess. Now, will you excuse me?" He turned and began to walk away, but was brought up short by her hand on his sleeve. She flung him around to face her. Her eyes were blazing.

But then her gaze softened, and she said quietly, "Owein, I have called you a fool, and that was wrong. I am the fool."

"You? Do not dare to call yourself that," he said fiercely. "Never."

"But I was. Ever since Elphin died, I have lived a half life, gnawing the bones of what might have been and never even seeing what could be. And now, I do see. Perhaps I see too late. If so, that is my punishment, and a fitting one. But, Owein, I must know. Once you offered me your hand in marriage and I scorned it, fool that I was. And yet, if you could find it in your heart to forgive me, perhaps we might begin again."

"Might begin again," he said slowly, gazing into her eyes, trying to read and believe what he saw there. "My golden girl," he said softly, "is there any hope for me?"

And though she did not answer in words, Owein was satisfied.

TRYSTAN STOOD AT the entrance to the cave where Rhiannon and her daughter had spent so many years. Many of the others were still gathered there, reluctant to retreat back into the forest for the night.

Queen Morrigan stood next to her brother, Arthur. Their mother, Ygraine, stood to one side, smiling at her children as Morrigan chattered happily to her brother.

Prince Lludd and his party were just leaving for the night, and the Prince stopped in front of Arthur and bowed. Morrigan smiled at the Prince, and Lludd, visibly shaken by the charm in that smile, retreated with his people beneath the waterfall and out into the forest. Prince Rhiwallon and his people followed, but there was no sign of Owein.

King Rhoram and Prince Geriant seemed to have taken charge of Rhodri, and were doubtless catching up on the news. Myrrdin was talking quietly to Elstar and Elidyr, and their sons, Llewelyn and Cynfar, had the full attention of Cariadas and Gwen.

Gwydion sat apart on the hearth in silence. But he was watching Rhiannon as she spoke quietly with Dudod. His gray gaze never left her, but his face was stern.

And then Trystan saw her, talking quietly to Sinend, for the two Druids still felt awkward in the company of the others. Sabrina's dark hair fell to her shoulders, and her startling blue eyes were kind as she listened to Sinend. He made a move to join them, when he felt a hand on his sleeve.

"My husband, as you know, Trystan, is not here. He is too unwell to travel," Esyllt the Bard said softly. He turned to look at her. Her luxurious brown hair glowed. And her beautiful blue eyes promised him a night of what she would no doubt call love.

But he knew better. At last, he knew better.

"You should have stayed with your husband, Esyllt," he said wearily. "I brought him out of Caer Erias so that he might be with you again. He loves you. He needs you."

"As you do not?" she challenged with a slow smile.

Trystan turned his head slightly, and saw that Sabrina was looking at him. She glanced at Esyllt, then looked away, but not before he had seen the shadow in her eyes.

"No, Esyllt. As I have been telling you for some time, no. I do not."

"So you have said, Trystan, but your eyes follow me just the same."

"You are mistaken, Esyllt. But that is like you. For you never took any thought beyond what you wanted. Years I spent, waiting, hoping, begging, that you might divorce March and be with me. But you never did. You promised you would, and on every Calan Llachar, I waited and hoped. But each time, you did not. You wanted me as your lover, and I was. But you never wanted me as your husband. And what I once felt for you is gone."

"Gone," she repeated. "Gone? Ah, no, Trystan, do not say that."

"It is true. Did you think you could toy with me forever?"

"I never toyed with you! I was confused. But now I know you are the man I want. Calan Llachar is six months away. And I swear to you, on that day, I will divorce March. I swear it!"

"Don't, Esyllt. Because I am done with you. Done."

He walked away from her without even glancing back. He went to Sabrina and stood close to her. He smiled at her, and took her hand and kissed it. And thoughts of Esyllt did not even cross his mind as he looked into Sabrina's blue eyes.

GWYDION SAT BY himself on the hearth. He spoke to no one, for he did not trust himself to speak. Today he had taken one of the last steps in his task. Within the week they would be in Cadair Idris, and Arthur would undergo the Tynged Mawr. Surely the boy would survive the test. And he would be High King. And Gwydion's task would be finished.

Oh, he would continue to use every weapon in his command to fight the enemy and help drive them from the land. But the leadership of the Kymri would belong to Arthur. Was this not true even now? And his task, given him long ago by the gods, would be complete. And then, oh, then! Then Gwydion could follow his heart. He would lay down his burdens and tell Rhiannon ur Hefeydd that he loved her.

But would he? Perhaps it would be too late by then. Perhaps it was already too late. Would she ever understand why he had forced the wall between them? Would she ever understand that his coldness had not been capricious, but rather devotion to his duty? Would she understand that, even when he had been his most cold, his most vile, he had done so only because his burdens could not be cast away?

Now, after all this time, would Rhiannon find the knowledge of his love a burden? Something she would far rather never have known? Perhaps best, then, to say nothing at all, even when Kymru was free. Lost in these musings, he did not realize that someone had come to sit beside him on the hearth until the man spoke.

"Gwydion ap Awst," the man said, "are you perhaps lost in a dream?"

"A dream that may never come true," Gwydion said, before he even thought. "One that, perhaps, should never come true."

And then he realized whom he was talking to, Rhodri, the one-time King of Gwynedd. Rhodri had been married to Queen Rath-tyen and had hated the man whom the Queen had truly loved—Gwydion's father, Awst. The Queen had starved herself to death after hearing of Awst's death, and Rhodri had left Gwynedd and hidden himself away so many years ago. Gwydion turned to look at Rhodri. The blue eyes reminded Gwydion of Ellirri.

"I loved your daughter, Rhodri," Gwydion said quietly. "She was kind to me."

"And my son?"

"You know what Madoc has done."

"I do. It is one of the reasons I have returned to the land of the living. Who but his father could show Madoc the error of his ways?"

"He was Uthyr's death."

"A fact for which I am sorrier than I can say. Sorrier, perhaps, than you might ever believe. Which brings me to what I have to say to you. I hated your father, for it seemed to me that he had taken from me the woman I loved. But I know now that he took nothing from me. Rathtyen loved me. And then the enemy came. And my daughter died beneath their axes. And my son became a trai-tor. And the Smiths were brought to Caer Siddi and forced to make enaid-dals. And I knew I could no longer hide myself. And so I have returned. And I offer to you the Dreamer, and to Uthyr's son all that is left of me. Saving only one task that I alone must complete."

"And that task is?"

"To kill my son."

The stark determination in the old man's voice startled Gwydion. "You would really kill him?" he asked.

"Ah, Gwydion, I am not surprised that you do not believe me. Did you think that my hatred of your father would cause me to embrace the enemy? Only now, at the end of my life, do I see what my selfishness has led to. If I had not run away to nurture my wounds, perhaps I could have taught my son better. I have much to make up for, and not much time to do it."

"Rhodri—"

"I understand I have a granddaughter in Gwynedd," Rhodri broke in. "Queen Morrigan tells me that Tangwen is ashamed of her father. That she helps the Cerddorian as much as she is able."

"She does. A brave girl."

"Who needs her granda. I will see to her. And now, Gwydion, I must leave you. I go with Rhoram and Geriant to the forest to camp for the night. I have one thing left to say to you."

Rhodri stood and looked down at Gwydion. The blue eyes that Gwydion had always thought so cold were warm now. "The walls you have built, Gwydion, must come down. I have suffered from their building by my own hand. Do not let that happen to you. Tear them down. The gods do not mean for us to be cruel. Not for any price. This is what I have learned. Do not learn it too late, as I did."

Meirwdydd, Cynyddu Wythnos—early evening

HAVGAN DRANK DEEPLY of his wine. He had worked hard today—listening to the latest reports from his men, visiting the Doors of Cadair Idris, participating in war games with his soldiers, and making love to Arianrod all afternoon. Ah, he had earned his thirst. And, in truth, the thirstiest work had been his lovemaking.

Of course, his wife had not been pleased. Not so much with his constant bedding of Arianrod, but with the deference he gave the Kymric woman in public. But what was Aelfwyn to him? What had she ever been? Merely a stepping-stone to power. Steorra Heofan, they called Aelfwyn, Star of Heaven, for her beauty. But her beauty was cold and distant. And she had never relished his bed.

Since she had come to Kymru without his invitation, he had kept a close watch on her. But what her scheme was, he had not yet determined. Though since the time when Arianrod had come to him almost two months ago, he often forgot that he had a wife.

Until, of course, moments like this, when it was all too evident.

"Perhaps my Lord would care to switch to ale now," Aelfwyn said in her carrying voice. "Or maybe a smaller cup for your wine would be better."

He lowered his cup of gold and rubies, and smiled lazily at her, as the conversation at the high table halted. "Your worries that I will be unable to perform due to drink are without foundation, wife," he said mockingly. "For it is no business of yours. Yet, I do believe that it will not be a problem. Not with the partner I have for my bed." He reached out to his left where Arianrod sat, and ran his hand through her honey-blond hair, turning her face to his and kissing her passionately.

Aelfwyn took in the sight with outward calm, her green eyes cool. Diamonds, hard and cold, were sprinkled through her beautiful light blond hair, which was braided and bound in shimmering coils. Her gown was flowing white with a girdle of diamonds. Only the merest tightening of her mouth gave even a hint that she was displeased.

Sigerric protested. His dark eyes were sad, as though in mourning for one who had died. "My Lord," he said quietly, "there are those here who owe their loyalty to the Emperor in Corania—not to you. May I remind you that to insult their Princess is an insult to the Emperor, and an insult to the Emperor is punishable by death."

"My wife has not been invited here to Kymru," Havgan said, "but she is here just the same. And uninvited guests must take what they are given."

Sledda sat just to the left of Arianrod, and chose this moment to do his usual toadying. "General Sigerric, I do not believe that our Lord needs any advice from you." The wyrce-jaga's remaining eye was baleful, and his sharp features spoke of his disdain for the General.

"You see less than you did when you had both eyes, wyrce-jaga," Sigerric spat with contempt. "You are a fool!"

Havgan opened his mouth to call them to order, but the command never came. Shouts from the back of the hall drew his attention. But he could not see what had raised the shout. The dining hall in Eiodel was immense. It could feed over three hundred warriors at once, and they were all gathered there now for the evening feast. Bright banners worked in threads of silver and gold and scattered with jewels hung from the dark walls. Hundreds of torches glittered to fill the hall with smoky light.

Havgan leapt to his feet, and the torchlight glittered around him. His tunic and trousers were pure white, and gold glittered at his belt and at the hem and neck of his tunic. The shoulder clasps of his golden cloak were made of gold and fashioned in the shape of boars' heads. Rubies glittered at the cuffs of his white boots. His tawny hair was held back from his brow with a circlet of gold and rubies.

"Silence!" he roared, and his warriors were quiet. "What has happened?"

The Captain of his guard came running through the press of warriors and came to a stop before the dais where the high table rested. He stood before Havgan stiffly, at attention. In his hand he held an arrow of gold, fletched with red and black feathers. At the sight of the arrow, Arianrod gasped.

"What is it?" Havgan asked her. "What does it mean?"

"The arrow of the Dreamer," she said stiffly. Her amber eyes were dilated with fear, and the skin of her beautiful face tightened. "His challenge to you."

"Gwydion's challenge," Havgan said, then laughed. "Gwydion, the man who betrayed me, the man who once called me brother. I am glad for the challenge, then, for it means he at last comes out of the shadows to face me."

"No, it does not mean that," Arianrod said. "A challenge from the Dreamer is not one from an ordinary man. It is a challenge from the Shining Ones themselves. You must treat this very seriously. For what would drive a Dreamer, one who sees the future, to make a challenge of which he is not sure of the outcome?"

"A challenge from your Shining Ones does not frighten me. My god is the only god. And he is on my side. Where did this arrow come from?" Havgan asked his Captain.

"Over the walls of Eiodel, my Lord."

"Over the walls!"

"Just a few moments ago. It screamed as it raced through the heavens to land at my feet."

Havgan took the arrow and stared down at it. "And the challenge, Arianrod? Does this arrow tell me anything about that?"

"You will not have long to wait, Havgan," she said softly. "He will come."

And he did. A glow in the air from the center of the hall had the warriors backing away in fear. The air glowed opal and onyx, tourmaline and pearl, then solidified. And Gwydion, Dreamer of Kymru, and Rhiannon, Dewin of Prydyn, stood there, staring gravely at Havgan.

They were both dressed for war in laced tunics and trousers of leather. Gwydion wore black, with the Dreamer's collar of opals around his neck. Rhiannon wore sea green, and her Dewin's torque of silver and pearl. They had daggers in their belts, and both held short spears.

"Dreamer," Havgan breathed. "False brother."

"No, Havgan. Never was I your brother," Gwydion answered. His gray eyes were cold.

"Golden Man," Rhiannon spoke, "we have come to give you one last choice. Leave Kymru. Now. Before it is too late."

"It is already too late, Rhiannon," Havgan said with a twisted smile.

"Then, Bana of Corania, hear our challenge," Gwydion said, coldly, implacably. "Tomorrow the Cerddorian of the countries of Prydyn and Ederynion, of Rheged and Gwynedd, will meet you at the crossroads of Sarn Achmaen and Sarn Ermyn. If you do not come, then we shall come for you. We shall storm the very walls of Eiodel, if you are coward enough to remain behind them."

"Coward?" Havgan shouted, enraged. "You dare to call me that?

I will meet you at the crossroads, Gwydion ap Awst. And I will see you spitted on my spear!"

"Come for us, then, Havgan, son of Hengist. And you shall see the Kymri fight." Then Gwydion began the war chant of Kymru:

"We fight through the strength of the Shining Ones;

"Light of Sun, Radiance of Moon,

"Splendor of Fire, Speed of Lightning,

"Swiftness of Wind, Depth of Sea,

"Stability of Earth, Firmness of Rock."

"COME TO US at the crossroads, Golden Man," Rhiannon called as their figures began to fade. "Come to us there, and meet we who are the children of the Shining Ones Come to us, and meet your fate!"

Chapter 25

Cadair Idris
Gwytheryn, Kymru
Ywen Mis, 500

Calan Gaef—late afternoon

Gwydion, Rhiannon, Gwen and Arthur were at the head of
the procession that slowly, silently, made its way through
the forest.

The rulers and their heirs followed them—King Rhoram and his
children, Sanon and Geriant, and his uncle, Rhodri; Prince Lludd;
King Owein and his brother, Prince Rhiwallon; Queen Morrigan
and her mother, Ygraine.

The Dreamers came next—Dinaswyn and Cariadas, then the
Bards—Elidyr, Master Bard, Esyllt, Susanna, Talhearn, and Dudod. The
Dewin followed closely—Elstar, Ardewin, Myrrdin, Neuad, and Cadell.
Last came the only two Druids in the party—Sabrina and Sinend.

Earlier that day the Dewin had Wind-Ridden to Cadair Idris,
reporting that Eiodel, Havgan's fortress, was all but emptied, but that
Havgan had increased the guard over Cadair Idris before he had taken his
Coranians and gone northeast to take up Gwydion's challenge.

The party, large as it was, moved quietly through the trees of
Coed Llachar, the Bright Forest, which stood to the west of Cadair
Idris, ending merely a quarter of a league away from the steps to the
mountain. It was Ywen Mis, and the days were short. Already long

shadows had begun to gather across the plain before the mountain. The dry, brown grass bowed and shook beneath the wind that drew swirling patterns through it. Overhead the sky was gray, and off to the east storm clouds gathered.

At last they reached the edge of the forest and Gwydion held up his hand, silently calling a halt. The guard around Cadair Idris was twenty strong, scattered along the eight broken steps before Drwys Idris, the great Doors of the deserted Hall of the High King.

"Elidyr," Gwydion breathed, "what news from the battle?"

The Master Bard smiled, but his smile had a twist to it. "My son Speaks to me that our Cerddorian are holding the attention of the Coranians. Havgan and his men are trapped at the crossroads, and we shoot them from the trees. He says that it won't last much longer. Achren and Angharad are difficult to control —their thirst for vengeance is not yet slaked. Trystan and Cai are ready to follow orders."

"Good. Tell Cynfar that it will not be much longer now."

Elidyr nodded, and his eyes took the far-off look of a Bard who is Wind-Speaking.

"Dewin and Druids, to the front," Gwydion ordered.

Elstar, Neuad, Cadell, Myrrdin, Rhiannon, Sabrina, and Sinend moved silently to stand beside Gwydion, awaiting the signal to begin.

Gwydion signaled again, and King Rhoram, Prince Geriant, Prince Lludd, King Owein, Prince Rhiwallon, and Queen Morrigan silently made their way to stand before Gwydion. Each one wore a sword at their belt and daggers thrust into their boots. They wore tunics and trousers of serviceable leather—Rhoram and Geriant in dark green, Lludd in sea green, Owein and Rhiwallon in red, and Morrigan in blue. The three rulers—Rhoram, Owein, and Morrigan, also wore the jeweled torques of their kingdoms around their necks. Gwydion nodded, and the six dropped to their bellies and began to make their way through the long grass. Taran's Wind, which was already rustling the long stalks, hid the sounds of their movements as they cautiously made their way closer to the steps of Cadair Idris.

Suddenly, Ygraine and Sanon, both dressed in leather tunics and trousers, leapt from the edge of the forest and dropped to their bellies, following the six who had gone before.

Gwydion began to step from the trees after them when Rhiannon's hand on his arm pulled him back.

"Let them go," she breathed.

"I did not say that they could do this," Gwydion said between clenched teeth.

"They need to do it," she said simply.

"Yes," Gwydion replied, after a moment's hesitation. "I suppose they do."

As the rest waited, the mountain stood still and silent on the plain. Tall and commanding, the mountain seemed to soar to the sky, unmindful of the doings of the humans at its base. The overcast, threatening sky lowered overhead.

Gwydion Wind-Rode, keeping an eye on the rulers and their heirs as they positioned themselves as close as they could to the steps. The guards had not spotted anything amiss yet, so cautious was the approach of the Kymric rulers, so well hidden were they in the long grass. At last, they were ready.

"Druids," Gwydion said to Sabrina and Sinend. "Now."

The two Druids, both dressed in their robes of green and brown, turned to face the steps where the guards stood. As they stared, a rumble was heard. Soft at first, it became louder and harsher. The steps of Cadair Idris began to shake. The guards cried out as they fell to their knees—half of them tumbling off the edge of the steps and falling heavily to the ground.

In that instant, the eight Kymri were upon them. Rhoram took the first one, slitting the man's throat. As he did, he gave a mighty cry. "For Anieron!" he shouted. King Owein took up the cry as he plunged his sword into the breast of another guard. "For Anierion!" Morrigan cried fiercely as she killed her man. Prince Lludd echoed the cry as his sword whistled through the air, sending a guard's head flying. Geriant and Rhiwallon, too, screamed Anieron's name as they killed their men.

But Ygraine, as she rose up out of the tall grass, sword in hand, called out the name of her dead husband as she spitted a guard with the blade. "Uthyr!" she screamed, and she laughed a terrible laugh as the guard's blood drenched her hands.

And Sanon—pale, quiet Sanon—laughed, too, as she called out the name of her dead lover and killed a guard. "Elphin!" she cried, her face flushed and fierce.

Rhoram, Owein, Morrigan, and Lludd each killed the four remaining guards who had fallen to the ground. The ten guards who had been standing on the plateau before the Doors remained. With a cry, they lunged down the broken steps, their weapons drawn.

"Dewin," Gwydion called. Elstar, Neuad, Cadell, Rhiannon, and Myrrdin closed their eyes and Wind-Rode, their shimmering, insubstantial forms coming to rest before the guards. The guards cried out in terror and pulled back in confusion. And that was all it took for the rulers and their heirs to finish the job.

Within moments all the guards were dead, and the way was clear. At Gwydion's signal, the rest of them stepped from the forest and made their way past the dead and dying bodies to stand before the steps leading to the Doors.

The steps, which, in the days of Lleu Lawrient, the last High King, had been white and shining, were dim and broken. Rockrose and white alyssum twined through the broken stone now streaked with Coranian blood. Gwydion, with Rhiannon, Arthur, and Gwen beside him, mounted the steps to stand before the Doors.

"Elstar?" Gwydion asked, as the rulers and their heirs took up their positions, with swords drawn, at the base of the stairs, allowing the Druids, Dewin, and Bards to follow Gwydion.

The Ardewin, whose eyes had had the unfocused look of one who was Wind-Riding, blinked. "No movement from Eiodel, Gwydion," she said.

Gwydion nodded and turned to face the Doors. Drwys Idris glowed dimly in the uncertain light. Jeweled patterns swirled on the surface of the doors, arranged in the pattern of the constellations of the god or goddess that each jeweled group represented. The constellation of Modron, the Mother and Y Pair, the Cauldron, was outlined in glittering emeralds. Taran, King of the Winds, and Y Cleddyf, the

Sword, sparkled with sapphires. Nantsolvelta, Queen of the Waters, and Y Llech, the Stone, glowed softly with pearls. Mabon, King of the Sun, and Y Honneit, the Spear, flashed in fiery opals.

The constellations of Cerrunnos, Master of the Hunt, and his mate, Cerridwen, Queen of the Wood, the Protectors of Kymru, shone bright topaz and dark amethyst. The rubies of Y Rhyfelwr, for Agrona and Camulos, the Warrior Twins, winked blood. The black onyx of Annwyn, Lord of Chaos, and the bloodstone of his consort, Aertan, the Weaver of Fate, shone dark and cool. Diamonds shimmered for Sirona of the Stars and dark garnet glimmered for Grannos, the Healer. In the center, the constellation of Arderydd, the High Eagle, the sign of the High King, outlined in emerald, pearls, sapphires, and opals, glowed fiercely.

A voice, light and musical, which seemed to come from everywhere and from nowhere, began to chant softly.

> *"Not of mother and father,*
> *When I was made*
> *Did my creator create me.*
> *To guard Cadair Idris*
> *For my shame.*
> *A traitoress to Kymru,*
> *And to my lord and king.*
> *The primroses and blossoms of the hill,*
> *The flowers of trees and shrubs,*
> *The flowers of nettles,*
> *All these I have forgotten.*
> *Cursed forever,*
> *I was enchanted by Bran*
> *And became prisoner*
> *Until the end of days."*

An empty silence followed the song. The wind moaned and, from far off, distant thunder sounded. And then the voice spoke again. "Who comes here to Drwys Idris? Who demands entry to Cadair Idris, the hall of the High King?"

"It is I, the Dreamer of Kymru, who asks for entrance," Gwydion replied.

"The halls are silent. The throne is empty. We await the coming of the High King. He shall be proved by the signs he brings. Have you the signs?"

"Bloudewedd, one-time High Queen of Kymru, we have."

"You have," the voice whispered through the ragged ends of worn hope.

"And soon you shall be freed," Gwydion said gently.

On the horizon, lightning flashed, as the storm from the east gathered strength. The wind moaned again, swooping down from the sky, tossing the long grass mercilessly. Light began to glow from the Doors, gathering strength, until the jeweled patterns flashed and glittered and shone forth, strong and sure.

"Have you Y Llech," the voice called, "the Stone of Water, Gwyr Yr Brenin, Seeker of the King?"

"I have," Rhiannon replied as she pulled the pack from her back and freed the Stone, laying it at the foot of the Doors. The pearls on the Stone glowed softly.

"And what, Rhiannon ur Hefeydd var Indeg," the Doors spoke, "have you learned in the seeking?"

Rhiannon was silent for a moment, for she knew the question was an important one. "To face pain. To stand before it and not run," she said at last.

"Then you are truly the one born to find the Stone of Nantsovelta. It is accepted. Have you Y Pair, the Cauldron of Earth, Buarth Y Greu, the Circle of Blood?"

"I have," Gwen said, pulling the Cauldron from the pack at her back and setting the golden, glowing bowl next to the Stone.

"And what, Gwenhwyfar ur Rhoram var Rhiannon, have you learned in the seeking?"

And Gwen answered boldly, for at last she knew the truth. "To forgive," she said, putting a hand out to her mother. "To love." Rhiannon grasped Gwen's hand, and the two stood together.

"Then you are truly the one born to find the Cauldron of

Modron. It is accepted. Have you Y Honneit, the Spear of Fire, Erias Yr Gwydd, Blaze of Knowledge?"

"I have," Gwydion said, stepping forward with the Spear in his hand. He placed the glowing opal-trimmed Spear next to the bowl.

"And what, Gwydion ap Awst var Celemon, have you learned in the seeking?"

"That fear, Bloudewedd, is the killer of the spirit. It must be acknowledged and faced with courage and truth."

"Then you are truly the one born to find the Spear of Mabon. Have you Y Cleddyf, the Sword of Air, Meirig Yr Llech, Guardian of the Stone?"

"I have it," Arthur said firmly, unbuckling the Sword from his belt and laying it before the Doors next to the Spear.

"And you, man who would be High King, what have you learned?"

"That no eagle can fly with broken wings."

"Then you are wise, indeed, Arthur ap Uthyr var Ygraine," the voice said softly. "And truly the one born to find the Sword of Taran. It is accepted."

On the horizon thunder rumbled, and lightning flashed. The wind keened, and the grass bent and rustled. Far overhead, from the west in the darkening sky came the sound of a hunting horn. "Cerrunnos and Cerridwen hunt tonight," the Doors said. "Tonight is Calan Gaef, and the Otherworld lays very close to this one. You have the signs. You may enter here."

And the Doors, closed for so many, many years, opened silently inward. Darkness pooled beyond the Doors. Gwydion turned to face the men and women who clustered around the steps.

"Drwys Idris bades us enter, my friends," Gwydion said. "And so we must."

Gwydion, Rhiannon, Gwen, and Arthur each took up their Treasures and, one by one, they all entered Cadair Idris, stepping into the darkness. When Myrrdin, the last one to enter, walked in, the mighty Doors swung closed. And Cadair Idris was once again silent, waiting. Only the sounds of the wind, and of thunder, could be heard on the plain outside the mountain.

TRYSTAN AND CAI withdrew slightly from the fight at the cross-roads, taking momentary refuge behind a small hill. Both men were splashed with blood, but they moved easily, for none of the blood was their own.

"Any time now," Cai panted, "and we can leave. Cynfar says that they are inside the mountain. He says that Gwydion has ordered us to withdraw."

"If we can get Angharad and Achren to pay attention to that order," Trystan retorted. "I believe that they are having too much fun."

"Well, they have had enough fun for one day. I, for one, will not risk the wrath of the High King if we do not withdraw. We were ordered not to sacrifice the lives of our people needlessly."

"But the Cerddorian have enjoyed it mightily, my friend," Trystan pointed out. "After all these years of striking in the shadows, it is a joy to fight in the open air again."

"I feel it in my bones, Trystan, that we should leave. The storm is almost upon us. And I do not think we would be wise to be here when Taran's Wind and Mabon's Fire come to the crossroads."

"We have done well," Trystan said. "Almost a third of Havgan's forces killed."

"And only a fraction of ours. I will have Llewelyn sound the retreat."

"As you will, friend Cai. As you will."

THE DOORS CLOSED behind them without a sound. The silence within the mountain was heavy and oppressive, and the darkness was complete.

"Gwydion," Myrrdin called. "Some light here, boyo."

But before Gwydion could even begin to call fire, there was indeed light. All at once, the hallway where they stood became as bright as day. The walls glittered with signs, spirals and circles etched on thin sheets of silver and gold. Jewels sparkled in the golden light.

A low exclamation of wonder came from their throats as the light dazzled them. The glow extended down the hallway, as, somehow, light after light from some unknown source flashed on. In the distance, a deeper golden light beckoned them on.

Owein shouldered his way to the front of the hallway, his sword drawn. He bowed to Arthur, then said, "I beg, High King, that you let me go first. There may be things within this mountain that would harm you. And that must not, for all the world, happen."

At his words, Queen Morrigan, Prince Lludd, and King Rhoram came to stand beside Owein, their swords also drawn. At Arthur's nod, the four rulers led the way down the long corridor, toward the golden light.

When they reached the end of the corridor, they stood on either side of a closed, golden door, their swords at the ready. Gwydion came to stand before the glowing door, and turned his back to it. He lifted his hands and spoke. "Behold Brenin Llys, the High King's hall, a sight that has not been seen outside of dreams for over two hundred years. Behold, Arthur ap Uthyr, your inheritance."

So saying, Gwydion turned and put his hands on the door. With the merest touch, the door opened, and the sight that met their eyes stunned them into silence. The hall of the High King was sheathed in gold, and golden light spilled out into the corridor. The walls, the pillars, the floor were covered with gold. Eight steps led to a raised dais. Each of the steps was covered with a precious stone—amethyst and topaz, emerald and pearl, ruby and onyx, opal and sapphire.

On the dais sat a golden throne. The armrests were molded in the shape of eagle's heads, their outstretched wings forming the high back of the throne. A huge torque made of twisted silver and gold rested on the throne. There were no jewels in the necklet—only four empty places to show where jewels had once rested, surrounding a figure eight studded with onyx.

A yew tree, the tree of Annwyn, Lord of Chaos, stood behind the throne. By its side stood a hazel tree for Aertan, Weaver of Fate. The yew branches, covered with tiny evergreen needles, bent over the golden chair, and the branches of the hazel that spread from its twisted trunk were covered with spiny, yellow flowers.

Within the center of the hall a golden fountain bubbled, the water somehow clean and fresh. A large, four-sided cup stood on the rim of the fountain. Eight alcoves were carved into the walls, four on each side of the throne.

"Here," Gwydion said, pointing to the alcove to the left of the door, "was the place where the rulers of Rheged would stand." The recess held a hawthorn tree, covered with tiny, white flowers. The banner on the wall behind the tree was of a rearing white horse with eyes of fiery opal on a field of red.

"Owein, Rhiwallon," Gwydion gestured, "this is your place."

The two men sheathed their swords and took their places within the niche. Sanon, whose rightful place should be with her father and brother, pushed determinedly through the others and came to stand, somewhat defiantly, next to Owein.

But King Rhoram smiled at his daughter and Owein. "Well, boyo, kiss her. What do you think she's waiting for?"

Gentle laughter greeted Rhoram's remark, and Owein, red-faced, softly kissed her.

The next alcove held a birch tree, and its shining white trunk glowed. The banner behind the tree was a white nightingale with sapphire eyes on a field of blue. "Elidyr, Talhearn, Esyllt, Susanna, and Dudod," Gwydion called. "This is the alcove of the Bards." They took their places in the alcove and Gwydion moved on.

The next alcove held a banner of a black wolf with emerald eyes on a field of green. The hazel tree's wavy, thin trunk was twined and bent.

"No need to tell us, Gwydion," Rhoram said briskly. "This is the one for Prydyn." Rhoram and his son, Geriant, took their places in the bay. At Rhoram's gesture, Rhodri came to stand with them.

The next alcove held a rowan tree with bright red berries hanging in clusters from its branches. The banner behind the tree was a black raven with opal eyes on a red field. "The Dreamers," Gwydion said, and Cariadas and Dinaswyn stepped into the niche.

Gwydion passed the throne and came to stand before the alcove on the far side. The banner was a rearing silver dragon with eyes of pearl on a field of sea green. The tree was ash, and the whitish-gray, smooth bark glowed. "The Dewin belong here," Gwydion said, and Elstar, Neuad, Cadell, and Myrrdin went to stand in the niche. Rhiannon began to follow, but Gwydion stopped her. "Your place is with me," he said.

In the next alcove the smooth bark and the shining dark green leaves proclaimed the tree to be an alder. The banner behind the tree was a brown hawk with sapphire eyes on a field of blue. "Gwynedd," Gwydion called, and Queen Morrigan and her mother, Ygraine, took their places.

An oak tree stood in the next alcove, and the banner behind the tree was a brown bull with emerald eyes on a field of green. "Druids," Gwydion said, and Sinend and Sabrina came to stand in the bay.

On the wall of the last alcove was a banner of a white swan with pearl eyes on a field of sea green. It held an aspen tree and the leaves shivered momentarily as Prince Lludd of Ederynion took his place in the niche.

At last, only Gwydion, Rhiannon, Gwen, and Arthur were left standing in the center of the hall, next to the fountain. At Gwydion's gesture, they each put down their Treasures next to the water.

Arthur, casting a look at the fountain, exclaimed, "There's something in there!" He reached out to put his hand in the water, and Gwydion leapt toward him, gripping Arthur's arm and shoving him back.

"No!" Gwydion cried.

"What is it?" Rhiannon called. "What's in the fountain?"

"A sword," Arthur spat. "Why can I not touch it? Do you want it for yourself?"

"The sword," Gwydion said, between clenched teeth, "belongs to the High King. Which you are not."

"Not yet," Arthur challenged. "But soon."

"We hope," Gwydion said shortly. "After we celebrate Calan Gaef, you will begin the Tynged Mawr. And if you pass the test, if you are still alive, you may take the sword in the fountain. It is called Caladfwlch, and it means Hard Gash. It was fashioned for High King Idris by Govannon, the First Archdruid of Kymru, he who fashioned the four Treasures. If you take the sword before the Tynged Mawr, it will kill you."

For a moment, Arthur said nothing as he gazed at the pool. Then he lifted his dark eyes to his uncle's face. "Once again, Dreamer, I have misjudged you."

"It happens often enough, Arthur," Gwydion said.

"You would do well, sometimes, to wonder why."

"I know why," Gwydion said softly. "But it is not always possible to change."

"You think not?" Arthur said, just as softly. "I think otherwise."

"You are young," Gwydion replied.

"And like not to be any older if I fail the Tynged Mawr. It could kill me."

"It could," Gwydion admitted. "But it is not likely. My heart says that you are the one. And always have been."

"But have you seen, in your dreams, beyond this moment?"

"No," Gwydion admitted. "I have not."

"Then let us celebrate Calan Gaef, and then to this Great Fate," Arthur said. "For I am anxious to see the end of this waiting."

"Very well." Gwydion went to the yew tree and stripped off a few branches, piling them at the bottom of the steps leading to the throne. He then went to the hazel tree and did the same, piling the branches next to the yew. From the bag at his belt he took a small jar of wine, a piece of bread, a container of salt, and a honeycomb wrapped in clean linen. Gwydion stood on the first step and began to speak.

"This is the Wheel of the Year before us," he called. "One flame for each of the eight festivals when we honor the Shining Ones." As he pointed to the top of the arch of each alcove, gouts of flame sprouted up, burning brightly. "Alban Nos, Calan Morynion, Alban Awyr, Calan Llachar, Alban Haf, Calan Olau, Alban Narth, and Calan Gaef, which we celebrate tonight. We gather to honor Annwyn, Lord of Chaos, and his consort, Aertan, Weaver of Fate, who together rule Gwlad Yr Haf, where the dead await their next turn on the Wheel."

"We honor you," the people gathered in Brenin Llys intoned.

"Let the Shining Ones be honored as they gather in Gwlad Yr Haf to witness the calling of the dead to a new life. Taran, King of the Winds; Modron, Great Mother of All. Mabon, King of Fire; Nantsovelta, Lady of the Waters. Cerridwen, Queen of the Wood; Cerrunnos, Master of the Hunt. Y Rhyfelwr, Agrona and Camulos, the Warrior Twins. Sirona, Lady of the Stars; Grannos, Star of the North and Healer."

"We honor the Shining Ones."

"We celebrate this time," Gwydion said, calling on Druid's Fire to ignite the branches of yew and hazel, "around the yew branch, which is the Tree of the Dead. It is the end of the old year, and the beginning of the new. Annwyn and Aertan now walk the Summer Land, and choose who shall be reborn. These spirits who are remembered will surely be sent back to us. Let us call out now the names of the dead whom we beg will be sent back for the next turn of the Wheel."

"Anierion, Master Bard," Dudod called.

"Uthyr, King of Gwynedd," Ygraine said.

"Olwen, Queen of Ederynion," said Lludd, the dead Queen's son.

"Urien, King of Rheged," Owein cried.

"Ellirri, Queen of Rheged," Prince Rhiwallon said.

"Elphin, Prince of Rheged," Sanon called out, her arm entwined firmly in Owein's as she did so.

"Cynan, Ardewin!" Myrrdin called, naming the Ardewin who had been killed by Havgan when the Coranians first came to Kymru.

"Now let us remember the names of the heroes and heroines of Kymru, that they may return to us if there is need," Gwydion called.

"Taliesin, Fifth Master Bard," Arthur cried. "Guardian of the Sword!"

"Mannawyddan, Fifth Ardewin," Rhiannon called. "Guardian of the Stone."

"Arywen, Fifth Archdruid," Gwen cried out. "Guardian of the Cauldron."

"Bran," Gwydion called. "Fifth Dreamer, Guardian of the

Spear!"

The names mounted up, tumbling one after another from the throats of the Kymri. Cariadas called out for Llyr, the first Dreamer, and Sinend for Govannon, the first Archdruid. Elidyr called for Math, the first Master Bard, and Elstar for Penduran, the first Ardewin. Then Rhoram cried for Pwyll, the second King of Prydyn, and Owein called for Rhys, the first Ruler of Rheged. Morrigan called for Gwynledyr, the first Queen of Gwynedd, and Lludd for Edern, first Ruler of Ederynion. Gwydion and Rhiannon called out Amatheon's name at the same time.

And then Arthur called out again. "I ask for the return of Idris, the first High King of Kymru!"

The others fell silent at this, as the name of Idris seemed to reverberate throughout the hall. The golden walls seemed to shiver, then to glow even brighter.

At last, Gwydion went on. "We invite the dead now to feast with us." He threw the bread into the fire. "I give you grain, for the element of fire. I give you wine, for the element of water," he continued as he tossed the contents of the small jar into the flames. Then he threw the salt into the fire. "I give you salt, for the element of earth. I give you honey, for the element of air," he said, as he unwrapped the honeycomb and threw it into the fire. "May this feast seem good to the dead, and may they be drawn back to us. Let us rejoice. One year is turned, and another begins."

And then they all began to sing:
"In Gwlad Yr Haf are fruit and fish and pools.
In Gwlad Yr Haf sweet are the cries of dappled deer.
In Gwlad Yr Haf are blue-eyed hawks, woods and flowers.
There await graceful, pearl-like women,
There await strong, diamond-hard men.
There the dead await
Aertan's nod,
Annwyn's touch,

To be born again."

Had this been another time, they would have begun the dancing and singing that the festival required. But Gwydion called for silence.

"Arthur," Gwydion said gravely. "It is time."

"I DON'T LIKE it," Havgan said. "One moment they're fighting us tooth and nail, and the next they vanish."

From the sky overhead thunder rumbled and lightning flashed. In the murky light, only Coranian warriors, nursing their wounds, could be seen at the crossroads.

"We heard them sound the retreat," Sigerric agreed. "But why?"

"And where was the Dreamer?" Havgan demanded. "He should have been here. It was his challenge."

"Perhaps," Sigerric said slowly, pulling the boar's helmet from his sweat-soaked head, "Gwydion was busy elsewhere. And this battle—"

"Was simply a distraction. To get us away from—"

"Cadair Idris," Sigerric finished.

"The Treasures," Havgan breathed, fire and hate in his amber eyes. "They have found them. And gone to Cadair Idris. And the Doors will let them in." Havgan shouted for his horse, and as he mounted, he called out to Sigerric. "I will see them die this day. I swear it!"

"How?" Sigerric called as he mounted his own horse. "The mountain will never let you in!" But Havgan was already gone.

"It will never let you in," Sigerric whispered, as he followed Havgan from the field of battle. "Never."

GWYDION REACHED FOR the cup that stood on the rim of the fountain. It was a large, four-sided cup, fashioned of gold. Each side contained the sign etched in jewels for the four gods and goddesses of the elements. One side was covered in pearls, for Nantsovelta of the Waters; one in sapphires, for Taran of the Air. One side glittered with emeralds, for Modron of the Earth; and the last with opals, for Mabon of Fire. Gwydion dipped the cup into the fountain, filling it with the sweet, clear water. He opened the pouch on his belt and drew out the leaves of Penduran's Rose that he had collected months ago in Gwynedd. He crushed the leaves between his palms and put them in the cup.

And then he handed the cup to Arthur. "When you are ready, drink. Penduran's Rose will prepare your mind to receive the power from the Treasures."

Arthur took the cup and stared into its depths for a moment. He glanced at the others who waited—the rulers and the Y Dawnus in their alcoves, here to witness this event. He looked at Gwen, and she smiled tremulously at him. He looked at Rhiannon, and her green eyes were calm. He looked at his mother and sister as they stood in the alcove and saw their love for him in their faces. He looked at Myrrdin, and he saw the rightness, the sureness of it all in his teacher's eyes.

Lastly, he looked at Gwydion, into the gray eyes of the man he had hated for most of his life, at the man whose plans and schemes had brought him here, ready to risk his life on this throw. And Arthur did not, at this last, resent it. He was neither angry nor afraid. He was beyond all that now. Instead, he accepted what must be, what had been marked for him since the day of his birth.

And so he drank.

He set the cup down on the rim of the fountain. At first, he felt no different. But then something began to happen. He felt his senses sharpening. His sight became unnaturally clear, his hearing sharper. His sense of smell heightened, and he could taste the Rose as it lingered at the back of his throat. He ran his fingers over his tunic, and marveled at the feel of it.

Gwydion nodded toward the Treasures gathered before the throne. "You know what to do, Arthur," Gwydion said.

"You have not told me," Arthur replied dreamily.

"You do not need to be told. It is in you, this knowledge. Do as Idris did, as Macsen did, as Lleu Lawrient did. Do as you were born to do."

Gwydion was right. He did know what to do. As if in a dream, Arthur picked up the Sword of Taran and guided its tip into an almost invisible slit within one of the silvery junctions on the Stone. The Sword slipped into the Stone with an audible click, and both Stone and Sword began to hum. The sound was low pitched, and then it began to build. The Sword and the Stone began to glow. Arthur reached for the Cauldron and held it in his left hand. He placed his right hand into the bowl, and felt a tiny prick on his finger, as he had somehow known he would. The bowl shimmered, and began to dance in his hand. When the Cauldron stopped spinning, he picked up the Spear. With the Cauldron in his left hand, and the Spear of Fire in his right, he mounted the Stone, standing to the right of the upright Sword.

The Treasures pulsed and glittered. The humming grew louder. Those watching were bathed in the strange light of the sapphires, the emeralds, the pearls, and the opals. The figure eight, sign of Annwyn, Lord of Chaos, etched in onyx on all four Treasures, glowed darkly, a glittering shadow.

IN HIS MIND'S eye, Arthur saw the pure white stag bound ahead of him, shooting across the plain of Gwytheryn.

Cadair Idris rose at Arthur's back as he leapt after the stag. He skimmed through the long, green grass. Wildflowers dotted the plain, shimmering in the golden light.

Arthur ran, the earth firm and fruitful beneath his feet. The wind whistled past his ears. The golden sun warmed him as, laughing, he jumped across a sparkling stream.

He followed the stag as it neared the lake of Llyn Mwygil. The stag leapt high, impossibly high, in the air and sailed across the water, landing lightly on the island of Afalon, the holy place of Annwyn and Aertan.

Determined to follow the stag, Arthur leapt through the clean, cool air, soaring across Llyn Mwygil and landing lightly on the island.

The isle was quiet. The stag had disappeared. Emerald green trees flashed in the golden light. The waters sparkled.

He could no longer hear the stag. Indeed, the golden afternoon was now completely silent.

And then the agony took him.

In Cadair Idris, Arthur stood unmoving, his dark eyes wide, his face without expression. Ygraine took a step toward him, then stopped. Gwen stood stiffly, her hands clenched into fists with the effort not to reach out for him. Gwydion reached out and took Rhiannon's hand.

The strange light intensified. The Treasures throbbed with a rhythm that spoke of another time and place far beyond Cadair Idris, in another world.

Just at the edge of vision, four figures suddenly appeared.

"Oh, Gwydion, they have come," Rhiannon whispered as she saw them.

The Guardians of the Treasures had, indeed, come to Cadair Idris to witness the Tynged Mawr.

Mannawyddan, the Ardewin, watched calmly with his mild blue eyes. Arywen, the Archdruid, watched with hazel cat eyes, her long black hair like a shadow. Taliesin, the Master Bard, his green eyes sad and wise, watched unmoving. And Bran, the Dreamer, the man who had set these events in motion with the death of his High King so long ago, watched with his gray eyes blazing.

Suddenly, from nowhere, from everywhere, a bright, white light cut through the air, pinning Arthur where he stood. Within that light, Arthur's body began to shake, and he cried out in agony.

When the pain came, Arthur stiffened and cried out. His cry cut through the still air over the island, startling a flock of crows that suddenly took wing. They wheeled overhead, echoing Arthur's cry.

The pain twisted through his guts, and he fell to his knees, clutching his belly. He threw his head back to scream again, and it was then that he saw them.

The Shining Ones had come, bringing darkness with them.

IN CADAIR IDRIS, Gwydion said softly, with tears in his silvery eyes, "Oh, gods, I did not know it would be like this."

Sweat and tears poured down Arthur's face. His features were twisted in pain. Again, he cried out.

"No!" screamed Ygraine. "Stop! It's killing him!" She took a few running steps toward her son, but Morrigan held her mother back.

"Leave him be!" Morrigan cried. "Let him finish!"

"Get him out of there!" Gwen called out. "Gwydion, get him out!"

And Gwydion took a step forward, but Rhiannon held him back.

"Wait!" she called. "Don't touch him. Wait!"

ANNWYN, LORD OF Chaos, was cloaked in writhing black, as though the shadows themselves had come to veil him. His hands were stained with blood. His dead-white face was patterned with spirals and circles of tiny onyx beads. His dark eyes sparkled wildly. He held a yew branch in his red hands.

Aertan, Weaver of Fate, was clothed in misty white. Her eyes were bloodstone—green chalcedony flecked with red jasper. Her thin hands were crisscrossed with a dizzying array of threads. Her fingers flashed in and out among the threads so quickly he could not follow her movements. But from her hands a tapestry was taking shape, trailing from her fingers and spilling to the ground behind her. Arthur caught a glimpse of horsemen and battles, of sweet lovers and long summer days, of bloodstains and grinning skulls.

"Child of Idris, child of Macsen, child of Lleu Silver-Hand," Aertan called. "You have come to us at last."

"What is happening?" Arthur gasped, clutching his head as a spike of hot pain shot through his skull.

"It is the Tynged Mawr," the Lord of Chaos said, his voice like the screams of the dying. "It is the magic of the High Kings. It is unleashed inside you. It courses through your veins. It seeks to know you, to test you. To see if you are worthy."

"The pain," Arthur gasped. "I cannot—"

"You must."

"Lord of Chaos," Arthur whispered through his agony, "why do you seek to torment me?"

"Ah. Arthur ap Uthyr var Ygraine, how little you have listened to your teachers. Do you think me evil?"

"There is blood on your hands."

"And that matters? Ah, but you are young. How but by dying do men reach the Land of Summer? How but by suffering is wisdom gained?"

"You have not understood, Arthur ap Uthyr," Aertan said, bright threads flowing through her fingers and flashing in the sun. "My Lord's mark is on the Treasures. It is he who grants you the gifts of the High Kings. It is he who stands with you to rid Kymru of the enemy."

"Your torments, Arthur, are of your own making," Annwyn said softly. "It is made of those times you thought to run. It is fashioned of those times you have turned away. It is shaped by those times you had thought to be less than you were meant to be."

"Your pain, Penerydd, is of your own making," Aertan said gently.

Arthur gasped, again clutching his belly. "Please make it stop. Make an end to it."

"Ah, young one, that we will not do," Aertan said. "For a destiny must be allowed to unfold. As yours does now."

"Please," Arthur begged, tears streaming from his eyes, sweat pouring from him. "Please."

And then he saw the truth in their strange, glittering eyes as they stood before him, silent and still. They would not help him because they could not. The pain was his. He alone had fashioned it in his refusals to embrace his destiny, in his insistence on his own rights, his own freedom.

And so, at last, he relinquished his own desires and instead embraced his place on the Wheel. He rose, ignoring the pain, and faced Annwyn and Aertan. He bowed to them and raised his face to the sky, spreading his arms in surrender.

"The struggle is finished," he whispered through his pain. "It is done. I will be what I was born to be."

IN THE HALL of the High Kings, the white light began to dim, and the throbbing began to fade. Slowly the light died; the hum quieted. And Arthur still stood on the Stone, the Spear and the Cauldron in his hands, the Sword by his side. His shaking had stopped, and he made no sound.

Slowly he stepped down from the Stone. Slowly he set the Cauldron and the Spear on the floor. Slowly he grasped the Sword and pulled it from the Stone, then set the Sword down.

Arthur turned to Rhiannon, Gwydion, and Gwen, his face still wet with sweat and tears, his dark eyes filled with pain and wonder. "Give me the rings," he said, his voice hollow.

Without comment, the three took the rings off their fingers and handed them over. Arthur took the rings, and stripped off his own ring. He turned to the throne, then stopped, facing the shades of the Great Ones of Lleu Silver-Hand who still watched. "So now will I return to the High King's Torque the jewels taken from it by you four long ago."

Arthur strode to the throne and lifted the Torque. One by one, he plucked the jewels from the rings, setting them within the Torque. Then he laid the Torque down, and went back to the fountain. He plunged his hands into the clear water, and grasped the sword that lay at the bottom. When he pulled the sword out, it was dry and gleaming in the golden light. The hilt, made of silver and gold, was an eagle's head with eyes of bloodstone and wings studded with onyx. The scabbard was etched with the sign for each of the four gods and goddess of the elements—the sign for Modron, the Great Mother, in emerald; for Nantsovelta, Lady of the Waters, in pearl; the sign for Taran of the Winds in sapphire; and the sign for Mabon of the Sun in opal.

Arthur hooked the scabbard to his belt, then returned to stand before the throne. He held the Torque in his hands, and said to the people gathered there, "I have survived the Tynged Mawr, and the powers of a High King are now mine. That which was once closed in me is now opened. I can harness the power of the Druids, and call fire and fog to confound the enemy. I can direct the power of the Dewin, scouting out the enemy across all of Kymru at a moment. I can bring together the power of the Bards, and speak mind to mind on the wind. I am your High King. And I stand in Cadair Idris, my home, at the heart of my country. I will lead you in this fight to free our country from the enemy that crushes us beneath their heel.

"My first command is for the Great Ones to depart," Arthur went on, turning to face the four men and women from the past, who had guarded the Treasures for so long, for love of the last High King of Kymru. "Go now," he said softly, "to your rest. You have served your High King well. May I have friends as loyal as you."

And the shade of Bran, his gray eyes at rest and calm at last, answered, "You have, Arthur ap Uthyr var Ygraine."

"So I have," Arthur agreed with a smile. "Go now."

And the four shades, smiling and at peace at last, faded away.

Then Gwydion began to sing the song of Anieron. And the others took up the song, until they were all singing, as Arthur stood before the throne, the High King's Torque in his hands.

"Shall there not be a song of freedom
Before the dawn of the fair day?
Shall this not be the fair day of freedom?"

ARTHUR RAISED HIS Torque, and clasped it around his neck. And as he did, from some unknown source, all the lights within the mountain of Cadair Idris began to glow.

HAVGAN AND SIGERRIC, weary from battle, neared Cadair Idris. Overhead, the storm had begun to abate. A full moon rode the sky. The mountain was in their sight, when they heard the fierce, undaunted cry of an eagle, and the faint shimmering of hunting horns in the sky.

"Their Wild Hunt," Sigerric said quietly. "It rides."

"It is nothing," Havgan replied shortly. "Their gods cannot

stand against our God."

As they neared the silent mountain, they saw, by the light of the moon, the dead guards, scattered on the broken steps.

"They have, indeed, been here," Sigerric said. "And gone into the mountain. Drwys Idris has opened for them."

Havgan did not answer. He was staring up at the Doors, which stood closed and implacable, as they had always been for him. Again, they heard an eagle's cry and the faint sound of hunting horns from overhead.

Then suddenly, shockingly, the Doors lit up. The jewels scattered there began to glow and shimmer. A low hum filled the night sky, and the once dark and silent mountain shimmered in the night, empty and forsaken no longer.

And at the sight, Havgan threw back his head and cried out in rage to the uncaring sky.

Epilogue

Cadair Idris and Eiodel
Gwytheryn, Kymru
Ywen Mis, 500

Gwaithdydd, Disglair Wythnos—night

Arthur ap Uthyr var Ygraine sat in Taran's Tower, the topmost level of Cadair Idris. In the past three nights since he had survived the Tynged Mawr, Arthur had come to this chamber to be alone, to plan for the freedom of his country, to come to terms with his own imprisonment.

For never again would he be simply Arthur, a shepherd of Dinas Emrys. Never again would he spend his days in the clean, clear air of the mountains of Gwynedd, guarding his sheep against danger, eating his simple meals perched on a rock, watching hawks wheel high overhead on the wings of the wind.

Never again. For he was High King of Kymru now, and any freedom he had once had was gone, never to return. But he thought that he could live with that. If that were the price of freedom for the Kymri, then he would pay it. He had not always been able to say that. But now he thought he could.

He remembered what Gwydion had told him of the dream his uncle had the day before Arthur was born. How Cerrunnos and Cerridwen, the Horned God and the White Lady, who led the Wild Hunt across the skies, had taken from Gwydion a young eagle, and had chained him with links of silver and gold. How they had said that it was not for the eagle to be free, but rather for him to take his place on the Wheel.

He remembered the look in his mother's eyes when she had made Neuad tell Arthur of his father's last battle. He remembered the pinched look on his sister's face when Morrigan spoke of Uthyr. He remembered Dudod's despair when he had whispered farewell to his brother the night Anieron, Master Bard, had died. He remembered Anieron's song, heard the length and breadth of Kymru that night, and the call to freedom.

And he knew that the price of freedom for Kymru was only his happiness. And that did not matter. It never had, though he had not always known that.

For now Cadair Idris was alive again. The mountain, deserted for so long, was once again home to the High King of Kymru. It astonished him, this mountain. Built by High King Idris over four hundred years ago, it was a mystery. For the air was still clean and fresh, somehow circulating after all these years. More wondrous still, all over the mountain there were lights that mysteriously went on and off when one passed a hand over a kind of metal plate set in each chamber, except for Brenin Llys, the hall of the High King. The glowing, golden lights, which shone from some unknown source, never went off in that room.

Perhaps the most astonishing thing of all had been how the Stewards of Cadair Idris had simply entered the throne room that night. An old man had introduced himself as Rhufon ap Casnar, a descendent of Illtydd, the Steward of Lleu Silver-Hand. He had brought with him his entire family, some fifty or so men and women. Just how they had entered, Arthur was still not entirely sure. They had brought with them foodstuffs, as well as other supplies, and had set to work ensuring that the rooms throughout the mountain were habitable. It had been Rhufon who had given Arthur his first tour.

There were eight levels within the mountain, and each level was perfectly round, the level below always slightly larger than the level above it. The first level, the level of Cerrunnos, contained Brenin

Llys and the corridor that led to it from the Doors.

The second level, the level of Cerridwen, was a huge banqueting hall, surrounded by kitchens and storerooms. The walls of the hall were hung with the banners of the four kingdoms—the white horse of Rheged, the black wolf of Prydyn, the silver swan of Ederynion, and the brown hawk of Gwynedd. There were banners, too, of the four Great Ones—a silver dragon for the Ardewin, a blue nightingale for the Master Bard, a brown bull for the Archdruid, and a black raven for the Dreamer. Over the main table hung the banner of the High King. It was an eagle outlined in dark onyx, with sapphire eyes, wings of pearl, a beak of fiery opals, and emerald wing tips. Just looking at the banner—his banner—as it had shimmered in the sudden, golden light had made him shiver.

The third level, the level of Aertan and Annwyn, was a garden, and this was truly a marvel, for the trees, the shrubs, the flowers that had been planted there had not died, but had remained as fresh as they day they had been planted. A bubbling fountain sprang in the middle of the chamber. Seven small chapels outlined the indoor garden, each chapel marked with the sign for the god or goddess to which it was dedicated—Mabon of the Sun; Taran of the Winds; Y Rhyfelwyr, the Warrior Twins; Aertan, the Weaver, and Annwyn, Lord of Chaos; Cerridwen and Cerrunnos, the Protectors of Kymru; Modron, the Great Mother; and Nantsovelta, Lady of the Waters.

In the garden were small tables set with musical instruments and board games. A particularly fine chess set had caught his eye there. The pieces were made of gold and silver. And he was quite sure that the face carved for the High King was his own. And the face of the High Queen? Arthur had thought he had recognized her. But he had said nothing to the others, and, if any one of them thought the features familiar, they did not say.

The fourth level, belonging to Y Rhyfelwyr, the Warrior Twins, contained apartments for the High King's warriors, his teulu, as well as training rooms and an armory. The armory had, indeed, yielded some fine swords, daggers, and spears that he had given to the rulers of the four kingdoms before they left.

The fifth level, the level of Modron, was made up of the High King and High Queen's apartments. A formal reception room stood in the middle of this level, and, once again, the eagle banner that stood above a high-backed chair canopied in purple and gold had confronted him. A huge, round table stood in the center of the room.

The sixth level, the level of Mabon, contained apartments for important visitors, each apartment decorated with the colors of those for whom it was reserved—the rulers of the four kingdoms, as well as the Ardewin, the Dreamer, the Master Bard, and the Archdruid.

The seventh level, the level of Nantsovelta, was made up of further apartments for the High King's officials, servants, and other guests. A glorious fountain stood in the center room, and the iridescent walls were sheathed in mother-of-pearl.

The chamber where he now stood, the eighth level, the level of Taran, was small in comparison to the other levels. It stood at the peak of the mountain, and the smooth walls, covered in silver, were incised with the constellations that wheeled over Kymru. One section showed the spring sky, and another the summer sky. One was for the autumn sky, and the last for winter. The constellations were perfectly executed, and the stars that belonged to each one were represented by twinkling jewels.

But that was not the wonder of Taran's chamber. For the roof was made of a glasslike substance, and the starry night sky streamed in. Gwydion said that there was a roof just like it at Caer Dathyl, set in the ceiling of Ystafell Yr Arymes, the Chamber of Dreams. And as Gwydion had said that, Arthur caught the longing in his uncle's voice for the Dreamer's home. Once he might have taunted Gwydion with that loss. But such things were past. He had no time for them now.

He was grateful to be alone with his thoughts. The others were in the garden room, resting for a few moments, waiting for the next move in this game. There were not many here now; it was nothing like it had no doubt been in the days of the High Kings. Not including the Stewards, only eleven people were still here. There were Gwydion and Rhiannon and Gwen, of course. There were Cariadas,

Gwydion's daughter, and Dinaswyn, Gwydion's aunt.

The two Druids, Sinend and Sabrina, had also stayed. Sabrina had not wanted to stay, had wanted to follow Trystan back to Coed Coch. But Arthur had insisted that she stay because he needed the Druids. He needed Sinend and Sabrina and even Gwen's raw and untrained talent. He needed to learn to harness the High King's power, and he could not master it without Druids to help him.

Rhodri, the one-time King of Gwynedd, along with Dudod the Bard, had also stayed. Arthur knew that soon Rhodri would be on his way to Gwynedd to deal with his traitorous son. But Arthur had told the old man that the time was not yet. He wanted nothing to upset the precarious balance until he had learned his new powers. And Rhodri, too, had obeyed without protest.

The Ardewin, Elstar, and her husband, Elidyr, Master Bard, had also stayed at Arthur's orders. With Rhiannon and Elstar for the Dewin, and Elidyr and Dudod for the Bards, he could practice mastering that part of the powers. So the Ardewin and the Master Bard had stayed, making Cadair Idris their headquarters. The web of Bards and Dewin that spanned Kymru was back into place, and there was little information that Arthur did not know.

The four rulers had begun their journey to return to their head-quarters—Rhoram to Haford Bryn in Prydyn, Owein to Coed Coch in Rheged, Lludd to Coed Ddu in Ederynion, and Morrigan to the new place at Cemais in Gwynedd. He had not wanted to say good-bye to Morrigan, or to his mother. But he had understood, and so had they, that they needed to return to Gwynedd with their warriors and prepare for the final battle.

He knew there would be one. And he even thought he knew, now, when it would be—almost six months from now, on Calan Llachar. It was his name day, and he would be eighteen years old. But the fact it was the day of his birth was not the reason he knew that would be the day when Kymru made its bid for freedom. It was because, this year, on Calan Llachar, there would be a total eclipse of the sun, as there was on the day of his birth. The eighteen-year cycle would come to a close then, and he felt deep inside, that this would, indeed, be the day.

He sat cross-legged on the floor of Taran's chamber, the High King's sword, Caladfwlch, resting on his thighs. He gazed above him at the night sky. He saw the five constellations that always rode the sky—Math, named after the first Master Bard, and Llyr, named after the first Dreamer. He saw Draig, the Dragon. He saw Beli, named for the doomed husband of Don. He saw Llys Don, the Court of Don, named after the woman who had been creator of Llyr and mother of Penduran, the one who had made the four Treasures.

And then he gazed at the constellations that appeared at this time of year. Mabon, for the God of the Sun. Cerrunnos, for the Master of the Hunt. March, the Horse. Cerridwen, the Lady of the Wood. Nantsovelta of the Waters. Y Honneit, the Spear of Fire. Abwyd, the Worm. And Aertan, the Weaver of Fate.

And what, he wondered, was Aertan weaving for him this night? What would his fate be? Would he succeed in freeing Kymru, or would he die? The answer to this, no one knew. Not even the Dreamer. For Gwydion had seen nothing in his dreams beyond Arthur coming to Cadair Idris for the Tynged Mawr.

As if thoughts of Gwydion had aroused the Dreamer, Arthur's uncle suddenly stood at the open door of the chamber.

"Come in, uncle," Arthur said.

Gwydion sat cross-legged on the floor by Arthur, but did not speak. For a time the two men sat there, gazing up at the sky. At last, Gwydion spoke. "You hold Caladfwlch well."

"The sword you paid so dearly to find. The sword for which you lost your brother."

"Amatheon would be so pleased, if he were here," Gwydion said quietly.

"I wish I had known him."

"You would have liked him. Few did not. If you are rested now from the test," Gwydion went on, "you must begin."

"I have begun, uncle," Arthur said quietly, as he laid a hand to his chest. "It is in here, and it is ready."

"Good. The Dewin, the Bards, the Druids are ready to begin to work with you."

"And the Dreamers?"

Gwydion's brow rose. "What could you hope to get from the Dreamers? The others, I understand. With the augmented power of the others, you could do mighty things. But the Dreamers?"

"The Dreamers are the Walkers-Between-the-Worlds, uncle," Arthur pointed out. "And that is a path I may need to take."

"Be careful," Gwydion warned. "It is dangerous even for born Dreamers to walk near to the Otherworld. It would, perhaps, be even more dangerous for you to be with us when we do."

"But I shall. When the time is ripe. And we will call for those who can help us."

"What, then, are your plans, my King?" Gwydion asked quietly, his gray eyes steady.

"They are these," Arthur said, ticking the points off on his fingers. "To kill Sledda, the Arch-wyrce-jaga, for his part in Anieron's death. To rescue the Master Smiths from Caer Siddi and bring them here to Cadair Idris to forge weapons of war. To rescue Queen Elen of Ederynion and Queen Enid of Rheged. To bring down the Archdruid and take his Druids back into the fold. To rescue the captive Y Dawnus from Afalon. And, finally, to throw the Coranians back into the sea."

Gwydion's mouth twitched, but his eyes remained grave. "Those are a great many tasks to accomplish, Arthur."

"What else is a High King for?"

A LEAGUE AWAY, Havgan gazed at the stars from the heights of Eiodel. At home, in Corania, they would have different names than here, but they were the same. There was Wuotan, the God of Magic. And Fal, the god of Light. Holda, the goddess of Water, and Nerthus, the Mother. Draen, the Dragon, and Mearth, the Horse. Donar, the god of Thunder, and Sif, the goddess of Plenty. Flan, the Arrow, and Skeggox, the Axe.

Suddenly, for the first time since he had come to Kymru, Havgan longed for his country, for Corania. Longed to be away from this strange land where he somehow felt more at home.

Most of all, he longed to see the last of Cadair Idris, the mountain that had defied him still. It shone now across the dark meadow, glowing with a faint, golden light, a light, which, Arianrod said, meant that the High King had returned.

Things that had once been under his control were under his control no longer. The broken network of Y Dawnus had been repaired—the latest reports of caravans attacked, temples burned, and wyrce-jaga slain were enough to tell him that. Three days ago, a third of his troops had been killed at the crossroads. The testing tool they had captured many months ago had found no fresh Y Dawnus. The ones he had captured suffered terribly on the nearby island of Afalon, but there were not enough of them to satisfy him. His cold, beautiful wife was plotting against him, and his General, once his friend, always looked at him with pity in his brown eyes. The Treasures, so eagerly sought for and followed across Kymru, had eluded him and Cadair Idris had refused to open for him.

And yet, in spite of those things, Havgan would not give up. He would not go home—because he no longer knew where home was. Was it Corania, the land in which he had grown up, the land that had always been strange to him? Or was it Kymru, the land of the witches, the land he had come to conquer and that had somehow, perhaps, conquered him?

The faint scent of honeysuckle came to his nostrils. She had come to him, as he had known she would. She came to stand by him on the battlements, and, for a while, did not speak. When at last she did, her words rocked him.

"I carry your child, *cariad*," Arianrod said softly.

Cariad. He knew that Kymric word. It meant beloved. That she should use that word to him told him much of her. Told him, too, much of himself. For he had longed for that word from her. Though he had not known it until now. He reached for her, enfolding her in his strong arms. She rested her head on his heart.

"*Cariad*," he said to her, at last breaking the silence. "Wife of my heart."

She was quiet for a time, and he felt a dampness on his breast. She was crying. He let her go and framed her face with his hands, gently forcing her to look up at him. Her amber eyes—so very, very like his own—were swimming in tears. But she was smiling.

"It will be a boy, Havgan. A son," she said.

"You know this?"

"I am Dewin," she said simply. "I know."

"We will call him Sigefrith, after Sigerric's father, my first Lord."

She shook her head. Her honey-blond hair—so like his own—stirred beneath his strong hands. "In Kymru, the task of naming is given to the mother."

He smiled. Once her opposition—anyone's opposition—would have enraged him. But no more. For she was the woman he loved as he had never loved any other woman before. She was the Woman-on-the-Rocks, come to him at last, facing him, gifting him with her heart. She would never leave him. And he would cling to her for the rest of his life.

"What will be his name, then?" he asked smiling.

"We will call him Medrawd. It means 'skillful.'"

"And in my tongue, what will that be?"

"Mordred," she replied.

Glossary

Addiendydd: sixth day of the week

aderyn: birds

aethnen: aspen tree; sacred to Ederynion

alarch: swan; the symbol of the royal house of Ederynion

alban: light; any one of the four solar festivals

Alban Awyr: festival honoring Taran; Spring Equinox

Alban Haf: festival honoring Modron; Summer Solstice

Alban Nerth: festival honoring Agrona and Camulos; Autumnal Equinox

Alban Nos: festival honoring Sirona and Grannos; the Winter Solstice

ap: son of

ar: high

Archdruid: leader of the Druids, must be a descendent of Llyr

Arderydd: high eagle; symbol of the High Kings

Ardewin: leader of the Dewin, must be a descendent of Llyr *arymes*: prophecy

Awenyddion: dreamer (see Dreamer)

awyr: air

bach: boy

Bard: a telepath; they are musicians, poets, and arbiters of the law in matters of

inheritance, marriage, and divorce; Bards can Far-Sense and Wind-Speak; they

revere the god Taran, King of the Winds

bedwen: birch tree; sacred to the Bards

Bedwen Mis: birch month; roughly corresponds to March

blaid: wolf; the symbol of the royal house of Prydyn

bran: raven; the symbol of the Dreamers

Brenin: high or noble one; the High King; acts as an amplifier for the Y Dawnus

buarth: circle

cad: battle

cadair: chair (of state)

caer: fortress

calan: first day; any one of the four fire festivals

Calan Gaef: festival honoring Annwyn and Aertan

Calan Llachar: festival honoring Cerridwen and Cerrunnos

Calan Morynion: festival honoring Nantsovelta

Calan Olau: festival honoring Mabon

cantref: a large division of land for administrative purposes; two to three commotes make up a cantref; a cantref is ruled by a Lord or Lady

canu: song

cariad: beloved

celynnen: holly

Celynnen Mis: holly month; roughly corresponds to late May/early June

cenedl: clan

cerdinen: rowan tree; sacred to the Dreamers

Cerdinen Mis: rowan month; roughly corresponds to July

Cerdorrian: sons of Cerridwen; the hidden organization of warriors and Y Dawnus working to drive the Coranians out of Kymru

cleddyf: sword

collen: hazel tree; sacred to Prydyn

Collen Mis: hazel month; roughly corresponds to October

commote: a small division of land for administrative purposes; two or three commotes make up a cantref; a commote is ruled by a Gwarda

coed: forest, wood

cynyddu: increase; the time when the moon is waxing

da: father

dan: fire

derwen: oak tree; sacred to the Druids

Derwen Mis: oak month; roughly corresponds to December

Dewin: a clairvoyant; they are physicians; they can Life-Read and Wind-Ride; they revere

the goddess Nantsovelta, Lady of the Moon

disglair: bright; the time when the moon is full

draig: dragon; the symbol of the Dewin

draenenwen: hawthorn tree; sacred to Rheged

Draenenwen Mis: hawthorn month; roughly corresponds to late June/ early July

Dreamer: a descendent of Llyr who has precognitive abilities; the Dreamer can Dream-

Speak and Time-Walk; the Dreamer also has the other three gifts— telepathy,

clairvoyance, and psychokinesis; there is only one Dreamer in a generation; they

revere the god Mabon, King of Fire

Dream-Speaking: precognitive dreams; one of the Dreamer's gifts

Druid: a psychokinetic; they are astronomers, scientists, and lead all festivals; they can

Shape-Move, Fire-Weave, and, in partnership with the High King, Storm-Bring;

they revere the goddess Modron, the Great Mother of All

drwys: doors

dwfr: water

dwyvach-breichled: goddess-bracelet; bracelet made of oak used by Druids

eiddew: ivy

Eiddew Mis: ivy month; roughly corresponds to April

enaid-dal: soul-catcher; lead collars that prevent Y Dawnus from using their gifts

eos: nightingale; the symbol of the Bards

erias: fire

erydd: eagle

Far-Sensing: the telepathic ability to communicate with animals

ffynidwydden: fir tree; sacred to the High Kings

Fire-Weaving: the psychokinetic ability to light fires

gaef: winter

galanas: blood price

galor: mourning, sorrow

goddeau: trees

gorsedd: a gathering (of Bards)

greu: blood

Gwaithdydd: third day of the week

gwarchan: incantation

Gwarda: ruler of a commote

gwernan: alder tree; sacred to Gwynedd

Gwernan Mis: alder month; roughly corresponds to late April/early

May

gwinydden: vine

Gwinydden: vine month; roughly corresponds to August

Gwlad Yr Haf: the Land of Summer; the Otherworld

gwydd: knowledge

gwyn: white

gwynt: wind

Gwyntdydd: fifth day of the week

gwyr: seeker

haf: summer

hebog: hawk; the symbol of the royal house of Gwynedd

helygen: willow

Helygen Mis: willow month; roughly corresponds to January

honneit: spear

Life-Reading: the clairvoyant ability to lay hands on a patient and determine the nature of their ailment

llachar: bright

llech: stone

lleihau: to diminish; the time when the moon is waning

lleu: lion

Llundydd: second day of the week

llyfr: book

llyn: lake

llys: court

Lord/Lady: ruler of a cantref

mam: mother

march: horse; the symbol of the royal house of Rheged

Master Bard: leader of the Bards, must be a descendent of Llyr

Meirgdydd: fourth day of the week

meirig: guardian

Meriwdydd: seventh day of the week

mis: month

morynion: maiden

mwg-breudduyd: smoke-dream; a method Dreamers can use to induce dreams

mynydd: mountain

mynyddoedd: mountains

naid: leap

nemed: shrine, a sacred grove

nerth: strength

neuadd: hall

niam-lann: a jeweled metallic headpiece, worn by ladies of rank

nos: night

ogaf: cave

olau: fair

onnen: ash tree; sacred to the Dewin

Onnen Mis: ash month; roughly corresponds to February

pair: cauldron

pen: head of

Plentyn Prawf: child test; the testing of children, performed by the

Bards, to determine if

they are Y Dawnus

rhyfelwr: warrior

sarn: road

Shape-Moving: the psychokinetic ability to move objects

Storm-Bringing: the psychokinetic ability to control certain weather

conditions; only

effective in partnership with the High King

Suldydd: first day of the week

tarbell: a board game, similar to chess

tarw: bull; the symbol of the Druids

tarw-casgliad: the ceremony where Druids invite a dream from

Modron

telyn: harp

teulu: warband

Time-Walking: the ability to see events in the past; one of the Dreamer's gifts

tir: earth

triskele: the crystal medallion used by Dewin

ty: house

tynge tynghed: the swearing of a destiny

Tynged Mawr: Great Fate; the test to determine a High King

tywyllu: dark; the time when the moon is new

ur: daughter of

var: out of

Wind-Riding: the clairvoyant ability of astral projection

Wind-Speaking: the telepathic ability to communicate with other humans

wythnos: week

yned: justice

Y Dawnus: the gifted; a Druid, Bard, Dewin, or Dreamer

ysgawen: elder

Ysgawen Mis: elder month; roughly corresponds to September

ystafell: the Ruler's chambers

ywen: yew

Ywen Mis: yew month; roughly corresponds to November

TOLTECA

K. MICHAEL WRIGHT

CHAPTER ONE
ONE REED

The Island Named Paradise, the Eastern Sea
The Toltec year One Reed, the season of the quetzal—May 455 AD

When night had grown long, and the fires of the village had died, Topiltzin, alone, climbed the high cliffs at the sea's edge. With warm salt air in his lungs, he knelt and searched the stars before dawn swallowed them. At least the skies had not changed. He had never been certain how far they had traveled through this ocean before reaching the island; but he knew at least that these were the same stars he had studied from the Hill of Shouting when he was young. Through all the years of his exile, Topiltzin had

1

watched this sky. He had carefully tracked the path of the Blue Stars against the horizon. He had marked the days.

He was old—fifty and two years, the same age his father would have been when Topiltzin left for his last rubberball game in the Southland so many years ago in Tollán. Topiltzin's skin was aged; his beard, long and white-gold; the tangled locks of his hair along the sides were silvered, but his eyes were still a steady, sharp, blue ice as they searched the face of the sea.

Topiltzin heard a rustle, and turning, he discovered Paper Flower had followed him. She was there, suddenly beside him. That was her way, jaguar eyes, silent, a soft wind you did not notice until you felt it lightly brush your skin.

When Topiltzin had died his first death, when the Lord of the Shadow Walkers had slain him, Paper Flower's had been the first face he had seen from death's abyss. He was certain death had already tasted his flesh, accepted it, and Topiltzin had nearly slipped away forever—there seemed no reason to remain—but when he looked back one last time, he saw her. She had been dabbing at his blood with a wet cloth, and when she realized he was watching, she gasped, startled. Glancing at her now, Topiltzin remembered that moment so clearly—her face that first time, how it cut against the acid blue of the sky behind her—her sharp features, her raven hair, the small lips, her eyes, quick, tender. In that moment, it had been as though Paper Flower reached across the quiet of death, touched Topiltzin's heart, gently, softly . . . and brought him back.

One score years and four had passed, yet she looked this night more beautiful than ever; her jet hair was now silvered in streaks that played in the moonlight. They had grown old here, upon this isle of the sea. They had born children beneath the white sun. They had laughed, they had wept. Life had played itself out in measured breath, and now Paper Flower was a part of him, their flesh one flesh. There was now a little of Topiltzin in the eyes of Paper Flower, and she in his, a warmth, a knowing touch, a tenderness almost like a wound.

Topiltzin turned back to the horizon. It was there, the talisman, the Morning Star. It ran herald of the sun, and Topiltzin knew she had traced its path as carefully as he had. He knew how she had feared this particular dawn for many years. They simply had never spoken of it. Yet it had come in the night like a thief, and now it was as though the future were kneeling there with them, as though part of what they were had already become memory.

"The Son of the Morning passes through the house of the Raven," Topiltzin said. "This is the year One Reed."

She quickly brushed aside silent tears, as though irritated with them. "Is there no way I can touch your heart?" she whispered.

Topiltzin kept his gaze upon the horizon—partly because he did not want to see her tears, he did not want to break. He had broken inside over the past few days many times and now he was determined to be strong and so he kept his gaze on the sea, the face of it, like blue leather, rippled with the rose of dawn. "You *own* my heart," he said, quietly.

"And yet you are going to leave."

"I have no choice in that, Paper Flower."

"You have choices. Choice is what you gave us that day on the beach when the Lord of the Shadow Walkers came for our souls. It was your gift to us, but also, it was our gift to you. We gave you life, we offered you choice, and now comes the moment you must choose. Choose between us and your ghosts, Topiltzin."

He sighed, finally turned to her. Paper Flower's eyes searched his, angry. He touched her cheek, but she pulled back. He could sense her anger, but all he felt in response was sadness, far, a sadness that just watched. "Somewhere," he said, softly, "love is marked—all we have shared—as love could ever be."

She shook her head. "No. Not this time. You speak with a silvered tongue, my prince, but there are no words to make this pretty."

Another tear crossed her cheek. Topiltzin reached to catch it, but Paper Flower angrily brushed his hand aside.

"You want to take my tears? You could. You could take them all if you wished. It is a simple thing to take them. But if you do what you are thinking, Topiltzin, then I shall keep these tears." She waited for a response and when she didn't sense it forthcoming, she turned away sharply, slipping over the steep side for the climb down.

"Wait! Paper Flower!"

He reached for her, but she was too quick, and she did not look back. For a time he stared after her, sadly, but then he turned to look again at the sea and forced the sting of sadness away. There was no time for it; there could be no weakness in him now. These many years, Topiltzin had listened to the silence that carried across these waters, but what was more, what he could not turn from—he had also listened to the screams. Perhaps that day on the sand—long ago in the land of Tollán, when he had faced the Shadow Walker—perhaps he had cheated death. Topiltzin had taken these years like a thief, but now it had turned, time had curled about the earth in full circle. The dawn sun would mark the Bundling of Years. It was time to return to Tollán.

⫐⫑⫐⫑⫐⫑⫐⫑⫐⫑⫐⫑⫐⫑⫐⫑⫐⫑⫐⫑⫐⫑

Paper Flower crossed the white sand of the beach beneath the cliffs. She had first started toward her hut; but knowing Topiltzin would come later, she decided he should find it empty. He should get used to empty; empty was his choosing now. She had loved him these many years, full and rich and with all her heart, and their sons and daughters, they were like sparkling jewels. She had tried to teach him to forget, but she had failed, and in failing to reach Topiltzin's heart, it seemed she had failed in everything. Her sadness was as endless as the sky this night.

She made her way to the wide, half-moon beach where the sand glittered as though diamonds might have been tossed. It was one of the most beautiful places she had ever known, and there were memories here—good memories, cherished.

Near a shelf of blue rock that curled fingers against the dark, ancient stone of cliffs, she slid onto one of the ledges and sat back, searching the curl of the waves for an answer, for comfort, for anything they might offer.

He had been a good father, Topiltzin. When his sons, born of thirteen queens, had grown old enough to touch manhood, Topiltzin started to train them. Paper Flower watched as their children first played mock games, wrestling for control of hillocks or groves of coconut trees; and in the beginning, she had smiled. It seemed the games built strength and courage, teaching them well. They laughed as they struggled in mock battles; but as they grew older, Topiltzin's sons carried shields that were as well crafted as any she had known in Tollán. They fashioned deadly spears and bows that could sink their oiled shafts deep into the trunks of palm trees; and not long after, the laughter—their innocence and youth—started to leave their eyes. More and more the peaceful valleys of the island they had named Paradise filled with the chilling echoes of the Flower-Song, the words the ancient heralds had given war in the Land of the Reeds. Then she knew; she realized what he was planning. Topiltzin was going to return. And he was going to take their sons.

ISBN# 9781932815467
Hardcover Adult / Paranormal
US $26.95 / CDN $35.95
Available Now

LYNDA HILBURN

Denver psychologist Kismet Knight, Ph.D., doesn't believe in the paranormal. She especially doesn't believe in vampires. That is, until a new client introduces Kismet to the vampire underworld and a drop dead gorgeous, 800-year-old vampire named Devereux. Kismet isn't buying the vampire story, but can't explain why she has such odd reactions and feelings whenever Devereux is near. Kismet is soon forced to open her mind to other possibilities, however, when she is visited by two angry bloodsuckers who would like nothing better than to challenge Devereux by hurting Kismet.

To make life just a bit more complicated, one of Kismet's clients shows up in her office almost completely drained of blood, and Kismet finds herself immersed in an ongoing murder investigation. Enter handsome FBI profiler Alan Stevens who warns her that vampires are very real. And one is a murderer. A murderer who is after her.

In the midst of it all, Kismet realizes she has feelings for both the vampire and the profiler. But though she cares for each of the men, facing the reality that vampires exist is enough of a challenge… for now.

ISBN# 9781933836232
Trade Paperback / Paranormal
US $15.95 / CDN $19.95
Available Now
www.LyndaHilburnAuthor.com

HOLLY TAYLOR

Night Birds' Reign

The legend is as old as time ...

The High King is dead. The land is in peril. A child has been born to save his people. But a traitor lurks with evil in his mind and murder in his heart, dogging the footsteps of those who protect the babe who would be king.

But magic is at work, high magic.

Gwydion the Dreamer awakes, screaming, from a prophetic dream of tragedy and loss, a dream peopled by kings of the past. Though he thinks he is not ready, the Shining Ones lay a task upon him: protect young Arthur; and locate Caladfwlch, the lost sword of the last, murdered High King of Kymru.

Dodging assassins to find the woman who holds the key to unlock a horrible secret, and fighting the longings of his own shattered heart, Gwydion sets out upon his odyssey. And finds that fate cannot be fulfilled without sacrificing the life of someone he loves ...

ISBN# 9781932815535
Trade Paperback / Fantasy
US $14.99 / CDN $18.99
Available Now
www.dreamers-cycle.com

The Piaras Legacy

Scott Gamboe

LONG AGO, SO THE LEGENDS SAY, THE NECROMANCER VOLNOR invaded the continent of Pelacia. His legions of undead soldiers ravaged the land unchecked, until the three nations united and pushed their evil foes back into the Desert of Malator.

But that was centuries ago, and few people still believe the tale. Other, more worldly matters occupy their time, such as recent attacks by renegade Kobolds. But Elac, an Elf who makes his way as a merchant, is too concerned with his business affairs to become involved in international politics. Until a marauding band of Kobolds attacks Elac's caravan and he finds himself running for his life.

Befriended by an Elven warrior named Rilen, he travels to Unlry, the seat of power on the Pelacian continent. There he is joined by a diverse group of companions, and he sets out on an epic quest to solve the riddle of his heritage and save the land from the growing evil that threatens to engulf it.

ISBN# 9781933836256
Trade Paperback / Fantasy
US $15.95 / CDN $17.95
APRIL 2008
www.scottgamboe.net

For more information

about other great titles from

Medallion Press, visit

www.medallionpress.com